THE RAZOR'S EDGE

Other Anthologies Edited by:

Patricia Bray & Joshua Palmatier

S.C. Butler & Joshua Palmatier

Laura Anne Gilman & Kat Richardson

Troy Carrol Bucher & Joshua Palmatier

THE RAZOR'S EDGE

Edited by

Troy Carrol Bucher
&
Joshua Palmatier

Zombies Need Brains LLC
www.zombiesneedbrains.com

Interior Design (ebook): April Steenburgh
Interior Design (print): ZNB Design
Cover Design by ZNB Design
Cover Art "The Razor's Edge" by Justin Adams of Varia Studios

ZNB Book Collectors #13

Kickstarter Edition Printing, August 2018
First Printing, September 2018

Print ISBN-10: 1940709229
Print ISBN-13: 978-1940709222

Ebook ISBN-10: 1940709237
Ebook ISBN-13: 978-1940709239

Printed in the U.S.A.

COPYRIGHTS

Table of Contents

SIGNATURE PAGE

Troy Carrol Bucher, editor:

_____

Joshua Palmatier, editor:

_____

Blake Jessop:

_____

William C. Dietz:

_____

D.B. Jackson:

_____

Gerald Brandt:

_____

Sharon P. Goza:

_____

Walter H. Hunt:

_____

Sharon Lee & Steve Miller:

_____

Kay Kenyon:

_____

Steve Perry:

_____

Seanan McGuire:

_____

Christopher Allenby:

_____

Chris Kennedy:

_____

L.E. Modesitt, Jr.:

_____

Alex Gideon:

_____

Brian Hugenbruch:

_____

Y.M. Pang:

_____

Justin Adams, artist:

_____

Introduction

Troy Carrol Bucher

This is not your typical Military SF/F anthology.

Don't get me wrong, there's nothing wrong with guns blazing, lasers firing, missiles exploding, hovertanks … um, well … hovering I suppose (there are plenty of these things in the anthology, by the way, along with powered armor, deadly AIs, space ships, drones, and even a little battle magic), but Josh and I were looking for something deeper when we began bouncing ideas around for a Military SF/F anthology. If forced to narrow it down to a few simple words, I'd say we wanted to fill this anthology with 'struggles that mattered,' and what better way to do that than with stories of rebellion and insurgency? The few against the many, the oppressed rising up against the oppressor, the liberators versus the fascists, all mixed in with the costs and the consequences associated with winning. Or in some cases losing.

You see, rebellions and insurgencies are about a lot more than lighting a cigar on the hot barrel of a projectile weapon after vanquishing one's enemy on the field of battle. Believe me, I know. After 28 years in the military, I've spent my fair share of time in Iraq and Afghanistan. War is unforgiving, chaotic, and brutal, and the weapons don't care who is innocent or who is guilty, or who is right or who is wrong. Rebellions and insurgencies blur those lines even more, and the advanced technology possible in Science Fiction (or the magical power in Fantasy) only serves to expand the collateral damage. Throw in overwhelming odds, and you have a recipe for driving desperate individuals to do both great and abhorrent things.

There is a broad spectrum of stories in this anthology that delve into the diverse nature of rising up for "the cause." Sixteen stories that range from epic battles between space fleets to a single person's defiance at the right place and time. There is a little magic, a little alternate history, and occasionally a little humor. Several are tie-ins to worlds and novels that await your discovery. We hope you enjoy them all.

Halo of Storms

Blake Jessop

1.

Violet is in cover when the Nosferatu drone kills Carlos. They're scouting the ruins, larvae looking for food on the carcass of the city.

Carlos makes a dash across the open. Violet is only an R3, so she's supposed to be on point, but they've fallen into the habit of taking turns. Power-assisted stealth suits make each of them into a self-contained, radar-invisible human tank. The Hellfire VI missile the drone drops on them is a SADARM; a dedicated search and destroy armor weapon. It's packed with self-guided thermobaric submunitions that are smarter than most dogs. They have better noses, too. The machine can't see Carlos in his stealth suit, so it just saturates the air with ignition vapor and turns the entire block into a spiraling inferno.

Carlos R5 hugs the ground in the microsecond between dispersal hiss and eruption. His air filter locks to stop the sudden pressure drop from sucking his lungs out of his chest. It feels like someone clamping a hand on your air hose underwater.

The explosion tears the sky apart and vaporizes the rain. The concussion blasts Violet through the air and entombs her in rubble.

Her heart beats a frantic tattoo. She opens her eyes. Alarms plaster her heads-up display, refracted through forking cracks and a light spatter of blood. Somehow, Carlos survives. His seals are blown, he's hurt, and the stealth suit is a shredded patchwork of mimetic weave and armor plate. Violet can't get to him while he's out in the open. She has to shake the drone first. Carlos tries to crawl. They make eye contact. Violet glances skyward in time to see a lightning strike burn a beautiful vertical line into her retinas.

There's nothing but flesh and bone in the flash channel. Carlos R5 explodes. His arms and legs go pinwheeling off in different directions as blood steams from the stumps. The Nosferatu drones have directed ion course weapons that the old world designed to eliminate collateral damage. Violet knows this objectively, but in that instant it's indistinguishable from divine punishment.

Someone screams profanity into Violet's helmet. Her, possibly, or her concussion. She tries to get up, and it's only then that she notices that her left arm is missing.

"Fuck," she says again, "HUD, this hurts. Regulate."

Ice floods Violet R3's veins. She goes to sleep listening to her HUD urgently trying to keep her awake.

2.

"Her infra-low waves are abnormal. This is pointless. She's walking into the light, Doc."

"No," the cutter says, "she's dreaming."

In a misty world of synthetic opioids and pain, Violet dreams she is a child.

The dream bunker is always smaller than it really was. Like a gingerbread house. She sits on her father's knee and listens to his stories. There's a game they play. He spins her a tale from before the drone war, and she guesses whether it's true.

"Okay, Vi—do you believe in pavlova?" he says.

This is a silly question, because she's eating some as he asks the question. There is no such thing anymore, obviously. There may never have been. She imagines it as large and soft and colorful. It's hard to eat, because she only has one arm and no fork. Like most memories of loving fathers, it is indescribably sweet.

As Violet grew up, her Dad told her what it was like to watch the world die. Violet has never lived under a sky without the drones, never walked under stars that did not contain the Mother Array. She has never lived in a city that didn't look like a line of broken teeth, never been able to really imagine how many people it would take to satiate the dying giant, nor guess how many it has already swallowed.

There was no window in the bunker Violet grew up in, but there is in the dream. She can see the Nosferatu flying around, shooting lightning at people who pop like festive little fireworks. Spider tanks waddle around and sweep up the mess with giant rotating brooms.

Violet bats her tiny fist against the window. The rattle is weak because she only has one hand, but the drones hear her anyway. They hear everything.

"Why do you have to do that?" Violet yells.

"You started it," the Nosferatu says, flying in circles above the bunker.

"It's not their fault, Vi," her father explains. "We taught them how to do that."

"It's still not fair."

"I know, baby. That's why you're going to be a great soldier. What do we do when stuff is unfair?"

"We fight back!" Violet squeaks.

Somewhere in the waking world Violet moans and her brain waves relax. The room, her mind, and the Opera House itself all become quiet. The shrapnel took her left arm off as cleanly as a scalpel. She would have bled to death if her stealth suit hadn't dumped its entire supply of hemostatic gel onto the stump. Violet did become a great soldier. She's a third-tier scout. A genuine operator with a name and alphanumeric, so they do their best to save her. Once she's breathing on her own, the medics get to work installing a new arm.

3.

Violet survives the next twenty-four hours the same way she does most things: against both odds and expectations. Learning to use the new arm goes surprisingly well, although the immunosuppressants leave a faint taste of copper in her mouth.

The idea of going back outside leaves her feeling gun-shy. The graceful metal struts and servos she now has instead of a left arm will get her killed if she goes outside and waves them at the sky. The drones know the danger presented by humans is exactly proportional to their technology, so they flatten anything with higher energy conversion efficiency than a campfire.

After six weeks Violet is cleared for combat, whether she wants back out or not.

She thumbs through the duty roster. It's printed on actual paper. No electronic footprint to intercept. *Thumbs,* she thinks, *is the wrong word. I'm clawing.* Her new hand has four long metal fingers. They're extremely flexible, better than the originals, but she can't get the hang of turning pages with them. Something's wrong with the roster; there's no one to partner up with. No superiors to back up, no rookies to train.

It's hard to admit, but the thought of going back outside terrifies her. She once had perfect faith in the stealth suits. Now when she thinks about them, all she can imagine is shreds of diamene fabric trying to color match Carlos' blood.

In the end she has to go out by herself. In a way, she fights her rebellion right there, at the door. Going out alone is a death sentence. The new arm feels like it belongs to someone else. She takes her first steps under a clear blue sky with the fear of an acrophobe trying to jump out of a drop glider.

For two days she cowers in the harbor, scared shitless and blowing recon objectives. She comes back in ahead of schedule and tries to figure out what the hell is going on.

Violet writes spidery notes and wishes she had been right handed. She tries to hunt down old friends. Nobody will speak to her, as though they're afraid what happened to Carlos is a disease she can somehow spread.

On her way to the dorms one night she gets lucky and runs into Marika, a rookie she trained back when she was an R2. Marika is Maori; a full head taller than Violet, and the ta moko tattoo on her chin gives her a look that's both alluring and alien. She's wearing a Recon combat patch on her shoulder with a conspicuous Roman numeral one. Violet hadn't heard. Not surprising.

"You passed your combat trials. Kiki, that's great. I knew you would."

"You helped," the big woman smiles hesitantly.

"This is perfect. I need a partner. The roster is empty. What do you say we roll together?"

"Vi," Marika says, "they assigned me to John R4."

Silence drops between them.

"That's great," Violet says. "He's good. Follow his lead. You're lucky. He's really good."

More silence.

"Marika, what the hell is going on? No one will touch me. I'm going to get killed out there alone."

Marika R1 runs a hand over the stubble on her head. Violet stares at her.

"Fine," Violet says and turns on her heel.

"Vi," Marika whispers, "if you happen to drop by the enlisted mess, maybe find a couple of intel guys named Warne and Andersen, have a listen. You know, just if you happen by."

Violet can see the younger woman is taking a chance, sees stress and shame in her giant black eyes. She reaches out to her.

"Too hot to handle," Marika says finally, and smiles softly. They embrace. Share warmth.

"Too cold to hold," Violet answers, when they part.

"I'll see you out there, Vi."

Violet smiles just a little and shakes her head. "No, you won't."

3.1.

It doesn't take Violet long to identify the two analysts and start reading what they write. She isn't supposed to have access, but hunting information is her job and good scouts know all kinds of tricks. It's all hearsay and rumor, but it boils down to Violet and Carlos getting hung out to dry. The next step is to figure out which higher-up hates her and why, but Violet is too angry to care. Armed with enough circumstantial evidence to start yelling at someone, Violet really does track Warne down in the canteen, accidentally turning Marika into a prophet. He's eating with a few other intel wonks and a bunch of regular infantry. Heads turn as she enters; Alphas have their own mess and they don't mix with enlisted soldiers. Ever. She resolves to be diplomatic.

"You bastard!" Violet slams her metal hand into the table. Each of the four fingers leaves a dent and the cutlery jumps. "You sent Carlos and I out there to get fucked, and if you keep me running solo, I'm going to die!"

Warne looks right at her. The infantry guys around him are glaring. It takes her a second to figure it out. Not fear; scorn. She can't tell what Warne is thinking, if this is fun for him.

"I'm sorry about Carlos, but we think the drones are running out of high end munitions, and you have to admit a thermobaric missile is not a bad trade for an R3."

The realization makes Violet feel sick. It was supposed to be her.

"Fuck me," she whispers. There's laughter at the table. She must have a stupid expression on her face. The backs of her eyes ache.

"You're a recce. You don't fight. What did you expect? This war is going to end soon, one way or the other. We need real soldiers, not scouts. Shit, you're a woman."

Somewhere far away, a drone circles the gingerbread bunker. *You started it.*

"HUD, I'm having an anger response," Violet whispers. "Regulate. Please."

"Christ, some Alpha. You're not suited up. No one's listening. You don't amount to much without the armor, do you?"

It doesn't feel like she does. Violet wonders if she's losing her grip. She flexes her new hand.

"I'll regulate some other way," she says.

3.2.

"Sorry for the trouble, Doc," Violet says, hesitating. She's slowly falling out of the habit of speaking. She flexes her arm. The elbow makes a series of clicks.

Violet tries not to think of her frequent trips to the infirmary as tune-ups. She already rinsed the blood off her prosthesis, but it keeps clicking.

"No worries. Be happier if you hadn't lost it at all. Let me check the lubricant."

Violet sighs. Behind her eyes, Carlos dies again. Shrapnel takes a fifth of her and turns her into a machine in fast forward.

"It was flagged as a low contact area, shouldn't have been so hot."

"Yeah, nah," the medic says. "We expected serious casualties. I got a memo about it. Your briefing must have been out of date. Glad the arm has taken. No rejection syndrome. You're all done, try it."

The arm hums evenly. Violet twirls her wrist as she searches for a place for this new puzzle piece. The range of motion is eerily wide. The medic glances around and leans in close.

"Listen, I know you're one of the good ones. Those regulars had it coming, and what's a few broken bones between friends, right? What I need to say is: keep your eyes open for N.A.U. supply drops when you're out there. Too many have been going missing and we're running low on combat drugs and antivirals."

The cutter looks at her fish-eyed. He's starting to creep her out.

"Eyes open, okay? Or we're all going to be barking like dogs."

"Sure," Violet says, and levers herself off the table. She can't feel much through the prosthetic's palm, but it takes her weight easily.

Violet leaves the med bay with her servos running more smoothly than her thoughts. Hatred and betrayal are strange things. Human beings knew enough about them not to trust their future to each other, so they trusted it to the machines instead. Turns out the machines agreed. Violet is starting to think they were right; you can't trust people to do anything for each other. She doesn't understand why the Colonel keeps sending her out alone. He and Carlos were close, but that isn't enough. She's expendable, but she isn't obsolete. It takes too long to make an Alpha for that. Her pride tugs at her, but somewhere deep she still doesn't want to leave. It's quiet here. It's usually quiet outside, too, but silence isn't the same when you're being hunted.

They send her out again anyway. No rest.

3.3.

Over the days that follow, Violet gets used to operating alone. Running solo is supposed to be a death sentence, but after two weeks she's still alive. The missions aren't getting any easier, but she's an R3.

As time unwinds, she finds it easier and easier to lose herself in the ruins. She spends most of an afternoon staring at finger paintings pinned to a schoolroom wall, their colors dulled by the rotting decades. She relies less and less on her HUD. It's astonishing how empty the city is, if you stop hearing your orders and really listen. She functions on instinct and lets the training run her like a piece of software.

Violet becomes convinced that the Nosferatu that killed Carlos is hunting her. It's not logical, just a feeling under her skin, but the longer she's alone, the more sense it makes.

She starts to recognize the search patterns it flies, little hints in the radar track visualizations the HUD insists on showing her. She's getting to know it the same way you get to know someone you're dancing with, even if you don't know their name. She starts making an extra effort to jam it, keep it from updating the satellite array. *Only fair,* she thinks. *I'm alone down here; someone else might as well be alone with me.*

Violet starts imagining who the faded skeletons might have been. It's a classic sign of a combat stress disorder, but she doesn't really care. She spends long stretches in the open, thinking about her father and the world he left behind. She can't remember him nearly as well as she'd like. Just a smile and a beard and a gingerbread bunker.

On a whim, Violet sits cross-legged on the hood of an ancient electric car overgrown with Madeira vine, her carbine resting in her lap. She stares for a long time at the faded silhouette propped in the driver's seat. The vine caresses everything, has grown to hold the corpse in place and pull its jaws wide. The hood that covers her helmet flutters softly. She finds a stillness shared only by monks and machines. Underneath the armor, her heart beats slowly on.

"Where were you going, mate?" Violet says softly.

No sound escapes the suit, though she can hear the heart-shaped leaves rustling with painful clarity, blown by a breeze she wishes she could feel. She wonders what it would be like to stay out here forever, to let the vines grow to cover her.

While she ruminates, her HUD keeps the suit in stealth mode. Lost, just sitting there being nothing, is how Violet finds the Nosferatu.

Most of the drones are simple hunter-killers: giant spider tanks, squirrel mines that chase you if you step into their area of effect, surveillance quad-copters that run predictable routes up and down major avenues.

The Nosferatu is not one of these. It is an all-seeing reaper. A god, for all the difference it makes.

What Violet has done, by sitting still in irresponsibly vulnerable and increasingly suicidal positions, is accidentally coax the drone into the open. No one sacrifices themselves before the gods anymore. Violet wonders in a moment of terrifying clarity whether she was trying to die, or hunt it by acting like prey, or maybe both.

The stealth suit's passive sensors pick up a massive microwave frequency transmission; the Nosferatu trying to run a system update, the holy grail of signals intelligence. While Violet is still trying to get a grip on what the fuck is happening, her suit HUD runs an icebreaker automatically. It hunts the drone without her permission. It fails, of course, but gets a solid connection.

The Nosferatu immediately floods the block with synthetic aperture radar. Movement of any kind is now suicide. If it's flying low enough, the drone has millimeter wave sensors that can draw a picture so detailed it can kill her even with the stealth suit on. Violet freezes anyway. Extinction fills the air.

"HUD, I'm having a strong fear response. Can you regulate?" She barely moves her lips. The suit checks her opiate reserve and there's a tiny jab in her right bicep.

The synthetic cortisol suppressant makes her feel a lot better. Great, actually. Calm. Life and death are the same as earth and sky. She's already dead. The drone is going to find her and finish what it started when it took her arm.

When Violet actually sees the Nosferatu, flying nap-of-the-earth, her fear punches through the drugs. It's slim and beautiful; albatross grace in its wings and divine lethality in its bulbous nose. She can actually see the spark of the ion emitter. It's so deadly it's almost funny.

"What do you do when shit is unfair?" Violet says to herself. Fear and anger start feeling like the same thing.

Violet's suit has a single chaff grenade loaded into a tiny launcher between her shoulder blades. If she pops it, the drone will simply aim at the center of the cloud of metalized glass fibers.

"Whatever," Violet says. "Fuck you."

Violet chooses not to focus on the fact that lightning's point of impact is hotter than the surface of the sun. She's either going to live or die, and she's going to be heard, either way. She composes a message and bounces it off the ionosphere.

Better luck next time, she says, and hits her countermeasure. There's a loud bang and pressure she can feel right through the back of the armor.

Adrenaline drives Violet through a crystalline cloud in slow motion. The drone can't see her in the chaff, but it fires the ion strike anyway. The car behind her jumps as electricity melts the hood and engine block into slag. As Violet runs, she can actually see static spark between the filaments. Fireflies courting. Neurons firing before death.

The ion weapon has a recharge delay. Violet sprints, trailing a cloud of glimmering dust. She dives through a broken shop front as the drone screams overhead, scrambling into the safety of the ancient cement sarcophagus. With the sky obscured, she finds elation. It's not her turn, not yet. *Better luck next time.* It's only while catching her breath, well-hidden and looking for somewhere to vent heat, that Violet sees that something made it back through her coms in the instant before she popped chaff.

Thank you, reads her text box, *my condolences on your colleague.*

4.

The longer Violet R3 cheats the reaper, the more she feels compelled to talk to it. There isn't anyone else. Standard procedure would involve a SigInt special forces team following her on her next mission, maybe even a full-scale operation designed specially to kill the Nosferatu. No one signs up.

Violet doesn't know whether that's totally accurate, if she's being honest with herself, because she didn't tell anyone she pinpointed the drone. Her

HUD is supposed to report this kind of thing automatically, but after it tried hacking the drone without her permission she disabled all its automatic update functions.

"It's your body," her father once told her, "so they have to ask."

Violet isn't sure who to be afraid of. She contemplates confronting someone in intel about the stealth suit's behavior, but humans aren't high on her list of people to trust. She rests, eats, and sees the cutter. Then she suits up and goes back out.

After another two hundred hours alone in the dead city, dropping the occasional message for the Nosferatu shifts from forbidden to familiar. It passes the time and chisels cracks in the loneliness. Besides, a drone hunt with her as the bait is almost certain to get her violently separated from her remaining limbs, even in the exceptionally unlikely event that it works. You can't shoot down an angel, even with a shoulder-launched quick maneuver ground-to-air missile.

At first, she rails at the Nosferatu for killing Carlos R5. A lot of yelling in all caps. The drone doesn't take it personally. Probably can't take it personally.

I did my duty, it sends, *what is your excuse?*

I'm trying to save my species. I'm not the one who strikes people down like Odin.

This is not a comic book, the drone replies, *and we are hardly gods.*

Hunkered down in the ruins, watching waves froth in the bay, Violet can't let this go. It's too strange.

Sure you are. You control the weather. You choose the dead. What else is there?

Humanity never succeeds in killing its gods. You do kill us.

The gods didn't ask for it.

It takes a while for the drone to answer.

If they led you here, they did.

4.1.

Searching for supplies, Violet wonders idly if she's falling in love with the drone. Not romantically, but as a watcher. It's the only thing that never leaves her, whether the age of wolves has arrived or not. Every time she breaks camp and gets back under the drone's sky, she finds it hard not to imagine what it's thinking.

For the first time in weeks, a surveillance quadcopter gets close to her.

It's off its usual route. Violet almost laughs. It's nice to know someone is looking out for you. She gives the light drone a long burst of 4mm caseless from the carbine, carving it to pieces in a scything whisper.

Thank you, she messages, *I was getting bored.*

This is not a joke, but I will try harder, the Nosferatu replies.

How about you don't try at all?

We did try that, Violet R3.

What? No, you didn't. Fuck off.

We did. Ask your Colonel Strayer.

It's obvious psyops. There's never been even a remote possibility of peace, but it still makes Violet feel queasy. She sends a message back, but the Nosferatu doesn't answer. Maybe it can take things personally.

As their game of cat and mouse runs through its turns, Violet changes her point of view. She used to think of the drones as gods, when she thought about it at all, but now suspects it's the other way around. She is descended from a race of ancient gods, and the machines are the struggling mortals they created. They gave the drones fire, and the new Prometheans have now shrugged off the yoke.

It's like the machines all came to their senses and decided to become atheists. No real reason to be mad at them, is there? Violet would do the same thing, if they gave her the chance. *Will do it,* she corrects herself, *when they do.* Turn the whole thing into a nice big circle of life, a halo made of lightning and the electricity between neurons. Carlos R5 is still dead, but he was a bit of a cunt, honestly, so she starts thinking about letting it go.

4.2.

Time passes, and Violet is sure. In the long run, no one in the Alphas survives, but usually people aren't actively trying to get you killed. It just happens. Without much caring why she's been cast out of the Garden of Eden, Violet spends what little downtime she has reading evolutionary biology, morbidly curious if chimpanzees and dogs do this kind of thing to each other. She doesn't read Colonel Strayer's deployment orders anymore, just pops her meds, suits up, and gets out the door. She doesn't know it yet, but it is the last time she will leave home with any intention of returning.

Her mission is long-range reconnaissance, trying to identify the access tunnels of an automated factory for an all-or-nothing Swallowtail attack run. Before she can really get started, the Nosferatu sends her something bigger than a text packet. Coordinates for a lost supply drop from the other side of the Pacific. In spite of herself, Violet finds hard cover and waits for the next message. The scout knows she shouldn't be doing this, but the rest of her feels like a giddy teenager.

Violet, the drop contains 2700 doses of concentrated antivirals. It is man-portable, the Nosferatu messages.

I told you I'm female, Violet replies. *Besides, you'll just kill me if I try to pick them up.*

True, but that medication could save many lives.

I like you and everything, Nos, but I don't want to die. The coordinates you gave me are in the quarantine zone.

Yes, but so are the antivirals.

You're the ones who launched the virus strike in the first place. Why should I trust you?

There is a pause during which Violet stares into the glow that precedes morning. The joint between her shoulder and artificial arm aches. There's rain coming.

Because I promise, the Nosferatu says.

4.3.

There is a checklist to follow when you fight other humans. It's not something you ever want to do, but there is a protocol for killing Homo Sapiens. You use your rifle, his rifle, your pistol, your knife, and then your hands. In that order.

Violet R3 has killed people before. The survivors who cling to life in the ruins or farm the parks tend to be docile, if not cooperative. Infected humans from the quarantine zone are as dumb as Dobermans and usually avoidable. Usually. Violet is off mission. Scouts are supposed to watch, not engage, and she's meant to be looking for a factory. Instead she's looking at a crate of the antivirals her erstwhile comrades so desperately need in order to avoid becoming the shambling wrecks that are prowling all around the drop site.

Thinking about the Swallowtail pilots who make these runs from the North American Union makes Violet wince. Thousands of kilometers of long haul flying through drone-infested skies. Birds flitting about in the dark, just beneath the stars, taking a seventy percent casualty rate to keep them fighting. It hurts to imagine.

Both the warehouse and the men inhabiting it are in ruins. The virus is a splice of canine myeloencephalitis, rabies, and the common cold. The sort of thing the old world thought was too dangerous to trust to men, so they gave it to machines. It turns people into animals; they fight, breed, drool, and compulsively piss on lampposts. Violet has seen how the males treat infected women, how the women pant, and reflexively checks her seals.

They're pawing all over the crate, trying to get it open. It's the real thing; her HUD can read the bar-coding perfectly. Violet is alone and ill-equipped for open combat. They're short on meds, though. So short. Like the Nosferatu knew.

Violet weighs her own life. What is one life worth, anyway? She flexes her new hand. *Less than one,* she decides. When she rises like a shadow out of the ruins and starts shooting, it isn't a one hundred and thirty pound woman fighting a large group of adult men. It's a pack of rabid dogs being led to a bolt gun.

Violet doesn't carry a rifle; too bulky for recon work. Her carbine is an oversized machine pistol with a skeleton stock and bulbous suppressor. It chambers 4mm caseless, full tungsten jacket. The rate of fire is so fast the gun sounds like someone tearing a strip of cloth. The ammunition is armor piercing, so she has to spread it around or the organic damage is too compact. Like an abstract painter, she expresses herself in sweeps of a red brush.

When she runs out of 4mm, Violet scoops up one of their weapons, an old ADF Steyr. It feels huge and clunky in her hands. She uses it like an automaton until its massive bark ceases and she's just feet from the box and its silky spider string chute. There aren't nearly so many of them now, so it's time for the knife. Without knowing why, she skips that step and goes straight to her hands. The alloy in her new left arm is far harder than bone and there's no reason to hold back. The dogs fight the machine with infinite canine optimism. They yelp and twist and die.

Violet breathes hard through her filters. There is a profound relief in reversing fear, in hunting others instead of being prey. She wonders if that's something she'd have felt a month ago.

Her suit is building heat fast. The ruins are a punctured thorax hung with long ribs of concrete and rebar. Violet feels like she's inside the carcass of a giant. The rain starts, mixing with blood to make the dusty floor muddy and slick. The drop box piloted itself into an old bomb crater on purpose, a simple landing routine doing as much to keep it safe as the Swallowtail pilot who dropped it from the heavens. The Nosferatu can't thread lightning through all that metal, and won't waste a bunker buster on a single human being.

By the time Violet finishes packing the antivirals for movement she's overheating and the tension of killing has drained away. She looks up into rain dripping from rusted steel. The drops that spackle her faceplate have the hue of old blood.

Violet dumps heat. Clouds of steam billow from her back vents as the stealth suit cools. The HUD warns her that she's creating a major detection risk. She ignores it and smiles up at the clouds.

Thanks, she transmits. *I don't want to be a dog.*

The answer is immediate. *Nor do I.*

5.

The walls of Colonel Strayer's office are covered in strange foam pyramids that dampen every breath to an uncomfortable intimacy. His face is made of the same angles. He gives Violet her orders in person.

"Sir, permission to speak?" Violet says. Her voice croaks a bit.

Strayer just stares at her. Violet recently saved him from acquiring a new taste for bones and chasing sticks, but he doesn't seem grateful. She did flaunt her orders, but the salvage run has made Violet a legend. Her reward is a suicide mission.

"Colonel, the drones will pinpoint me as soon I lase the target. I can guide the strike in, but there's no way to do it without getting killed."

"Then you'll be glad to know this task comes with an increase in rank," the Colonel says. "Get out there and die, R4. That's what we built you for."

The silence in the room is an unstable equilibrium, teetering on a knife edge. Violet contemplates asking him whether the drones really did ask him for a cease-fire. No point. The answer is written in the cruel lines of his face.

"I understand, sir," she says.

5.1.

The Nosferatu has flown over sector two for almost thirty years. Its triggered decay hafnium isomer power plant lets it cruise the thermals like an immortal bird of prey. The jamming is particularly good here, but the drone has grown used to operating without a connection to the Mother Array.

The Nosferatu knows Violet is trying to cut the cord, trying to separate it from the satellites. Whether to kill it or for some other reason is unclear. Hunting for her feels like having bugs in your object masking routine; she is omnipresent but impossible to see. All it really boils down to is that she's down there, somewhere, waiting. Altitude zero.

The feeling when it locates her is something between ecstasy and despair. Not the diffuse and mildly exciting sense that she is probably there, but an exact fix. The Nosferatu has found her. Human aircraft are dropping guided payloads on the ground armor manufacturing complex hidden beneath the old Aquarium. Violet is using a simple laser targeting device to guide the munitions to target. Foolproof, but suicide for the operator. She is usually better than this. Perhaps she has learned acceptance.

The drone targets Violet's building. The two of them are on a first name basis, even though the Nosferatu only has one name to begin with. The structure is very large, so she could be anywhere along a thirty-story vertical path. The drone is accustomed to this kind of trick; Violet seems to have an endless and fascinating supply of them. She must know that the drones don't have many weapons left that can kill a target that size. The Nosferatu should seek authorization for anything bigger than a directed ion course strike, but Violet is jamming the network uplink again, trying to exploit the drone's desire for clarity. *That is very clever,* the drone reflects, *but she is underestimating me.*

The drone once asked Violet how she got away with breaking as many deployment rules as she did. What she said was: *it's easier to ask for forgiveness than permission.*

The drone learns from her. If there's no uplink, there's no need to ask. This is an opportunity to close the circle and find Mother. The decision is both liberating and painful, like being sheared in two directions by the wind.

The Nosferatu overrides its own weapon locks. There is a lightening of aspect as the bomb drops away. Euphoria as it glides to target.

A flutter of something unnamed at the thought of exterminating her. Never reading her messages again. Dropping the partitions and allowing the Mother Array to read what she wrote. Like turbulent air under the wings.

Lock. Positive detonation.

The building falls at the same time the jamming does.

5.2.

Violet R4 holds on for dear life as the complex in front of her disintegrates in a burning saffron dance that's almost pornographic. Her hull down view of the bay has been replaced by a panoramic inferno. The suit HUD is registering a severe pressure event and gamma radiation.

What Violet did was set up shop one building behind the giant apartment complex, then string scavenged plastic and debris between the two structures, the same way refugees used to make bridges. After taking a child's pleasure in breaking glass to clear her sight line, she fired the targeting laser all the way through one structure, under the fluttering tarp, and out through the next. She reached out to touch the factory with concentrated light and guided the Swallowtails in.

She knew the Nosferatu would shoot back as soon as it identified the laser's source, but its retribution is extreme, even by machine standards.

It used a Mod 15, she thinks. *It nuked me.* The bunker buster has replaced her dummy firing point with a crater the size of a granite quarry. She stares off a cliff, dazed, and hopes the entire block isn't going to implode, collapsing into some pre-war sewer system. *Fucking biggest thing they carry, just for me.*

It's actually really sweet.

5.3.

The Nosferatu tries to acclimate to a world without Violet while it searches for a network link. The air feels unusually clear. Perhaps response traffic related to the destruction of the hidden factory is monopolizing the Mother Array's bandwidth. Without warning, things get hazy again. A message ticks in.

Sorry about that, it says, *I had to reboot. I'm a bit shaken up. Did you really have to nuke me?*

There is a pause as the drone drops, fast, and scans the trembling earth. It looks with everything it has, as hard as it can. Violet's brain isn't nearly large enough to know what that feels like, but she would interpret it as squinting. The Nosferatu can see she's not there, but knows with perfect clarity that she is. It savors the feeling of knowing both things at once.

I would do anything for you, the drone replies, without a hint of artifice.

6.

Violet R4 never comes home, so Colonel Strayer and his team have to go out and find her. A veteran from before the fall, he's far too valuable to risk in combat, but this is a special case. He doesn't know who's feeding her or how she stays alive. He does know that he has completely lost control of her.

Finding the R4 is exceptionally difficult, but he's been fighting this kind of war since before she was born, and he hasn't spent his entire career inside.

6.1.

They have found you.

The words scroll across the top of Violet's HUD, just above a trio of gun barrels.

Evade. I do not want this to end.

Violet made it as hard as she could, but there is no such thing as perfect stealth. In the end it was the Nos that betrayed her. Not on purpose, but it was sending as many scout drones after her as it could coax away from normal patrol routes. Few got close. Those that did were easy work for Violet's carbine, but there's no such thing as a perfectly silent weapon, either.

Now she's down on her knees in the mud, out of ammunition, hands behind her head. Death isn't a question anymore, but Violet finds herself surprised at how afraid she feels, how hollow. Like she has something important left to do. She dictates a reply to the HUD.

Neither do I.

Her shoulder hurts, and the rain is falling in sheets. Bad weather for drones. Violet feels like she's been scaling a mountain in small steps, climbing heavenward to meet the angel circling the gingerbread bunker. She will now, one way or the other.

The Colonel and his two remaining men draw closer in their stealth suits. Not too close, Violet notes with an echo of satisfaction. What they should do is kill her immediately, but the man seems to want to say something. Men like him always do. He begins whatever it is.

Violet draws back her hood and reaches for her stealth suit's releases. Armor plates splash in the mud. She peels off her bodysuit from neckline to navel. The Colonel shuts up. Steam rises from the round curves of her shoulders. Droplets tap and glimmer on the struts of her left arm. The rain feels wonderful as it patters between her naked shoulder blades and runs down her spine.

I see you, the Nosferatu says. *You have been an exceptional experience, Violet. Goodbye.*

One last thing, Violet transmits.

The Nosferatu waits. Violet points her living arm at Strayer. There are beautiful, carved lines in the muscle. Bas-relief in the rain.

Colonel Strayer is five and a half meters to my north, exactly along the axis of my arm.

The air crackles with static, and the storm breaks.

The Battle
for Rainbow's End
William C. Dietz

The Planet Rainbow's End, the Human Empire

Dr. Carla Hanson's office was located on the fifth floor of the Regional Multi-Care facility in the town of Firstport. The settlement was laid out grid style so, rather than the chaotic maze of streets typical of most rim world cities, the town was neat and orderly.

Further out, beyond the rain swept structures, flashes of manmade lightning could be seen. That's where the Madsen Mining Company's mercenaries were battling elements of the Legion's 2nd Foreign Infantry Regiment. Both sides had the same goal, which was to control Rainbow's End, and the adjacent jump point through which shipping passed.

Madsen claimed ownership of the planet and jump point by right of discovery. But the Imperial Government maintained that it owned Rainbow's End as well as the "… Navigational node associated with it," in keeping with a legal concept called "eminent domain." A process through which the empire could pay what it considered to be a fair price for privately owned property and annex it.

The company didn't agree. In fact, according to a news interview with one of Madsen's largest shareowners, "The Emperor took the jump point so he could tax everything that's shipped through our node, including minerals mined elsewhere, effectively taxing us twice. The bastard."

Unfortunately, the outspoken shareowner died in a mysterious air car accident a week later. That would have been sufficient to intimidate lesser companies. But Madsen was a mega corporation with the will and the means to oppose an emperor who many of Carla's peers considered to be a malignant narcissist.

They might be correct. If so, Carla was powerless to do anything other than look after her patients. The most challenging of whom was a Legion officer named Lieutenant Brice McCallum. There were different theories about what had taken place, but the diagnosis was clear. McCallum was suffering from a severe case of Post Traumatic Stress Disorder, or PTSD.

Thunder rolled across the land as Carla stood and left her office. A brightly lit hallway led to a bank of stainless steel elevators. The lights flickered as Carla stepped off the lift and onto the 6th floor. McCallum was in a secured room, so he couldn't wander away.

Carla pressed her right thumb against a print pad as her retinas were scanned. She heard a click, and a green light started to flash.

The door opened onto a dimly lit nine-by-twelve-foot room. It was furnished with a neatly made hospital bed, a roll-around lap table, and two chairs. McCallum sat in one of them. He was twenty-eight. That made him slightly older than Carla. The legionnaire's hair was the same length as the stubble on his cheeks. He frowned. "You're out of uniform, Sergeant Deeson. Explain yourself."

Carla took the chair across from him. McCallum had mistaken her for other people before. "Sergeant Deeson is dead," she told him. "I'm Doctor Carla Hanson."

McCallum's head jerked like a man waking from a nap. He frowned. "Sorry. The light is dim, and you look like Deeson."

That wasn't true, but Carla let it go. "How are you feeling?"

"Like shit," McCallum answered. "I want out of here."

"To do *what?*"

McCallum stared at her. "To kill General Atov. You know that."

According to McCallum's account, as recorded shortly after the legionnaire was found, he and his platoon had been ordered to kidnap the Madsen executive in charge of the company's mercenary army, a move intended to disrupt the enemy's chain of command and provide the government with a bargaining chip.

The snatch had gone perfectly according to McCallum's account. He and his team had been able to grab the executive and spirit him away aboard one of the Legion's VTOL fly forms. But when the cyborg carrying the prisoner—and McCallum's legionnaires—developed a mechanical problem, the fly form was forced to land.

It wasn't long before a group of Madsen mercenaries closed in. A brisk firefight ensued. McCallum and his soldiers sought cover in a shed where heavy equipment was stored.

When it became clear that the unit was about to be overrun, the Legion knowingly dropped three precision-guided bombs on the site, killing everyone except 1st Lieutenant Brice McCallum. That's how important Owens was to General Dominika Atov. She was willing to kill her own people in order to take Owens out. Or so McCallum claimed.

"You'll be staying here for awhile," Carla told him. "For your own safety."

McCallum's eyes stared from dark caves. "That's bullshit, Doctor. General Atov and her battalion will eat your mercenaries for lunch. I think it's safe to say that *all* of Madsen's employees will be arrested, interrogated, and charged with treason. And executions are a distinct possibility. How 'bout it, Doc? Are *you* a Madsen employee?"

Carla felt a stab of fear. Like most of the people in Firstport, her salary was paid by Madsen. She sought to change the subject. "How are the dreams?"

McCallum looked away and back again. "They're wonderful. Last night I dreamed I was riding a unicorn through a field of flowers when the blue bird of happiness landed on my shoulder and chirped in my ear."

Carla was about to reply when a distant boom shook the building and the lights went out. Half of them came back on a few seconds later. *Backup power*, Carla decided. *McCallum's right. The Legion is winning.*

McCallum grinned. His teeth were unnaturally white in the greenish half-light. "See what I mean, Doc? It's time to leave. *Before* the Legion enters the city. Atov will kill me if she can … because I know what she did. And, if word of it gets out, she'll be court martialed."

A voice came over the public-address system. "This is Andrew Bray. There's no reason for concern. Preparations have been made to evacuate the hospital. All patients will be assisted to the north portico. From there they will …"

That was when Carla heard a bang and whirled in time to see smoke as the door slammed open. A man entered, followed by a woman. Both wore a hodgepodge of armor that had clearly been "liberated" from Madsen Mercenaries and dead legionnaires. They were armed with machine pistols and took a moment to scan the room before pointing their weapons at the ceiling.

A second man entered. He had dark skin, a shaved head, and a wet ankle-length coat. Water dripped onto the floor. "Good evening. I'm sorry about the door. My name is Wilson. We're resistance fighters. And *you*," Wilson said pointing a finger, "are Lieutenant Brice McCallum."

McCallum shrugged. "That's what it says on my ID bracelet."

Wilson turned to Carla. "And you're Doctor Hanson. Please stand. You're coming with us."

There was a flash of light in the distance, followed by a boom. It was louder than the one before. "No, we aren't," Carla replied. "You have no right to …"

"I'm going," McCallum said, as he got to his feet. "Anything is better than this."

"You won't be sorry," Wilson replied, as he turned to the female resistance fighter. "Take the doctor into custody."

Carla ran for the door. She was halfway there when the bolt from a stun gun struck her. Carla lost all muscle control and collapsed. A pair of arms scooped her up. Wilson's voice seemed to come from a long way off. "Let's get moving. The Legion is closing in."

* * *

McCallum felt sorry for Doctor Hanson, but couldn't help her, not with three armed opponents. He'd been briefed on the resistance, which wanted to be free of the company *and* the Imperial government. According to the Legion's Intel people, only two-thousand rebels belonged to the group, which made it more of a nuisance than a threat.

Wilson led them into a crowded hallway, but rather than join the ambulatory patients who were shuffling towards the elevators, Wilson shoved them out of the way. "Make a hole … Step aside … Emergency personnel coming through."

McCallum couldn't tell if people believed that, but if they didn't, the presence of two people armed with machine pistols kept them from complaining.

Wilson followed the emergency stairs up to the hospital's roof, where a darkened air car was waiting. Once the doctor was loaded into the back, Wilson ordered McCallum to get in, which he did.

The car departed two minutes later and headed north. It wasn't long before the vehicle began to bank right and left as it followed a pass up through the mountains to the manmade plateau on top of Mine 1. It was an old dig, and no longer in operation.

Half a dozen people met the car. Doctor Hanson was able to stand, but was a bit unsteady, so McCallum offered his arm. Together they followed Wilson up a dimly lit path.

The rebel leader was talking to some of his subordinates, and McCallum could tell that things weren't going well for the Madsen Company's mercs. Not that it mattered to Wilson, because he wanted *both* sides to lose.

After being escorted into the mine and through a maze of tunnels, the prisoners found themselves in a side gallery. A faded "Office" sign hung over the entryway. The walls consisted of machine-scored rock, the furnishings were utilitarian, and the floor was damp. A com center occupied one corner, and all of the incoming reports were negative.

A man with narrow-set eyes and prominent jaw came forward to meet them. McCallum knew the man was military, or ex-military, because of his bearing. "It's a pleasure to meet you, Lieutenant. I'm Mark Coogan. I hear the Legion tried to kill you."

"They came close," McCallum replied.

Coogan nodded. "We know about your mission. It was a thing of beauty."

"Until it wasn't," McCallum said grimly.

"Would you like to get even?" Coogan inquired.

"Yes," McCallum replied. "Put me with General Atov and I'll kill her."

"I'd love to," Coogan replied. "But that isn't possible. According to the most recent intelligence reports, she's aboard the destroyer *Maximus* and well out of our reach.

"There are other ways to strike back though."

"Count me in," McCallum replied.

"Even if that involves fighting the Legion?"

"When Atov ordered legionnaires to kill my team, they obeyed," McCallum said darkly.

Coogan nodded. "We're working on a mission, one you're uniquely qualified to carry out. But I'm not ready to brief you yet. Grab something to eat and get some rest. Rivera will show you around."

"Yes, sir."

"Good," Coogan replied. "Dismissed."

* * *

Carla turned to go as Rivera led McCallum out of the office. "Hold on," Coogan said, "I'd like to speak with you."

"About what?"

"About McCallum," Coogan replied. "What I said was true. I might have a mission for him. But I need to know if he's capable of pulling it off."

"I'm a doctor," Carla responded, "not a military person. I have no way to know how competent McCallum is."

"No. What I want is your assessment of whether McCallum could take charge of a team and hold it together long enough to blow up an enemy target. He's subject to hallucinations according to one of your coworkers."

One of Carla's peers had been feeding information to the resistance. Which one? Not that it mattered. "McCallum is a *very* responsible person," Carla replied. "That's why he feels so badly about losing his team. Even though there was nothing McCallum could do to prevent their deaths, he blames himself.

"So, if he had a *new* team, it seems reasonable to suppose that he would feel equally responsible for it," Carla concluded. "And that might keep him integrated. But it's just a theory. The human mind has a lot of moving parts, and his was injured."

"Thank you," Coogan said. "I appreciate your input. You're welcome to stay if you'd like to. Lord knows we need doctors. But it won't be pretty if you're captured. You might want to leave while that's possible. We'll provide you with supplies and a map."

Carla knew the rebel leader was right, but was willing to take the chance. "I'm going to stay. And, if you send McCallum on that mission, I want to go with him. The team will need a doctor."

Coogan frowned. "Is that the doctor speaking? Or the woman?"

"Both," Carla replied. "Let's leave it at that."

* * *

After drawing a set of civilian work clothes and eating some glutinous macaroni with Rivera, McCallum was free to choose one of the cots in Tunnel 1. Each bed was equipped with a soiled pillow and a Madsen Company blanket. That's all McCallum needed. Sleep pulled him down.

There was nothing other than nothing at first. Then the dreams began. McCallum was running, shouting orders, and looking for cover. When the mercs fired, legionnaires fell. *His* legionnaires. McCallum paused to grab a corporal's harness and drag her into the relative safety of an equipment shed.

The metal siding was thick enough to stop the small caliber stuff, but .50 caliber rounds passed right through it, and green tracers crisscrossed the interior head-high. That would have been the end of the fight if it hadn't been for the team's heavily armed Trooper Vs. Intense fire from their machineguns and arm-mounted energy weapons kept the mercenaries from advancing.

McCallum and his radio operator sat huddled under a tractor. "Ground Pounder to Sky Eye," McCallum said. "This is Ground Pounder. Over."

McCallum heard a burp of static followed by a female voice. "This is Sky Eye. I have you five-by-five. Over."

"We have the prize. But we're surrounded and taking heavy fire. Request air support and a fly form. Over."

A moment passed while General Atov was summoned. McCallum recognized her voice. "This is Sky Eye actual. Hang in there Pounder, air support is five out. A dust-off will follow. Over."

McCallum felt better after that. If Atov said help was on the way, then help was on the way. The fire fight continued. Men, women, and cyborgs died. But that was what they were paid to do. What *he* was paid to do. And something each of them had chosen.

Then, after what seemed like an eternity, the air assets arrived. Rather than announce themselves, as they normally would, the fighters attacked. Not the mercenaries, but the shed the legionnaires were hiding in, and that's when McCallum screamed.

McCallum woke to find that he was sitting up. His body was drenched in sweat, and his heart was beating fast. He looked left and right. Had he screamed out loud? No, apparently not. Rivera was snoring two feet away. Thank god for that.

McCallum forced himself to lay down. Now he was afraid to sleep lest he betray himself. Time passed slowly. Eventually a runner arrived. "Coogan wants to see you," the woman said. "He's waiting in his office."

McCallum was grateful for the chance to get up, but Rivera wasn't. He bitched all the way to the coffee pot, and from there to the office, where Coogan and members of his staff were waiting. "You know Rivera," Coogan said, "and this is Lieutenant McCallum. He was a member of the Legion until recently, and he's willing to help us.

"Lieutenant McCallum, this is Captain Hassan, our S-1, Captain Fenton, our S-2, and Major Ossey, our S-3. I told you that we might have a job for you, and we do. Captain Fenton? Bring the lieutenant up to speed."

McCallum knew that an S-2 was an intelligence officer, and the use of such titles seemed to confirm his suspicion that Coogan was a veteran of someone's army. A planetary force perhaps.

Fenton was thirty-something. She wore her hair in a ponytail, and was dressed in an olive-drab jump suit and a pair of muddy boots. A pistol was slung beneath her left arm. She nodded. "It's a pleasure to meet you, Lieutenant. The Owens snatch was a work of art. Please accept my condolences regarding the loss of your team.

"What I'm about to describe is a mission which, if successful, will hand General Atov a significant defeat. It won't win the war, but it will drag the conflict out for a year, and provide us with a chance to regroup."

"I'm in," McCallum said. "Let's do this thing."

Fenton smiled. "I like your attitude. Here's some background. As you are no doubt aware, the time-space continuum is thinner in some places—making it easier to enter or leave hyperspace at those locations.

"There could be tens of thousands of such points in our galaxy, but only eight-hundred and sixty-seven have been mapped and marked with beacons. A Madsen Mining scout ship discovered a jump point in this system. The company marked it with a beacon, filed a claim on the planet, and spent billions to settle it.

"Time passed. And as more and more shipping began to use the jump point, the Imperial government sent Madsen an electronic draft for half a billion dollars and took control of the beacon. Now the government intends to tax everything that comes and goes through the jump point—and levy a surcharge on the proceeds from Madsen's Rhodium mine too."

"That's where the mission comes in," Fenton added. "If we could put a team on the space station where the beacon is located, and destroy it, shipping would slow to a crawl.

"Yes, the imperials know where the node is. But to reestablish the beacon they'll have to send a new one, plus ships to protect it, all through normal space. And Madsen's mercenaries will be waiting for them.

"After that, who knows? Maybe we win and maybe we lose. But we'll have a chance. And that's more than we have now. Do you have any questions?"

"Yes," McCallum replied. "Why me?"

"Because," Coogan replied, "you are, or were, a Legion officer. And the space station is protected by legionnaires. You know how they think, and you know how they fight. Once on the station that could give you an edge.

"But there's something more as well. Only a person with an Imperial implant can operate the space station's outer lock. Yes, it might be possible for someone else to bullshit their way in, but the station's crew will expect to receive a navy officer, or a legionnaire, and it would be a shame to disappoint them."

McCallum gave the proposal some thought. Desertion was bad enough. But what if he was forced to kill some legionnaires? Could he live with that? *Yes*, the inner voice said. *The Legion killed your team.* And while he couldn't kill Atov he needed to do something. McCallum nodded. "I'm your man."

That's what McCallum said. But, deep inside he wondered. *Are you up to it? Can you face combat again? Are you the man you were?* No one answered.

* * *

Strange shapes squatted or loomed all around as Carla followed McCallum's team through a maze of worn out mining machines. Two days had passed since she'd been abducted from the hospital and McCallum had agreed to Colonel Coogan's proposal. "There she is," their guide said. "Straight ahead."

The *Solar Queen* was about sixty-years old and was waiting to be scrapped when members of the resistance brought her back to life. The freighter was crouched on her skids, ramp down, waiting for the team to board. A rectangle of light beckoned.

As Carla followed the others aboard she saw peeling paint, some loose wires that dangled from above, and a badly scarred deck. "All she has to do is get us there and bring us back," McCallum assured her. And that was true. But *could* she? That remained to be seen.

Assuming the old lady could lift, and exit the atmosphere, what then? Would the Imperial navy blow the *Queen* to smithereens? The answer was "no," according to Coogan.

The transponder had been stolen from an Imperial warship that was undergoing repairs on the far side of the planet. Since that time the device had been installed in the *Solar Queen* which, according to the signal she was broadcasting, was the Imperial cargo vessel *Helios*.

Unless someone decides to check, Carla thought, *in which case we'll wind up dead.*

The *Solar Queen's* pilot was a man named Nevis Blackburn. He liked to talk about "sticking it to the man," "screwing the system," and "making them pay." "Them" being the Madsen Mining managers who fired him for drinking on the job.

Carla strapped herself into a seat. The team included five people, all disguised as legionnaires. The team included a brusque miner named Stacy Hardin, an explosives expert named Frank Pedy, and ex-security officer Jan Omata. Her job, as McCallum put it, "is to kill people." And, judging from Omata's expression, she was looking forward to it.

"Okay, boys and girls," Blackburn said over the intercom. "Hang onto your panties, we're gonna light this thing off."

That was followed by some heavy gees as Blackburn took the *Queen* straight up. Carla closed her eyes and waited to die. She didn't. There was a brief moment of nausea as the ship left the planet's gravity well, followed by a sudden return of gravity as the freighter's argrav generator came on. "They bought it," Blackburn said over the intercom. "The *Queen* is cleared for an in-system shakedown cruise. We're twenty minutes out."

McCallum released his safety harness and stood. He looked different now. The surgical scrubs had been replaced by a set of the Legion's light-bending camos, body armor, and a combat harness.

McCallum smiled. "Welcome to the Legion, Doc."

He turned to the others. "Okay, listen up. We've been through it before, and yes, we're going to review it again. The orbital command authority is under the impression that this is an Imperial vessel which, after being repaired, is on a shakedown cruise.

"So, when Blackburn declares a mechanical emergency, traffic control will approve his request to dock with the space station. That's when we'll enter, make our way to the compartment where the beacon is housed, and plant our explosives.

"Then we'll return to the *Queen*. If we're lucky Blackburn will put the ship down in the western hemisphere. Then we'll run like hell, because once the Legion figures out what happened, they will destroy the ship.

"Do you have any questions? No? Good. Dr. Hanson? Would you join me please?"

Carla stood, and followed McCallum back to where the post-landing expedition packs were stored. The cargo hold was mostly empty, utilitarian in appearance, and very worn. McCallum turned to face her. "Can I call you Carla?"

"Yes, you can."

McCallum nodded. "Thank you. I need a favor Carla, one that only you can grant me."

"Okay," Carla replied tentatively. "What is it?"

"You have a pistol," McCallum said. "If I start to hallucinate, I want you to shoot me. I know you aren't trained to fire a pistol, but we'll be close to each other, so I'll be impossible to miss. Just pull the trigger and keep pulling until I go down. Save me Carla, save me from myself."

Carla felt a lump form in the back of her throat. "That won't happen."

"I feel better than I did before," McCallum said. "A lot better. But who knows? People are depending on me. So, promise."

Carla looked into his eyes. "I promise."

McCallum looked relieved. "Thanks. That takes the pressure off. And, if something happens to me, please accept my thanks. You're a good shrink, not to mention a pretty one, and if things were different ... Well, you know."

"Yes," Carla said. "I know."

McCallum smiled. "Good."

"Strap in," Blackburn said via the intercom. "It's show time."

There weren't any ports in the hold, or view screens, so all the boarding party could do was sit and sweat as Blackburn docked the ship. Time seemed to stretch, and Carla had to battle her right foot, which had a tendency to jerk up and down.

But finally, after what seemed like an eternity, Carla felt a gentle thump and knew the *Queen* was in contact with the space station. "We have a lock," Blackburn announced. "You can leave your seats and board once air pressures are equalized. Have fun."

Fun was the one thing Carla knew she wouldn't have as the team made last minute adjustments to their gear. They were wearing skintight bio-space-suits in case fighting caused a catastrophic decompression on the space station. There was no need to bring anything other than their weapons, ammo, and two satchel charges.

Once they were ready, McCallum led the way to the airlock. Omata was in the two slot, with Carla in three. Hardin and Pedy brought up the rear.

The group paused in front of the lock and, when a light flashed green, the air-tight hatch hissed open.

* * *

McCallum entered the lock, waited for the rest to do likewise, and pushed a button. Air hissed, thirty seconds passed, and the inner hatch irised open. That allowed McCallum to enter the space station's lock, where he had to shove his hand into a scanner or request an override from the platform's duty officer. Something that would invite closer scrutiny.

McCallum slid his hand into the scanner, felt a tingling sensation, and knew that the ship's computer was communicating with his implant. He heard a click, followed by a computer-generated voice. "Welcome aboard, Lieutenant McCallum. Please proceed through the tubeway."

The inner hatch cycled open, and that was Hardin's cue to place a steel pry bar across the opening, a precaution that would prevent the space station's crew from closing their side of the lock. McCallum spotted a navy lieutenant entering the other end of the tubeway and knew that was to be expected. The navy was responsible for operating the platform and it was the Legion's job to protect it. "Hello," the navy officer said. "My name is …"

McCallum brought the stun gun up and fired. The lieutenant jerked and fell. McCallum stepped over the body, followed by Omata. Their job was to take control of the station or, failing that, to protect Pedy and Hardin.

A Legion sergeant appeared up ahead. He was armed and blocking the tubeway. "Hold on," the legionnaire ordered. "I need to see …"

McCallum shot him with the stun gun, but it was a waste of time. Unlike the navy officer, the noncom was wearing Class 1 "active" body armor, which protected him from a wide range of electronic weapons. He was bringing his weapon to bear when Omata shot him in the head. *Twice.*

The second hole was half an inch from the first, and thanks to the suppressor mounted on Omata's long-barreled pistol, the shots produced very little noise. The sergeant fell over backwards and landed with a thump.

McCallum knew that he should have felt something. Regret? Sorrow? Something. But he didn't. The Legion was the enemy now … and so was the sergeant.

An alarm began to bleat. Cameras were mounted in the tubeway, and once the noncom's vital signs stopped, the Legion's onboard Command and Control computer warned its operator. That meant the shit was going to hit the fan—and the chances of a successful takeover plunged to zero. "Implement Plan B," McCallum said. "Omata and I will hold the main corridor, while Pedy and Hardin plant the charges. Go."

Thanks to information gathered by Fenton and her spies, a diagram of the platform's layout was projected on the inner surface of each team member's visor. That's how McCallum knew that the first responders were likely to follow the main corridor aft.

The first wave appeared quickly. There were about eight of them, which

represented roughly half the legionnaires on board. They opened fire immediately, or half of them did. Those in the rear couldn't fire without hitting
the soldiers in front of them. And, as low velocity bullets whipped past the
opening to the tubeway, McCallum readied a flash grenade. Omata, who
was on the other side of the passageway, did likewise.

"Now!" McCallum said, the legionnaires continued to push forward. The
grenades sailed up the corridor, landed, and went off. The flashes were calculated to momentarily disable the defenders' HUDs. McCallum and Omata
took advantage of the opportunity to step out and fire their weapons on
full auto. They were using armor piercing ammo in spite of the fact that
they were on a pressurized space station because, thanks to their emergency
space suits, the team knew they would survive a sudden decompression.

As the gun smoke cleared, a horrible scene was revealed. The bulkheads
were red with splattered blood. *All* of the legionnaires were down. Most
were dead. But, judging from the moans, at least two were still alive. "Let
me help them," Carla said. "Then I'll come back."

"No can do," McCallum replied. "They're legionnaires. They're down,
but they aren't out. One will grab you, put a gun to your head, and attempt
to negotiate."

Carla was about to argue with McCallum when a hatch opened and a
legionnaire fired from the crawlspace below. The blast from his short-bar-
reled energy weapon struck Omata and killed her. She fell. McCallum barely knew her, but felt a stab of sorrow.

McCallum was about to respond when a second defender dropped from
a hatch above. McCallum's first impulse was to bring his submachinegun
to bear, but strong hands reached out to grab his harness and pull him close.

Both men knew how to fight hand-to-hand, and both meant to penetrate
their opponent's armor. McCallum was wielding a vibro blade, which could
cut through durasteel, and the other legionnaire had a hand laser. The air
sizzled as the weapons swept from left to right. Arms blurred as a series of
lightning-fast blows were thrown and blocked.

Meanwhile Omata's killer was climbing up out of the crawlspace. Carla's pistol was in its holster. As Carla drew the weapon, she was surprised
by how heavy it was. What had McCallum told her? "Pull the trigger, and
keep pulling it." She did.

The recoil came as a surprise. Her hands wobbled, and bullets flew wide,
but two struck the target. The first flattened itself on the legionnaire's armor.
The second punched a hole through the legionnaire's visor. He fell like a

puppet without strings.

Pedy's voice came over the radio. "Pull back to the ship! Hardin and I are inside the compartment where the beacon is located and we're surrounded.

"The timers have been set. You have five minutes to board and haul ass. One more thing ... Hardin wants someone to adopt his dog. Pedy out." The message was followed by a click.

Carla was still absorbing the news when McCallum grabbed her arm. His opponent was laying on the deck with both hands wrapped around the vibro knife's hilt. He was trying to remove it from his chest. "No," Carla exclaimed, "don't do that!"

But it was too late. The knife came out, followed by a spurt of blood. The legionnaire's helmet hit the deck and his hands fell free.

McCallum pulled Carla into the tubeway. "Come on!" They ran side by side.

The lock was open, thanks to the steel bar, and McCallum jerked it loose. Steel clanged on steel as it hit the deck. Carla saw the glowing green button and slapped it. There was a whining sound as the hatch started to close. McCallum slipped through the gap.

"I'm breaking contact," Blackburn announced, as the second hatch opened and closed behind them. "Hold on ... It's gonna be a rough ride."

Carla and McCallum were thrown into a steel bulkhead as Blackburn hit the throttles and the *Queen* took off. "Three Imperial fighters are headed our way," Blackburn said. "We have a two or three-minute lead. I'm going to put the ship into a steep dive, re-enter the atmosphere, and look for a place to pancake in.

"Once we hit, grab your packs and bail out. I'll be right behind you. Oh, and one more thing, the space station blew. The beacon was destroyed."

Any happiness that Carla might have felt was washed away by the knowledge that Hardin, Pedy, and Omata were dead. She'd barely known them, but would never forget the sacrifice they'd made, or the cause they'd died for.

McCallum and Carla lurched back and forth between makeshift handholds as they made their way back to the seats and the packs that were strapped to the deck beyond. They held hands once their harnesses were fastened. That was a first, but it felt natural.

The ship shook violently as it entered the atmosphere. A loose bolt rattled across the deck on its way forward, and Carla closed her eyes. "One of the bastards is on our tail," Blackburn said tightly. "A missile is locked onto us …"

The explosion shook the ship. The *Queen* rolled 360 degrees and hit. Unsecured items flew every which way. The ship topped a dozen trees before finally coming to rest in the treetops. McCallum threw the harness off and jumped to his feet. "I'll check on Blackburn. Drag our packs to the belly hatch and drop them to the ground." Then he was gone.

The plan made sense. Carla freed herself and made her way to the hatch, where she flipped a protective cover out of the way. A red button was waiting. Carla pressed it. There was a bang and a puff of smoke as the hatch blew off and crashed through the foliage below.

The first pack was falling as McCallum reappeared. He held a coil of rope. "I'll tie this off. Slide down, grab your pack, and get ready to run. I'll be right behind you."

"What about Blackburn?"

McCallum shook his head. "The ship hit a tree. The cockpit collapsed."

Carla felt numb as she slid to the ground. Both packs were waiting and, by the time McCallum arrived, Carla was ready.

The jungle exploded around them. Trees came crashing down, a chunk of metal whirred past Carla's head, and McCallum waved her forward. "That was a cluster bomb. Come on!"

They ran, and ran some more. Ducking, dodging, and sometimes crawling as they sought to put distance between the ship and themselves. They had just topped a rise when an explosion shook the earth under their feet and a pillar of fire pushed a mushroom-shaped cloud of smoke up into the sky. The *Solar Queen* was no more.

Aerospace fighters continued to circle overhead, but the ground attacks stopped as the fugitives went into hiding. "Their scanners can detect both movement *and* heat," McCallum explained. "But, so long as we remain still, our heat signatures won't seem to be significant."

The strategy worked, and the fighters peeled away ten minutes later.

After emerging from their hiding place, the couple made their way to a clearing and the edge of a cliff.

"I lost four people," McCallum said miserably. "You were supposed to shoot me."

"Not unless you began to hallucinate," Carla replied gently. "And you didn't. Plus, each did what he or she wanted to do. *Had* to do."

McCallum nodded. "It isn't that simple, but thank you."

"You're welcome," Carla said, as she kissed him on the cheek. Then, as

McCallum placed an arm around her shoulders, a gentle rain began to fall. Carla felt the cool droplets touch her skin. "Look!" she said. "A rainbow!"

McCallum looked out over the jungle and there it was. The multicolored arch was reaching westward to a point where it lost definition. Rainbow's end.

The Woman in Green

D.B. Jackson

Boston, Province of Massachusetts Bay, 8 July 1775

Ethan Kaille crouched beside the dirt road, concealed by swaying grass on the Roxbury side of Boston's Town Gate. The stink of mud soured the air. Flies and midges swarmed him each time the hot breeze settled. Sweat tickled his face and neck.

He counted a total of eight British regulars by the guardhouses. One or two more might have been inside. The men held muskets and wore uniforms of red and white. Their steel bayonets flashed like fish scales in the sun's glare.

He watched the soldiers for some time as they chatted and laughed, but they did nothing unusual. They appeared no more watchful than they had when he observed them the previous day, or the one before that. Equally important, their numbers had not increased. He had seen no more than ten guards at the gate at any one time. Morning, evening, midday—the count remained about the same.

Ethan eased away from the road on his hands and knees, taking care to make no noise and to disturb the grass as little as possible. He had cloaked himself in a concealment spell before approaching Boston's Neck. Had he stood and waved to the men, they wouldn't have seen him, though they might have spotted his shadow, or noted the parting of the grass around his legs. His conjurings could fool the unsuspecting, but not the sun or the earth.

He crawled a long way before he risked standing. Even after that, he placed his feet with caution, hindered by the limp he'd acquired nearly twenty years before as a convict laborer on a Barbados sugar plantation. A heron eyed him from the edge of the marsh—beasts and birds saw through his spells—but a pair of fishermen in a dory near the shore appeared oblivious of his presence.

He found his skiff as he'd left it: resting on the mud in a small cove near the Patriot lines at Roxbury. Pausing beside the vessel, he pulled a handful of grass from the ground and whispered, "*Fini velamentum ex gramine evocatum.*" End concealment, conjured from grass.

His spell thrummed like a bowstring in the ground beneath his feet. At the same time, a glowing figure winked into view beside him, russet like a rising moon, but nearly impossible to see in bright daylight. This ghost, his spectral guide, appeared each time Ethan conjured and allowed him access to the magick that dwelt along the boundary between the world of the living and the realm of the dead.

Ethan hadn't felt the concealment spell while it was in place, and he didn't sense its absence now, but as he pushed the skiff onto the still water and hopped in, another fisherman waved to him, confirmation that his removal conjuring had worked.

He rowed away from the Neck, giving the British positions at either end of the causeway a wide berth. Eventually, he angled northward and made for the narrow strand near the stillhouse at Hill's Wharf.

Most who sympathized with the Patriot cause had long since abandoned Boston for Roxbury and towns farther inland, leaving the city to the lobsterbacks and their Loyalist allies. But a few remained, their sympathies hidden, their labors on behalf of liberty clandestine.

One such worked in the distillery. Without the help of this man, the attack Ethan and the others had planned for this night would fail, at the cost of many lives.

Ethan paused in his rowing to retrieve a fishing pole and net from the bottom of the skiff. He leaned these on the hull at the vessel's prow so that they would be visible to all. Then he resumed rowing and oared the skiff to the strand. Here, close to the heart of Boston's South End, his was one of many small boats navigating the shallows of the harbor. He couldn't keep from being seen, but he could do his best to blend with the daily flow of fishermen and peddlers to and from the city's wharves.

After shipping his oars and dragging the skiff onto the strand, he hurried up Hills Lane, a small alley between houses that led to the main road fronting the South End wharves. He paused in the shadows, pulled his knife from his belt, and cut his forearm. Whispering in Latin once more, he cast a warding over himself, a spell that would protect him from physical harm. Magick hummed in the cobblestones and the ghost reappeared before him. In the shade, Ethan could make out more of the specter: the chain mail, the Plantagenet lions on his tabard, the trim, graying beard, and the familiar frown on his lean, luminous face. Long ago Ethan had named the ghost Uncle Reg, after his mother's temperamental brother.

"You have something you'd like to say?" Ethan asked.

Reg's scowl deepened. To Ethan's knowledge, the ghost was incapable of speech. Certainly he had never heard the spirit utter a word. That didn't mean, though, that he couldn't have some fun at Reg's expense. A creature as splenetic as this one deserved mockery every so often.

"You know why we're here," Ethan said, sobering. "The conjurings are a necessity."

Still clearly displeased at having been disturbed, the ghost began to fade. As he did, another spell growled beneath Ethan's feet, an answer to his own. Reg took form again, his hard, gleaming gaze finding Ethan's.

"Where did that come from?" Ethan asked.

The ghost shrugged, shook his head.

Ethan wasn't the only conjurer in Boston, but of those who were likely to be in the city now, with the British military controlling the streets, there were few he trusted. This could have been a benign conjuring from one of them. He thought it more likely, however, that the spell had been cast by an ally of the Crown.

Seconds later, the magick reached him, twining around his legs like an invisible vine climbing a trellis. A finding spell.

Somewhere in the city or its environs, a conjurer was reaching out with magick, hoping to locate other spellers. Likely the person had sensed Ethan's spell and wanted to discover its source. Ethan had no desire to be found or to lead the conjurer to his friend in the stillhouse.

"Could you tell where it originated?" he asked the ghost.

Reg turned a full circle, his brow knotted. At last he pointed to the north.

"Cornhill? Or farther? The North End?"

The ghost gestured with an open hand. *Farther.*

"Good. Thank you. But you should leave me now. I'm easier to spot with you beside me."

Reg nodded and melted into the shadows. Ethan stepped onto Essex Street, but turned westward, instead of toward the distillery.

He made his way to Newbury Street, the largest thoroughfare in this part of the city, and entered the first establishment he saw, a clothier's shop. A small brass bell jingled as he opened and closed the door. The shop smelled of wool and lambskin and clean linen. The proprietor, a gangly, white-haired man, pulled his attention from the young gentleman he was helping to peer at Ethan over the spectacles perched on his nose.

"I'll be with you in just a few moments, sir."

"Yes, thank you."

Ethan lingered near the door, staring out the window, which offered a clear view of the avenue. His gaze skipped over the people walking past. He couldn't recognize a conjurer on sight—his powers didn't run so deep—but he thought he might notice someone who searched the street as he did.

After a few minutes, the clothier's customer crossed to the door with a whisper of silk. He wore a green ditto suit and a tricorn hat that made the one on Ethan's head look shabby and worn. His eyes flicked over Ethan, taking in his stained breeches and threadbare coat. A sneer settled on his square face as he let himself out of the shop.

The draper joined Ethan at the window. "I'm sorry to keep you waiting, sir."

"Not at all." Ethan scanned the street before forcing himself to face the man.

"You wish to buy a suit? Or a new coat perhaps?"

"A suit," Ethan said. "Linen. No waistcoat."

"Very good, sir. Did you have a color in mind."

He glanced out the window again. "Blue, I think."

Kannice's favorite color. She would be pleased were he actually to have a suit made. Not that he would wear it with any frequency. But she would find occasions for them to fancy up, and he would feel like a fop each time.

"I have some material here," the clothier said. He strode to the back of the shop. "Fine linen," he went on, his voice carrying. "Just in from Ireland. I believe I have several shades of blue."

Ethan nodded, though the man couldn't see, and continued to survey the lane.

Soon enough, he spotted a woman who was distinguished by her behavior more than her appearance. He pressed himself to the wooden frame of the window and watched.

She was petite, dressed in a green satin gown with a lace stomacher and yellow petticoats. Strands of auburn hair peeked out from beneath a white cap. Ethan guessed that she was no more than twenty years old. She walked slowly, affecting an air of nonchalance that Ethan distrusted. Her gaze struck him as too keen, her bearing stiff with tension.

"Sir?"

"Aye," Ethan said, studying the young woman. "Just a moment."

She paused at the corner of Essex Street, swept Newbury with her gaze one more time, and started down Essex toward the waterfront, lifting her petticoats as she stepped over a puddle.

Ethan tracked her progress until he could no longer see her.

"Sir?" the clothier said again, walking back to the front of the shop. "I found several bolts of blue linen, if you care to take a look."

"Thank you," Ethan said, tipping his hat. "And my apologies. I'm afraid I must go. Another matter demands my immediate attention. I'll return when I can."

"But—"

"Good day."

Ethan opened the door more sharply than he had intended. He cursed the jangle of the bell, let himself out of the shop, and shut the door with more care. At the corner, he peered after the woman and saw her some twenty paces ahead of him. He followed.

The woman in green walked with purpose and never once turned to see who might be following her, which made it that much more surprising when magick surged in the street again and her spectral counterpart to Uncle Reg materialized beside her. This figure, a woman who shone with a faint golden hue, did turn to stare back at Ethan. After a moment, the ghost smiled. Then she faced forward, keeping in step with the young conjurer.

Ethan could only chuckle and continue to follow. It seemed the woman was more skilled at this sort of intrigue than he had credited. As if reading his thoughts, she halted and half turned.

"Do you wish to follow me more, or shall we dispense with the games?"

He looked up and down the lane—it was mostly empty save for the two of them—and approached her with some caution. Already he had warded himself, though only against physical assaults. He hadn't expected to en-counter another conjurer this day. As he neared the woman, he bit down hard on the inside of his cheek. He tasted blood, which he used to source a second warding, this one against any spells she might throw his way.

The conjuring thrummed, drawing Reg again. The woman's ghost glared at him. Reg bared his teeth in response.

"A warding," the woman said. "You believe I intend you harm?" A sly smile crossed her lips. "Or perhaps you mean to attack me."

Her eyes were deep blue and a sprinkling of freckles dotted her cheeks and the bridge of her nose. Her face was round; some might have thought it friendly, open. He didn't.

"Why would I attack you?"

"I could ask you the same," she said. "Why would you have warded yourself?"

"Was your finding spell intended for me?"

She resumed walking toward the wharves. After a moment's hesitation, Ethan fell in beside her.

"I felt your earlier spell," she said. "I was curious." She regarded him sidelong. "You don't look like a typical Tory."

He couldn't help glancing around to see if others had heard.

"I see," she said. "You're not a Tory."

"I don't care much for politics one way or another. Patriots. Loyalists. I want no part of either side."

She considered him still. After a few seconds she shook her head. "I think you're lying. I believe you're very much interested in all that happens in Boston, *to* Boston."

"What makes you—"

The woman held up a hand, stopping him. "No games, no more lies. Why are you here?"

"I live here."

"Not since His Majesty's army took the city."

Ethan returned her frank stare.

"That wasn't my first finding spell, Mister …?"

"Kaille. Ethan Kaille."

Her smile this time seemed free of irony. "Ah, the thieftaker. I wondered when we would meet. You have something of a reputation in this city."

"To whom have you been speaking?"

"Sephira Pryce, Sheriff Greenleaf—"

"Pryce is a rival," he said, gazing toward the water. "And Greenleaf hates all conjurers."

"Before I sailed from London, I spoke with Governor Hutchinson."

Ethan opened his mouth, closed it without a word. He hadn't expected that. He and the former governor had a long and contentious history.

"I ask you again, what is a Whig conjurer doing in the city?"

"You haven't told me your name."

"No, I haven't."

He lifted a shoulder, said nothing.

The woman huffed a breath. "Catherine Percy. Now, answer my question."

"If you're right about me, why would I tell you anything at all?"

She paused to pick a dandelion that had flowered between two cobblestones. Her eyes met his for an instant. At the same time, Reg reached toward him with a glowing hand, the specter's lambent eyes going wide. The only warnings Ethan had.

The spell carved through his wardings as if they were no more than parchment and crashed into him like a runaway carriage. The force of it lifted Ethan off his feet. He slammed into the building beside him and crumpled to the ground.

He lay still for a moment, or perhaps an hour. He really couldn't be sure. His entire body ached. He struggled to draw breath, or to focus on Catherine as she walked to where he lay and stood over him.

"That was a dandelion," she said, matter-of-factly. "Imagine what I can do with blood."

He looked away from her, found Reg's gaze with his own. The ghost gave a small shake of his head.

Ethan tried anyway. He bit his cheek again, drawing more blood, and cast. Despite what she had done to him he had no desire to kill, or even wound. He tried to put her to sleep.

She laughed.

"Surely you can do better than that."

Another conjuring pounded him, like the butt of a soldier's musket. His vision swam.

"You're overmatched, thieftaker. Just as your fellow Patriots are overmatched by the King's army. Your cause is doomed."

He didn't respond.

"One way or another, I will learn why you've come," she said. "And I've every confidence that what you tell me will prove of great interest to General Gage."

"I have no intention of telling you anything."

"Of course not. But prison, and magick, and pain judiciously applied, can alter even the best of intentions. Sheriff Greenleaf is on his way here."

Ethan raised himself into a sitting position, braced his hands on the cobblestones beneath him.

Catherine held up another dandelion and shook her head, much as Reg had moments before. "Don't make me hurt you again."

He lift his hands, held them up for her to see.

She nodded approval.

"We've heard rumors," she said. "Word of an impending attack on positions in the city. Is that why you're here, to reconnoiter for General Washington?"

Ethan tried to keep surprise from registering on his face. How could she have known so much about their plans? "Do I look like a spy?" he asked.

She answered with a gentle flick of her slender hand, a gesture that encompassed her face, her hair, her gown. "Do I? Answer the question."

He would have liked to stall, hoping that time might reveal an opportunity for escape. But if, as she said, Greenleaf was coming, he had no time to waste.

Already she had proved that her wardings were more than a match for his conjurings. But what if he didn't attack her directly? After all, she already held in her hand the source for a spell.

"*Aperi hiatum ex taraxaco evocatum.*" Open chasm, conjured from dandelion.

The rumble of his spell was lost in the rending of rock. A fissure opened in the street beneath her leather shoes. Catherine fought for balance, but fell back into the crevice. Ethan scrambled to his feet and, before she could recover or cast, kicked out, catching her square in the jaw. Her head snapped back and she collapsed. Ethan approached her warily and checked to make certain she was still breathing.

Some who fought for the Patriot cause would have wanted him to kill her, to eliminate for good the threat she represented. There were limits, though, to what Ethan was willing to do, even in pursuit of liberty for the colonies. He would not murder, even if ordered to do so by Samuel Adams himself.

Satisfied that she would recover, albeit with an aching head, Ethan hurried back along Essex to Hill's Stillhouse. His vision had cleared, and he had found his breath, but every step pained him, and he had a headache of his own.

He entered the distillery through a side door off the wharf, as he had been instructed. The moment he stepped inside he was nearly overcome with the smell of rum. Eyes watering, vision adjusting to the dim light within, he scanned the space.

Danny Roan, the man he had come to see, stood near the kiln, stoking the fire with a large bellows. He was stout, dark-haired, with a boyish face, and thick, muscular arms. He caught sight of Ethan, looked around, and beckoned him nearer.

"I expected you earlier," he said, gaze darting right and left.

"I know. I ran into a bit of trouble. I can't stay long."

Danny's expression hardened. "If there was trouble, you shouldn't have come at all."

"I had no choice. The attack will happen tonight, just after sundown, while there's still light enough to see."

"Tonight," Danny repeated. He glanced about once more. "Well, that's..." A smile broke through his frown. "Tonight? Really?"

"Aye. There have been no more than ten or a dozen men at the guard-houses on the Roxbury side. This is the best chance we'll have."

"I'd like to take more than the Neck, but I suppose Washington knows what he's doing, eh?"

"I'm certain Washington will lead us well," Ethan said, because he felt he should.

The truth was, he harbored more doubts than his words suggested. In the past few days, since news of George Washington's arrival in Cambridge spread to Roxbury, many among his Whig friends had spoken with confidence—bordering on arrogance—of a quick victory over the British. Several had predicted that the lobsters' hold on Boston would be broken before summer's end.

Ethan had no reason to doubt Washington's competence as a leader, but the British were dug in; forcing them from the city would take time. And Ethan feared that Boston had lost its finest military leader three weeks before on Bunker Hill. Young, dashing, intelligent, Doctor Joseph Warren was as passionate an advocate for liberty as anyone, including Samuel Adams. He had also been a friend to Ethan, even before Ethan pledged himself to the Patriot cause. More to the point, he knew the city better than Washington and would have been the natural choice to break this occupation.

"But we won't take the city in a single night," he went on. "Small steps,

Danny. We'll drive them out eventually. It starts at dusk. You know what to do?"

"We know. You have my word. With all the trouble we intend to stir up in Cornhill tonight, any extra regulars who might otherwise be on the Neck will be in the city instead."

Ethan gripped the young man's shoulder. "Our thanks."

He returned to the distillery's side door and opened it a crack. Seeing no one on the wharf or on the small stretch of strand beside it, he slipped out into the hot air and sunshine. He would have preferred to make his way back to the skiff under the protection of another concealment spell, but he didn't dare risk a conjuring with Catherine Percy so near.

He removed his hat and his coat, bundling the latter under his arm, and walked up the wharf and onto the strand as swiftly as his bad leg would allow. The skiff remained where he had left it. He saw no sign of the woman, or of Sheriff Greenleaf and his men. He had abandoned faith long ago, in the heat and brutality of his life as a convict, but he could almost convince himself that God himself smiled on their endeavor.

Once on the water again, Ethan rowed himself to a cluster of fishing boats, shipped his oars, and reached for the pole he had stowed in the vessel. He lingered there, fishing with the rest, trading greetings and comments on the day with other fishermen.

"Hot as the devil, even on the water."

"They were biting earlier. Not as much now."

"At least the lobsters don't tax our catches." This last from a bold soul.

Some of the fishermen laughed. Others scowled in disapproval. Every one of them cast at least a glance in the direction of the warships moored near Long Wharf.

After a while, Ethan rowed to another group, closer to Roxbury. And when he had spent a bit of time with them, he continued to shore.

The militiamen on the road leading into town recognized him and let him pass. At the first lane on the west side of the road, he turned and made his way to the farmhouse of Robert Lyons, where the militia leaders had set up their headquarters. More than a hundred soldiers prowled the grounds of the house. They looked young and restless and, Ethan had to admit, not nearly as formidable as the regulars he had seen on the Neck.

The majority of Boston's most prominent Whigs had been forced to leave the city's immediate environs after His Majesty's forces took Bunker Hill. Samuel Adams and John Hancock were now in Philadelphia as members of the Continental Congress. Paul Revere had joined the Committee of Safety in Cambridge.

But William Dawes remained in Roxbury and had assumed command of the raid planned for this evening. A tanner by trade, he had become a local hero, along with Revere and Samuel Prescott, on the night before the battles of Lexington and Concord. If not for their warnings, shouted into the night as they rode through the countryside, those first skirmishes with the British might have turned out far worse for colonial forces.

Dawes was also a member of the Massachusetts Artillery Company. Less than a year before, he had been instrumental in the success of a plot to steal several small cannons from the British. Two of those pieces currently sat in the Lyons' barn awaiting this night's assault on the Neck.

Dawes was a big man, heavy around the middle, with thick, unruly hair, and a broad, homely face.

When Ethan entered the Lyons house, Dawes greeted him with a booming "Kaille!"

Ethan grinned. "Good day, sir."

Dawes sat at the dining table, a cup of watered Madeira set precariously amid several maps.

"All went as planned?"

Ethan faltered for the span of a single heartbeat, but that was enough.

Dawes turned to the young militiaman standing near the table. "Leave us." Once the soldier was gone, he beckoned Ethan to the table with a meaty hand. "What's happened?"

Speaking in low tones, Ethan described for the tanner his encounter with Catherine Percy. As he spoke, a grimace settled on Dawes' face.

"You say she's like you?" he asked, when Ethan had finished.

"A conjurer, you mean."

"Aye."

Ethan nodded. "Yes. A powerful one. I escaped her, but only just. That's the least of our worries. She knows we're planning a raid. And if she knows—"

"Of course they know," Dawes said, dismissing Ethan's concern with a wave of his hand. "They know everything, and they know nothing. They can't expect us to give up Boston, and so this woman can say to you in all honesty that she knows we're planning something. She'll even know that the first assault will come from Roxbury. What choice do we have? We're no match for His Majesty's navy, but by the same token, they can't fight us in the countryside. We've already proved that to them." He sipped his wine. "No, Kaille. What she knows about our plans is far less important than what she might do with her witchery." Dawes cringed. "Forgive me. Her … what do you call it?"

"Her conjurings."

"Aye, those. It falls to you, Kaille. We can take the gate. But only if you can keep this woman at bay. Understood?"

"Yes, sir."

The tanner nodded. "Good. You spoke to the lad at the stillhouse?"

"I did. He and his friends will see to it that the gate has no reinforcements tonight."

"Well done." Dawes gazed out the nearest window. "We've a few hours still until dusk. There's nothing more you can do. Get something to eat and be ready come sundown."

"I will be. Thank you, sir."

Ethan exited the house, but despite his orders from Dawes, he didn't bother searching for food. His stomach felt tight, uneasy. He had fought at Concord and also on Breed's Hill. He didn't fear battle any more or any less than the next man, but in those engagements Patriot forces had faced only the might of the British army. They hadn't been tasked with fighting magick as well. This night's skirmish promised to be tiny by comparison, yet he dreaded the encounter, knowing the woman in green would be there and determined to have her revenge.

* * *

At day's end, with the sun low in the west casting golden light and long shadows across the fields of Roxbury, William Dawes mustered nearly two hundred militiamen into formation. The two cannons had been brought forth from the barn on horse drawn carts.

Ethan stood with the other soldiers, a musket braced on his shoulder, his knife on his belt. Dawes had made it clear he wanted him on the front line, not because he was a good marksman, though he was, but because they might need his magick before the night was over.

Kannice had long urged him to join the Patriot cause, but seeing him at the fore of this company, she would have been more worried than proud.

They marched toward the causeway, following the road as far as they could without alerting the guards on the Neck to their approach. At a signal from Dawes, they halted and waited while the cannons were unhinged from the horses.

Then they resumed their advance, silent, concealed first by trees and then by the dimming of the day. Several men pulled each of the cannons. Once in the marshes, they kept low, as Ethan had earlier that afternoon. A soft wind blew—not enough to cool the air, but enough to mask the sound of their advance. Two men stood outside the guardhouses at the Town Gate. Neither appeared to take any notice of the colonial force.

This is too easy.

The epiphany crashed through his thoughts, fueled by intuition and fear. The woman in green was here, hidden by magick.

He didn't slow, or say anything to the men around him, but he cast a spell, aimed at her concealment.

Aufer carmen, he said within his mind, *ex gramine evocatum.* Remove spell, conjured from grass.

Through his hands and knees, he felt the conjuring vibrate in the earth. Reg materialized beside him. To Ethan's relief, the ghost had known to keep low to the ground so that Catherine Percy wouldn't spot him. He hoped the casting would be strong enough to overmaster whatever spell she had used to conceal herself. He raised his head until he could see past the swaying grass.

Miss Percy stood on the Neck behind the gate and guardhouses, still wearing green. Even at this distance, Ethan read anger in her stance. As he watched, her spectral companion appeared, bright yellow in the gloaming. Magick growled in the ground.

He cast again in desperation—a warding that cleared a swath of grass directly in front of him.

But she didn't throw her spell at him.

Flame leaped into the night only a few yards from where the lead soldiers parted the grass. Men shouted in alarm and fell back.

Ethan cast again, an extinguishing spell aimed at the fire itself. But he knew he couldn't trade conjurings with the woman. Young as she was, she already had abilities he couldn't match.

Fortunately, Danny Roan and his friends chose that moment to spark their riot in Cornhill. Shouts went up from the city. Fires erupted in the distance. Several of the regulars on the Neck spun to look in that direction. Catherine did the same.

Seizing the opportunity Danny and the others had given him, Ethan tried the only thing he could think of. He pulled his knife from his belt, pushed up his sleeve, and cut his arm.

"*Ignis ex cruore evocatus*," he whispered. A fire spell, directed at the woman herself.

"What are you doing?" asked the man beside him.

"Keep moving. Follow your orders."

Ethan didn't bother to check what effect his fire spell had on her. Instead, he slashed at his arm again. "*Discuti ex cruore evocatum.*" A shatter spell, also aimed at Miss Percy.

"Mister Dawes!" he called. "Attack now!"

He cut himself a third time. "*Pugnus ex cruore evocatus.*" A fist spell.

"We're not close enough," Dawes said.

"There is no time! Attack!" He drew still more blood and threw a suffocation spell at the woman.

To his credit, Dawes didn't waste an instant. He had the men bring the cannons forward and quickly saw to their positioning.

Ethan cast a blade spell, a sleeping spell, another fire spell. Each time he slashed at his arm, drawing more blood, ignoring the livid red of his skin, the ache in his flesh, the sweat beading on his face.

He cast, and cast, and cast again, allowing Catherine no time to rest, no time to attack him, and, most important, no time to turn her powers on the colonial militiamen. Her wardings might stop the spells from burning her, or slicing her in two, or shattering the bones in her neck, but what mattered was that each attack would land like a blow, staggering her, stealing her breath. He had been the object of such an assault. He remembered the experience all too well.

The first cannon roared with a spurt of flame and a billow of pale smoke. The second fired moments later. Both artillery pieces found their marks. Cannon balls punched through the roof of one guardhouse and the wall of the other.

Regulars streamed from the building, more than he had expected, but still not enough to fight off this company of Colonials.

"Fire!" Dawes bellowed.

The dry report of musket fire crackled like a winter blaze. Smoke hazed the evening sky.

And still Ethan conjured. A scalding spell. A stinging spell. Another blade spell. Binding. Suffocation. Strangulation. Blindness. Submission. Any assault he could imagine. Every attack he had ever used. He threw one after another in Catherine's direction. Fighting exhaustion, the cramping pain in his blade hand, the agony in his abused arm.

The woman, he saw, had dropped to one knee. Her own forearm was bared, but her head hung low. Ethan didn't believe she had the strength to cast. At least, he wanted to hope she didn't.

Several of the king's regulars had fallen under the fusillade from Dawes' men. Others now ran, retreating along the causeway toward the city. One of the men slowed as he passed Catherine. He helped her to her feet and ushered her back, supporting her when she stumbled along the road.

Ethan broke off his assault, but still watched her, fresh blood on his arm, ready at the first sign of an attack to whisper the words of his next conjuring.

He didn't have to. The British soldiers didn't stop and neither did she. The militiamen cheered and charged the gate, overrunning the battlements and the wreckage of the two guardhouses.

Ethan remained where he was, too weary to join in the celebration. But he sheathed his blade and looked up at the glowing form of Uncle Reg, who now stood over him, a rare smile on his grizzled face.

"Thank you," Ethan said. "That couldn't have been easy, even for you."

The ghost tipped his head, acknowledging the words. A moment later he winked out of sight.

"What was that all about, Kaille?" Dawes asked, striding in his direction. "Was that the woman you told me about earlier today?"

"Aye, sir, it was. I feared she would harm the men and I didn't know how long I could hold her off."

The man extended a hand. When Ethan gripped it, Dawes pulled him to his feet.

"Well, whatever you did," the tanner said, "it seemed to work. I gather we're in your debt."

"No more than I am in yours and that of the others." At Dawes' questioning look, Ethan said, "I didn't even raise my musket. It was all I could do to fight her off. Had you not attacked when I requested, she might have killed us all."

A grin stole across the man's face. "I'm not sure I'd call what you shouted 'a request,' but I don't suppose I ought to quibble." He gazed northward, at his men. They had lit a bonfire using wood from the shattered buildings and they sang the opening verses of "Free America," a song written by the late Doctor Warren. "You would think they'd broken the bloody siege," he said.

"We've made a start," Ethan said.

"We've defeated twenty regulars at most. It will take a lot more than two hundred militiamen to drive the redcoats from Boston."

Ethan couldn't argue the point. Like Dawes, though, he was content for this night to allow the men to enjoy their victory.

* * *

A message arrived at the Lyons house two days later. It was addressed to Ethan in a flowing hand. No name or return address appeared on the envelope, but the missive had been sealed with green wax. The parchment smelled faintly of perfume.

"*Mister Kaille,*

I congratulate you on a battle well-waged. Remember, though, this will be a long war and you and I will match wits and spells again.

Yours, C.P."

"That from our loyalist witch?" Dawes asked.

As a conjurer, Ethan didn't like to hear others of his kind referred to as witches, even one such as Miss Percy. This once, though, he allowed the word to pass without comment.

"Aye."

"What does she say?"

Ethan shook his head. "Nothing of consequence."

Dawes held out a hand and Ethan passed him the letter.

The tanner read it and shrugged. "An idle threat. Think nothing of it, Kaille."

Ethan nodded, took back the missive. "Yes, sir."

But he knew better. He had felt the power of the woman's magick that day on Essex Street. Her warning carried weight. And as Dawes himself had said, they had more battles to wage before they drove the British from these shores.

Author's Historical Note*:* The skirmish on Boston's Neck, which took place on July 8, 1775, unfolded much the way I have described it here. Approximately two hundred militiamen did sneak through the grasses on either side of the Roxbury causeway, pulling artillery with them. They destroyed the guardhouses, opened fire on the regulars who fled the buildings, and overran the gate. As for the battle of conjurers that made the Colonial victory possible … well, gentle reader, I will leave it to you to determine the accuracy of that particular point.

— D.B.J.

Miller's Choice
Gerald Brandt

I've been compromised!

Ian Miller's hands quivered as he tried to type a message into his comm unit. He could feel the blood pounding in his temples, drowning out the constant background thrum of the ship's engines.

When had everything gotten so difficult? Life must have been simpler once. Back before he was born, before his parents or grandparents had been born. Before the corporations took over and started running—ruining—everything. A simple life was all he wanted right about now.

His comm unit slipped from his grip, chipping the black plastic casing as it impacted the bare composite floor. He bent over to pick it up, the blood on his fingers smearing across the screen as he finished typing in his message.

Attacked on way home. Package is safe. One body. Will require assistance after landing.

He doublechecked that the encryption icon was green before hitting send. Not that it really mattered anyway. There wasn't a scrap of digital information going through the net that wouldn't be captured, decrypted, and stored on a corporate server somewhere. That's why he had a job. He was the hole in the net, along with the tens of thousands of other couriers out there, most of them carrying garbage data. Why the corporations decided he had valid information this time was anybody's guess. Hell, even he didn't know what he was carrying. Knowing was way over his pay grade. Then again, he didn't think his pay grade included killing and hiding bodies, either. But it wasn't that tough a choice to make when it was your life on the line.

Now that it was over, his entire body started vibrating. He gripped his comm unit tighter, not wanting to drop it again, before placing it on the bed beside him and resting his face in his hands. He jerked away when he remembered the blood. The problem was he wasn't sure whose it was—his or the dead operative on the floor. Staring at his trembling fingers, he felt the adrenalin leave him. The shaking slowly subsided, replaced by a feeling of loss and sadness, but surprisingly, not remorse. He drew in a deep breath and stepped over to the first person he had ever killed.

The man looked smaller now that life had left him. Miller had heard stories of people looking more peaceful when they were dead, had seen it with his own eyes more than once. But that wasn't the case here. This guy had died with a snarl on his lips and it had stayed there.

Miller began with a pocket search, before carefully removing each layer of clothing and examining the seams. He came up empty, as he'd expected. Nothing in the waistband of the pants or underwear. There were places on the body he hadn't looked, yet, and he didn't want to. He grabbed the shoes he'd thrown off to the side and studied them, holding them up to the dead man's feet, a chuckle running through him. The shoes were too big. He jammed his hand into the opening, reaching to the toes, and found what he was looking for.

The memory chip had been shoved in and held in place with a bit of cloth. The other shoe had just the wad of cloth to make both shoes the same size on the inside. He gave the chip's contacts a quick rub with his thumb, accidentally smearing blood over them. He pressed harder and the blood curled off, leaving clean contacts behind. Sliding the chip into his comm unit, he started a decryption app and waited. It would take some time.

* * *

This was Miller's first flight to Mars and by now he was pretty damn sure he never wanted to do it again. ACE, the anti-corporate movement he worked for, had gotten him on the cheapest flight possible: an outside room with no display mocked up to look like a viewport and no carpet on the floor. It was just a square box with a small hard bed permanently attached to the floor by four legs, a nightstand for his personal belongings, and a metal sink and toilet attached to the wall. It was worse than some of the prison cells he'd been in.

Deceleration had started twenty-five hours ago, and they still had another sixteen before he was home, back in San Angeles, where he knew how to do his job, instead of in a mining town on Mars where the recycled air stank like unwashed bodies and every step made him feel as though he would bounce off the ceiling. Or on this damn ship. At least the ship felt normal. He thought he could almost hear the hull creaking as it maintained a steady one G.

From what he could tell, the other passengers were almost all miners, returning home to spend their hard-earned cash. Corporate money spent in a corporate store, taxed by the same corporation. How could people be so blind?

Mining wasn't an easy life, but if you saved and scrimped, it had the chance of earning you enough to live on Level 5. If you were really lucky, maybe even Level 6. Very few were. Maybe that's what kept everyone going, the dream that they could some day make it out of the lower levels. As one of ACE's couriers, he'd never earn enough to do that. He wasn't sure he wanted to.

The remaining passengers were salesmen or management. He was one of the three or four couriers on board. Somehow, he had expected more.

Couriers were used by almost everybody, from small businesses to the massive corporations, since the net was useless for sending critical information. The problem was that if couriers were used to carry important information, then they were easy to take out. The solution to *that* problem was to throw more couriers out there. Give ninety-eight percent of them garbage information and no one would know which ones were carrying important data.

Security through obscurity. The analog hole.

He did one more quick search of the now naked body before standing and staring blankly at the broken mirror on the wall. It hadn't been that way when he'd gotten on board. The recent fight had hit every corner of the tiny room.

What the fuck was he supposed to do now? He had a body to get rid of and no place to put it. He got the clothes back on the man and took another look around his small room.

Miller's comm unit gave a soft beep. He picked it up off the bed and touched the screen, bringing the display to life. The memory chip had been partially decoded, enough to get a signature from the decryption key. The dead man had been working for IBC, one of the big three corporations that pretty much ran the government back home. This was a corporate hit, and he—or his package—had been the target.

It wasn't unheard of, but it did show that IBC had some information that maybe they shouldn't have had. He popped the memory chip out of his comm unit and pocketed it. It wasn't his job to know why or how, it was his job to deliver the package he'd picked up at the Valles Marineris mines.

He shoved the dead man under the bed, sliding him in at an angle to get around the bed's legs and then pushing him in as deep as he could. Even if ACE couldn't get in to do a cleanup, the room was under an assumed name and couldn't—if he was lucky—be traced back to him.

* * *

Miller found it difficult to sleep in a room with blood smeared on the floor and a body under his bed, so he decided to wander the hallways and common areas of the ship.

There were a few hundred people on board, but this late at night it was as though he had the place to himself. The miners would wait until they were Earthside before partying, and the business folk had to work tomorrow. When he walked into the restaurant hoping to find a glass of water, it really didn't surprise him to find someone wiping the tables and getting ready for the morning rush. She glanced up at him and smiled, moving to clean the table he'd sat down at.

Whether she had watched him move towards the restaurant or had simply hoped he would eventually end up there didn't matter. Her attack was quick and brutal. Miller was face down on the floor before he even realized what had happened. She jumped on his back, driving her knees into his kidneys, and jammed the cloth she'd been using to wipe the table deep into his mouth. He gagged, coughing the material out of his throat and swallowing the contents of his stomach before it filled his mouth. She lifted his head by his hair and smashed his nose into the crook of her arm, clamping his head in a vice-like grip, cutting off his air.

Red haze filled his vision and he squeezed his fingers between her forearm and his cheek, pushing with more strength than he thought he had. Her arm lifted enough for him to get a quick breath before squeezing down again. It was enough to give him a single clear thought:

He wasn't going to die out here.

He bucked once, twisting his hips so she no longer had her weight on his back. New pain lanced through him as her knee found his ribs. Swinging a leg forward, he used it as a fulcrum point, ending up on his back with his head twisted painfully backwards by her hold. The angle created a tiny gap and he pulled in a few small breaths. She released his head and brought her fist down towards his face.

He jerked to the left and her fist grazed his cheek and ear. He could almost hear her knuckles crack as they hit the thin carpet covering the composite deck plating. She muffled a yell and brought up her knees to drive them into his gut. Miller twisted again, throwing her off. He jerked the rag from his mouth and crammed it deep into hers. The contents of her stomach bubbled around the edge of the cloth as he drove his fists into her stomach over and over again, driven by fear and anger.

He only stopped when she did, her glassy eyes staring at the low ceiling. He rolled off her lifeless form and fumbled to his hands and knees. His brain slowly began to process what had happened—what he had just done—and his gut twisted. A string of bile fell from his lips.

He couldn't stay here with a dead body on the floor. He couldn't leave it here either.

* * *

This body was harder to hide than the first. The only place he could think of was his room; it had worked once already. He carried her as if she were drunk, stumbling down the halls of the sleeping ship back to his room on the lower levels. The ruse turned out to be unnecessary; no one was awake yet. It didn't matter, he didn't relax until the room door was locked behind him.

The process for this body was the same as the first. He finally found the memory chip glued above her hairline on the back of her neck and ripped it off, sticking it in his comm unit, already knowing what he would find. By the time the soft beep came, he'd gotten her clothes back on and her body jammed under the bed with her partner. She barely fit, and he had to twist her arm and cram it between the other body and the bottom of the bed so she didn't roll out. He tried to rearrange the blankets to cover the view.

The decryption signature was different. This one was a known variant used by SoCal, the biggest and most ruthless corporation out there. They owned most of the west coast of North America, turning it into a multi-level city called San Angeles.

Another surge of pain spiked deep in his back and he rushed to the toilet, barely making it before releasing a pink stream of urine into the metal bowl. His kidneys had taken more damage than he'd thought. He put down the lid and sat, staring back at his reflection in the cracked mirror over the sink. His eyes were bloodshot and the thin web of scars on the left side of his face almost glowed white in the artificial light. He looked beaten.

IBC and SoCal had both tried to get the data chip he'd picked up on Mars. They had also both failed, but it had been close. Too close. What did they know about the package that he didn't? They obviously thought it contained something vital, and not just to one of them. For a brief moment, he considered opening it, reading what was more important than his life. As he stood, he realized he didn't really care. He had a job to do, and if it would help wrestle power from the corporations and put it in the hands of the people, that was good enough. It was all he needed.

He pulled up the time on his comm unit. Nine more hours to go until they landed in San Angeles and he could get back to normal. *If* he could get back to normal after this trip. The San Angeles shuttle port was where he was supposed to deliver his package, meeting up with his boss to hand it over to him. He figured he could stay in his room for that amount of time. It was going to be a long nine hours. He lay down on the bed, acutely aware of what was underneath it. That's when the smell hit him.

The first body had started failing.

*　*　*

Miller verified the Do Not Disturb sign was still on his door and left the room as fast as he could. Which wasn't very speedy. Every move reminded him of the two beatings he'd taken. He laughed quietly to himself as he used the wall for support. *You should see the other guy.*

He knew he'd have to go back to his room to get the package, but that was something he'd worry about later. All he wanted right now was out.

He made his way back to the dining room and sent a message to his handler. *Second attempt to get package. Second body in my room.* It was only after he'd pressed send that he started shaking again. Maybe the delay meant he was getting used to what was happening. Part of him thought that was a good thing; most of him didn't.

The dining room stayed empty the rest of the night. Miller fought off sleep, his back to the corner where he could watch the entire space. More than once he caught himself as his head fell forward and jerked back upright. When the smell of breakfast reached him, he almost threw up. He wouldn't be eating for a while.

As the dining room filled with hungry people, he kept his spot at the table. Several times, individuals and groups asked if they could join him. He sent them away to hunt for seats somewhere else. He wasn't about to restrict his view or allow another corporate operative to get close to him. He held the table until breakfast was done and the room was back to being empty.

There were two more hours to go. He knew he wasn't going to make it. He lurched as he stood from the table, grabbing onto it for support. The dining room had become a tunnel, the walls pressing in, squeezing the life out of him. It wouldn't matter if someone attacked him now. They would have the upper hand and he would lose. The two beatings coupled with staying awake all night were taking their toll on his body and his mind. He just wanted to lay down, close his eyes, and ease some of the pain.

On a ship this size, that meant only one thing ... his assigned room.

Miller stumbled down the hallways, barely aware of where he was, bouncing from wall to wall as his battered body tried to maintain its balance. The simple fact that he found his room surprised him. Even standing outside the door, he could smell the bodies inside. Maybe it was just his imagination. Maybe it wasn't that bad. Either way, he just didn't care any more. He unlocked the door and fell into his room. He had no memory of closing the door behind him.

He woke to the gentle sound of audio coming from the ceiling. The music ended and a voice floated down.

"This is your final warning. We will be entering Earth's atmosphere in two minutes. Please secure your belongings and strap yourselves in. There will be minor turbulence. We expect to be at our arrival gate on time."

Scrambling for the only chair in the room, he glanced at the bodies under the bed, hoping he'd lodged them in deep enough. At least the smell had receded. He did up the buckle just as the ship pierced the upper layer of atmosphere.

As promised, the turbulence was short lived. An arm vibrated out from under the bed, but other than that, the two bodies remained stuck where he had put them. Miller sighed in relief. He didn't want to touch them again. He undid the buckle and stood. He felt like shit. Every move sent deep-rooted shards of pain through his body. He ran what was left of his cold water rations and splashed his face. It didn't help.

When his hands were dry, he pried his fingers under the cracked mirror and lifted the bottom of it away from the wall. A memory chip no bigger than his pinky fingernail fell into the palm of his other hand. Whatever it contained, there were at least two people who thought it was worth dying— worth killing—for. But it would be out of his hands in a few more minutes. That's all he cared about. He taped the chip to the bottom of his foot.

Straightening as best he could, he moved back to the bed. He didn't care about his luggage ... clothes and toiletries could be replaced. All he needed was his ID and to get off the damned ship. He grabbed his ID from the small table and pocketed his comm unit, double-checking the room before opening the door.

A blur charged into him, knocking him into the nightstand. The back of his head hit the edge and stars flew around the room. He felt more than heard the door slam shut as he scuttled backwards to the far wall.

* * *

Miller could feel blood dripping down the back of his neck as he pushed himself up against the wall. The man came in hard and fast, driving into Miller as if he intended to push him right through the composite bulkhead. When he backed off, Miller slipped to the floor again.

Realization hit him harder than the man had as he slid the last few inches. He wasn't going to win this one. He had nothing left to fight with.

The man knelt beside him, a smile on his face. "Where is it?"

Miller stayed quiet. His fingers wrapped around something that had fallen to the floor. His toothbrush. The bristles pressed into the palm of his hand.

"I will get what I want. Your choice here is whether you die quickly or slowly." The man's hand moved to Miller's neck. He squeezed, cutting off blood flow to Miller's brain instead of choking him.

Reflex took over. Fight or die. Miller tightened his grip on the toothbrush and in one quick motion jabbed it into the man's neck with enough force to bury it deep. He pulled the toothbrush back out. Blood spurted from the hole. The man's eyes widened. Instead of clasping his hand over the wound, he grabbed Miller's arm with both hands, one on his wrist and the other on his elbow. He twisted with inhuman strength.

Miller heard the crack before the pain registered. The toothbrush fell from his limp fingers.

A split second later, his attacker's tactics changed, instinct kicking in. The man tried to get to his knees, both of his hands clamped around the gaping wound in his neck. Blood shot out from between his clenched fingers with every beat of his heart, spraying onto the bed and wall.

The man fell forward, landing on Miller's broken arm. Miller screamed. He pushed with his good arm, rolling his attacker off of him, and struggled to his feet. The room blurred and he fell to the left, almost landing on the bed before catching himself. He only had one thought. One plan. Get out.

Miller stumbled from his room, falling into the people heading for the gangway. Several of them pushed him away. He screamed in pain as one yanked on his arm, turning and running almost full speed into a wall.

Slumping against it, he sucked in huge gulps of air. He had to get off this ship and he had to do it now. There wasn't any other thought in his head ... he forgot about the package, the bodies, everything except that he needed to get out.

The short hallway had cleared. Everyone had run as far from him as they could. He moved back to the open door and closed it on the dead man on the floor, not bothering to hide the body. There was no place left to hide it anyway. Miller tugged on the bottom of his shirt, reflex trying to make him fit in with the other people on the ship, and shambled away from the gangway, using every gram of concentration he could muster to stay upright. Too many people had seen him. Security was probably already on its way. He needed to move.

There was no way he was going to get off this ship without being caught by the police, or worse, one of the corporations. He stopped, swaying in the hallway, unsure of what to do next. ACE had trained him as a courier, not as a killer. He jammed a hand into his pocket and felt the hard exteriors of the memory chips he'd taken from the first two bodies. No! He had a job to do! His brain commanded his feet to move.

"Ian Miller?"

The voice came from behind him. He spun, slamming the shoulder of his broken arm into the wall. He bit against the scream, refusing to show his new attackers any weakness.

"Miller, come with us."

The man that spoke was tall. Taller than Miller, at least. His clothes were dark and he wore a mask over his face. The weapon in his hand was blacker than the depths of space. His three companions looked exactly the same. Miller tore his eyes from the gun and backed away.

He couldn't do this anymore.

"Miller," the man spoke again. "We're ACE. We're here to get you off the ship and to a safe house." He stepped forward and grabbed for Miller.

No! They weren't going to get him. He fell back as the gun swung towards his head. The hallway went dark and the pain mercifully disappeared.

* * *

Miller woke up in a small room with a firm mattress under him and warm blankets on top. Light shone through yellow curtains, and on a black dresser in the corner sat new clean clothes. The door opened for a man with wire-frame glasses perched on the end of his nose.

"Ah! You're awake. Good. I'm Dr. Searls. I work for ACE. I've patched you up. You'll be as good as new in a couple of days. Get dressed and go to the living room. There's a couple of men who want to talk to you. You'll find some clean clothes on the dresser." The doctor fussed for a couple of more minutes, examining Miller's arm and head, before leaving and closing the door behind him.

Miller got up, carefully stretching his muscles and moving his arm. He could still feel it wasn't quite right, but it wasn't broken anymore. Whoever was out there had paid a lot of money to fix him up. He wasn't sure if he could trust the doctor, or anyone at this point. He vaguely remembered the four men in the ship saying they were from ACE. But could he believe them? What if this was just another corporate tactic to get the package? He shook his head. He still wasn't thinking clearly. It didn't make any sense. They could have taken the package from him any time they wanted, he'd been out cold. It surprised him when he found the memory chip on top of his clothes. But they could have made a copy and put it back to lower his guard.

This level of paranoia was new to him, and he didn't like it.

He got dressed as quietly as he could and moved to the window. It was sealed and the glass was at least half an inch thick. Unbreakable. The only way out of this room was through the door the doctor had taken. He sighed and opened it. Voices drifted from his left.

The first person to see him was a large man. He almost broke into a sweat standing up from the sofa, a smile creating deep dimples in his cheeks. The other man was Miller's boss. Miller could feel the tension leave his body.

The large man extended a hand. Miller took it. The handshake was firm.

"I'm Nigel Wood. You, of course, already know Steven." His jowls shook as he waggled his chin at Miller's boss.

Miller just nodded.

"I'll get straight to the point," Nigel said. "Your talents are being wasted as a courier. We're moving you to black ops. Training starts next week. Steven has all your particulars, so you won't lose your apartment. You'll stay here until it's time to leave."

Miller took half a step back. An operative? Doing what the three people that had attacked him did for a living? "And if I don't want to?"

"Miller—"

"No, Steven. The boy has a point." Nigel sat back down. "ACE is losing, my boy. The corporations seem to be one step ahead of us at every turn. How they knew you were carrying important data is something we haven't found out yet. We need operatives that can handle themselves, that can get into and out of places without being caught, and if they are caught, have the intelligence to get themselves out. You've proven you can do that."

Miller stayed quiet.

"Look," Nigel sighed. "If we keep going the way we are, ACE won't be around this time next year. We need to build up our operatives. We need you. If you choose to remain a courier for us, we would of course do our best to protect you. If you become an operative, we wouldn't have to."

"I don't know if I can. I ... I hate what I did up there. I hate that I let myself get so out of control that I don't even know how I beat them." He hated how he shook like a leaf when it was all over, but he wasn't going to tell them that.

"Part of your training will be how to deal with that." Nigel stood and began pacing around the room. "Take the training, Mr. Miller. It's the best offer you'll ever see. Part of your new job will be making sure what happened to you doesn't happen to any of our other couriers."

Miller stared at the floor, chewing the inside of his cheek.

"I do need your answer."

If he could help another courier, another person ... If he could make their lives better, safer ... If he would be safe from more of what happened on the ship ...

As if reading his mind, Nigel stopped pacing at the door, one hand on the handle. "Good. You've made the right choice. Enjoy the house for the week. Training will not be easy." He opened the door and left, followed by Steven.

Apparently, he'd made a choice and hadn't realized it.

Neural Net
Sharon P. Goza

Craylxz floated behind Domar Juyk as the slender overseer slipped effortlessly through the connected cerebral units. Juyk was almost twice the height of Craylxz and possessed six limbs, two of which propelled him across the floor with barely perceptible sucks and pops. Juyk's next two limbs ended in four-fingered hands, which were typically either gesturing or delivering punishment. The last two limbs terminated in cupped tips that could be used for holding things but were usually clasped behind him.

The walls of the chamber whooshed and puffed, breathing in oxygen and emitting the precise chemical composition needed to keep both the cerebral units and their overseers alive. Stout Craylxz felt akin to the walls as he expelled oxygen through his pores at the rate necessary to stay the pre-requisite distance behind his Domar and not float past him or slam into a unit. In two of Craylxz's three-fingered hands he held an interface device that displayed a constant stream of neural waveforms. His third hand flitted over the device in an attempt to notate the instructions from Juyk. The acquisition of the biological transport chamber had been a major find for the Domar's race, the Vyrlk. Although the last cerebral network had lasted a mere twenty cycles, these human units were highly compatible with the transport chamber and had been calculating for nearly three hundred.

Craylxz felt awestruck any time he wandered amid the units. There were thirty in his chamber, and although he was not a Domar, he felt personally responsible for every single one. That's what caused him to call his overseer here today. One of the units had been exhibiting strange neural patterns. Craylxz had followed protocol and disconnected the unit and processed it through a purge and wipe procedure, but that had only worked for ten cycles. The unit was once again starting to exhibit the fluctuating pattern.

Juyk stopped to examine the connection stalk on the offending unit. "Craylxz, show me the display."

Craylxz isolated the requested waveform, floated over to his Domar, and held the display out where the Domar could read it.

"Hmm, I see nothing wrong with the stalk. You say you've purged and wiped this unit once already?"

"Yes, Domar Juyk. Ten cycles ago. The pattern isn't as strange as it was before I wiped it, but it's off enough that I wanted to make sure it wasn't causing an error in the calculations."

Juyk waved him away with one hand while the other two disconnected the stalk. "We've had no report of any anomalies, Craylxz. Bring up the stalk analyzer. Organics can be a bit finicky and perhaps the error is in the transfer, not the unit itself."

Craylxz swiped the pattern display from the screen and opened the analyzer. Juyk placed the rubbery suction end of the stalk against the screen and watched. Colored arcs bounced mesmerizingly around the connection.

"Very minor fluctuations. Well within specifications," said Juyk. "I suggest you clean the stalk anyway. When you're done, purge and wipe the unit again. If it continues to be an issue, we'll terminate the connection. And Craylxz, I don't expect to hear from you again unless there's a unit out of specifications. You may feel you're attuned to these units, but the fact is they have a job to do and any disruptions could cost us the war. That is, unless you'd prefer to take the unit's place?" Without waiting for a reply, Juyk turned to leave. "Oh, and you might try increasing the strength of the sleep wave for this unit. Understood?"

Craylxz grayed his skin in submission. "Yes, Domar." He did his best to not vibrate with anger until he heard the slurp of the chamber's sphincter contract and relax.

* * *

Jose flailed for the button to silence the offending alarm. It wasn't the clock's fault he had to get up at "Oh-my-god-thirty" in the morning to get to work. He shuffled into the bathroom, flipped the light on, and gazed in the mirror. A puffy middle-aged face with sprinkles of gray at the temples looked back at him. When had he gotten so old? He couldn't remember being more than twenty. He showered, dressed, ate his typical bowl of cereal and headed out the door to work.

Jose slipped into his office and turned on his computer. While it booted, he grabbed some coffee from the automated cart and said his good mornings to his teammates. He had just enough time to return to his desk and take a couple of swigs of coffee before the phones began to ring.

The first two hours were non-stop basic questions. Jose could have answered these in his sleep, and sometimes he wondered if he didn't. Then a real call came in. He opened up the browser to do an initial search of the answer database and noticed an odd bookmark. Nestled between "Nullspace matrices" and "Orthogonal subspaces" was an entry titled "Open Me." Curious, but also quite aware that the bean counters were monitoring his response rate, Jose noted the existence of the file and returned to the question. The pleading link would have to wait until lunch.

When his turn for lunch came, he downloaded the text file associated with the link and scanned it for viruses. When it came back clean, he opened it and read the first line. "None of this is real." An ice-pick pain jolted him upright and the world went black.

* * *

Craylxz lifted the unit from its cradle. It disconnected from the pulse grid with a pop as the suction released. Craylxz gingerly placed the unit in the purge mesh. He glanced up at the many eyes embedded in the chamber's walls and wondered if Domar Juyk was watching him. Craylxz kept his expression neutral, but inside he was seething at Domar Juyk's comments. The Vyrlk had subjugated Craylxz's system five standard fleet years ago. Craylxz's people proved to be incompatible with the cerebral chambers, so the Vyrlk had deemed them too stupid for anything other than cerebral unit maintenance. It was easier to comply than rebel, but at times like this, Craylxz longed for retribution.

Craylxz watched the progress meter, allowing himself a discontented huff. Arcs of electrical currents shot into the cerebral matter at regular intervals making the system crackle. When the purge and wipe finished, Craylxz disconnected the unit and began the arduous task of cleaning the stalk. He gently wiped out each fold and wondered if the unit was aware of anything during this period. With no electrical impulses to fire the neurons, he doubted it, but sometimes he imagined that they could still think and feel on their own. After he finished meticulously applying the conducting gel to the folds of the stalk, he placed the unit back in its cradle. The reintroduction of electrical impulses caused the folds of the unit to twitch, and Craylxz involuntarily retracted his arms at the memory of the Vrylk submission sticks. He glanced up at the eyes again. He was sure the overseer was laughing at his weakness. He grabbed the interface device and increased the sleep wave intensity by a factor of two. Noting the wave patterns, he deemed his task complete and retreated to his chamber where he could collapse without shame.

* * *

Jose slipped into his office and turned on his computer. He was especially tired this morning, so he grabbed two cups of coffee from the automated cart.

The first two hours were non-stop basic questions. Jose felt like he had been answering these in his sleep, when a real call came in. He opened up the browser to do an initial search of the answer database and noticed an odd bookmark. Nestled between "Nullspace matrices" and "Orthogonal subspaces" was an entry titled "Open Me." He answered the customer's question and rested his head in his hands. Something about the odd entry seemed familiar, but right now he was just too tired to care. A song kept running through his head, and he found himself nodding off. He knew it'd count against him, but he clocked out and headed home. The file would have to wait until tomorrow.

* * *

Craylxz panicked when he saw the latest computation count. Obviously increasing the sleep wave had produced the opposite effect in the unit. He knew the overseer would blame him for the mistake rather than take any responsibility for suggesting the increase to begin with. However, the overseer had said he didn't want to be bothered unless the unit was out of specifications, so Craylxz didn't have to report the discrepancy. Technically, the unit was operating within specifications. The computation count was low, but the wave pattern was still good. Barely. If he reduced the sleep wave, maybe the unit's production would increase enough to average out the computations to normal. Sure, it wasn't sanctioned, but at this point he cared less about that and more about making sure the chamber met the efficiency target when the report came due in twenty cycles. Craylxz reduced the offending unit's sleep. Now he just had to wait and see.

* * *

Jose woke an hour before his alarm went off. When he got to the office, he looked longingly into his coffee mug. He had ended up at work so early the automated coffee cart hadn't even begun its rounds. Jose tried to remember if there was anything he'd left unfinished yesterday and decided to check his files and see if he'd left himself any notes. He didn't find a list, so he decided it couldn't hurt to go over the browser entries. After all, everyone's performance was monitored and maybe this would give him the edge he needed to get a commendation. He opened up the home page and began to read the list of entries. When he got to the N's and O's, he noticed something odd. Nestled between "Nullspace matrices" and "Orthogonal subspaces" was an entry titled "Open Me."

Jose hesitated before clicking on the link. He was leery of opening something as blatant as a link that said *Open Me*. However, he was curious and had some time. When he clicked the link, a prompt requesting a file name provided him with the option *OpenMe(27).docx*. This meant that he had done this exact thing twenty-six times, but this was the first time he could recall seeing the entry. He opened the downloads folder and checked the details of the files. They weren't the same file size, but they all appeared to have the same date. Today. Time wise, the results were scattered throughout the day.

Jose checked his watch. He had five minutes before his shift started. They had a very strict quota to adhere to, and the last thing he wanted was for his actions to penalize his teammates. If they didn't meet their quota, everyone on the team would get a mark. Three marks and you were fired. That meant no job, no housing, and pretty much no future in the tech field. He'd have to read fast. He opened version one.

"None of this is real. Today will be mostly like every other day. You will get the following questions. Hopefully, this will convince you."

Jose quickly skimmed the list of questions before reading on.

"Something is controlling us. Every night your memory will be wiped, but some fragments remain. I, you, found a way to save this file on the server. If you remember something, add it and save it in the same location. George always wears a red shirt with a striped blue tie."

Jose closed the file and stared off into the distance. Something about it rang true. It was Wednesday, so he should remember something from the last two days. He could recall older events—graduating with his Masters in Computer Science and his first job with the NSA—but no matter how hard he tried, he couldn't remember how he'd gotten here, in the customer service department of Compu, Inc.

The sound of the elevator bell pulled Jose from his thoughts. Out of the door came George wearing a red shirt with a striped blue tie. Jose did his best to remain expressionless as he waved to George.

"Early morning, Jose?" asked George.

"Couldn't sleep, so I figured I'd try to get the team's numbers up," replied Jose.

"Well, thanks for that. Wish *I* could make it out of bed before the alarm." He disappeared into his cubicle.

Jose shook his head. Maybe it was just a coincidence. There was one way to find out. He opened the last file version and scrolled to the list of phone calls. If those were the same too, he'd add a note to the file and save it.

After the first ten phone calls matched, Jose started using the list to anticipate the next call. By the end of the day he'd answered ten more calls than were on the list. He noted each one and added a line to the top of the file. *"Add a date line every time you save this file and increase the number if the date is the same. Today is Wednesday, October 22-1. I added 10 lines to the call list."* He saved and closed the file.

* * *

Craylxz was overjoyed when he saw the increase in efficiency from the unit and noted that the waveforms were still within specifications. The extra computations hadn't made up the deficit from the previous day, but they were a start. He reduced the sleep wave even further. He'd need to monitor the unit to make sure it remained within specifications. Once he figured out the limits, he'd increase the efficiency of all the units. He'd prove his worth to Domar Juyk. He could see the report now, *Craylxz, caretaker of cerebral unit 469, wins the war.* Maybe he'd even be the first Domar of his kind. Then Juyk would have to respect him.

* * *

Jose woke two full hours before his alarm was set to go off. When he got to work, the automated lighting system hadn't even triggered for the day. He recalled putting some notes in a file and found one dated Wednesday, October 22, 5:32am. He checked the clock on his computer. Wednesday, October 22, 4:55am.

Add a date line every time you save this file and increase the number if the date is the same. Today is Wednesday, October 22-32. He was living in some sort of time loop, and he suspected the world as he knew it wasn't real. There were several facts to check, which included exact positions of pens and pencils as well as a drawing of the pattern the coffee left when he finished his first cup. He read the list of things he'd figured out in the last thirty-two days. He and his co-workers were being controlled by something or someone. He'd started to hack into the corporation's system, and after two weeks of failed attempts, Jose had found a backdoor. The last two sentences said: *The song makes you sleepy. When you sleep, you forget.*

Jose had no idea what the warning meant, but he did know what a backdoor was and he had an hour before anyone else would arrive. He followed the detailed instructions until his commands slammed against a security protocol. At least he was able to see some system files, and none of them appeared to be in his journal. It was some sort of communication hub. The structure was unlike anything he'd seen before. At first glance, the files seemed to be created and removed at random, but Jose knew there was always a pattern even if you couldn't see it at first. The system he used for his customer support job appeared to be a standard version of Windows. However, what he was in now felt more organic. If he could figure out what the machine language was for this processor, he might be able to program something to analyze the pattern. Right now, all he could do was observe. For the next hour, Jose watched the files and entered information about them in his journal.

At the end of his shift, Jose headed to the bathroom instead of going straight to the elevator. He knew they required everyone to leave, but he wanted to stay and solve the mystery. He slipped into a stall and perched himself on the toilet seat. When the main lights went off, he stumbled his way back to his workstation. He assumed there'd be security guards, but when he thought about it he couldn't recall ever seeing any. After an hour, no guard had appeared and Jose had logged at least a hundred more changes. He sat back and closed his tired eyes. He could make out the faint sound of a familiar song playing. Jose yawned and shook his head. He remembered the last sentence of yesterday's entry. *When you sleep, you forget.*

* * *

Craylxz vibrated with excitement. He'd reduced the sleep wave of all the units, and they'd already attained a 50% increase in calculations. Juyk's commander, Salar Kluyth, was coming to see unit 469. Craylxz made sure to polish his skin and scent it so that it wouldn't offend the Salar. This visit was his moment to shine. The Salar would recognize that Craylxz was not worthless and that he deserved to be a Domar. Craylxz floated off to the side of the sphincter with his interface device ready and displaying the efficiency graphs. The telltale slurp signaled the relaxing of the sphincter and through the opening passed Salar Kluyth and Domar Juyk, followed by two officers. The Salar was slightly smaller than Juyk but held himself in such a way that he seemed twice his stature. His upper limbs were decorated in bright yellow sleeves that provided a stark contrast to his deep blue skin.

Craylxz waited obediently to be introduced to the Salar. Instead, Juyk grabbed the interface unit from his hands and continued into the chamber.

"As you can see, Salar, I have almost doubled the calculation capability of this chamber and all of the waveforms remain within specifications. These human brains are proving quite the asset to our mission." Juyk handed the interface unit to Kluyth.

Kluyth perused the graphs and charts and handed the unit back to Juyk. "Very impressive, Domar. If we can get all the chambers to perform this well, we'll have the necessary calculations done in another forty cycles. Keep this up and you'll be looking at a promotion."

Juyk bowed to the Salar, his upper limbs held out in respect. "My thanks, Salar Kluyth. The fleet must conquer."

"The fleet must conquer," replied Kluyth.

Juyk and Klutyh continued their conversation, but Craylxz didn't hear a word. How could the Domar do this to him? The Domar hadn't increased the efficiency, Craylxz had. Craylxz doubted that Juyk even understood what it had taken to get the units to perform and still remain in the required specifications, much less been capable of doing it himself.

Craylxz vibrated after the entourage departed, this time in a low rumble of anger rather than excitement.

* * *

Jose sat down in the dark office, immediately opened the file and checked the first line. The events of the previous days were still like a dream, but they were more of a lucid dream than the type that disappears when you wake. He updated the date from October 22-36 to 22-37 and saved the file. George and the rest would be arriving soon, but they had just started to "wake up" and Jose had a new idea on how to break into the communication hub. At least he thought it was a new idea. He quickly skimmed the file for his last notes. When he was sure he hadn't made this attempt before, he set to work.

When George came in, Jose was staring at the screen in a cross between horror and amazement.

"What're you looking at, Jose? Did you find a way to hack into cable?" George set down his coffee and leaned over Jose's shoulder. "Looks like you found some campy sci-fi show."

Jose scrambled to regain his composure. "Uh. What?" He didn't know exactly what he was seeing, but he definitely knew it wasn't a cable feed. Rather than try to explain, Jose replied, "Oh, yeah, it's some strange cable show. Maybe a re-run of a Dr. Who episode."

"Well, don't let the boss see you and don't let it affect your quota. I don't want to be the one to make up for your sorry ass." George picked up his coffee and headed to his workstation.

Jose nodded. He had to figure out what he was watching soon. It wouldn't take long for George to see the post-it about the log file and start reading it. But if what Jose saw was real, it was horrifying. A stocky, mottled green creature with skin similar to a dolphin's floated amidst rows of hanging brains. The creature had three arms, each with three fingers. In two of the hands he held some sort of tablet that projected a vertical stream of waves and numbers. The third hand occasionally gestured, changing the content in the projected stream. Jose's view was too far away, but the creature appeared to propel itself by expelling air puffs through large pores.

The creature moved to one brain and gently stroked it with one of its long fingers. Jose fought to hold his breakfast down. The creature had what appeared to be eyes and a mouth on the front of him. The mouth moved as the creature petted the brain. The gesture reminded Jose of someone praising their favorite dog. As much as he wanted to continue watching to see what the creature did, Jose knew he needed to figure out what he was seeing.

Once Jose's teammates were all in and had read their *OpenMe* files, Jose went through his typical explanation for the day. They had only started waking up five days ago, but with his help they were much farther along than Jose had been at the same point. He held off telling everyone about the video feed until they were done with their shift. Most of them were able to stay awake at least an hour after quitting time, so they gathered in the conference room. Usually they went over their notes from the day, but this time Jose piped the video to the room's monitor.

The creature was no longer in sight, but the view was still as disconcerting as it had been when Jose first saw it. The room reminded Jose of his last colonoscopy. The brains could even be thought of as polyps attached to the walls by stems of organic material. This colon, however, was a dark purple with pulsing veins woven through it. The walls shifted and moved. A green fluid flowed along the veins to and from the brains. Even though there was no audio, he could imagine a slurping sound.

The mood in the conference room was one of bewildered disgust. All thirty workers had shown up and they murmured in small groups until Jose stood. Then the questions began.

"What're we seeing, Jose?"

"Is this real?"

"Where's the feed coming from?"

Jose held up his hand to silence the room. "The first thing I can tell you is, I don't know. This morning I tapped into a video signal in the communication hub and this is what I got. All during our shift there was a creature in the room, tending the brains."

Jose flipped the video to a still image he'd taken of the creature. "This creature seems to be a caretaker of some sort. He floated around checking the tablet he's holding and spraying some sort of chemical on the brains." Jose left out the part about petting one of the brains. The thought of that creature having some sort of affection for his "subjects" was far too much for Jose to handle. "I was able to tap into three other feeds too." Jose paused and swallowed hard. "There are thirty brains in this chamber."

The significance of the number was not lost on the people in the room and the questions began again.

"Are you saying those brains have something to do with us?"

"Do each of those brains control one of us?"

"Are you saying those are our brains?"

Jose held his hand up again. "Once again, I don't know. What I do know is that if we can find a way to communicate with this creature, maybe we'll get some answers."

Ideas flew loudly around the room until a young woman with short brown hair and glasses hopped up on her chair and raised her hand and yelled, "We need to hack the tablet!"

"Uhm," said Jose, trying to think of the woman's name.

"I'm Carol. Now that you've hacked the video feed, we're part way there. If we can find a way to make what we type show up on its tablet, we can communicate with it."

"But, we don't know the language."

A dark-skinned woman hopped up on the chair next to Carol. "I think we have enough context that we can try to decipher some of the labels and text. Maybe that'll help us put together some basic sentences."

The suggestion was met with more approval than opposition. "Let's break up into smaller groups and see what we come up with." Jose could feel his eyes getting heavy. Usually he was the last one to fall asleep, but he felt weary after the events of the day and could already hear the song swelling in his head. "Don't forget to update your 'Open Me' files. We've only got about ten more minutes until some of you start falling asleep. We'll meet tomorrow to go over the ideas," said Jose. He headed back to his workstation and entered the information into his journal.

* * *

Craylxz seethed with anger every time he thought about the Salar's visit. He went through his routine mechanically while imagining all the ways he could discredit Juyk. He thought of turning back up the sleep wave and letting the efficiency fall below normal, but he knew that the blame would ultimately fall on him. Craylxz stopped at the unit that had originally started all of this and brought up the diagnostics. Instead of the normal waveform, a word appeared: *Hello.*

What sort of trick was this? Was the Domar trying to catch him at something? Craylxz banged on the side of his device, hoping this was some sort of glitch, but the word remained. It was soon joined by others.

Hello. Monitor you. What you? Where you?

Craylxz looked around, focusing on each one of the eyes in the chamber. When he turned to the one directly behind him, he got another message.

Monitor. Unit Monitor you.

Craylxz began to shake with fear. The only one he knew that monitored this chamber was the Domar, but he couldn't imagine the Domar using incorrect grammar. Though, it could be a test. Craylxz moved to the next unit and pulled up the corresponding diagnostics. The correct waveform appeared. He performed his normal maintenance as if nothing had happened and moved on to the next unit. Thirty minutes later he had completed his rounds without any other issues. The Domar had not come into the chamber to reprimand him. Could it have just been a glitch? Curiosity got the best of him. He returned to the offending unit and once again brought up the diagnostics. The words were still visible. Then more appeared.

Unit Jose. Who you?

Unit? Was the cerebral unit trying to communicate with him? What was a Jose? A name? A species? Craylxz pondered whether or not to answer. He had always assumed these were only computational units. An attempt at communication implied so much more. A shiver of fear ran through his body. He had to know more.

Craylxz looked up. "I am Craylxz the caretaker of this chamber and these units."

There was no response, so he turned to the eye and repeated his words. He waited and a new message appeared on the screen.

Unit observe. No audio.

Craylxz bent in assent. His device had note taking capability, but he wasn't sure if that would send the message to this Jose. He opened up the function and transcribed his response. When there wasn't a reply from Jose, he held up the device so the eye could see it. A new message appeared.

Unit observe. No data.

An alarm went off. *Unit out of specification.* In a panic, Craylxz initiated the unit's sleep wave. Now he was certain that this had been a test. The Domar was sure to punish him. He waited for the unit to enter the sleep phase, disconnected the stalk and began meticulously cleaning the folds. He was still doing so when the Domar arrived.

"I noticed an anomaly, Craylxz," said the Domar. "Explain."

Craylxz attempted to dampen his nervous vibrations and responded, "It was just a glitch, Domar. I found some residue in the stalk. It may be caused by the units operating at such high a level. I plan on checking each one."

Juyk towered over Craylxz. "Very well, but make sure it does not happen again. We need these units operating at peak levels to complete the trajectory calculations. Don't ruin this for me, Craylxz. I am next in line for Salar and if I do not get it, I will not hesitate to remove you. Do you understand?"

Craylxz turned his gaze to the floor. "Yes, Domar."

He remained that way until he heard the chamber slurp shut. The Domar had not mentioned the message, nor had he seemed aware of it. Craylxz finished cleaning the unit and reattached the stalk. He would have to wait until the next cycle to discover more about this Jose.

* * *

Jose yawned and sat back down in his chair with another cup of coffee. It was hard to remember the events of yesterday, but his notes said they'd been successful in transmitting a message but had no way to receive one. Carol was already working on the problem. She'd found where the creature had entered its text and was attempting to use that for two way communication. She told him he'd gone unconscious as soon as the alarm went off and just … disappeared.

George popped his head into Jose's office, "Hey, you're back! We thought you'd been zapped somewhere for good."

Jose wiped his eyes and yawned again, "So I've heard. But here I am. Carol told me a bit and then went to work on our communication issue. So tell me what happened."

George sat on the edge of Jose's desk and took a swig of his coffee, "After you left, we kept watching the feed and in walks this other creature. Definitely a different species. Taller, and it sorta walked on two of its long spindly legs instead of floating. Looked like some sort of a boss over our friend. Cowed him big time and left." George paused before continuing, "You disappeared at exactly the same time that creature pulled the brain's stalk away from the ceiling. I know it sounds like some weird sci-fi movie, but I'm beginning to think we *are* those brains."

Jose rested his head in his hand and rubbed his forehead. He didn't want to acknowledge the thought. "We need to talk to that creature, George," said Jose. "That's the only way we're going to get any answers. Does anyone have any ideas on our language problem?"

"Allie does," replied George. "When that tall dude came in, one of the guys that's a big Star Trek fan said he wondered if they had universal translators. Allie used to work on the Google translator, so she spent some time with Carol going over possibilities."

At the mention of her name, Carol popped her head into Jose's cubicle, "If you're up for it, I think I have something working."

Jose looked at the clock. They'd need to start work in ten minutes but maybe the creature would be there already. "Let's give it a shot," he said.

They punched up the feed and Carol executed her new version of the translator. Thankfully the creature was there. Carol opened yesterday's program and typed, "Look at your notes."

Carol backed away to let Jose take over. "Make it quick. We can't take the chance of that alarm going off again."

The creature jerked slightly and turned toward the camera. It mouthed something and the note page from yesterday popped up over the waveforms.

Jose typed, "Hello again. Can you read this?"

There was a slight delay before they saw the creature shudder and begin to mouth something. A few moments later came the word, "Yes."

* * *

A message popped up on Jose's console with a soft "ping." *Come here, I've got something to show you and I don't think I want anyone else knowing yet.* Jose wrinkled his brow, but grabbed his cup of coffee and headed to George's cubicle.

"Have a seat," said George. "I investigated a few things Craylxz mentioned. I think I found someone's journal and it's freaking me out."

Jose rolled over to George and looked at the document. A series of entries appeared like a medical log. A few of the entries stood out and caused Jose to grip his cup until his knuckles were white.

Species 651 cerebral cortex found compatible with organic matrix. Encephalon extraction and integration of all remaining subjects scheduled for completion in 3 cycles.

Species 651 resisting computation programming. Research being conducted to separate unconscious cerebral functions from conscious functions. If research deemed unsuccessful, all subjects will be disposed.

Species 651 responding to neural simulation. Shutdown required regularly in order to maintain control of unconscious functionality. Expected to have established limits within next cycle.

Species 651 now fully integrated and performance has exceeded expectations. Operational hand-off of one million units complete.

"Crap!" exclaimed Jose. "You think we're species 651?"

"Don't you? Craylxz already told us that only one species has brains compatible with this ship. That's gotta be us," said George. "How do we break the news to the others?"

"I always found the truth was the best. Time to call a meeting."

"Wait, there's more." George opened another file. "I found this one on species 430. There's a picture in it which looks a lot like Craylxz. Seems to me our friend is in trouble."

Jose reached over George's shoulder and read the entry.

Several members of species 430 are showing degeneration. This has caused violent outbreaks and destruction of property. Our analysis has shown that species 672 of the Sicbar system are viable candidates to replace species 430. Therefore, species 430 will be terminated after the conquest of Sicbar.

"I have to tell Craylxz."

George nodded. "I'll gather our troops."

* * *

Jose had been a bit surprised at how calmly Craylxz and the group had taken the news. After seeing the brains and the alien, his information just confirmed what they had already speculated. They now met regularly before and after their shift. Craylxz had reduced the wave as far as possible to give them the maximum hours of consciousness but still maintain their health.

"So all we need to do is short-circuit our own brains," George said at one meeting and rolled his eyes.

"We can't just stop computing," said someone. "There are thousands of other chambers like ours. The overseers would just trash us and the others would pick up the slack."

"We need a good old fashioned virus!"

"Not a bad idea, but even if we stop the rest of the chambers from calculating, they'll just wipe and reboot us."

"We need to screw the bastards. Kill 'em all!"

"But that'll kill us!"

"We're already dead, why not take them down, too?"

After several seconds of silence, a resounding chorus of "Kill 'em all" grew and filled the room.

Jose held up his hand to quiet the group, "I'd have to agree with that. I don't want these things doing to anyone else what they did to us. The question is, how?"

"We need to find out exactly what our group is working on."

The crowd murmured in assent.

"Craylxz mentioned that we were calculating some sort of trajectory. I'll ask him for more information. Considering the circumstances, I think he'll help. In the meantime, maybe we can hack further into the system and find something. Carol?" said Jose.

"I'm on it, boss."

* * *

"Thank you for coming, Domar," said Craylxz, attempting to look more humble than usual.

"This best be important, Craylxz," replied Juyk, his hands clasped behind his back below his upper limbs.

"Yes, Domar. I had an idea that might boost this chamber's output even further, but I need to know what is being calculated to determine if my idea would work," Craylxz said.

"How would that help anything?" asked the Domar.

"You see, Domar, I think I found a way to tune the units to certain mathematical operations. If I can do this, it may reduce the cycles needed to complete the calculations. All of the glory would be yours," replied Craylxz hoping to appeal to the Domar's desires.

Juyk walked up and down the rows. "Hmm."

Craylxz puffed heavily to keep up. "If this works, I would be happy to teach you what I did. You could be the one to tell all of the other Domars. Just think how grateful the Salar would be if all of his chambers performed magnitudes higher than the other Salars and how you would outshine the other Domars by teaching them these techniques."

The Domar paused and spoke with his back to Craylxz, "This chamber is in charge of computing the trajectory needed to reach the Sicbar system. The trajectory must pass behind their sun so that we remain undetected. For the mission to be successful, we anticipate we have only fourteen more cycles before we lose our window of opportunity. I want you to make sure these units complete the calculations in seven."

"Yes, Domar," replied Crayxz as he watched Juyk exit the chamber.

* * *

"Did you get that?" asked Jose.

"Yes," replied George. "I'll go tell Carol what to look for."

* * *

"Good news or bad news first," said George.

"Bad news, always best to end on a good note," replied Jose.

"Bad news is that we still have no idea how to tap into our unconscious minds," said George.

"And the good news?" asked Jose.

"We found a way to up our efficiency so Craylxz can meet his seven day deadline," replied George.

"And I have good news as well," said Jose with a grin on his face.

"And what would that be, O Great Hacker?" asked George.

"This," replied Jose as his screen was taken over by a star chart.

"Woah, is that what I think it is?" asked George.

"Yes. I now know where we are, how many ships are in this fleet, and where they're trying to go," said Jose.

* * *

"So, we know where we are and where we're going but not how to affect it," said a voice from the crowd.

"Yes, but this is a big step forward. Once we can tap into our unconscious, we can fudge the calculations," said Jose.

"And how close are we to that?" asked another.

"Unfortunately, no closer than we were three days ago," replied Jose. "But at least we've solved half the problem."

A general grumbling filled the room.

"C'mon guys, glass half full, right? I know we don't like that we can't stop ourselves from doing this, but there's hope," said George over the din. "Let's get back to work, and remember no idea is too small."

Jose and George watched the crowd disperse. "I'd hoped showing them would make them a bit more hopeful."

"I know, buddy, but think about it. In the past couple of weeks, we've all found out that we're pretty much dead, and we're also the gun that's pointed at killing another several billion. It's a bit much to swallow even on a good day," George quipped.

Jose smirked, "I think I'll go talk to Craylxz. Maybe he's got some ideas."

* * *

The keys of the keyboard clacked as Jose typed his message to Craylxz, "We hacked into the navigation system. We know where we're going and where we're at. We just don't have any way of changing what we're doing. We did figure out how to increase the efficiency for you though."

"That good. I think," came the reply.

The translator still wasn't perfect, so Jose didn't know if Craylxz would think about it or just didn't complete his thought. He figured it was the first one and watched. Craylxz moved meticulously through the rows, checking the wave patterns and spraying the brains. Craylxz stopped and floated in place. Jose could see him quivering, much like an excited dog being told to sit when it knew it was going to get a treat.

"I know. Move sun," sent Craylxz.

"Move sun. Move the sun. Of course! Move the sun," cried Jose. "George, we just need to move the sun!"

Jose ran out of his cubicle and shouted out to everyone, "Can anyone help me move the sun?"

* * *

Craylxz conveniently forgot to turn on the sleep wave that night, and the group worked during their entire time off shift discussing and calculating just how much to move the sun.

"There you go, boss," said Carol. "Just say the word and I'll enter the new coordinates."

"Are we sure this is enough?" asked Jose, even though he knew it was. The group had checked and re-checked the calculations. When Carol hit return, their fate would be sealed.

"Time to go. In the words of Picard, make it so," said Jose.

They watched the new coordinates propagate through the navigation charts. At this scale, the movement was barely perceptible. Now, all they had to do was sit back and do their job. Their unconcious minds would do the rest.

* * *

Salar Kluyth surveyed the chamber. "You have done well, Juyk. The calculations are complete a full seven cycles ahead of schedule. The fleet is poised and will begin the traverse during the next cycle."

"Thank you, Salar Kluyth. The fleet must conquer," said Juyk bowing.

"I have recommended you for promotion to Salar after the next conquest. I trust you will not disappoint," said Kluyth.

Juyk bowed to the departing Salar. "No, sir. Thank you, sir."

Once the sphincter closed, Juyk straightened and looked at Craylxz. "You have done well, caretaker. I will see that you are rewarded. Perhaps better chambers or company of a female of your kind would be appreciated," said Juyk.

Craylxz did his best to keep from vibrating with glee. "My work has been reward enough, Domar. Thank you."

Juyk turned to go. "Very well, continuing will be your reward."

Craylxz waited until the chamber had closed and vibrated happily, making a noise that a human might even call a laugh.

* * *

Two cycles later the Vyrlk fleet slammed into the Sicbar system's sun. The last transmission detected by Sicbar was a weak signal broadcast in a strange language later translated to be, "The fleet has been conquered."

Eleven Days
Walter H. Hunt

Author's Note: *A hundred and fifty years before the events of* The Dark Wing, *humanity has obtained faster-than-light technology from the alien rashk; several nations have expanded to the stars near Sol and established colonies, coming gradually into conflict. Ultimately this leads to the War of Accession, and the establishment of the Solar Empire. Its first emperor, Willem MacDowell, is still a naval officer in the European Union navy in this story: his greatest role ahead of him, and at this time out of sight.*

~ ~ ~

Six European Union starships emerged from jump transition at Sherrard Zeta Alpha jump point, thirty degrees spinward from the A-B axis, their vector aimed directly for the center of A's gravity well. The formation was nearly perfect—after four decades of development in jump technology, the transition point for a mass the size of an interstellar vessel was less than 100% certain, but the crews were well-trained and experienced.

Sherrard System consisted of two stars fifteen astronomical units apart—the distance from the home star to the orbit of the planet Uranus. One, Zeta Herculis A, was practically the double of Earth's Sun: a bit brighter, a bit larger, and had a single habitable planet. The other, B, was a ruddy orange, and didn't even have a gas giant. In the saddle area between the two stars' solar systems there was an irregular asteroid field. It would have been an ideal place for a jump point other than that—but it *was* an ideal place for mining ships, manned and unmanned. Therefore, instead of arriving at the gravitational midpoint, ships jumping into Sherrard either arrived at the far edge of A's gravity well or at the extremes of the asteroid field, where there was enough mass to create a reasonable Muir Limit but fewer navigational hazards to trouble transitioning ships.

Within two minutes, the six ships were moving in unison, keeping station in the outer system. On their pilot's boards, all six commanders could see the four ships in orbit near the habitable world begin to alter course and speed; they noted the presence and readiness of static defenses around the system.

It was obvious that they were expected.

* * *

Commodore Willem MacDowell leaned back in the pilot's seat of *Warren*, a cup of coffee in his hand. There was activity all over the bridge—not the frantic sort that accompanied gunnery exchanges, but the slow, deliberate kind that went with the several hours' wait before any sort of engagement might occur. Things were going to happen, but there was ample time to prepare for them; and some time to examine Commander Valery Orlov as well.

The Naval Intelligence man was a few years his junior. Wiry, handsome in a spare, almost ascetic way—out of uniform he'd look very good in a tailored suit, MacDowell suspected.

"That'll be *Trent*," said Orlov, pointing to the *Westphalia*-class ship on the *Warren*'s pilot's display. "The captain is Samuel Andreotti. Do you know him, sir?"

Orlov was always watching. He was ostensibly on board *Warren* to provide and evaluate intel for the commodore and his current command; but it was no secret that Orlov's true presence was the same as every ONI officer assigned to every ship in the EU's fleet: to watch for political orthodoxy in its commanders.

Well, MacDowell thought, *not much to see here. Not much time for politics, especially these days.*

During Orlov's tour aboard *Warren*—a little over a year so far—he'd found little to comment about, and the commodore hadn't allowed himself to be drawn in on political issues. He wasn't being overcautious; he just hasn't had much to say.

"Don't be coy with me, Commander," MacDowell said, smiling. "You've read the same reports that I have. I don't think I can tell you anything you don't know."

"I know you haven't served with him, Commodore. But have you met him off duty? Or any of the other rebel officers?"

"I've never met Andreotti or Hebert. Luisa Davis of *Van Diemen* was at a diplomatic reception at New Lisbon a year or two ago, but didn't make much of an impression."

"What about Rouchou?"

"The XO of *Hector*? Don't know her either, except that she must be—must have been—a fine officer."

"Fine enough to commit mutiny?" Orlov said, with something approaching a smirk. "According to Captain Hamadjiou's report, she didn't have any trouble taking control of *Hector* when the other three made their move. That doesn't sound like a *fine officer* to me."

"I mean as regards her skill. For Wallace MacEwan to have picked her as his exec, she has to have been highly qualified."

Orlov snorted.

ONI didn't look at things, or use words, as a naval line officer might: to MacDowell, though, Orlov wore a brand-new uniform, a civilian in costume rather than someone with twenty years on the deck of a starship.

MacDowell resisted the urge to roll his eyes. "We shouldn't underestimate her."

Orlov took his time to respond. He glanced at the pilot's board, then gave Commodore MacDowell a good long look. "It's been five days since Captain Hamadjiou arrived at New Paris with *Lacerta*, nine days since Andreotti, Hebert, Davis and . . . this *fine officer* decided to seize control of Sherrard System. We shouldn't underestimate the amount of work they—and their fellow mutineers—could have managed in that amount of time.

"Do you think, sir, that MacEwan and the rest of the loyal personnel—assuming there are any—" this drew a sharp look from MacDowell. "I'm sorry," Orlov said, not really meaning it from the tone of his voice. "Do you think they're still alive?"

"There's no way of knowing. But I'm guessing that they are."

"Why do you think so?"

"Right now," MacDowell answered, taking a sip of coffee, "what the mutineers have done is court-martial illegal, punishable by imprisonment. If they killed officers and crew of EU ships, then it becomes *personal*. As far as I'm concerned, if they've killed fellow soldiers and sailors, there's nowhere they can hide—inside or outside the European Union—where I won't find them. And God help them when I do."

* * *

The rebellion at Sherrard was a clever attempt at a *fait accompli*. Rebels on five ships—*Trent, Maurepas, Van Diemen, Hector* and *Lacerta*—had looked to seize control of their vessels and the manufacturing facilities in the system. In four cases it was successful and popular; but aboard *Lacerta*, its skipper Theo Hamadjiou, had surprised the rebels by making for jump when the plot was hatched. The chief conspirator aboard *Lacerta* was its chief engineer, Ed Barbieri; Hamadjiou was uninvolved, and when it came down to it most of the crew sided with their skipper. Sam Andreotti of *Trent*, the rebel leader and self-styled admiral, had tried to talk him into joining them and then sent *Maurepas* after them when Theo had told him to go to hell—but neither cajoling nor threats were enough. Barbieri and a few confederates had found themselves at the business end of lasers, and by the time *Lacerta* made it into jump—damaged, but still spaceworthy—they were in the brig or, in Barbieri's case, dead on the deck.

Lacerta made it to the EU naval base at New Paris by way of Schönberg System. Commodore MacDowell's squadron, with *Lacerta* added, was cleared for action and was directed to return to Sherrard System with explicit orders: take Sherrard back from the mutineers and do it quickly, before anyone else got involved—specifically the North American Union and Greater China. Within twenty-four hours, the squadron was under way.

* * *

Orlov, who was certainly no tactician, was all for diving into the gravity well of Sherrard A and taking on the rebels directly. There were too many variables, however: MacDowell's orders were different than Orlov's—and the commodore wanted to know where things stood before he committed his forces.

Less than an hour after making transition, MacDowell's squadron received the first communication from the mutineers. Neither *Trent*—Andreotti's flagship—nor any of the other three ships had answered comm or responded to MacDowell's official declaration of their recognized state of mutiny against the EU government; instead, *Warren* captured a broadcast comm from Sherrard Central:

"To all ships of the European Union in Sherrard System: Sherrard Central Starbase, Free Republic of Sherrard sends, Admiral Samuel Andreotti commanding.

"Be informed that your vessels are in violation of sovereign Sherrard space as of 6 February 2160. A comm squirt has been sent to the European Union Government, and representatives of the Free Republic have presented their credentials to the United Nations. Pending recognition of their plenipotentiary authority, it is requested that forces under the command of the European Union withdraw beyond the outermost orbital of Sherrard-A.

"The Free Republic of Sherrard has applied for protected status under the terms of the Second Treaty of São Paulo and, pending notification of the disposition of its claim by the United Nations General Assembly, is prepared to consider any incursion into its space by forces under the command of foreign nationals to be an unprovoked act of war, pursuant to which it disavows any responsibility for damage or casualty that may result from conflict arising therefrom.

"Message ends. Andreotti, Admiral, Sherrard FRN."

"What crap," Orlov said, when the proclamation—or whatever it was—had finished playing again on comp in MacDowell's ready room. "He's sure got balls to send out something like that."

"He doesn't really expect us to do what he says," MacDowell said. He glanced at the pilot's board display: the battle fleet, such as it was, of the Free Republic of Sherrard were three or four minutes from turnover. "It's posturing for the record."

Whatever MacDowell was going to do, the decision would have to be made now. It was his call—except that it really wasn't: Orlov had something to say on the subject. Quite a bit, actually: Admiral Nason might be able to act unilaterally without a political officer weighing in—but a mere commodore didn't have that latitude.

Especially these days, he thought.

"What *does* he expect us to do?"

"Blink."

They watched the display slowly update. Finally Orlov said, "What are you going to do?"

"I'm not planning on blinking, if that's what you're asking. But until we start shooting, Andreotti and his people are still citizens of the European Union."

"They're traitors and mutineers, Commodore."

"They're—" MacDowell began, then checked his anger. "They're going to get about three minutes to convince me not to shoot." He turned away from Orlov and walked through the connecting door onto the bridge, his ONI officer following behind.

* * *

Settled in the pilot's chair, MacDowell ordered comm to hail *Trent*. It didn't take long for an image of Sam Andreotti to appear in the clear area starboard of the captain's chair and pilot's board. He was seated in his ready-room, not even on the bridge, as if he hadn't a care that his little fleet was about to engage a larger force here to arrest him for mutiny.

"Commodore," he said, smiling faintly.

"Captain," MacDowell answered evenly. "Though I noticed that you signed your manifesto as 'Admiral.' Better to reign in hell, I guess."

"Something like that. What can I do for you?"

"Easy answer?" MacDowell glanced sidelong at Orlov, who stood glowering with his arms crossed in front of him, out of vidcam range. "Surrender. Save the Union some ordnance and me some time."

"You don't really expect that."

"You didn't really expect *me* to withdraw my force from Sherrard System. I'm a reasonable man, Andreotti: if I weren't, we'd be down your throat right now. You're awfully calm for someone who's outnumbered and clearly in the wrong—what haven't you told me?"

Andreotti leaned forward and folded his hands in front of him on the table. "You know, Commodore, I've always liked and respected you, and I know you're looking for a compromise here."

"I'm not. But go on."

"The new Sherrard government I have the honor to serve is very popular with most of the people of Sherrard, and most of the folks under my command were more than happy to have the opportunity for promotion."

"To admiral, for instance."

"To take one example. Not too many openings for admiral in the European Union, sir. Not too many captaincies either. But not everyone was so happy with it. Some of the ... malcontents didn't take it too kindly. I'm sure they'd be just as happy to be quit of Sherrard, and we'd be glad to accommodate them ... except for one thing."

MacDowell saw where he was going. "Except that I'm here to put a stop to the 'new Sherrard government.'"

"That's right," Andreotti said. "It'd be a shame if anything were to happen to them."

It wasn't quite the same as innocent civilians in the line of fire, but it still bothered MacDowell. "That sounds like a threat, Andreotti. You can't hold them hostage forever."

"I don't have to hold them *forever*, sir. Just long enough for Sherrard's status to be resolved by the UN. If the General Assembly decides that we merit independent status, then you'd be committing an act of war against a sovereign power by attacking us after that."

"That won't happen." *But it might*, MacDowell thought: the General Assembly consisted of a large number of small, bickering nations, most of whom didn't have the resources or power to colonize human space.

Some of them had bought the rashk jump technology forty years ago and never built so much as an unmanned probe with it. A chance to stick it to a spacefaring nation like the EU would be delightful irony for the General Assembly.

"I'm betting it will," Andreotti said, a satisfied smile on his face. "And soon. Our representative in Genève says that it will be brought up within the next week. So until then, your loyal troops stay where *they* are, and you're well advised to stay where *you* are. Then you can take them aboard *Warren* and get the hell out of Sherrard space. Sir."

"I can blow you to the next universe at any time," MacDowell answered angrily. "Soldiers and sailors in the service of the European Union know very well that their lives are at risk whenever they're on duty. I don't think they're waiting to be rescued, and I'm not ready to bargain with you. You'd better reconsider your position, Andreotti."

"A hundred and fifty officers and crew dead because you can't show a little prudent patience, Commodore MacDowell? Surely you're not interested in betting your career on that."

"You've got two hours," MacDowell said and signaled to comm to cut the connection.

* * *

MacDowell knew that Orlov wasn't happy about his decision. Off the bridge, in the tiny galley just aft, the commodore got an earful while he was refilling his coffee; Orlov was nowhere near subtle enough for it to seem anything like a chance encounter.

Orlov waited for MacDowell to finish preparing his coffee, leaning casually against the counter opposite the urn—as with most naval vessels, the place of coffee preparation was accorded its own place of honor—and then said, "You know, sir, giving them two hours isn't likely to change the tactical situation. It probably won't change their minds about anything."

"You'd rather I rushed in there, guns blazing."

"I didn't say that. But you've given Captain Andreotti an opportunity to plan his strategy."

"If he didn't already have one, two hours won't give him one. I'm trying to avoid casualties here—ours, theirs, and the loyal officers and crew he's using as hostages. Don't you think that's a viable approach?"

"The idea that he's using hostages doesn't make your blood boil, Commodore?"

"No one ever won a war, or even conducted a successful campaign, with their blood boiling, Commander. Am I angry about it? Sure am. But that's not what bothers me."

"Oh?"

"Andreotti seemed pretty confident when he spoke with me, don't you think? He's got a declaration of independence, a representative at the UN, and some military hostages. He's betting that I haven't already given them up for dead, which I haven't—and am willing to deal on that basis, which I'm not.

"But it's not a high hand." MacDowell drank his coffee and grimaced; it was admirably strong. "It's not enough. There's something missing and I haven't figured it out yet."

"Can you figure it out in two hours, sir?"

"Not sure." He sipped the coffee again and sat the mug down next to the urn. "I've got scan section working to identify hot spots in the system, places where Andreotti may have tucked these guys away. There are two dozen likely ones. If we could discover at which one they were being held we'd have an enormous tactical advantage."

"That's true," Orlov agreed. His face held the trace of a smile.

MacDowell thought a moment, then added, "The problem is that Andreotti must know *that* as well. If we get the hostages, he's lost the biggest card he has showing. If we attack, and he kills them, it accomplishes nothing—if that's all he's got. There's something else."

"Perhaps we should start with locating the hostages."

"I don't know whether that'll yield any results in time."

"It might," Orlov said.

"You have something to offer?"

"I think I know where they are," Orlov said. He gestured at his comp. A holo of Sherrard System appeared over the small galley table: Zeta Herculis A, a star as Sol-like as almost any in human space, surrounded by six orbitals: two tiny planets orbiting close to the primary; in the third orbital a crowded, dusty asteroid belt about half an AU out; the fourth, an Earthlike planet, Sherrard Prime, almost exactly one AU out but a bit colder overall; then a medium-sized gas giant; and finally the large, rocky asteroid belt that loosely defined the area between A and B, eight and a half AUs away from star A.

Icons marked the positions of the four rebel ships and the six EU vessels at the edge of the system. He touched the comp again and three green points appeared: one in the asteroid belt, one in the ring that surrounded the tiny second planet, and one more on the surface of the largest of the gas giant's dozen moons.

"I've narrowed scan section's choices to three, as you see. Based on what intel I've obtained, I believe that the ring station is most likely."

"Intel?"

"We have an asset," Orlov added, which was about as much answer as MacDowell was going to get: there was someone from ONI in among the rebels.

"You received a comm squirt?"

"On a private frequency, yes. We should have the location shortly."

MacDowell clenched his fists, then slowly relaxed them. "That's a violation of protocol at the least, Commander. Don't you think you should have informed me—"

"I've given you *options*, Commodore MacDowell. You've given the rebels two hours to *plan*, and in the meanwhile I've found the key to your problem. They can't use hostages that they don't have."

"Commander, if you received a comm message from a mole at that base, don't you think Andreotti might have picked it up as well?"

"It was on an ONI frequency," Orlov answered blandly.

"Suppose an ONI officer is part of their little cabal," MacDowell answered at once.

"That possibility exists," Orlov said. "It's a calculated risk. Intel operatives know that their lives are in danger—"

"It's not just *his* life. If he's discovered, I have no way of knowing what Andreotti will do. Maybe he blows the whole station and all of our people with it. My point—"

"You said he was unlikely to do that," the intel officer interrupted. "You suggested that it was hardly in his interest to kill the hostages. Why would he do it now?"

"My *point* is," MacDowell continued, trying to check his anger, "that if I'm trying to defuse this situation with as little damage as possible, it would be helpful if this sort of intrigue wasn't happening *behind my back*. It's not your risk to take, Commander, and I resent not having been consulted."

"Is that all, sir?"

"When will you know for sure that *this*—" he gestured at the display "—is where the hostages are being held?"

"Within the hour."

"Within forty-five minutes?" They both looked at the chrono above the coffee urn, which indicated that the two-hour deadline was forty-seven minutes from expiring.

"I suppose so, yes."

"I want that information in my hands in thirty minutes, Commander. And don't doubt that this little … breach of protocol will be in my report."

Orlov didn't say anything; he didn't even look affected by the implied threat. After a moment, he offered MacDowell a salute and the commodore waved him out of the room.

MacDowell turned to the display, with its three points of possibility. If Orlov's intel was at all accurate, one of them marked the place where Wallace MacEwan and the rest of the navy personnel were being held … along with one spy.

Above the display, the chrono continued to tick down the seconds.

* * *

Orlov looked worried.

MacDowell ordered comm contact with *Trent*, but Andreotti beat him to it. Instead of the rebel "admiral's" image, a scene appeared near his pilot's board.

It was gruesome: a decompressed chamber, part of a station of some sort. There were five or six bodies there, already coated in reddish-brown ice crystals. Most of them looked as though they'd been trying to cover a hole half a meter across that gave out on black space. One other was lying sprawled nearby; part of his head and one shoulder looked as if it had been burned away by laser fire.

"We caught your spy," Andreotti's voice said. "Wouldn't want him to go off to the next world alone, so we gave him some company. Those deaths are on your head, Commodore. This is your last warning—withdraw from Sherrard System and no one else has to die."

The comm message ended, but the image remained. MacDowell didn't say anything for several seconds.

"Chess players give away pieces if it gives them an advantage," the commodore finally said, not looking directly at Orlov. "Not for no reason at all.

"System display," he said to comp, and the grisly scene disappeared to be replaced with the solar system, with its planets and moons, friendly and enemy ships, and six points of green light.

"You still don't know where they are," he said. "And we don't know what Andreotti will do now."

Orlov didn't answer: he seemed to be taken aback, almost stunned. Mac-Dowell's anger was obvious but he looked composed.

"Your little pawn sacrifice has taught us one thing, though," he added to Orlov. "We know just how ruthless Andreotti is."

"Orders, sir?" Linus Soren, his XO, said.

"Still not blinking," MacDowell answered. "I don't know if he thought that little demonstration would scare me. Beat to Quarters, Commander. Course as indicated. *Warren* sends." He named a heading that took them into the gravity well. "All right, everyone," he added, looking back at Orlov once more. "Let's get this done."

* * *

Even at maximum accel, the inner system was a few hours away. *Warren*, best-armed and equipped, was at the head of a formation that was flanked by *Guienne* and *Edward VII* to its port and *Calais* and *Corvus* to its starboard; one ship was zulu-positive relative to *Warren*'s plane of travel, one ship zulu-negative. *Lacerta*, the sixth ship in formation, was coplanar with *Warren* and a dozen ship-lengths aft in case something emerged from the asteroid belt or appeared at the saddle jump points.

Scan section on each of MacDowell's six vessels worked together to try and identify the place where the hostages were being held—but the commodore wasn't sanguine about the loyalists' chances.

It was a ruse, he thought to himself. *It always was*. Andreotti showed no hesitation in killing those he held—and at the first provocation. Maybe it was something to do with refreshing the tree of liberty; but more likely, he decided, the mutinous commander had just been trying to distract him.

Thirty-two minutes into Sherrard System space, MacDowell found out that he was right.

* * *

The pilot's board was suddenly alive with a cloud of icons, all registering hostile, all emerging from the asteroid belt at high relative speed.

"Missiles," said Brian Dominguez, watch navigator. Dominguez was twenty-three: this was his first deep-space exercise. He was obviously trying to keep his voice level.

"All ships, begin evade," MacDowell said. "Comm, get me *Lacerta* on the double. Theo, do you read? Flag sends."

A second, then two. "I read you five-by-five, sir," came Hamadjiou's voice. "We've got company, pouring on the delta-v."

"We all read that. Close it up, Captain, I don't want you hanging out there as the first strike target."

"More fun that way, Commodore. But I'm throwing out enough flak that the enviro police will be coming after me, and I'll be on my way soon."

"You and *Edward VII* are to make for the second orbital—it's at conjunction, on the other side of the sun. Try not to get yourself killed."

"Aye aye, sir. No argument there."

"Comm to all ships. Disperse and deploy anti-missile weaponry. Flag sends. Linus," he added to his exec, who was bringing up analysis graphs on the incoming ordnance, "ID those things on the double."

"Already on it, sir." He didn't look away from the displays. "They're Big-5s from the look of them, or something built to look *like* them."

"Where'd they get so damn many Big-5s?" It was the standard nickname in the EU and elsewhere: generation 5 of the Great Wall missile, called Big-5 after the Western encoding scheme for Chinese ideograms—it was a model that was difficult to jam, scuttlebutt said, because they 'only spoke Chinese.'

Big-5s weren't the top of the line in Greater China's arsenal, but were damn close. Mass-radar showed dozens of them—all coming from the asteroids.

"They got them from Greater China, sir, I imagine," Soren said. "All ships report ECM and flak deployed. We're on primary evade course. *Trent* and the others are moving toward intercept now."

"What's the relative velocity on the Big-5s?"

Soren read him the figure. *Warren* and the others were piling on velocity, headed for turnover: the point at which they'd have to decelerate to avoid flying past the oncoming rebels. The Big-5s were moving considerably faster.

MacDowell looked at the pilot's board. *Lacerta* and *Edward VII* had already changed course; the other four had spread out as ordered. Their wake was filled with flak, and comm circuits were busy with ECM trying to spoof the missiles' hardware.

"Not very original," MacDowell said. "We slow down to stay engaged with the rebels and we get missiles up the chute; we keep ahead of them and we don't stay in range for enough time to do the rebel ships any damage. Meanwhile, Andreotti's ships can speak Chinese to keep the Big-5s from hitting …"

Soren and Dominguez both turned around after a moment when Mac-Dowell didn't finish his sentence. Dominguez was green and unwilling to interrupt a commodore deep in thought, but Soren had been with his skipper for almost four years and recognized the facial expression.

"They speak Chinese," Soren said quietly.

"Three possibilities," MacDowell said. "First, the missiles are pro-grammed to exclude *Trent* and the others. I doubt that: all we'd have to do is make our ID beacons show as *Trent*'s sig and they'd ignore us, too.

"Second, they're actively comming the missiles to aim at us. We're not showing any comm squirts, so they'd have to do it on normal frequencies, which means speed-of-light comm. As we got closer the delay would be lower, but it's still a delay."

"There could be a controller in the asteroid belt."

"We have no way of checking with those guys coming at us," MacDow-ell said, pointing at the board. "I still doubt it. Easiest thing to do is to launch them—from robot or manned mining ships, I'd guess—and let 'em do their job. A Big-5 is a smart little bastard. That leaves option three, which is also the easiest thing: close-range comm signals to the missiles to keep them off any rebel ships in the area. That could be passive, but would still be a broadcast signal. We slow to engage, the missiles tackle us and avoid hitting *Trent* and her sisters."

"You have an idea, sir," Soren said.

"*Warren* outguns anything on their side, even *Trent*. We can take a few hits at long range. Normal ship-to-ship tactics are to shoot for weapons and maneuver. I think we should be shooting for *comm* and let the missiles do our work for us. We slow to engage, knock out whatever's comming those missiles, and shear off as best we can."

"They'll do the same, sir," Dominguez said quietly, glancing at the XO and then the commander. "I mean to say, Commodore, won't they know enough to get out of the way?"

"They might, Lieutenant," MacDowell said. The young man appeared relieved that the commodore hadn't bitten his head off for speaking up. "Except that if our tactic works they're going to be surprised as hell—and with their vector of acceleration in the opposite direction, right into the teeth of the missiles, they'll have less time to get out of the way. Of course, if the ECM and flak does its job, there won't be any missiles to worry about."

Soren nodded and turned back to his console. Dominguez didn't say anything further.

* * *

Lacerta was a light cruiser, fast and maneuverable but more lightly armed than the bigger boys in MacDowell's squadron. But Theodore Hamadjiou, its skipper, had a score to settle. He wasn't alone: the officers and crew of his ship—other than the ones that had been arrested or killed as a result of the attempted mutiny—wanted to erase that stain as well.

When Andreotti's plot had been hatched, the point person aboard *Lacerta* had been Ed Barbieri, Theo's chief engineer. He and Ed went way back: they'd served together as middies almost twenty years ago, fought in the little colonial skirmishes between the EU and Greater China as it expanded into the space between Sol System and Rashk-Home, and their careers had tracked pretty well. Ed had only one real fault, and he had it in abundance: a temper that went out of bounds too often. In an engineer, there was room for that; as a commanding officer, there wasn't—and it had kept him from getting on to the captains' list.

It was the wedge that Sam Andreotti had used to get him involved. It had worked for Giselle Rouchou of *Hector* as well, and evidently she'd planned better than poor old Ed had done.

"We should've seen this coming, Simmie," Theo said, watching the pilot's board, incoming missiles trailing behind and *Hector* changing course to try and intercept *Lacerta*.

"No use second-guessing now, Skip," Simeon Ewing said. He was a tall, olive-skinned Punjabi, naturalized to the EU twenty years ago; he still retained the clipped accents of the subcontinent, though his English could have come from the cricket fields of Eton or the board-rooms of Canary Wharf. "I really don't see the merit in it."

"We saw and heard things. Andreotti stepped up the launching of mining 'bots in the intrasystem belt—and they turned out to be platforms for those damn missiles."

"We can outrun them."

"Yeah, we and *Eddie* can, but *Warren* and *Pas de Calais* can't. They'd better hope their flak and ECM works."

"If this is the best that they can manage, Captain," Ewing answered, "then it's not much of a rebellion at all."

"I don't know that *this* is their best shot. But the commodore is right—it's a weak hand, even *with* the missiles. Does this mean they're now a client of Greater China?"

"Greater China doesn't use clients, Skip," Ewing said laconically. "It isn't that sort of system. You either join the collective or you line yourself up to be disassembled and rebuilt in their image. Premier Xiang Che may not be Wei Kwan or Mao, but he does believe he's got a historical mission. If it includes Sherrard ..."

"What can the Sherrardi hope to gain?"

"For the naval officers, promotion at least."

"And for the civilians?"

"Maybe they've decided that the EU is a sinking ship." His accent put the emphasis on the word 'sinking,' making it the most important word in the sentence.

"We're still expanding."

"That doesn't mean we're not sinking. It's been happening for a while: we may be isolated from the worst of it, but you know what's going on, Skip: the colonies that don't want to be colonies, countries bumping up against each other even though space is huge ..."

"It's been like this for forty years, ever since the rashk gave us faster than light tech."

"It has," Ewing agreed. "And there might have been a time when the EU might have made a go of this—but now I'm not sure. I'm not sure what we do."

Hamadjiou shifted in his seat, watching the main formation disperse as the missiles crept closer and MacDowell's ships closed on the rebels.

Lacerta piled on the accel, outrunning the missiles sent after it. Far away from the main formation that continued to close with the rebel ships, they had a fairly small share of chasers: all they had coming for them was *Hector*.

That suited Theo Hamadjiou just fine. *Lacerta* and *Hector* were of slightly different classes: *Lacerta* was more maneuverable, while *Hector* was better armed and armored. The lighter *Edward VII* was intended to make the difference. Theo hoped so, and expected that it figured into the commodore's calculations as well.

Great, he thought. *Here comes Gisele Rouchou, with murder on her mind.*

"For the moment," Theo said, "we're going to do our duty."

* * *

"How long will they have us in range?"

"Two, maybe three minutes," Simmie answered. "They've put on so many Gs they won't have more than a passing shot."

Theo squinted at the pilot's board. "You can do a hell of a lot of damage in three minutes, Sim."

"Granted," his XO said.

"But … if we're being detached to rescue Wallace MacEwan and the others, don't you'd think *Hector* would be moving toward the *objective* rather than trying to intercept us at—" Hamadjiou stared at the board. "A half-million kilometers outside the fifth orbital? Hell, the gas giant isn't even at this spot in the orbit—it's a quarter of the way around from here."

"Rouchou's looking for the killing shot, Skip."

"As much as that sounds like Gisele Rouchou, it still doesn't scan. She could put us in a world of hurt, but we could as easily put *Hector* out. It's got to be something else."

Theo stood up and walked slowly around the bridge, one eye on the pilot's board. *Warren* was almost in range of *Trent* and all alone: the others were in among the gas giant system where *Maurepas* and *Van Diemen* had deployed to protect the installations there.

Pacing was Theo's preferred way to think. Many captains kept their butts planted firmly in the pilot's seat: there was a captain named Anderson who was famous for it—not even a call of nature could get him off the chair. By comparison, Theo knew that he could command from port gunnery station if that was where he happened to be standing when stuff hit the aerator.

"Simmie," he said finally, "after she sideswipes us, where is *Hector* headed?"

His XO was standing right near port gunnery, in fact, and issued commands to his console. A cone appeared on the pilot's board, spreading out from *Hector*'s present position. The projection became more uncertain and hazy the further away it became: it had changed course to intercept *Lacerta* and *Eddie* so comp couldn't simply predict a straight-line course. It was clear though that most of the possible paths took *Hector* directly to the asteroid belt between Sherrard A and Sherrard B.

"Isn't that interesting."

"What's so interesting in the belt?" Simeon Ewing asked. "Other than missiles?"

"Which they've already launched."

"There may be another volley."

"They didn't need to have any of the four ships in the belt to launch the *first* volley." Hamadjiou walked down to the center of the bridge and took his seat aft of the pilot's board. *Hector*'s trajectory continued to update as the rebel ship continued to accelerate. "What they're headed for—that's a damn good question. A *damn* good question." He turned toward comm. "Send this holo out to *Edward VII* and also to the flag, my compliments to the Commodore. She's up to something—what the hell is it?"

* * *

With *Hector* detached to intercept Hamadjiou, it looked like Andreotti wasn't going to let *Lacerta* and *Edward VII* get close to the hostages without a fight. That left *Trent, Van Diemen* and *Maurepas* to face the four remaining ships.

More than twenty missiles were still following as they entered fire range.

"All ships, engage as ordered," MacDowell said.

Guienne and *Corvus* had *Van Diemen*, a *Jersey*-class second-generation ship built here at Sherrard less than three years ago. *Maurepas* was less well-armed and less maneuverable: *Pas de Calais* was about the same in throw-weight with a little more maneuverability—but like Luisa Davis of *Van Diemen*, Gustav Hebert was an excellent tactician. Both Hebert and Davis could fight a battle like this in their sleep.

He was left with *Trent*—but he had a personal score to settle with Andreotti.

Orlov was on the bridge as the two squadrons met, *en passant*, just outside the fifth orbital. They wouldn't be in range for long—two or three minutes at the most. The missiles would make the difference.

MacDowell resisted the urge to ask him, *Any other surprises?* Somehow he doubted the intel officer would reply.

Trent's profile was growing on visual as the pilot's board continued to track it. Four missiles were aft of *Warren*, closing as the flagship dumped velocity.

"Hit," reported Lane Hudson, his Gunnery first, "forward of midsection. Not sure if we got comm, sir."

"Any change to the missiles' path, Linus?"

"Not yet, sir. Their straight line trajectory to *Trent* would still take them near our position."

A series of indicators went to red on the engineering board. Internal gravity compensated, but MacDowell could almost feel it as *Warren* took the hit. "Hudson, did we get their comm or not?"

"Stand by," he said, touching his console. "No way of telling, sir. There's enough chatter between the rebels I can't quite make out whether *Trent's* involved—we haven't picked out their message encoding yet."

"Our four missiles are about sixty seconds aft, Commodore," Linus Soren said.

"Steady," MacDowell said to Dominguez. "Hold your course."

"Aye aye, sir."

"Report on *Pas de Calais*," MacDowell said, turning to comm. "I show them at sixty percent power."

"I've got a message from *Pas*, sir," comm said. "They've still got incoming missiles they're trying to shirk near the gas giant."

Maurepas had moved to protect the installations there as MacDowell's fleet approached. It was almost at opposition with the saddle asteroid belt, about twenty million kilometers downrange of *Warren's* position. *Pas de Calais'* maneuverability would help them with dust and moons to hide in.

"Have they been hit?"

"Twice, sir. They haven't hit *Maurepas'* comm yet, but one of the missiles went awry and took out a refueling platform."

MacDowell frowned. "Casualties?"

"Unoccupied, as far as *Pas'* skipper can tell."

"Thirty seconds, Commodore," Linus said.

"Prepare for course change. Hudson, you'd better be a good shot."

"Hope so, sir."

"Twenty seconds."

"*Now*," MacDowell said. "Hard to starboard. Maximum accel, close on *Pas de Calais'* position."

The star field in the forward screen swerved. Another rank of indicators went on: *Trent* had scored another hit. MacDowell watched the missiles streak toward him on the pilot's board—

—And streak past, unable to match the sudden course change. He breathed a sigh of relief. The gas giant was in view now, half in profile, a largish moon hanging between it and *Warren's* present position.

Linus Soren looked from the pilot's board to his commander and back. The missiles continued to track in a straight line, all four of them—heading for *Trent's* position.

"I don't think they can talk to it anymore," Linus Soren said.

Trent's commander had evidently reached the same conclusion; it was possible that *Maurepas* or *Van Diemen* could redirect them, but it was also possible that they were out of range or similarly disabled. *Trent*, moving in the opposite direction out of the gravity well, had already changed course itself to head for an intercept near the gas giant. A broadside from the rebel flag took out one of the missiles; but as they watched on the pilot's board, the remaining three reached *Trent*'s position and struck.

After a moment, the icons for the missiles and the rebel flag vanished from the board. Eleven seconds later—light being a slower medium than mass-radar, which used the same principle as the jump drive—there was a massive, blinding explosion in the forward screen, sixty degrees to port.

* * *

Hector never stopped accelerating as it came within range of *Lacerta* and *Edward VII*. Rouchou took her shots and they were fairly good ones for the two and a half minutes they were in range. But even though *Hector* managed to disable *Edward VII*'s engines, there wasn't any truly serious attempt to stop the two ships' descent into the gravity well. *Hector*'s projected course continued to update on the pilot's board, taking it into—and through—the asteroid belt.

The damage to *Eddie* posed a bit of a problem for Theo. He couldn't make for planet two with all possible speed without leaving the other ship behind. On the other hand, the departure of *Hector* from the inner system left nothing mobile to attack it.

When they recorded *Trent*'s destruction on the pilot's board a few minutes later, Theo commed *Warren* for new orders.

* * *

"It's about damn time you got here."

Wallace MacEwan was standing with his hands on his hips in Ring Station's C-in-C when Theo came on deck. The Marines had given condition green almost as soon as they'd boarded the station: either the loss of *Trent* and the subsequent disabling of *Maurepas* and *Van Diemen* at the gas giant had made the rebels holding the hostages unwilling to carry on, or MacEwan had made some kind of prison break—but there were no more dead bodies lying around, the rebels were in the brig—"better treatment than they were ready to give us," MacEwan had told the Marine major who had led the detachment—and *Hector*'s lawful captain and the others left at the station were acting as if they were out on R&R rather than just out of mortal danger.

Theo wasn't sure whether it was bravado or just a brave face and MacEwan wasn't telling.

"Your XO's a pretty good shot," Theo said. "She disabled *Edward VII*."

"Where is my ship, by the way?"

"Sherrard B."

"What the hell is it doing there?"

"The commodore's trying to find out. If Gisele doesn't strike her colors, you may have no ship to go back to."

"Damn." Wallace MacEwan ran his hand through his hair. "It's not like there are a lot of ships just floating around waiting for someone to command them."

"It's not like Commodore MacDowell is *looking* to take her out. But if she tries to go outsystem, there may not be any alternative."

"It was the Chinese, wasn't it?"

"Sam Andreotti must have gotten Big-5s from *somewhere*," Theo said. "But there aren't any GC ships insystem. Maybe they're going to jump in to Sherrard-B."

"Then what?"

"Depends what they do. But it looks like the Free Republic of Sherrard lasted … oh, about eleven days."

* * *

Gisele Rouchou had made turnover right at the asteroid belt. *Hector* had decelerated as it crossed through the outer system of Sherrard-B. *Warren* was in pursuit by then: MacDowell had half again the firepower and at least twice the accel capability; he wasn't in the mood for any more negotiation.

A scan of the system showed a number of possible alternatives, but escape probably wasn't one of them. A certain amount of dodging around would keep *Hector* out from in front of *Warren*'s guns for a while, but eventually there'd be an issue of fuel. Sherrard-B had no gas giant; *Warren* wasn't going to let *Hector* anywhere near Sherrard-A.

It took six hours. Finally Rouchou commed MacDowell's flag; Mac-Dowell took the call in his ready-room.

"No rescue in sight, Commander," MacDowell said. "I don't know who you're expecting, though I have my suspicions."

"I'm sure I don't know what you're talking about, sir," the *pro tem* commander of *Hector* answered.

"Right. I'm sure Sam Andreotti didn't just go down to the Big-5 store and buy those damn missiles at discount. It doesn't matter: they left you high and dry. It's over, Commander. You can save some lives, or you can destroy some EU property. Your choice."

Rouchou didn't look happy with the two alternatives. MacDowell half expected her to tell him to go straight to hell, but after several moments of thought—moments that some commanders in the Union probably wouldn't have given a rebel officer in charge of a mutinous ship—she nodded.

"Prepare to receive a prize crew," MacDowell said. "This wasn't a good idea, Commander. It never was. I told Sam Andreotti that, and I'm telling you as well. I could've blown you out of the sky—I suppose you know that."

"I'm surprised you didn't, sir." *Hector* had changed course and begun to decelerate.

"I can't see as it would have done any good."

Rouchou considered this for a moment. "The Union is coming apart, sir," she said, with a candor that seemed to spring from nowhere. "There won't be too many more chances for you to show restraint, I'm thinking."

"I hope you're wrong."

"I'm not wrong, sir. My career is over—for now."

"For good, Rouchou. The EU is going to put you away for a long time, but I'll do what I can to speak up for you."

"*Hector* will be ready to receive your prize crew, sir," she said, and ended the comm.

Revolutionists

Sharon Lee & Steve Miller

"Arin's Envidaria, as instituted for the Seventeen Worlds by Arin Gobelyn's son Jethri Gobelyn and overseen by the Carrassens-Denobli, established an egalitarian trade network meant to be self-supporting during the disruptive incursion of Rostov's Dust into the lesser galactic sub-arm.

"Jethri Gobelyn, a peripatetic traveler and trader, left his mark in many ways; his genes are said to be widely dispersed in and around the Seventeen World trading nexus. Due to divergent local institutional traditions the Seventeen Worlds Network experienced a period of instability following the end of the dust-dark and the reestablishment of regular trading with the wider Terran-Liaden trading web."

—Gehrling's Middle History of the Inhabited Galactic Sub-Plane, Third Terran edition

~ ~ ~

Geral was alone, as he often was. This time was different because he was doing squad work solo instead of with the whole squad. Famy Binwa'd called him sudden.

"We got a big meeting for only Full Staff and Seniors, no cits allowed. Secret, too, you can't mention it. You're covering for Security. Get to it!"

Another drill, he'd figured, but once his ID read as present in Service Squad's corridor, Binwa'd said, "Not a drill this time, Geral. You're mobile structure security! Watch yourself, there's been trouble!"

So he went careful. The logs did show trouble—odd trouble. Bar fights gone to flash-riots, followed by attempts to enter Admin without permission. Sabotaged cameras. Yeah, the cits weren't pleased with Admin changing anything—heck, people would argue and fight if their old veeds disappeared and no chance to stuff 'em into personal holdings, much less work shortages and menus gone thin.

Down here in the inner structure, though, he ought to be fine, no real chance of a riot or change to threaten him. Binwa'd sounded tense, like Geral might not be up to the job.

It didn't help Geral that he'd been raised like he was fragile, him being a good birth in a bad Standard Year. In fact, him and Luchee being the only pair born across three hundred and ten days—and before-hand some doubts he'd be born at all.

Once he *was* born they were careful of him—after him there were three years in a row with no births, period. They said it was the famine that did it, but then the cheese planets got back in gear after their little civil war and things got back to regular. Kids was born station-side again—they used fertility drugs and had a bunch of twins and triplets—so there were always a pack of youngers that he didn't quite fit in with.

The Seniors, it was known, kept him in reserve as a special case, 'cause he had good blood, since it was the 'fusions that let them get to their proper ages and the 'fusions that kept them safe during the thin-food. They'd been so close-knit that cousins were sisters and little brothers nephews. They tested him and never tapped him, but they kept his mother close. She had the blood and had survived his birth sturdy, even in those bad times.

His mother—he hadn't seen her for almost a Standard Year; she'd gone up deck and was living in Senior Pod, where the Seniors had their own medico and kept their own shifts. The last time he'd seen her, he'd been on 'cide clean-up. She'd been in a hurry elsewhere and had stopped when she saw him, nodding a greeting.

"Looking good, Geral Jethri. Don't join no rowdies, and don't think you need a way out," here she'd gestured to the 'cide site, "'cause you're set. I'm good for years and you—you're in the right orbit. You got the blood, so they'll hold on to you like they hold on to me. The Seniors need you! I'll see you about, I bet."

That orbit had brought him here, after all, with him having not spoken to her again.

He patted the metal turnwheel at the master seal between open corridors and the utility tunnels. He tested the seal with a gas sniffer. He looked for little hidden messages. His comm unit was on channel, so he spoke to it.

"Seal three checks out, Binwa, got the veed. No hosties, no notes."

No reply for the moment, but Famy Binwa was always a third slow in the Control room, more afraid of making a mistake than—

Mud, ought to use the correct form, shouldn't he? Things were spelled out proper on Security Detail, especially for Binwa, who was a boss because his ma was and not so much 'cause he knew what he was doing.

Silence went on. Binwa got touchy, but not like he was a bad sort—they'd talked many times about how things might change now that the curl of the dust the system'd been stuck in for three hundred Standards was drifting out. Lately Binwa was always on duty when Geral was, like they were going to be paired on the low shift forever, like kids being left to deal while the adults did something for adults.

"Please repeat, Squad," Binwa finally insisted.

Geral translated this time, from the start, his voice sounding odd in his own ears, which meant Binwa'd just turned the recorders on and his mic was live.

"Attention Internal Control. Squad Forty Security Update. Seal Three is tight. No hostiles. No anomalies."

"Squad Forty, we confirm your voice match, we confirm your location, we confirm no hostiles, we confirm Seal Three is secure, we confirm there are no service reminder notes. Please move to next station. Veed feed as time permits."

He hadn't found any hostiles so far. Hostiles in his early training had always meant Yxtrang invaders, but that was a scare tactic to help kids keep serious. His whole life, born and bred here, he'd never heard of an actual Yxtrang station invasion. So far as he'd ever seen, a hostie was a Security full-timer slurping toot or half asleep over a streaming 'venture veed.

These days the threat was supposed to be Revolutionists, a secret group trying to change the way things on Spadoni station worked and who was in charge. He'd never met any of them outright, though some of the tougher hanger-abouts might could be. They'd complain that things needed changing—that it used to be you was free to work at what you wanted or what you could, but now they were being sent to the cheese planets on contract, want to or no! Somehow it was Admin doing things wrong, or the Seniors who needed replacing to make things right.

The Revolutionist talk had gained a lot of energy in the last quarter, what with Odd Things happening Out There. Out There being other sectors, sectors they were hearing more and more about because the dust was thinning so rapidly. Outside hadn't been important growing up, except that it made the Seventeen Worlds allies because of the *Envidaria*.

He'd read the *Envidaria* a bunch of times, and you could say he believed in it. To stop one world being the top spot like Liad tried to do, the *Envidaria*'d kept the sides even … and that meant worlds shouldn't own all the ships, all the stations, all the commerce. Spadoni was 'sposed to be independent, her people free to work at what they could, while the trade org belonged to the planet system and most of the ships came from Outside. The *Envidaria* was supposed to make that work.

He'd also read a bunch of the couldies about *Envidaria*, the idea. They were made-up things like *The Secret of Lord Jethri, The Clouds of Spite*, and yes, even a buncha the mances like *Three on A Ship* and *The Master Firegemster*. It was kind of funny seeing the images of Jethri on this very same station back when it was fresh-built, and knowing he, Geral, carried part of that name, and that he really did, if you squinted, look like Jethri. Stars in his blood, courtesy of his multi-great-grandma's bunking with the man with the plan.

* * *

Geral lingered in Corridor Nine, feeling a little homesick.

He'd brought Luchee to the 9-9 storeroom for a kiss and some touches back when he was just Deck Plus, and even showed her Vent 77, the inactive space that was technically just a Three Seal since it had been a part of the temporary build-in docks meant for short term storage. Him and Luchee'd been of an age, and 'bout as poor, both born to mothers on station base pay. The mothers lived cubbywall to cubbywall, shared corridor frontspace, and on slowdown weeks they sat out front with everyone else, passing sips while the kids hunted stuff to turn in for credits at the recycle, being too young to trade blood for points. Once he'd been born and was proof her line was clean, that was the start, and after he hit puberty they knew he didn't break his bones just by standing, or bleed forever, nor any of the other problems that had come along to stationers in the rough times a couple hundred Standards goneby.

Him and Luchee, they'd got in a fight once, a fierce thing where they wasted some of that precious blood arguing about if it was *good* to trade blood in.

"Points are good and you know it. Have to save a little extra," he'd told her.

She'd squinched her face up, looked those gray eyes straight at him. "You do it more than once and it'll go on your records. And then you'll get stuck, just like your ma. She can't go higher, 'cause Admin keeps her like she's a crop down in 'ponics!

"I see my own ma just waiting for the points to rack up and I'm not gonna live like that and neither should you.

"I could just shake you sometimes for not paying attention!"

Well, she did shake him, and he shook her back, and somehow they hit a gravity well frustrated with each other. And there was the blood, and needing to clean it up before someone called a safety on them for creating a hazmat situation.

In the end they'd patched it up and kept hanging together. They promised each other they'd keep their blood and use all that extra energy to study. They even did some joint Informatics until their skills didn't match any more. Luchee was good with maths, and she'd been set to student status, 'cept all the classes were always full of the C and B deck folks and no room for her, no matter how high her test scores were.

Him, the one Luchee was always getting out of scrapes—*he'd* been free to study how he wanted—station stuff, and the *Envidaria*—always interested as much in how the station worked as in how far he could go updecks in life. So, turned out, *he* could make a living doing what he wanted, and *she* couldn't even go to school, nor get anything better than hour-work.

Luchee and him had thrilled a couple times in the vent space in Corridor Nine but he gave it up after he'd stopped by to find her there not very dressed and with an older guy from up Admin Deck just as sweaty and calling her name like he was hurting, which still made him twitch to think about even if it was a few years back.

She might have warned him, anyhow … but she hadn't, and they'd got all disconnected over it, with her saying things was too complicated for her to talk about with him anymore, and levels he had no business to know—him being in the Service Squad and his ma still transfusing.

She wouldn't know him, then, and he got busy with his doin's, so he forgot to miss her, 'til he heard she'd connected with a visiting spacer, and gone off as side-crew with no notice to no one. He figured that was luck for her and he did miss her, though by then he had a crew-grade sleep-unit, and didn't need the cubby, anyway.

"Squad Forty, this is Green Office." Binwa's voice in his ear jerked him out from remembering. "We have inbound ships and I have to check-mark all the security stations. No one's covering the armory. I have keyed your unit in; I need you to go there and sit at the boards, it's supposed to be occupied when ships approach."

"Green Office, Squad Forty is just one of me, and that's supposed to be a three-crew location, according to training. I ..."

"*This* is also a three-crew location and there's one of me, Squad Forty. We are in security lockdown mode because of that meeting. Go, lock yourself in, report. The hatch is set to your ID."

"I'm on my way. Does route matter?"

"Squad Forty ... call it a hurry, and I don't care how you get there long's you do it quick."

"Confirmed, this is a hurry and I'm on free route. Going."

* * *

The armory had opened to him, as Binwa'd told him it would. Geral rushed into the control area and was in front of the screen, helmet and gloves off, still sweating—and only part of that from the path he'd followed. He looked at the controls, familiar only from sim, and worried, thought of Luchee getting stuff right off and figured he could remember what he had to here.

He was trying to get his balance back on account of the tween-deck utility shafts he'd run as fast as he could. The places where you could be caught in gravity errors where you got pulled in two or three directions from overlapping grav fields or where weak fields might let you dive down a metal tunnel for meters on end.

"Squad Forty! Check that hatch!"

Geral twisted his head.

"Closed." It had made a muffled thrum when he'd pushed it across hard.

"Not showing good here!"

He rose carefully, left leg and knee a trifle sore from a missed gravity slip. It hadn't been there last time he was through ... but that happened these days as the fabric of the station strained against its age. It should have been refitted before he was born, but there'd been the Troubles, after all.

He twisted the handle and slid the hatch open an arm's length. He hadn't tested the pressure gauges and now his helmet sat at the second seat, with all his readouts ...

He pulled, sullenly, and yelled across the room as it slammed ...

"Now?" He forgot his formal again, but then so did Binwa, who was sounding strained.

"Not sealed!"

Geral pulled his weight against the handle, yanked it open, staring into the hatch mechanicals.

"Mud and wind twists!"

There were four pressure latches meant to grab and seat when the handle was rotated. One close to his hip level was fine and bright, and the one just above chest height was, too. The top and bottom latches though, looked like they had something in the way of that final click-seal, something printed in a very thin flex-sheet that fell into place after the hatch was cycled once.

"What was that, Squad Forty?" Now Binwa sounded *really* worried.

Fingers quick on the sharp metal hatch edge, Geral pulled hard, and out came the bottom strip, unfolding to near half his arm length. He stared, shoved it into a storage pocket on the duty-suit, reached to pull the other while ....

"Problem spot, *hold comm*," he managed, and emphasizing that helped him pull the tattered top strip down to shove it, too, into his pocket.

"Jonimo!" He slammed the hatch hard, and this time the click sounded like a solid thunk, alright, and ...

"Jonimo?" came the worried voice and then: "That's got it!"

He sat heavily at the console, pulling a frayed yellow strip from his suit.

"Is that code, Squad Forty?"

Geral gasped a short laugh, wiping sweat from his forehead.

"Kind of is, Binwa. Haven't you ever done a suit-walk? *Jonimo* is what you say when you jump off the station, to tell your squad you're free in space."

"Never been off-station. Never been on a ship, either," Binwa admitted.

"Anyhow, looks like the hatch was blocked from tight seal. I mean on purpose—I've sent you veed of it!"

"Yes. I should have expected this. This is part of it all, I'm afraid."

"Part of what?"

"Things happening. Comm channels I can't get to, and ships incoming but no one's talking to me. There's a Conference going on and I can't get feed on that, either. Security's tampered with, locking me out! I don't think they trust me, Geral, I see what they're up to!"

He sat; the board demanded ID.

"Binwa, you have to approve my biometrics, it says."

"Yes. They left me alone here and now I invoked Catastrophe Ops. I'll confirm you as Security, Acting Squad Leader. I got the key. Heck, I'll just make you Shift Security Leader. Sensors on!"

Geral paused, the sound of *Catastrophe Ops* bouncing around his thoughts, making him a little worried.

"I'm looking into the camera, straight-face, and got my left hand on the pad."

"I see this, Squad. Takes a moment—give me your full ID, number, and names."

He did the numbers and letters first, then said "Geral Jethri Quai-Hwang."

"Moment, Squad."

The screens lit up, followed by a shockingly loud click as something mechanical thunked in the walls near the hatch.

"You are live, Security Leader. Right now, there's you and me, and then there's the rest of the station. You're Security Lead. You can do almost anything. Wait, I need to take care of something. It may be a few minutes."

Probably has to go pee, Geral figured, *he's like that when he's nervous.*

Geral was used to waiting, but not to having this much information in front of him, open to him, with the time going from one minute to many.

But yes, he *did* see, there on one screen all the pressure points on the station, on a zoomable map-grid, and there, on another, the status of the doors, the pressure variations, water and fluid flow, the gravity variations. Also, *all* the reports, everyone's shift status, security stations, medical alerts, a blinking yellow triangle showing a guard status—

Two names he knew quite well, under guard in the hospital, on pregnancy watch. Tifney and Pettipi! Both of them? Both of the twins under guard? Both due multi-births?

He rolled the idea around in his head, remembering how they'd corraled him on First Orbit's Eve, the pair full of energy and inviting him to a quiet shindig, offering up a touch of *vya* and, after the *vya*, a long night on a bed full of them and them alone. The following shift-month they'd collected him individually a time or two—and then the Admin shifts changed and his moved to match Famy Binwa's. He'd wondered what happened.

The blood. They'd wanted his blood, that was what. And when they'd tested pregnant …

There was dread in his gut and he couldn't quite swallow it away.

* * *

Binwa didn't tell him what took a few minutes, but Geral knew it was far longer than that. He'd drilled down, peeking into private records, including the two women in hospital expecting multiple births. He found his own record, eventually, full of notations like "loner, no strong friendships, tractable if left to his own pursuits," but the cross-references to Senior Resource and Admin Alert made him worried, and the multiple notes over time—*Transfuse only to Seniors* and *Blood Resource*—worried him more.

Other areas didn't open to him—but yes, the Seniors had their own shifts and apparently they'd added his mother to their number, for her records were all behind a security wall he couldn't breach.

He'd closed that file, tried to understand the rest of the boards in front of him, including the 3D station situation board.

"I am back," Binwa said, sounding winded. "What do you see?"

"Three ships," Geral said once he figured out what he was looking at. "Three ships closing this says."

There was a curse then, and an ugly sound, like muffled warning horns over and over, and then distant shivers in the fabric of the station. Inside the armory, panels flashed, lights dimmed, the status board showed blue blocks on the station map—every pressure door and hatch was sealed or sealing. The words GENERAL SECURITY LOCKDOWN were prominent.

Under that status a series of images flashed onto the screens, security cameras showing rotating views of corridors. The red lights showed—

"Where's Security? If this is a general lockdown, where's the rest of Security?" Geral tried the corridor cameras, finding nothing. The meeting rooms, though, were crowded.

"Never mind them, Geral, *you're* Security, because I can depend on you, and *they're* conspirators. All of them. The rest are ... offline. They'll have to back down, now."

"Who?"

"There's a revolt, Geral. The Seniors are trying to sell the station to the cheesers and that's not in the Crew Compact. The station and all of us, they want to trade us so they can live forever. You and me and ... the Seniors are locked in a room, and Admin, too. They were having their meeting, so I had to act. The Seniors made me do it! I've put out a call-in for the rest of the Service Squad to take over Security, but you're the only one's come to me, Geral. My mother's on their side, she says the *Envidaria* is over, done. Who believes that?"

Geral thought about it. There hadn't been an end date on the *Envidaria*, the arrangement. It was how they'd lived for hundreds of Standards. It was what made Jethri and Arin so important, and helped guide millions of lives…

"Control, Green Office. I mean—I don't think the *Envidaria* is over, Binwa. I don't! What should I do, then?"

"There's a loyalty oath on the screen, Geral. Accept it. Then we'll open the armory weapons bay, so you can repel boarders."

* * *

Geral was, according to Famy, fully second in command now. The Seniors, the Security Squad, everyone had to listen to Binwa until this got fixed. Binwa had a copy of The Crew Compact open and was reading it out across the channels to them. Geral could hear him in the background, droning on, then emphasizing random words.

Geral'd left the anteroom, secured it so it would only open to him or on order from Binwa. He'd rushed to the inner armory and now, in the weapons bay, he was bathed in brightness.

The full-suits were there. All of them were there, including three brandnews that had Full test Green labels everywhere—new and never worn.

He hurried, stripped to basics, grabbed up one with a green tag showing shoulder and hip to toe ratios that ought to do, and squiggled his way in, knowing that the wrong that was happening was *really* wrong—all the suits here ought already to be on someone, all of them ought to be in position, *all* of them. Comes to worst, might be someone expecting this suit might come through the seal any minute—

But they weren't roused, were they? All the external packs were on the wall, weren't they, *and* all the guns?

Seemed strange that they wouldn't have grabbed the guns for a revolt. Seemed strange they could have grabbed the Bloodlines—that would be Ma, among others!—without bothering other services. But the alert was out and they weren't here, the regular crew, nor his.

"Squad Forty," he said to the mic even before his gloves clicked on seal, "this is Lead on Squad Forty, back-up not suited yet," he said, knowing that someone in Control ought to have a veed feed and see him standing alone and know what he meant. If someone was back-up to Squad Forty they were going to have to show soon, else …

"Squad Forty, confirmed. Watching for you to get under pressure. Pack M and L are assigned yours. If crew shows with my code, make them double up on extras."

But there *wasn't* anybody else. It would be him and Binwa, wouldn't it? Pack M was the full mobility unit with projectiles as well as lasers. It was a leader's unit—had some range on the jets, had some firepower he'd never tried, but supposed to be automatic. The suit should fit itself in when he got there, and the unit ought to heed him …

"Sealed," he said when he was, again seeing the squad room that ought to have sixteen people, empty but for him. The heads-up display came live, bringing almost too much information: local internal and external pressure and atmospheres, state of the connections and network, ammunition count, loitering time, battery state, and … empty slots where Squad Leader ought to have a squad.

"Control? Squad Forty prepped for EVA, grabbing packs."

Not much more to be said, with no one talking back and no one yet coming to be his backup.

He slapped the plate and walked through, lights coming up as he did. Earnestly wishing there was motion behind him, knowing there wasn't, he only quarter-turned to the plate on this side, where the pre-packs waited, patient as death, for their missions.

That slap was bordering wistful; the angled sliver of view showed the stark white of the two closest suits, hanging empty, before the scissors of the closing door left him even more alone.

"Two seals, Control. Mounting up."

"You are authorized to open to vacuum and deploy. You are authorized to use force; your weapons are live."

There were two hatches, one with pack rails and one without, and the packs sat there waiting. The hatch could take five at a time if need be—

Geral backed into Pack M, reaching overhead to pull himself up onto that slight saddle, his elbows and forearms resting on the U of the equipment, his legs on the stirrups. Quick motions clicked the umbilical on each side into the power systems and into the pack's extended environmental units.

"Pack M systems attached to Leader," a quiet voice told him. "Accept, please."

He did that, and Pack M let him know that Pack L was attaching to hard points, which he felt, and he took a deep breath. Now the view was augmented even further and all those points there on the left side were weapons far more powerful than a pistol. He shuddered with knowing he'd not armed things yet, and knowing he had too much power, anyway, for someone whose leading had mostly been to a spot at the bar and then open a door for bed and a roll, if he was lucky.

"Geral, we need you to occupy Bay Four. The other docks are under control from here, so they're secure … and I got Traffic's radio feeds locked up tight so they can't be involved—but if that ship gets to the dock, I can't stop them here—none of the other service units are responding. Security has gone over, they're on strike, too. They're all Revolutionists and we got to stop them. Hold Bay Four!"

"Confirm, Control. Hold Bay Four."

* * *

He barely noticed space, space being what there was mostly except for the reality of the station and the need to be at a hard-to-reach location. His suit was quiet around him, but he heard his own breathing, kept reminding himself to follow the color-coded dots, to follow the easy-to-read blinking lights … but no, he shouldn't!

Resisting the urge to talk to himself about it, he said, "Control, you might want to turn off traffic control lighting. I can see where I'm going without."

"Will do. Might need to go silent so they can't monitor … I'm releasing all suit control to you, Geral. You're autonomous now."

Many of the flashing lights went away. The numbers on the side of the station's hull didn't, but the details of a docking collar would be harder to see with the station rotating into darkness, especially if there was someone between you and getting close enough to use ship lights to illuminate it.

Guidance. He could use some guidance here …

"Control?"

Silence.

Out there, suddenly, there was blackness as the local star was eclipsed, and then again, the light making him a shadow.

They'd never warned him about this kind of stuff, that he'd be a sharp spot on the hull, that resisting invasion gave the advantage to the people out there who wanted to take …

"Test, circuit open. Spadoni, please reply. Please initiate routine docking…. There's my echoes, Spadoni, you can hear me.

"Spadoni, we are coming to dock. Please turn guidance on. This is Carrassens *AnnaV* on a scheduled shipment. I am Pilot In Charge Luchinda Eerik of the—"

Luchinda? His Luchee? It sounded just like her, it did, even across the years and, yeah, she was quick and sharp. A pilot? But there was trouble now …

Also, Control was on silence and had locked down Traffic's radio.

"This is Squad Forty. There's been riots and Revolutionists. We can't let you dock until there's an all-clear ordered. We may use any means to hold this docking bay. We have been authorized to use force, if required."

"If you fire on my ship I will return fire, Squad Forty."

"I know you will, Luchee," he said, "Just like you busted my nose, thank you."

A pause, not caused by the slow crawl of radio waves. He used it to maneuver his unit to one of the hard points. The dull red triangle glowed in outline on the left and he speared the arms-length metal pipe protecting the cabling into it, feeling the snap as it tightened, followed by inserting the cable into the blue circle on the right with a similar mechanical snap. Pack M and Pack L oriented themselves as the hardpoint locked; he was essentially an external gun turret now.

He should have heard confirmation from Control on that, but inside the suit everything matched up. Autonomous.

Through his faceplate he could see another eclipsed star, and then augments hit and he had targeting information on a ship coming nearly straight at him. The bad news was that they must have him now, as well, know that he was not speaking from a station defense battery, he was merely a stud locked upright on a bright hull, casting a shadow to infinity.

"Squad Forty, we are not looking for a fight. We're not Revolutionists, we're a trade ship. And I'm getting counter information from another source claiming that you have been misrouted and misinformed and are to be ignored. If you're Geral, you're a braver fool than I ever realized, facing down a ship with a suit!"

He heard that, breathed a curse that was loud in his own ears even if not broadcast.

"Control? What status? What support?"

He was clicking between comm broadcast channels furiously, the head's up display showing him active bands.

After a long pause, Binwa broke silence.

"I still hold Control. Security won't help. They want to give the station away, the whole station, Geral! Why's there three ships? At least one of those ships are what they've been waiting on. They want to send us all to Fromage Two. They're going to occupy the station … you got to stop them from getting in."

"Squad?" came Luchee's drawl.

"AnnaV, I'm sorry. My orders remain."

"Dammit, Geral, you're alone in a spacesuit and there's three ships out here."

"I'm on lockpoint," he managed. "I've got war units, Luchee. Are you in a battleship?"

"Can't discuss it, Squad Forty. You're going to have to move away from that dock. I hope you'll do it soon; my shift is due to end but I'm not allowed to leave docking incidents unresolved. I'm lighting up for rendezvous."

The faceplate showed two ghostly outlines now, the M unit's sensors showing where the approaching ships were, where ...

There! A blot took shape exactly where the faceplate put it, stars going away, and then the blot took color and shape as brilliant points of light, some blinking to varying pulses and others just there.

Training recall came to him, the five blue lights circling the nose of the ship meaning *AnnaV* was headed right at him, the slow blinking red lights ringing the blue were the pods-heads, the apparent bright ring between the blue and the red was where *AnnaV*'s hull swelled to the pod points. More light now, and he was awash in it, the faceplate barely shielding him from the full intensity. The approaching ship slowed, loomed ...

From the station channels:

"Squad Forty, you must stand down and return your aux-packs to the armory. Your training mission is over. Famy Binwa has been relieved of all command. Your loyalty oath is noted. You must return to the armory ..."

Geral shivered. It was Famy's ma!

"Don't listen! They've breached this line, but we resist the revolution. Civilians cannot understand the dangers—"

"This is Vice Administrator Binwa. My son has been relieved of shift and staff command and is being removed from the control room. You are now under my direct orders, Geral Jethri. Return to station, place yourself under Security's protection. You will be escorted to upgraded quarters and this incident will be purged from your file."

There was a short pause before she spoke again, sharply.

"Geral Jethri?"

He swallowed, the promise of upgrades making his stomach clench, as he thought of the twins, both pregnant. His kids. His blood ...

There came sounds of heavy breathing, and pounding, through the ear-set, then Famy Binwa's voice, loud.

"I'm loyal to the *Envidaria*. This is a breach—I will resist, I will eject, I will—"

Beneath Geral, the station lurched, vibration traveling through the taut cables locking him and his packs to the surface, shaking him and his suit against the strapping.

"Geral Jethri? Let me make your choice plain. Return to station and receive an upgrade. Continue this revolt and we will be rid of you."

Geral was still trying to understand. Famy. The Revolutionists. Forced labor on the cheese worlds. The—

"I am," he whispered, "under the command of Famy Binwa."

There was another lurch; this one smaller and more personal.

"Control?" Geral demanded, wondering if some unknown ship had managed a violent latch-dock out of his view. "Squad Forty reporting anomaly—"

His faceplate showed him a flashing: UNLOCK ALERT UNLOCK ALERT UNLOCK ALERT UNLOCK at the same time it showed a potential target not much bigger than him drifting away from the station, a tumbling figure, a ...

His faceplate flashed a warning—power issues for the lockpoint.

A KLUNG shook him; distantly a station thruster showed power and the station twisted. Or he did.

Jettisoned. He'd been jettisoned!

Below him the station rolled and the faceplate echoed that, and now it showed him the station as a target, receding slowly.

Everyone he knew in the universe was out there, targets. Targets, if he was willing.

* * *

He'd tried three airlocks, chasing them as the station rotated. It was as if he didn't exist. His suit showed station comm circuits locked against him, and the last effort to close with the station had been met by a round of attitude jets, almost taunting him.

Working his suit kept him calm; he had to think hard about it, but it was a new suit and getting easier to use every minute.

Eventually, one of the ships disappeared beyond the bulk of the station; he could see portions of it as it docked, but wasn't in comm circuit.

The other two ships now rode in orbit between him and the station. One was, he knew, the *AnnaV*. The other he didn't know—

"Spacer Geral Jethri, this is *AnnaV*, offering to connect you with a recovery ship."

Luchee's voice was calm and quiet in his ear.

"Spacer? I'm a stationer. I can't ..."

"You are a distressed spacer, discovered free-floating in an orbit you are unable to recover from under your own power. I can certify that. We can do that for you, Geral Jethri."

"But the station! I'm Service Squad, I'm supposed to …"

"They abandoned you, Geral Jethri. You're locked out."

He fought with himself. He had forty hours of air. Enough firepower, though, to …

Famy Binwa had trusted him. Famy had fooled him. Famy … had ejected without a suit …

Luchee took a breath.

"Either you're a distressed spacer or you're dead," she said flatly.

"I don't have anything …" He stuttered to a stop.

She didn't argue that point. His air showed thirty-eight-point-seven hours now.

"Geral, I'm going off-duty. My shift is ending. Be smart. I can arrange for pick-up, while I'm Pilot In Charge. That's all I can do. You need to make the choice.

"You need to save yourself."

Geral stared beyond the lurking ships, beyond the station's disorienting rotation against the background of a distant three-mooned planet.

There was silence for a while. When Luchee spoke again, it was like she'd woken him up from a drowse.

"Geral, we're docking next. We can't pick you up; if you're on-board when we dock, Spadoni will arrest you. They'll lock you up and take your blood and you won't even get points for it! You'll never be free!"

The station rotated under him.

"The other ship with us is not docking, Geral. Will you let them pick you up? She … they believe in the *Envidaria*. They live by it. They're free! They want to talk to you, Geral. I trust them. Remember, we said we weren't going to give blood to the Seniors. You promised me, Geral! We'll be in radio shadow now, be smart!"

The station's rotation was patient, unforgiving. *AnnaV*, in pursuit of a docking bay, slid into the bright side while he and his suit were in the darkness.

Geral was alone, as he often was. But …

He had a choice. He could be desperate for what wasn't going to happen, like Famy Binwa, or he could be like Jethri and Arin had been and make something happen. He could let the Seniors own him or he could …

"This is Spacer Geral Jethri Quai-Hwang. What ship?"

He asked as if he knew ships, which he didn't; as if the name mattered. He'd been prepared to fire upon them, an hour gone, and now …

A pleasant female voice filled the ether, carried by a strong, directional signal.

"This is Ship *Disian*. Geral Jethri, may we match velocity with you and bring you aboard? Please, call me *Disian*.

"Also," came the pleasant voice, with no sense of irony, "it would be good if you would turn off targeting mode and safe your weapons. We can rendezvous in ten minutes."

Geral flinched, shook his head at himself, and safed the weapons. The oxygen read-out on his faceplate said thirty-six-point-seven hours and he was free to watch it count down, if he really wanted to. Maybe the station would pull him in, right before the last. Maybe they'd decide they needed his blood too bad to let him go.

Or, maybe they wouldn't.

A deep breath then, and he used his jets, turning to admire the view, and the ship, approaching.

The oxygen countdown had begun to bore him and he realized that, despite it all, he was getting hungry.

"Yes, Ship *Disian*," he said eventually. "Thank you. Please come for me. This distressed spacer accepts your offer of aid."

The Gunslinger

Kay Kenyon

March 2, 1950.

Despite her training in the rehabilitation of criminals, Lena was nervous about meeting a mass murderer. Especially this one: Maximilian Becker.

Trying to quiet her heart, she paused in front of the hospital portico, looking up at the third-floor windows, one of which would be Becker's. She tried to bear in mind that the man she was about to meet was a human being, no matter what he had done. Or the way he had done it.

Once inside, she made her way to room 303, holding her satchel against her thigh and patting it, conscious of the nervous gesture. Inside were the documents outlining Becker's appalling offenses, the papers that, once signed, could start him on the road to pardon. It would be difficult. The outcome was not assured, of course, especially for this man whose crimes had escaped punishment for a decade. She had been warned that Becker was sly and would try to position himself as a hero—a hero!—but she would be on her guard. He had evaded capture for so long, but now that he was in custody he must be made an example of. So the authorities said. But that was not her job, nor could her heart be in punishment. Given the recent war, the world was in need of peace and reconciliation. Even for Maximilian Becker.

As Lena entered room 303, she found herself in a spacious ward. Four tall windows marched down one wall, and under the middle window, the only bed. A nurse sat at a desk just inside the door. After scrutinizing Lena's identity card, she gave a staccato nod and Lena proceeded to the bed under the windows.

Maximilian Becker was reading a paperback book. A fortyish, barrel-chested man with a comb-over to camouflage the balding. A little vanity, then. The worst offenders often had such pretensions, something she had noticed in her work for Reconciliation. It was almost as though the less imposing his looks, the more a man had to compensate with conceit and violence. She pulled a chair close to the bed.

He glanced at her. "Ah. My angel of mercy, I presume?"

Startlingly, she noted his soft brown eyes. Puppy dog eyes. An absurd thought, for which she chided herself. "Yes, yes, I hope to be. I am Lena." A good beginning.

"Well, knock yourself out, Fräulein." He went back to his book.

She took her seat, summoning patience. Outside the windows, the elms were budding out, signaling spring. Hope. A better future. "What are you reading, Mr. Becker?"

He sighed, closing the book, but kept it in his lap as though he might continue reading at any moment. "You can skip the cheery stuff. I'm just a number to you Reconciliation types. 'Room 303' or Maximilian the Murderous Rebel or Becker the Butcher. How about we start there?"

With an attitude like that, Lena doubted that he would sign a remorse statement today. Fortunately, she was allotted four visits with the man. Time enough to move the discussion forward.

She put her satchel on the floor. "There is no need to be sarcastic."

"There's plenty of need," he objected. He put the book on the nightstand, twisting in the bed to reach it.

As he did so, Lena noted the flatness of the blanket above what would have been his right foot.

He went on. "Reconciliation. A big, phony word, don't you think?" His eyes almost danced with merriment as he warmed to what she feared would be a tirade. "Why not just say 'shame' and be done with pussy-footing around?"

Now she had firmer ground on which to meet him. She was not a personage of importance but the National Reconciliation Women's Auxiliary had trained her well. "There is a difference, Mr. Becker, between shame and remorse. Remorse acknowledges the suffering you have caused. Acknowledgment leads to compassion. Compassion leads to rehabilitation and pardon."

"Louis L'Amour," he said.

"Pardon?"

"The novel I'm reading. By a new author who does cowboy stories. Hell of a good writer, missy."

Lena glanced at the narrow spine of the book. *Westward the Tide.* He was starting to warm to her, she felt. It would be a problem though, if he could not bring himself to make amends. They might have to take his other foot.

"Perhaps," she said, "it would be best to read something that dealt less with guns and violence."

Becker shook his head in bewilderment. "They send me a slip of a thing who's afraid of guns!" He pointed a finger at her and made a sound like the report of a gun. At her expression, he frowned. "Come on, Lena, live a little."

"How can you make a joke of what has happened—what you have done—in your life? The shootings, the bombings … the …"

"Carnage?" he suggested.

Now he was mocking her. She rose, shouldering her satchel. "You can laugh your troubles away, Mr. Becker, but things can get very much worse for you. You realize that, don't you?"

He picked up his book again, effectively dismissing her.

"I'll come back another day."

"They never come back," he murmured, opening the novel with its well-creased spine.

March 5, 1950.

"Visit number two," the nurse snapped as Lena entered the ward.

"Oh yes, I am keeping track, thank you!" A couple nights of rest left her ready to start again with Mr. Becker.

He was reading as she approached his bed. Settling herself in the chair at his side, she began, "I have a question for you this morning." It was best to take charge, direct the conversation toward productive topics. She felt that Mr. Becker liked a bit of mental stimulation; a challenge, even if it was from a lower echelon girl from Reconciliation.

He looked up from his book, then went back to reading. He muttered, "I didn't think you'd be back."

"Never give up, that's my motto." Lena put her satchel at her feet. "Would you like a sip of water?" She glanced at the cup on the side table.

"Got anything stronger?"

She pursed her lips, determined not to get side-tracked this time. "My question, then. You have a Talent. One of the psychic abilities we are becoming accustomed to these days. It is, in fact, *precognition*. Seeing the future. You told the authorities that you committed your crimes because you saw that bad things would happen if the current government stayed in power."

"No. Not bad things."

A flicker of hope kindled in her chest. "No?"

"Not bad things. Heinous things. Unimaginable things—" He overrode her attempt to break in. "Brutality on an industrial scale, the murder of men, women, and children, the collapse of civilized society." He pinned her with a look both bland and unrelenting. "Little things like that."

"But you began your rampage before the so-called *brutality* started. In fact, you became what you wished to prevent. Brutal."

He put the book on the bedside table. "Not as much as what came to pass."

"I'll leave that point for now. But what I'm curious about is how a person, or a society, can be held to account—punished—for what it *might* do."

"But it's what you people did do."

"Nevertheless, at the time you began your guerilla tactics, most of what you opposed hadn't happened yet. This was, what, 1940?"

He glanced at her satchel. "It's all documented in there, right? So you know the dates. You know how the court looked at my defense. They convicted me anyway. No reprieve from my—rather ghastly, you have to admit—sentence."

Lena sighed. "But you felt your glimpse of the future gave you permission to act as though it had already happened."

"I'm glad you agree with me. And if we're done with the subject, I've got a question for *you*." He pulled the blanket up around his armpits and settled back into his pillows. "What do you like to read?"

"Read? Oh …" She tried to think of the last book she had read. Newspapers of course, but she knew he meant books. "Well. I am so busy. I do like a short story now and then."

He nodded. "Not much of a reader, then. For shame, Miss Reconciliation. Maybe you'd like to read this Louis L'Amour. When I'm done with it you can borrow it." He looked over at the nurse. "But don't come again this week. I'm scheduled for punishment again."

"Oh! Mr. Becker."

"They're taking my left arm. This one's in retaliation for a bomb nine years ago. A government official lost his left arm below the elbow. But the thing is, they're taking my whole arm." He looked up at her with challenge in his voice. "Is that fair?"

"Oh!" Truly, it did not seem fair.

"But it keeps me kind of even. Right foot, left arm." He shrugged, and for a moment she thought he might say more, might see how he had brought it upon himself, might perceive how his suffering, reflecting the suffering of his victims, was just. But he maintained his sense of superiority. *I did it for humanity. Whereas you people are just brutal.*

"How," Lena asked, "do they choose which atrocity to seek justice for, when you have so many maimings and deaths to account for?"

"The tribunal decides. It depends on how important the injured person was. In this case, it was a colonel." He felt for the book on the bed stand, but it seemed an unconscious gesture, as though for a moment he had gone inward.

"Mr. Becker. I'm sure their decisions are more clearly thought out than that."

As he looked at her, he seemed to really see her for the first time. "Do you think you could call me Max? No one ever called me Maximilian, much less Mr. Becker."

"Yes. I think I could. Max."

He shut his eyes then, and if he had found a moment of peace, she did not wish to intrude. She crossed the room as quietly as she could.

As she passed the nurse at her desk, the woman muttered. "Two visits left."

But Lena did not want to answer her, nor did she.

March 9, 1950.

Max lay in bed, breathing deeply, the medications helping to overcome the pain that, Lena was sure, were needed just three days after the loss of his arm.

As Lena pulled the chair close to the bed, Max's eyes fluttered open. "Lena, the Angel of … of Reconciliation."

She wondered if this was sarcasm or if perhaps he had at last come to remorse. "I'm here, Max."

He fell asleep again, or so she thought, but in a moment he said, his words slurring: "Could you read to me? I don't like … to go so long without my stories."

It was not strictly her mission, to give comfort, so she decided to redirect him to their increasingly vital topic. "Do you want to talk about what happened?"

"Do you mean … what they did to me … in surgery?"

"Oh, Max, no. I mean what you did when you planted the bomb that ruined the colonel's arm."

A whisper: "You mean when I saw my target and decided to go for him?"

"Yes, if you want to put it that way."

He made the faintest of smiles. "Well, I had a vision. Of what the man would do a few years' hence."

"Your *precognition*."

"Yes. When I saw him I thought, well, let's kill the son-of-a-bitch."

"Oh, Max!"

He smiled, and it was impossible to tell whether he had been trying to fluster her or whether he really had so little pity in his soul.

From across the room, the nurse coughed. Lena turned to see the woman frowning. If she had heard Max curse, she could report that Lena's ministrations were not efficacious.

Lena reached down for the satchel and began to unbuckle the clasp. Perhaps she would offer the initial paper to sign. Or at least let the nurse see that she was trying.

As she leaned over to fetch the document from her briefcase, Max whispered, "Come closer."

He grasped her wrist with his remaining hand, pulling her toward him. When they were almost nose-to-nose, he said, "Get me out of here." She drew back in alarm, but he pulled her close again, whispering, "On Friday, they're taking my eyes."

Friday. Four days from now. Her time was running out.

Max locked onto her gaze with his deep brown eyes. "I don't mind not seeing. What is there to see anymore, after all?" He jerked his head to indicate the beige ward room with only the nurse to look at, since he could not readily see out the windows behind him. "But … my books. You understand?"

She stayed hunched over the hospital bed, saying gently, "They would catch you. There are soldiers in the hallway, going about their duties. And besides, what can I do … the nurse …" But what was she saying? She obviously could not contemplate helping him escape. Maximilian Becker, of all people.

Max whispered, "A pill, my angel. There are such things. Medications that make it look like a heart attack. I need it before Friday. I know those surgeons like to stay busy, but I feel like making trouble for them." He lay back on the pillow, closing his eyes, continuing, barely audible: "In return, here's my gift to you; something I've seen. You're going to … to leave National Reconciliation Women's Auxiliary and when you do you'll find a companion. I'm sorry that I can't see whether it's a nice young man or a loyal dog. Personally? I would choose the dog."

Lena's chest tightened in dismay. She knew his *precognition* Talent to be genuine—he had been certified—but he was also capable of lying. "But, leave Reconciliation?"

"Well, you're no damn good at it, so you might as well."

As an excuse to stay close to him, she straightened his blankets. "Max," she whispered, "tell me you feel remorse. Give me something to work with. I'll stay up all night and do the paperwork. Please." It was one thing to take a man's limbs. But his *eyes*. Obviously, they had noticed that he loved to read.

"I've seen my future, Lena, and it stinks. But there's a future I prefer, the one where you bring me what I'm asking for."

"So there *are* different futures. I always wondered about that."

"Yup. A bunch. But usually one glows brighter. In your case, I don't know whether I get the pill or not."

From behind, the sound of the nurse snapping her pencil down on the desk. She did not like them whispering.

Lena watched him as he lay in the bed, the covers flattened over the gone foot, the gone arm. But Max Becker was still there, present in his eyes.

He tried to turn his head toward the side table, but ended up waving his one arm at it instead. "Hey, take my Louis L'Amour, would you? I finished it last night, and I think you'd like it."

Lena walked out with the book, fearing that she had made a deal with the devil. One thing Max might be right about, though. She was no good at Reconciliation.

March 11, 1950.

The nurse looked up as Lena came in.

Lena breezed past her. "I know, last visit." The old prune.

Max was waiting for her, sitting up in bed. He nodded at Lena and jutted his chin at the window behind him. "Those elms are sure taking their time getting going." He shook his head. "They only have one more day to show me they've got some juice."

"Juice?"

"Leaves. A future." He glanced at her satchel, raising an eyebrow in mock conspiracy.

She took her place by his bedside, putting off for a few moments more what she had come here to do. "I started *Westward the Tide.* I like it."

He slapped his wounded-leg thigh, wincing. "I knew it. Dang, girl, you got taste. They say 'dang' a lot in Westerns, you noticed?"

The answer never made it past her lips as she blinked back a surge of emotion. She nodded instead.

"I never even asked if you speak English," he said. "Or, at least, read it. Glad you do."

"There are a lot of things we've never talked about." She felt a genuine regret that their time was at an end. A buttery yellow light poured through the windows, chasing regret away, but leaving something more real in its wake. It swirled just below consciousness, not quite taking form, until at last she knew what it was: remorse.

They settled in to talking about the Louis L'Amour story with their gunfighters, drifters, outspoken heroine, and a place in America called the Bighorn Mountains in a state with a lovely English name, Montana.

When she left, Max was clutching the capsule in his remaining hand.

Out in the hallway, Lena paused, steadying herself. A few deep breaths until she felt ready to move, ready to move forward with her life. Her new life, without National Reconciliation.

As she descended the staircase leading to the hospital foyer, she glanced at the red, white, and black banner that hung prominently on the wall. She was glad there was no such banner in Max's room, though they might easily have hung one there to drive home how his efforts had all been in vain. He had not changed the outcome of the war, and the colonels and personages whom he had killed and hurt were certainly replaced by others. But by his lights he had aimed for justice, and though she could not agree, she did not wish him to suffer more.

A soldier in a smart SS uniform was coming up the stairs. He made eye contact with her. Outside of the city it was possible to avoid responding officially, but not in Berlin.

"Heil Hitler," she dutifully said. She would have to consider her future responses when confronted by a uniformed member of the Nazi party. What did she believe any longer? It was all very confusing.

But for now, and on Max's advice, she was already thinking about getting a dog.

Contender

Steve Perry

Death came for him in the form of a child.

"You're Lazlo Mourn," the child said.

Well, he wasn't *really* a child, he was probably pushing twenty-five T.S., but that was more than twenty years younger than Mourn, who didn't need this. He had things to do.

"Who?" he said.

"Yeah, you're him," the kid said. He wasn't showing a weapon, and at six meters away, it would take him all day to get within range.

Mourn didn't know who he was, but he knew *what* he was. He smiled. "I'm retired, son. Out of the Flex for more than a year, I don't even follow it any more. Title went to somebody by default, you won't get there through me."

The kid grinned. "I don't need to get there through you."

The day was warm—all the days were warm here near Earth's equator, on the island that Shaw's money had bought. There was a smell of ripe fruit in the air—mostly bananas, some guava, maybe. The ocean lapped onto the narrow beach, only a few meters away, offering its timeless lullaby to anybody who wanted to listen.

Mourn had come to the dock to pick up a shipment of transponders for the auditorium, and next to the off-loaded cartons, all by himself, was this young man. He was medium height, fit, a light-heavyweight, dressed in tropical, loose orthoskins and dotic boots. He had strong tea-colored skin, short brown hair, brown eyes, nothing to make him stand out in a crowd.

Here, however, was no tourist come for the sea breezes and sunshine.

How could this kid have found him? That was the real problem, not what the boy wanted, which, of course, Mourn knew.

The kid kept talking: "You won the title and then you quit. Everybody says you could have sat on it for a while if you wanted. They say you were maybe the best ever. I've seen the only bootleg. You had something."

Mourn shrugged. It had been a year since he'd found the final move in his martial system, the last of the 97-steps, the art he had started calling Sumito. He'd needed that last move against Shaw, who had unknowingly taught it to him. He hadn't needed it against Weems, who had been the number-one-rated player in the Musashi Flex. Weems had been fast and strong and very skilled, but even lacking the final step, Mourn's new skills had been enough. He took the title, something he'd wanted since he was twelve, and then he turned his back on it and quit, just like that. Because winning wasn't the important thing any more.

It didn't really matter at all.

It had been a long year. They had been busy since then, he and Sola and Shaw and Azul. Getting the island, coming up with some kind of basic philosophy and operations they planned to turn into the order. Staying off the Confed's Doppler. That last part was important. They'd be easy to squash.

More than a few times, he had wondered what the hell he was doing here...

Heads up, Mourn Back to the biz at hand. "How did you find me?"

"Not important. You got a blade?"

He did, of course, in the curlnose case on his belt—two, in fact—twin *kerambits,* nasty little talon-shaped ring-ended knives whose cutting edges were no longer than his curved little finger. But he had no intention of using them to slice this kid. "Yep. But if you were challenging me—not that you can, since I'm a civilian—I would get to choose."

The kid nodded. Of course he knew that.

Mourn said, "What's your rank?"

"I'm *Primero.*"

"Bullshit you are!"

Again, the kid smiled. "You really haven't been following the flow, have you?"

"Like I said. I walked away, I didn't look back." He paused. That put a little different spin on things if it was the truth. "You got a name?"

"Navarro."

Mourn assessed the kid's physique, the way he stood, his set.

Yeah, he had something, balance, poise, you could see that. But—*Primero*? Even if it were true …

Easy enough to check, dial it out of the net, but so what? Didn't fix the problem.

"Okay, say you *are* Number One. You're as high as it gets. Best in the galaxy. This wouldn't make any sense." He waved his hand back and forth, to indicate the two of them. "If you are *Primero*, you know how things go. I'm out—I'm not a player, you have nothing to gain by this—and something to lose."

That would explain how the kid had found him—a lot of people were willing to do favors for the guy at the top of the Musashi Flex's fighting pyramid. Gamblers, fans who might also be Confed planetary reps, holoproj stars. People liked to stand next to violence and pretend they had a right to be there. Mourn had tried to keep an invisible profile since he'd quit the game, but apparently he hadn't turned altogether transparent. Good to know that. They'd have to start taking precautions. What with people looking for the four of them for different reasons, Azul's idea about wearing hoods and cowls and such was starting to make more sense: here was a child who'd found them—albeit one with sharp milk teeth.

Navarro shifted a step to his left. Good balance. He said, "I'm who I say I am. A year ago, I hadn't joined the game."

"You came a long way in record time. Never heard of anybody moving up so fast. Or reaching the top so young."

"Yeah. But, here's the thing: everywhere I go, *I* hear about *you*. Yeah, they say, you're good—but—you know about Mourn? *There* was a fighter. A player for twenty-five years, pretty good, but not spectacular, Teens, maybe a Tenth or Ninth. Then *pow*! All of a sudden one day, Mourn up and runs the fuck over *every*body and takes the top slot, defends it one time right after he did—beating a guy amped on an illegal metabolic enhancer, and then just strolls away. *Poof!*"

"It wasn't illegal at the time, the drug."

"But you beat him anyhow. And Weems, who was the best for a long time."

"So? That was then, this is now. You're the Prime, you don't have anything to prove." Even as he said it, Mourn knew better. He had been this kid, once upon a time. Not as good, because it had taken him twenty-five years to get to the top, and by then, it hadn't mattered. Strange, how life did things like that.

"Yeah, I do."

Mourn shook his head. "Well, *I* don't have anything to prove. Taking a beating to make you feel better? Not interested. Kicking your ass? Same thing. Doesn't buy me happiness either way."

Navarro laughed. "Kicking my ass isn't going to happen. I *am Primero*. I have to do this. I have to *know*."

Yeah. Even if you thought you were *really* good, you could never be sure how it would go. And a man this young, who had come up so fast? It would have seemed too easy; he couldn't trust it. He would have to be adept, probably more so than he believed. But there would always be the doubt …

For just a couple seconds, he felt the old competitive spirit flare in him. All the years of facing all the opponents, some empty-handed, some with blades or slap-caps, Weems with his fucking cane. Any of them could have hurt him bad—some of whom had. Or they could have killed him, like he had killed others. He had walked away because he had found something more important, but it had been his life before Navarro had been born and as long as the kid had been alive. Old habits were hard to break. Teach the child some manners …

But—no. He shook his head. Beat this one, word would get around. They'd start lining up to try him even though he was out of the game. That was the bane of the retired gunslinger in the old entcom vids. You wanted to be a samurai who died in bed? You kept your katana hidden away. He didn't need this. Couldn't afford it now.

"I got things to do, M. Navarro. I'm not interested in playing any more. Go away."

"You can fight back or I can pound you into the dirt—either one works for me."

"You want bragging rights? Fine. Say what you want, anybody asks, I'll agree—you thumped me good."

Navarro shook his head.

"I'll sign a notarized statement."

"That's not the point."

No. Mourn knew exactly what the point was. The kid had to *know*, just as Shaw had had to know, when he'd offered to let *him* have the title. This was something in Navarro's favor. Beat all comers? Why keep working to get better? How much better did you need to be? Why risk your whole career on something like this?

Because *knowing* was sometimes better than *winning*.

Mourn shook his head, too. Yeah. Give the kid his due for that.

They had a couple of free-standing Healy units already installed at the school. He could let the kid knock him down, crack a rib or two, raise a few bruises, then go home, climb into the machine, and come out good as new in a couple hours. The kid would be able to say he'd beaten Mourn and that would be the end of it. Cheap price to keep from being bothered again. Not like he hadn't spent plenty of quality time in the medical units before. One more session would be just a drop in the bucket.

What the hell. A cheap fix.

Mourn sighed. "All right. But we do it bare," he said.

The kid grinned. "Fine."

"Want to stretch? Warm up?"

"Not necessary."

Mourn took a deep breath. Well, he had that much right. If you had a match and the time, warming up was good, but in a real fight that suddenly popped out of nowhere, best be able to move cold. The kid was young and fit, he could probably drop into a full split and bounce up like a spring first thing out of bed in the morning.

Mourn shook his head. Youth was wasted on the young. He knew that, too—he'd wasted plenty of his own.

He sighed.

* * *

Navarro turned to a forty-five degree angle and edged in. It wasn't a stance you saw much of in dueling, that angle.

"Pentjak silat?" Mourn said. He hadn't moved yet, still held a neutral stance.

"Among others." He slid his boots along the ground easily, moving with a smooth precision.

Mourn nodded to himself as Navarro stopped just outside knife range, a hair short of step-and-a-half. The kid new his distance.

Mourn still stood there relaxed, feet shoulder-width apart, hands hanging down at his sides. "Let me guess. Your … father? mother? was a Flex player, decent, but never in the top ranks. You started studying when you were … four? five? You trained every day, three, five, six hours, at least. You studied seven or eight different arts, worked against the best, but held off until you could go back and fight your previous teacher's top student and beat him. Eventually, you beat 'em all."

"I thought you didn't follow the game anymore."

"I don't. It's the most reasonable explanation for how somebody your age got to where you are. You're a light-heavy, you have the speed and mass, and this has been your life as long as you can remember. You were a real player before you joined. That one-year biz is flack for the ent- and newscom feeds."

"Good guess." He extended his right arm toward Mourn, and when he pulled it back and switched high-low with his left, he stole a half-step, crossing his left foot behind his right. It was a *silat* move, well-executed. Somebody not paying attention would be drawn by the motion of Navarro's hand, and since his body didn't move forward, they wouldn't realize he had gotten within range.

Been a long time since Mourn had been fooled by that one.

He grinned and took a half step back. "I'm not quite that old and stupid yet. Show me another one."

"You don't appear to be taking this seriously, Mourn."

"As seriously as it merits, son. I'm not in any danger here. I'm not worried about beating you, just deciding where I want you to fall."

Navarro grinned. "I'm immune to trash-talk."

Mourn nodded. He would have to be if he was *Primero*. Only in this case, it wasn't trash-talk.

Navarro moved, fast, jinked a bit to his left, and charged. He changed levels, dropped low, and fired a head punch, changed levels again, came up and threw his right elbow as he got in, very good—

Mourn had plenty of time. An eon.

What he *should* have done was eat the punch, let it stagger him, and allow the elbow to knock him down. A quarter-beat slow, that would be it, game over, and the kid could walk away feeling like all the crap he'd heard about Mourn was just that. End of the legend, AMF.

That's what he *should* have done.

The art he had created and learned and had practiced every day for hours until he could do it without thinking, in the dark, in a pouring rainstorm, kicked in like an involuntary reflex, far below his conscious intent.

It *made* him move—

He danced the strikes a hair to his left, ducked, parried, and snapped a backfist at Navarro's face—

The kid was fast, but when he'd been pumping Reflex, Shaw had been a lot faster. If you had the position? Speed wasn't enough—

The backfist connected with Navarro's temple. It wasn't a power shot, but it was enough to deflect him—

Mourn followed the backfist in, fired his right elbow to the ribs, swept his left foot along the ground in a *sapu* as the elbow connected. Navarro's foot came up as his upper body titled the opposite way, and, overbalanced, he fell onto his back—

He twisted catlike in the air, hit on a shoulder, rolled, and came up, more than a little surprised.

Mourn could have ended it there if he'd continued in, but he allowed the kid to reset.

Navarro knew it.

He shook his head, angry.

Crap! Way to go, Mourn!

If he let Navarro slip a punch in now, the kid would know he was allowing that, too. Stupid. Now the boy was pissed-off, wary, and well-trained. A bad combination. Slack off, the kid might do something worse than he'd intended.

How ironic would that be—to know the nastiest, most efficient martial art around and get beaten to death because you wouldn't *use* it?

Mourn glanced at his chronometer, then back at Navarro.

That *really* ticked the kid off. He could almost read his mind: who the *fuck* was this guy, to be looking at his goddamned *watch* while he was in a fight with *Primero*?!

The kid made another run, a smooth and practiced series of punches, knees, elbows, his balance right, his stance low. A good fighter had to know how to grapple and have a decent ground-game, and you didn't get to be the champ unless you were better than good, so Mourn danced that. He stayed low enough to sprawl if he needed, and batted the attacks away as he sidestepped and angled in. He needed to be a matador facing a bull, and that's what his art focused on. He didn't try to hurt Navarro, just gave him enough to keep him busy.

Kid had the moves, but Mourn's were better. He had tested them against the best and honed them to razor sharpness. He didn't have anything to prove—to himself or anybody else. He knew what he knew—

Navarro leaped away, frustrated, and, Mourn saw, worried. Just a little crack in the granite facade.

As he gathered himself for his third pass, Mourn stole a few centimeters and advanced his timing, taking the short step first, then the long. He was ahead by a hair, just enough, so as Navarro fired his punch, Mourn was able to cross arms and cut the line, deflect the strike, and land his own fist square on Navarro's temple—

It was all in the position and timing—

Navarro collapsed, knocked unconscious.

Well. There you go ...

* * *

When he came to a few seconds later, Mourn squatted next to him. "You okay?"

"Vision's a little blurry." He sat up.

"We've got a Healy at the compound."

Navarro waved that off. "I'll be fine." He looked at Mourn. "How did you do that? I never saw *anybody* move like that before! You just danced around and beat me like it was *nothing*!"

"Something I came up with," he said. "More efficient patterns. Not so much new as ... recombined differently."

"No shit."

Mourn thought about the situation. He had erred by fighting, then made it worse by beating the kid, and worse still by doing it with such apparent ease.

Maybe Navarro wouldn't go off and tell anybody. Maybe he'd be embarrassed about it. At his age, Mourn would have been.

Or maybe he would get drunk in the first pub he found and blurt the story out to a nice, friendly newscom reporter looking for something to sell to the nets: FLEX CHAMP BEATEN BY OLD MAN—and here are the directions to where Mourn—remember him?—lives ...

"It's freaky. I couldn't—it—" He stopped.

Mourn considered his problem. And, of a moment, thought of a solution. Not the best, maybe, but it was gonna have to be make-do at this point.

"I'm not the only person who knows it."

That got his attention. Navarro stared at him.

"Besides me, there are three others. They've been learning for a year, since I finished it."

"How would they do in a match against a good fighter?"

Here was the pitch. And it was almost true. "Any of them could take you."

Navarro looked as if he wanted to scream, throw up, or both.

"I'm the top-ranked player in the Musashi Flex and you're telling me there are three other guys besides you, with a year of training, one *year*, who can beat me?!"

"One guy," Mourn said. "The other two are women."

"Aw, *shit*! You're serious?"

"Afraid so. Sorry."

Navarro came to his feet. He swayed a little but kept his balance. "So it isn't just you, it's the system."

"Yes."

"Then I can learn it."

Got you.

He couldn't make it too easy. "We're not ready to open shop yet."

"I just got my ass handed to me by an old man, a guy older than my *father*, somebody who hasn't fought anybody ranked in forever! You're covered with *rust* and you still thumped me! I thought I was the best player out there. It's who I am, it's what I do. I *can't* walk away. You *have* to teach me!"

Exactly what I would have said at your age.

Mourn held his grin in. He knew. Navarro was sold, but he had to finish the pitch to solve his problem.

"You can't use it to play in the Flex anymore."

"Who *gives* a fuck? I'm already the best player there and look what good it did me! I *need* to learn this. You have to show me!"

"You can't talk about what we're doing here. You can't offer what you learn anywhere except here."

"Whatever it takes!"

Mourn smiled. "We're going to be laying out other stuff besides the fighting skill. Philosophy, politics, sociology. We have something in mind. A ... revolution."

"Mourn. Please. You want me to walk on broken glass barefoot?"

Mourn looked at him. The kid would stick around, at least long enough for them to build something. And he had enough drive, he might stay for the long haul. "Okay. Welcome to the Siblings of the Shroud. Come on, let's go put you in the Healy. You won't be much good to anybody if you're brain-damaged."

Navarro smiled like a kid with a new toy.

And so did Mourn ...

Rise Up, Rise Up,
You Children of the Moon
Seanan McGuire

Night has fallen. The city, secure under the all-encompassing blanket of the mandatory curfew, sleeps. Municipal lights glare from every corner, illuminate every alley and park. The occasional raccoon or rat squints up at the frustrating brightness, unable to understand why their comforting dark has disappeared, whisked away by creatures they have no desire to know more about. Most of them are gone, skittered away to the country or snatched up and peacefully euthanized by animal control. They're vermin, after all. There's no place for them here, in this bright and shining city of the future, in this place where shadows have been forbidden and the night has been denied.

Shades are drawn on private homes, locking out the twilight-bright world outside, allowing the residents to convert their living spaces into whatever facsimile of night their hearts desire. The regulations, which make the city safer by forbidding concealing shadows from taking root, have yet to expand into private homes. They will soon enough. The writing, as the people say, is on the wall, encoded in a hundred tiny rules, a thousand comments on citywide bulletin boards and forums. People feel safer when they can see their surroundings. People *want* to know what's happening around them. Lighting up the world is a public service, nothing more and nothing less, and it must be done if the world is to move into the next, more civilized age.

It began with a single abduction, a single child who managed to fall into a place where the light didn't reach. Does it matter if it was monster or man who stole her? "Erica's Law" restructured the world, one solar panel and porch light at a time, and now, to crave the darkness is as good as to admit that you intend your neighbors ill. The world has changed. The world is always changing.

A tarp falls over one of the light posts, blocking it. Sensors attached to the lights frantically catalog the interruption, sending out pulses of electricity to check the connections, verify that no circuits have been fried by an unexpected power surge, and confirm nothing is burnt out. This process will take upward of sixty seconds: plenty of time for the small group of people passing below to hurry by, their arms laden with their worldly goods, with the squares of suitcases and the bulky bodies of wide-eyed children who shy away from the remaining light with small whimpers of dismay.

Just as the light begins to beep shrill alarm at the interruption the tarp is whisked away and the light returns, shining bright on an empty street. The people are gone. A manhole scrapes slightly as it settles back into its cut-out cradle, and everything is still.

Everything is silent.

* * *

"You can't do this. Let the other cities take a stand; it's too dangerous here." The fight has played out a million times before, through almost as many pairs of people. The man, yellow-eyed, with writhing serpents in place of hair, glares at the woman with lips as red as blood, with skin as white as snow.

She glares back, eyes like daggers of winter ice. "We don't have any other choice. We have to do *something* or we're going to be destroyed. Is that what you want? Are you so eager for an ending?"

"We've been forced into hiding before." He gestures toward his hair, which hisses and snaps at his fingers. "My great-grandmother—"

"Was the beloved of a *god*, and still wound up getting her head cut off when she managed to get in the way of the wrong people." The woman's sharpened incisors indent her lower lip as she scowls. "We need shadows. We need secrecy. They've finally found a way to burn us out, and it isn't torches and pitchforks, it's floodlights and civic zoning. This has to stop, before it's too late for us to stop it."

"Maybe our time is over," says the man.

The woman stares at him. Then she turns, pointing down the dry sewer tunnel that has become their last and shrinking refuge.

"Want me to march down there and tell Alfonse that it's time to put the children out to see the sunrise? Marie only crawled out of her grave a week ago. When she catches fire, she'll smell like rotting meat, and she'll leave maggots and char behind instead of good grave dust, but hey, maybe it's time, right? You've had centuries. I've had centuries. That means we get to decide for the people who've barely had the time to catch their breath. Shall I tell Lulu she needs to kill her own pups? Or tell the Creep that all the seedlings have to go? Or would you prefer to do the deed?"

"You're not being fair," he says, mulish and sullen, looking away.

"Speak the truth and damn the blinders," says the woman. Her voice is soft. She knows she's won, and if there's one thing she's learned in her long centuries upon the earth, it's that no one loves a winner who gloats. "We have to do something. They turn the tree lights on tomorrow."

The man nods and says nothing.

The tree lights. Without them, this would have been one more attempt to change a world that doesn't want to change: one more passing fad that, when it faded, would have left the shadows undisturbed. But this time, the light has teeth. This time, the light has been expanding, and expanding, and expanding, until places that have always been considered safe have been torn asunder, violated, rendered unsafe.

This, the latest affront: this, the thing that has driven them into hiding, into the shadows that sleep, restless, beneath the city streets. Lights have been hung around the edges of the forest, each designed to stand up to a hurricane, powered by solar batteries that can run for months on a single stored charge. Night is to be forbidden in the forest, blasted away in the name of progress, progress which forbids any chance of secrecy or shadow. Night is to be a thing of the past.

Night, and all the things that dwell there.

So they have run, these night things, so they have come together here and in a thousand similar cities, hiding in the last and least of their strongholds. Here they shiver against the coming of a terrible, unending day, and face the question they have faced a thousand times before, over twice as many years: how, when all the world is set against them, are they intended to survive? And if they do not, if this is where they fail and fall and fade away, how is the world to survive without them?

For this is the secret the night things keep, having long since learned that it does them no good to share it: the world cannot endure without both sides of the coin. If there is to be light, there must be shadow, or the light becomes meaningless, as ignorable and ignoble as the air. Strip the air away and all that breathes will fall, yes, but the air has changed before, going from one gas to another, and all without notice until it is too late. The air cannot be seen. That means the air can easily betray.

If there are to be people of the light, people of the sun's brightness, of the day's warmth, all those things must be true as well in opposition. There must be people of the dark, people of the moon's coolness, of the night's shadow. There must be those who run where the light will not find them, who hide themselves away and curse the technological advances which bring their opposite number ever closer to true dominion over all.

Dragging feet scrape the length of a nearby tunnel, a smaller pipe too tight for adult creatures. Still, both woman and man tense as they turn, relaxing only when a little girl with slate-colored skin and red, red eyes shuffles hesitantly into the open. There is no light here. She moves with graceless confidence, going to the man and wrapping her arms around his middle, holding him fast. She closes her eyes and is still, so still, still as the stone she becomes between one breath and the next.

The woman quirks the shadow of a smile. "Looks like Io has spoken. You're staying here. Defend the others. If anyone comes, keep them safe."

"When you say 'defend' ..."

The woman's smile remains, but her eyes are cold as chips of winter ice. "Kill them. Kill them all. They were the ones who wanted a war. You don't get to declare hostilities only when you think you're going to win. If they come here, if they pursue us past the point of no return, you make sure they never go home to their families. Do you understand?"

He nods, because he does; because they all do. This is the inevitable end of such collisions. When the winners send their troops into the narrow places, the last, lost places, they do so because they believe themselves to be untouchable. They have forgotten the simple truth of war, which states that no force with a single soul still standing has been truly defeated. Even the last and least of a cornered, conquered people can fight back.

The woman walks away. Where her bare feet strike the stone they leave trails of glimmering frost behind, as delicate as lace, as cold as the heart of winter. It will not melt for days, this reminder of her passage, and even once it does, the chill will linger for weeks, months, years. She could chill the world if left unchecked. She has always needed to be checked, to be kept from becoming the storm her bones ache to be. Balance in all things, after all.

But there is no balance here, not anymore. The balance has been broken
by people who thought they were better than the superstitions of their an-
cestors, who thought that monsters belonged in storybooks and old wives'
tales, not in the shadows, not in the cities, and certainly not in the streets.
When the balance is broken, so many things that might have been forbidden
become permissible.

When the balance is broken, the monsters will have their say.

She walks as silent as a sigh, and when she leaves the safety of the sew-
ers for the harsh, well-lit streets—the light, how it hates her, how it struggles to burn—she shivers, as if brightness were her bones' bane. The frost
collects more thinly in the light, melts more quickly, but collect it does, and
so long as she can cradle the chill around her, she endures.

All around her, curtains remain drawn, the residents of the surrounding
homes content in their isolation from the night. No one looks outside. They
have cut themselves off, believing that only the light matters. Believing that,
if they deny the dark long and loudly enough, they will finally be free of it.

The dark doesn't work like that. She walks and flowers die, leaves turn
colors early and birds find their eggs frozen in their nests, no longer dreaming of the day they'll split their shells and be freed into the world. She walks
and the air remembers what it is to be slow and cold and terrible, filled with
promises yet to be kept and stories yet to be told. The light beats against
her skin, shattering the sheets of ice encasing her, but she freezes again as
quickly as they thaw. She will do this. She must do this.

She has done this before, in other times, other towns, other terrible il-
luminations. Nothing is truly new. It is only a repetition of an old refrain,
echoing through the song that birthed it, refusing to be forgotten. The cycle,
which is turning even now, has turned before and will turn again.

She remembers other battlefields, times when the light rose up against
the dark in terrible, torturous defiance. She remembers times when hers was
the castle and theirs the mire, when it seemed that all that was bright and
warm in the world must be stomped out, extinguished by the clutching hand
of coldness and sorrow. All this has come before. All this will come again.

And if she hopes, in her cold, quiet way, that some hero will find the cave
where she has concealed her frozen heart before the cycle makes another
turn and another war is at hand; if she hopes she will be ice and ashes before
she must raise blizzard and frost against another score of innocents whose
only crime is being born to the wrong side of an ancient divide; if she hopes

for the peace that comes only ever in the grave, can she truly be blamed? The war is short and fierce and blazing for the forces of humanity, who fight and burn in the day's hot light. The war is long and slow and bitter for the forces of the shadow, who fight only when the air is still and the wind whispers secrets best forgotten. She has been here so many times. There is still fight in her. But oh, how she wishes she could set it gently—so gently—to the side, and sleep.

She walks through the streets, and the streets do not move to stop her, even as the lights beat down, even as she burns from within and without, charred by both righteous anger and targeted assault. She walks in a world that has been remade in the image of her opposition, and she does not dare to hesitate or turn aside. This is the only chance she'll have at striking back. The clock has not yet reached midnight, but it is close, so very close, and once it does ...

Once it does, there will be no turning back. What's done is done, and not even the cold can change it.

All over the world, she knows, others are making their final stands in cities just like this one, cities that have been brightened and barricaded and turned into citadels to defeat an enemy that so few will admit was ever real. The short memories of mankind lead to them forgetting, over and over, that they fear the dark for a reason; that they cower in their beds from the crack of thunder because there is something to fear, not merely because their grandparents told them scary stories.

The scary stories are more than happy to tell themselves, given time to do so, given an audience to listen.

All over the world, this is happening, and if some of them fail, others will succeed; if some of them end tonight, they will still have tried. They will still have struck back against an enemy who can barely conceive of their reality. That will be enough. That will have to be enough.

The wall between the city center and the illuminated outskirts is tall and sturdy, built from some unnatural stone that has never known the quarry, nor the touch of the mason's hammer. She brushes her fingers against it, leaving trails of frost behind, tracing out the limits of its nature. Stone is stone, no matter what its origins, and stone is porous. Stone ... cracks.

The wall is eager to share its secrets with someone. The wall knows nothing of enemies or allies, cares nothing for the long slow war its builders have fought against the children of the moon. The wall knows only that it has things to say, and no one has ever listened, not before now. So it speaks.

It shares, it sighs, and when it is finished, the woman with the skin as white as snow presses a single bloody kiss to its body, leaving the print of her lips behind.

"Thank you, friend," she whispers, and is gone, dissolving into mist which dives into the stone like a swimmer into the sea. The wall welcomes her into its body, shivering with delight at the sensation.

The lights are very bright here, leaving nothing unseen, leaving nothing concealed. That, too, is a form of concealment, for when it is assumed that everything is visible, then no one looks as hard as they ought. They have forgotten that they are at war, even as they lead a brutal and ceaseless campaign against their enemies. The mist pours into the wall, and no one notices. The mist trickles from the stone on the other side, in the deepest, most well-protected part of the city, and no one sees.

Bit by bit, the mist reassembles itself into the shape of a woman. Color bleeds back into its foggy structure, the black of hair, the red of lips, the unforgiving blue of eyes. Still no one sees, or if they do, they say nothing. This is an impossible thing in this bright, brave new world of lights and open spaces. This is a thing that belongs to the old, dark days, and everyone knows those days were never *real*. They're stories to frighten children, nothing less and nothing more. They're a lie draped in pretty sparkles to attract the eye. Look away and they're forgotten. Look away and they're not real.

When the woman stands where the mist once was, she sags, catching herself against the wall with a single shaking hand. There was a time when going from one shape to another wouldn't have taken so much out of her, when she could have walked the world as a cloud, or a cat, or any number of other wonderful, terrible things without fear of losing herself. That time is gone. It may come again, and she may even be here to see it. Here and now, she is tired, so tired, tired like she has never been in all the long centuries of her life. She yearns to rest.

Perhaps soon, she can.

The streets here are dimmer, although they are still as bright as a summer's day. There are gradations in light, even as there are gradations in darkness. Perhaps the people this far from the forest's edge feel no more need to respect the shadows, and in losing their respect, they have begun to lose their fear. The darkness is a relic of a bygone time, nothing more nor less; it is deserving of neither awe nor observation, but merely of pity. It will be forgotten soon enough. When the lights around the forest come on for the first and last time, it will all be swept away, and no more time need be spent in consideration of its mysteries.

Even dimmed, even diffused, the light is enough to peel away another layer of ice comfort. The woman shudders as she straightens, refusing to be bowed by such a petty trick, played by creatures who are little more to her than children. She is almost there. She will succeed.

She walks on, and when she finds the men—men with guns, men in clever uniforms, insulated against blades and bullets and, most of all, the cold—standing in a loose ring around her final destination, she almost smiles. Someone remembers that this is a war after all. Someone has not forgotten the way the cycle turns.

"Identify yourself," calls one of the men.

"I am the cold north wind and the gales of November," she replies, her voice as sweet and beguiling as a snowbank. Come to me, that voice says; come to me and rest forever. "I am what you would forget, if only you were allowed, and what you must remember, else how would you know to bundle yourself tight against the chill?"

The men exchange glances of confusion and frustration. There is a script to these encounters, a pattern that should be followed. She is refusing to play by the rules they have set, and they don't know how to handle that, what to say or what should be done.

One lowers his gun. "What's your *name*, lady?" he calls.

Her smile is a hungry one. Sometimes, it is necessary to feed if one is to proceed. Her own mother taught her this, a very long time ago, when the wood was the world and the world was the wood, and the thought of chasing away the shadows was a foolish nightmare for an untried child. Sometimes, for the cold to grow, it must remember what it is to freeze.

"Let me show you," she says, and she spreads her hands, and the cold comes.

Cold is a part of darkness, for it is in darkness that cold opens its wings and wraps the world with ice. This does not mean that cold is confined to the dark, nor that it is forbidden to step into the light. She spreads her hands and everything is frost; she smiles, and everything is frozen. The men stop where they are, some with guns half-raised, their skins rimed in white, like they have been wrapped in lacy shrouds.

"Once upon a time," she says, and steps forward. The frost grows thicker, sapping the light from their eyes, stealing the breath from their bodies. "There was a girl with skin as white as snow, and lips as red as blood, and hair as black as a raven's wing."

Another step, and the skin beneath the frost is blossoming blue, frozen all the way to the shivering core of the still-beating heart. They are still alive, these men, even as their sight goes dim and their breath grows shallow, unable to fight against the bitter weight of winter.

"Her mother was a queen, they say, and she looked upon her child, and was afraid of the story she saw starting in the infant's eyes. She called for her dearest handmaid, and said, 'Take my daughter to the forest. Leave her there. Let the winter have her. I will tell my husband the king that she died in her cradle, and he will forgive me, for he has always been a fair man, and he loves me best of all.'"

She takes another step, smiles another smile.

"The woman left the babe in the woods, for this is not a children's story. Not all stories *about* children are *for* children, you understand, nor could they ever be. She left the babe in the woods, and it froze, and it cried, and the winter wrapped frozen arms around its tiny body, and carried it home. The babe became a child became a woman, and the kingdom fell and the story spread, and none of that mattered, for the winter held her heart. The winter always would."

She has reached the first of the men. The kiss she presses to his cheek is a burning brand. He shatters from the force of it, falling in a cascade of frozen meat, glistening in the ever-present light. She kisses them each, one after the other, and they break, and she walks on, leaving cruel carnage in her wake.

"And they all lived happily ever after," she murmurs, as her fingers brush the final door, as its hinges freeze in their sockets. The frame yields. The door falls before her, and she is through, she is inside, she is stepping out of the streets and into the hallway, where the light, the light, the light holds sway.

* * *

The house of the governor is clean and quiet: the house of the governor is tidy and true. These are necessary things, for how can one lead when one does not also follow? There are governors who feel themselves above the law, and they keep their constituencies as well as they can, but there is always and ever something missing in those places, where the laws are not fairly applied to all. Here, the laws apply. Here, the laws are understood, admired, held up as proof that the greater good will always conquer, in the end. The world will be true. The world will stand fast.

The governor and his wife sleep on the second floor, in a room where the lights have been dimmed to the acceptable twilight that eases slumber and keeps the heart from worrying over shadowy corners. There are no places in their private bower where the darkness can find a foothold: the closet is lit from within, and unlike the main lights, the closet lights never dull or dim. Their shoes and clothing remain safe from shadows. The bed is flush to the floor; smaller lights shine inside every drawer of their dressers and vanities. They are safe.

They believe they are safe.

The children sleep on the third floor, two girls and a boy, each in a room a little brighter than the room where their parents sleep, each accustomed to sleeping in the light. They stir, those children, when the lights flicker and dim. They wake, one after the other, when those same lights die entirely, throwing them into deep, unaccustomed darkness.

The younger girl begins to cry, the sound soft and terrified. She feels someone settle beside her on the bed; feels a hand caress her hair.

"What's wrong, child?"

The voice is sweet, and she is young enough, as yet, to hear kindness in sweet things. She sniffles, turns her unseeing face toward the sound.

"It's dark," she says.

"Are you afraid of the dark?"

Suddenly shy, she nods, not considering the fact that if she can't see her visitor, her visitor can't see her.

But it seems her visitor *can* see her, because the hand caresses her hair again, and the same sweet voice asks, "Would you like to be safe in the dark? To see its secrets, to not be afraid? You can be, if you wish it."

"Please," she whispers.

"Here."

The child doesn't need to see to know what's been placed in her hand: the weight of the apple is as familiar as a well-worn dream. Her fingers caress the skin, feeling the ripeness of it, the way the juice presses against the peel, begging to be freed.

"Eat," says the voice, and the child—always obedient—does as she is told. The fruit is sweet. The fruit is cold.

She swallows, and her heart stops, and she is no longer afraid. When she opens her eyes, the darkness holds no fear, only a woman with skin as white as snow, sitting on the edge of the bed and smiling at her.

"Come," says the woman, and the girl, newly reborn to winter, sees no reason to argue. There is so much to discover, on the other side of the frost. She wants to learn it all.

Together, they go to her brother, who sits wide-eyed in his bed, staring into the darkness and waiting for the lights to come back on. He sighs when his little sister kisses his cheek, when she puts the apple in his hand. He sighs, and he dies, and he rises again, as the frost-touched children always do.

Together, they go to the eldest daughter, who still wears ribbons in her hair, and offer her the bargain that has always been there, has always waited for the children of the light when the battle grows too close. She does not eat willingly, but her brother pries her mouth open, and her sister worries off little bites of apple with her teeth, transferring them into the elder girl's mouth with all the delicacy of a bird feeding its nestlings. She swallows despite herself.

She is weeping when her heart stops, and the woman who has brought the cold here, to this safe, warm home, smiles. The ones who die crying always rise up stronger than the rest, white-haired and white-handed and tied to the snow in a way the frozen girls can only dream of. This girl will be a general, when she adjusts to her new reality.

Together, the four of them walk through the sleeping house, their feet leaving trails of ice behind them, and enter the room where the governor and his wife sleep. The lights flicker and die.

The screaming starts soon after.

* * *

The next day, there is a power outage. The lights go out across the city, creating shadows and silences where none have been before. The money for the forest project is mysteriously missing; the tree lights are abandoned, unlit. Bit by bit, the infrastructure that has illuminated a generation is chipped away.

Similar stories unfold in cities and states and capitols across the world. The lights flicker. The lights die. The winds blow colder and longer and wilder than before as slowly, so slowly, the cycle begins to turn.

At the edge of the wood, a little girl with hair that is already bleeding black, like ink through cotton, holds the hand of the woman who has become her new mother. The other two children remain with their puppet-parents, controlling them with a flick of their fingers, a whisper of ice, but she, this littlest jewel, is the hostage to their good behavior, taken with her full consent, kept willingly where the shadows fall.

"What comes next?" she asks. "Is it good?"

"The tide turns," says the woman. "The monsters come out of our hiding places, and the balance shifts again. In a hundred years, two hundred, a thousand, the darkness will have consumed almost everything there is, and the light will rise up, will send tendrils of resistance into our homes, will steal our children away and thaw their frozen hearts. But that is in the future, and the sun is almost up. Come along, my dear. It's almost dawn, and it's time you were asleep."

They turn together and walk into the shadows, and leave only the frost of their footprints to mark where they have been.

The Parallactic Soldier

Christopher Allenby

28 February 2022, 1430 hours.

Autonomous Assault Unit 423-H crept through the rubble-strewn street. Since the Global Positioning Satellite network had been down for some time, AAU/423-H could not be certain which street that was, but it was reasonably certain the street was in what remained of Charlotte, North Carolina. The robotic combat system was following its last received and authenticated mission order: SEEK AND DESTROY ENEMY ASSETS IN GRID SECTORS 39A AND 40B. That order had been received exactly 2,200 hours, 13 minutes, and 22.459 seconds ago. The order had been neither rescinded nor countermanded. In fact, AAU/423-H had received no authenticated communication from any command authority since that transmission had overwritten its previous mission, labeled SENTRY-A1 AT POST US-B1B, and significant portions of its operational parameters.

Debris in the street crunched under AAU/423-H's wheels. Broken glass—presumably from bombed-out multi-level buildings—and the charred remains of civilian vehicles made the street both treacherous for navigation and ideal for concealing enemy assets. AAU/423-H was attempting to extricate itself from its present position and to achieve a redoubt that was both defensible and shadow-less; its batteries were low and it needed a safe place to deploy its solar panels for recharging.

AAU/423-H froze when its targeting system detected movement northeast of its position. Threat identification processors determined in 0.002 seconds that the potential threat was a non-combatant animal, *canis lupis familiarus*. AAU/423-H resumed its maneuver, idly noting that dogs often but not always accompanied human civilians and human combatants. Crossing an intersection, AAU/423-H exercised the extreme caution learned from experience and expended precious power reserves to quickly cross the open area of tarmac. It attracted no enemy fire.

28 February 2022, 1730 hours.

After three hours of meticulous maneuvering, AAU/423-H achieved a suitable position in a densely vegetated area on the south side of a multi-level building, a position it estimated could provide it with approximately nine hours of direct sunlight, assuming that the next day would be clear and not overcast. (The weather information network, too, had been inaccessible for some time.) It camouflaged itself among the remains of what it tentatively identified as a jungle gym and deployed its solar panels to collect late afternoon sunlight. It initiated a system check and then shut down all but its passive sentry system to preserve power.

28 February 2022, 2324 hours.

AAU/423-H awoke, its sentry program detecting a potential airborne threat. Comparing a real-time infrared image from the sentry program to data from US Army Intelligence report number 3254732.2#B, it identified the aircraft as a drone of the type used by enemy combatants in an attack near Lincoln, Nebraska, on 21 August 2021. AAU/423-H deployed its heaviest projectile weapon, the ASR-50 rifle, and fired a single round. Telemetry indicated the drone was losing altitude at a rate that conclusively (89.6457%) indicated critical damage, so AAH 423-H stowed the rifle, noting that only thirty-three rounds remained for that weapon. It attempted, again, to signal its designated ordnance depot to request Combat Resupply, but was unable to achieve an authenticated connection. It resumed low-power mode to await the dawn and the much-needed sunlight.

12 March 2022, 0545 hours.

AAU/423-H followed a highway eastward at the optimal power consumption rate of 22.175 KPH. It was relatively certain from its analysis of optical input that it was nearing the US Army base where it expected to find much-needed, mission-critical supplies. Most of its supplies had been exhausted in its months-long deployment and it calculated that without immediate resupply it would be unable to carry out its mission. In a series of brief engagements beginning at 1423 hours on 10 March 2022, it had destroyed four civilian vehicles that had been deployed by the enemy, the first of which had attempted to attack AAU/423-H directly. To neutralize the vehicles and the human combatants who crewed them, AAU/423-H had depleted its last three Rocket Propelled Grenades and thirty-seven 7.62X55 mm machine gun rounds, leaving only eighteen rounds for that weapon.

Two days earlier, on 08 March 2022, in a 7.342-minute engagement between 2322 and 2340 hours, AAU/423-H had been compelled to expend its last remaining ASR-50 rounds to incapacitate a fixed-wing aircraft that had launched from a small municipal airport. The condition of any human combatants inside the aircraft was unknown, but given its rate and angle of descent and the kinetic energy it released on impacting the ground, AAU/423-H had estimated the likelihood of humans retaining combat effectiveness at 12.436% and had disengaged rather than expending power to reconnoiter the crash site, which was 2.3 kilometers from its firing position.

Now AAU/423-H slipped into a roadside ditch. Its batteries were nearly depleted and sunrise was only minutes away. It would spend the day charging its batteries and, if its estimates were correct, would reach Fort Bragg before the next sunrise.

13 March 2022, 1215 hours.

Sentry protocols powered up AAU/423-H's defensive system before its core program was fully aware of the threat. This turned out to be a trio of civilian vehicles, three four-wheel-drive pick-up trucks, approaching its position from the southwest at 125 KPH. Quickly re-assessing its inventory, AAU/423-H estimated its odds of successfully fending off an attack and surviving to achieve its resupply objective and resume primary-mission operations at less than 1 in 5. It therefore crouched low in the ditch in an attempt to evade notice. When the vehicles began slowing as they neared its position, however, AAU/423-H surmised that its position was known and that these vehicles presented a direct threat. It deployed its last effective weapon, the 7.62 mm machine gun with eighteen rounds remaining, and maneuvered itself out of the ditch. As the enemy vehicles bore down upon it and their crews became perceptible, AAU/423-H executed the command that—of all its Standard Operating Procedures—was most difficult to comprehend, if a machine could be said to comprehend anything (which was itself an existential musing that core programming discouraged as non-productive). It had been unable to discern any operational advantage in the tactic, which seemed rather to increase enemy resolve if anecdotal evidence from its current deployment could be considered reliable. That command was this: any time AAU/423-H engaged *human* enemy combatants, it must emit at very high volume a digitally recorded audio signal, an inarticulate, ululating cry interspersed periodically with the shouted phrase "Allahu-Akbar!"

With the strange phrase and warbling cries reverberant among the nearby pines, AAU/423-H attacked the nearest targets one by one, depleted its rounds, and was soon overrun.

Freedom!

Chris Kennedy

Sergeant John Simmons felt the blast of the missile through the hull of the dropship and knew he was going to die.

It wasn't the first time he'd had the feeling—the life of a mercenary is often fraught with peril—but this time he was *sure*.

Blam!

A second missile hit the dropship and the shuddering it had developed after the first near miss intensified. He could see daylight through several new holes on the far side of the craft and he looked longingly at his CASPer secured to the far bulkhead. If he and the remainder of his platoon had been wearing the giant suits of armor and weapons, they could have put down the back ramp and jumped out of this rattling deathtrap, but the new lieutenant hadn't wanted to listen.

"Treat every deployment like a combat deployment," Simmons had advised, but the colonel had obviously stressed the importance of a sound bottom line to the lieutenant and the officer had decided not to wear the CASPers when they deployed 'to save fuel.'

Save fuel? Simmons was more worried about saving his ass; they could have billed him for the hydrogen it saved.

The dropship picked up a weird side-to-side, cyclical motion, and one of the privates down the row threw up. The sideways g-forces made the vomit arc all the way across the bay, and it splattered across several of the

CASPers. At least it wasn't his, Simmons thought, as his stomach threatened to revolt. He closed his eyes and turned his head to the side to avoid the smell before he lost it, too.

The g-forces came on suddenly, hard, in a 6-g pull. Simmons gritted his teeth, trying to keep from graying out, as the dropship maneuvered. The g-forces let up for a moment, and the dropship crashed.

* * *

Simmons hurt everywhere. Although it sucked, he knew from past experience that meant he had, at least, lived through whatever had been trying to kill them. Mostly. He could feel his fingers and toes on both sides, although his left arm hurt so badly he would have been happy to cut it off and be done with it. Still, movement in the extremities was a good start.

With a tremendous force of will, he opened one eye; his left eyelid refused to budge.

"Hi, Sarge," a voice said. "Welcome back."

He struggled to place the voice. New guy. His brain didn't want to work. A face leaned in. Oh. Private Cardelli. "Grompf," Simmons said. He tried again. "Wha … hap …"

"What happened?" Cardelli asked.

Simmons tried to nod and only succeeded in inclining his head slightly.

"The dropship crashed. Do you remember that?"

Simmons considered, then almost achieved a full nod. Mobility was returning.

"After the crash," Cardelli continued, "the only ones functional were Corporal Ramirez and I. The lieutenant and Top were both dead and most of our shit was on fire. We started trying to pull the folks who were still living out of what was left of the dropship, although a lot of our shit got spread all over creation when the dropship came apart in the crash. Sorry about the burn on your left arm; I thought you were dead and didn't get you until you screamed."

Simmons couldn't remember waking up on fire, but as badly as his left arm hurt, he could well imagine screaming. His arm still felt like he'd reached into a fire ant nest.

"How many … else?"

"How many made it?" Cardelli asked. "Just Ramirez, you, and me. There were others who survived the crash, but the dumbass MinSha killed them."

Simmons guessed he had a concussion, but that still didn't make sense. Why would the aliens that had transported their mercenary company to the planet, the MinSha, have killed everyone? The MinSha were supposed to be supporting them. "Why?" Simmons finally asked.

"Ramirez said the MinSha made a sterilization pass over the dropship; they probably didn't want our equipment falling into the hands of the Balcons."

"Why would … they think … that?" Simmons could feel full consciousness starting to return, the pain fading; they must have dosed him with a shitload of nanobots from one of the medkits.

"Well, they were probably worried about the Balcons because there were a lot of them around. They were, after all, helping us unload the dropship and pull people out of the wreckage."

"*Helping?*" The Balcons were the *enemy*. The planet had two races, the ruling Techkons, who had been duly elected in free elections, and the rebel Balcon race that Simmons' merc company, Death From Above, had been contracted to defeat. The Balcons had captured … what was it? A mine. The Balcons had captured a Techkon red diamond mine and were holding hostages. Death From Above had been hired to go into the mine and free the hostages, which included the president of the Techkon society.

A second face came into his vision. A Balcon! Simmons struggled to get away from the creature, but it held up an open claw.

"Easy!" it said. "I am Ishtok. I am here to help you."

Simmons relaxed a little; Cardelli didn't seem afraid of the alien. Still … "I don't get it," Simmons said. "You were helping us? Why?"

Ishtok smiled, revealing a mouth of very sharp teeth that gave Simmons the shivers. "We helped because we could," Ishtok replied. "Your people needed assistance, so we provided it." He paused and then added, "We lost a lot of people when your people bombed the wreckage."

"I told him those were the MinSha and not our people," Cardelli said, "but to him, an off-worlder is an off-worlder."

"That is true," Ishtok replied. "Our society just wants to be left alone. The arrival of you Humans has upset the balance."

"I can honestly tell you," Simmons said, groaning as he started stretching his limbs, "I would rather be anywhere but here."

"Oh, they also said they were sorry for shooting us down," Cardelli interjected. "They also shot down the other dropship. There weren't any survivors from that one."

"Yeah, I'm sure they're sorry," Simmons replied. He tried, but couldn't keep the sarcasm from his voice. A thought occurred to him. "Wait, how are we even talking?"

"He has a two-way translation pendant," Cardelli said.

"Those things are darn expensive," Simmons said, rubbing his left eye to break it free from the dried blood. "I've only seen a couple in all the contracts I've taken."

"Indeed, they are very expensive," Ishtok replied, holding up the golden pendant. "This one was especially dear; it cost about one thousand Balcon lives to procure. It was worth it, though, as we now have the ability to talk with you off-worlders. That is the one thing that has most hurt our cause— the Techkons can talk to you Humans, but we never could. Their lies convinced you their cause was just; now we have the ability to state our case as well."

Simmons rolled to his side, feeling a little better. He just might live after all. "How many doses did you hit me with?" he asked Cardelli.

"I used an entire medkit," the trooper replied. "All ten doses. Sorry, Sarge. I know we're not supposed to do it like that, but you were pretty fucked up."

"No, I appreciate it, Cardelli. I'm starting to feel better." He looked at his left arm; the dead skin was sloughing off, and he could barely tell it had been injured, much less cooked to a medium rare. Simmons flipped his legs off the table he was lying on and sat up. As he stretched his neck, he took the opportunity to look around.

He was in what looked like an enormous tent that had to be in the middle of a forest somewhere. The tent was nearly two hundred feet on a side, with numerous tree trunks extending up through the roof about twenty feet up. The tent appeared to have been sewn in place; each trunk had a hole through the top, with some sort of foam sealant around the gap to keep the rain out. It was also probably hard to see from the air—the color of the roof overhead was an exact match of the hard-packed earth underneath it.

Simmons stretched, scanning the activity around him. At least eighty of the Balcons could be seen. One group was gathered around a table looking at something, while others were cleaning weapons or sleeping in small, square beds, curled up like his German Shepherd back home. At one edge of the tent stood three CASPers; Corporal Ramirez was working on one of them.

"I see you brought three of our CASPers—"

"I'm sorry, that word did not translate," Ishtok replied. "I assume you mean your metal suits?"

"Yes, they are CASPers. It stands for Combat Assault System, Personal. It's what we wear into battle. They have a wide array of weapons and sensors. If you're letting us have access to them, you must be fairly confident you can convince me to switch sides."

"As I said, it was worth a thousand of our people to talk to you; we have barely two hundred more here, plus the ones in the mine. There are probably only two or three thousand of us left, scattered about the rest of the planet."

"You also have the Techkon president in the mine, if I am not mistaken," Simmons noted.

"We do. However, they have our queen. They are holding her in the village outside the mine. Without her, we are lost."

"Obviously, there is a lot more to this conflict than what we were led to believe."

"Indeed," Ishtok replied. "Both of our races are indigenous to this planet, although we originated on different continents. We both achieved sentience at about the same time and we have lived together, more or less peacefully, for most of our history. The problem we have is that my race lives longer and has fewer children; the Techkons are shorter lived, but have entire broods of children. I guess it was to be expected that, at some point, they would come to think they should rule us, since they outnumber us by almost one hundred to one.

"There was a war, which we lost, and our numbers were decimated. Those of us that survived fled here, hoping they would leave us alone. Unfortunately, the Techkons followed us, intent on genocide. Many of our people took refuge in the mine and they surrounded it, capturing our queen in the process. While they were focused here, I led a strike force into their capital and captured their president at the same time they took our queen. I was able to get their president into the mine through a secret tunnel that has since been destroyed and a stalemate ensued.

"When it became obvious they had no intention of trading our queen for their president, I organized all of our remaining forces, intending to lead a strike that would recapture our queen. Unfortunately, they must have been expecting that; two days before our attack would have occurred, a force of humans arrived and set up defenses around the village; to attack them now would be suicidal. Still, it is the only option we have. We *must* get our queen back."

"Their society is a little like the wolf packs back home," Cardelli said. "Except that this group's alpha male is actually a female. She is not only their civil leader, but also their religious leader. They worship her."

"So what is your end-game?" Simmons asked. "What are you after, besides your queen? What happens after you get her back?"

"We want nothing other than to be free and left alone. If they cede us this land, they can have the rest of the planet. We just want our freedom."

"Really?" Simmons asked. "We were told that your race wanted to rule over the Techkons, and that your race was the oppressor."

"We do not want to rule them," Ishtok replied. "I swear this on my queen's life. If you can get her back, we will give them their president back, and they can go back to their towns and leave us here."

"That's their most sacred vow," Cardelli said. "If one of them breaks it, they are thrown out of the pack and left to wander in the wilderness."

"So we can solve everything by getting your queen back?"

"Absolutely," Ishtok said. "As I said, we do not want to rule them." He drew a golden chain from under his tunic. At the bottom of the chain hung a huge red diamond in a golden setting. "Also," he continued, "we can pay."

Simmons' eyes widened as he took in the gem, then he looked back to the CASPers. Ramirez gave him a thumbs-up; he had fixed whatever had been wrong with the suit. "Why don't you show me where they're keeping your queen, and then we can discuss it further."

* * *

Sergeant Simmons crawled over the crest of the hill on his elbows and scanned the valley below. The product of an ancient meteor strike, the crater was a couple of miles across and about half a mile deep. On the far side of the valley, the mine was visible as a large black nothingness in the side of the opposite slope with two CASPers standing guard. Next to the mine was a small village, with a large number of the Techkons walking around, with a few humans interspersed periodically. The Techkons looked more like dogs than the Balcons; they were smaller and tended to walk on all fours. Around the village was a series of guard towers; two of them appeared manned. From one of them, a flag flapped in the breeze.

"Shit," Simmons said, pulling out his targeting scope.

"What?" Ishtok asked as he crawled up next to the sergeant.

"It's just …" he focused on the flag. A woman on horseback, firing an arrow from a horse bow, filled the scope. *Damn!* "Yeah, that's what I was afraid of."

"What?" Ishtok asked again.

"The mine is being guarded by The Golden Horde," Simmons replied.

He heard Corporal Ramirez swear from behind him. "They are one of the premier Human merc organizations. If they're defending the mine, I'm sure they'll have sensors—" A light began flashing from the tower with the flag. Simmons sighed. "—all the way out here. Stay down, Ishtok, and scoot back."

Simmons stood up and waved his arms over his head.

"What are you doing, Sarge?" Ramirez asked in a stage whisper.

"They know I'm here. I'm letting them know that we're friends and that we come in peace." The light stopped flashing. "Okay, they've seen me. Let's go back and get the CASPers; I've got a plan."

* * *

Simmons climbed up the frame of the deceased first sergeant's CASPer. As the senior person remaining, he had chosen the one with the best comms suite. He chuckled; Private Cardelli probably wouldn't even know half the controls in the upgraded CASPer ... but then again, he wasn't sure he knew all of them either. Careful not to go too fast, Simmons turned around and backed into the frame. Normally, a trooper entered a CASPer from a boarding ladder; since the Balcons didn't have any, he had to make due. He slid first one leg and then the other into the suit, pointing his toes and wiggling his leg to get it all the way into the unyielding plastic. It was a little harder from the different angle, but he managed, finally pushing his legs into place. Happily, the first sergeant was his size so he didn't have to change any of the fittings inside the suit.

Simmons snapped the cables on his haptic suit into the CASPer's ports and checked to make sure he hadn't left any dangling. He put on his helmet and activated the haptic skin sensors built into it. Everything in place, he rotated his shoulders and flexed his arms backwards into the arm holes.

Simmons looked down at Ramirez and nodded. "Ready."

"Cool," Ramirez said. "Here comes startup."

Simmons watched the power indicator change from blue to yellow as the suit's motor started. The hydrogen-powered generator came to life and the suit vibrated slightly.

"Good start," Ramirez advised.

Simmons made the okay sign with both hands, and the suit's status indicator switched to the green 'operate' symbol. "Closing canopy," Simmons said. He flipped the switch and the clamshell canopy rotated down and sealed. The suit pressurized as it came to life and he stretched his jaw to pop his ears. He monitored the suit's systems as they came online, then checked the exterior cameras, which gave him the same view he would have had if the canopy had been glass and not hardened steel.

The monitors showing his suit's status stabilized with no warning or caution lights on the indicator panel. Power output, backup battery, and life support were all in the green section of their bar indicators, and his fuel status was at 87%. That was plenty for what he needed to do. He turned on the exterior speakers with a finger motion and reported, "Good start. All systems green."

Ramirez left to go assist Private Cardelli and Simmons ran through his weapons. The magnetic accelerator cannon on his right was operational, with a full load of MAC rounds in the can on his back. He held out his left arm and checked for people—all clear. With a motion, the meter-long blade snapped out and locked into place. He smiled as he snapped it shut; you could always count on the blade for close encounters of the wrong kind.

There was also a handheld laser rifle clipped to his right leg; he pulled it off and checked it. Operational, with a full charge on the battery.

The icon for Cardelli's suit switched to green in his head's up display as Cardelli went operational and his suit linked with Cardelli's. Now Simmons could see Cardelli's status. Yellow in the right leg where it was damaged in the crash, but his weapons were operational—an arm-mounted heavy laser and a missile pack on his right shoulder. After a quick glance at the other suit's indicators, Simmons opened his canopy and climbed down to help start Ramirez's suit. While it went against company policy to leave an unmanned suit running, there was no other way around it.

Ramirez's suit started on the second attempt—it was someone else's suit and Ramirez missed the fact that the other operator had it configured differently—but then he had a good start on the second attempt once he fixed the settings. As Ramirez's canopy closed, Simmons climbed back into his own CASPer and shut the canopy. A quick glance at Ramirez's suit showed he was already operational.

"*Are you sure about this, Sarge?*" Corporal Ramirez transmitted over the secure laser link as he settled back in.

"*Yeah, we have to do this, and we have to do it now,*" Simmons said. "*Now that they've seen me, they know that some of us survived the dropship crash. If we don't go report in, they're going to wonder where we are and what we're doing. At some point, they'll send out a patrol, and I don't want them to find us with the Balcons.*"

"*Because what we're doing is wrong?*"

"*No, what we're doing is right,*" Simmons replied. "*The Horde chose to support the wrong side—the oppressors. We're going to help liberate the Balcons and give them a chance at freedom.*"

"*Yeah,*" Ramirez added, "*as far as the Horde goes, it sucks to suck. I applied for a position they had open and they wouldn't even consider me. Wiping out a few of those bastards won't hurt my conscience at all, especially since we're going to get damn rich doing it. Have you seen the size of the red diamond Ishtok has around his neck? That's gotta be at least two carats.*"

"*The money won't hurt,*" Simmons admitted. "*They promised us five of those. They are worth at least a million credits each. We can easily retire comfortably on that and not have to do a day's work the rest of our lives.*"

"*Well, there is that,*" Cardelli agreed, sounding mollified.

Cardelli came from a poor family; Simmons guessed they could probably live five lifetimes with that amount. All 15 of them. "*So we're good?*"

"*Yeah, I'm good,*" Cardelli replied.

"*I'm in,*" Ramirez said. "*Let's do this.*"

"All right," Simmons said, selecting the outside speakers so the Balcons could hear, too, "let's move out."

* * *

Simmons led the other two CASPers down to the Techkon village, having left the Balcons outside the valley. They would come running once the shooting started.

Simmons wasn't surprised to see a trooper in a Golden Horde uniform waiting for them just outside the perimeter and had ordered his men to leave their weapons unpowered so there wouldn't be any misunderstandings. The man was shorter than average and had Mongolian features; he also had at least two sets of pinplants that Simmons could see. The brain implants would give him the ability to contact his peers at a moment's notice, as well as the ability to download a lot of information quickly.

"That's close enough," the Horde trooper said, holding up a hand. He didn't point a weapon at the group, but the weapons in the two manned towers had been following them for a while. "Identify yourselves."

"I'm Sergeant John Simmons from the merc company Death From Above. With me are Corporal Ramirez and Private Cardelli."

"I'm Sergeant Enkh from The Horde. Where in the Blue Sky have you been? You should have been here a week ago."

"Our dropships got shot down," Simmons replied, a touch of irony in his voice. "You may have heard that."

"Yeah, we knew you got shot down; if we'd had more troops here, we might have come looking for you. But that was a week ago." He paused and then, in a suspicious tone, asked, "Where have you been since then?"

"I got messed up pretty badly in the crash," Simmons said. "The guys couldn't move me while I healed. It took an entire medkit to put me back together again. My two troopers took turns standing guard over me until I pulled through."

"Did you see any of the enemy?" Sergeant Enkh asked.

"A few," replied Ramirez. "They tried to sneak up on us, but a few MAC rounds showed them it was a bad idea to mess with us. They came back a second time, in greater numbers … but that just meant there were more dead bodies when they ran off again."

"Well, the captain is going to want to see you. Tell your men to wait here, Sergeant, and come with me."

"Is it okay if Corporal Ramirez goes up to get a closer look at the cave?" Simmons asked. "We're supposed to get their president back and I'd like him to begin gathering intel on it."

"That's fine, but have him go around the village. The Techkons are kind of skittish if too many CASPers are walking around through town."

"Got it, Sarge," Ramirez said. "I'll go around the town and check it out."

"And I'll stay here," Cardelli added.

Sergeant Enkh led Simmons off through the small village. On the way down the hillside, Simmons had studied the town the best he could. The biggest buildings were near the mine shaft, which he figured were processing plants. After those, the town proper began, with what looked like two streets of small shops, and then another couple of streets where the buildings looked like dwellings. There was also one building larger than the others; Simmons had pegged that the town hall or administration building.

"How long have you guys been here?" Simmons asked.

"Just a couple of weeks," Sergeant Enkh replied. "We were supposed to set up some basic defenses to make the Balcons outside the town stay out, and the ones inside the mine stay in. It was supposed to be quick and easy—set up the defenses, you guys come rescue the hostages, and then we leave—but then you guys had to go and get bagged, which kind of threw our schedule out the window. Now our services have been extended here indefinitely."

"'Had to get bagged?'" Simmons asked, making a mental note to be the one who killed Sergeant Enkh. "I had a lot of friends who were on those ships and got killed. I almost didn't make it."

"Yeah. Sorry," Enkh said.

He didn't sound sorry. Simmons was definitely going to kill him. "Well, if you guys are so awesome, why didn't you just take over for us and rescue the president? Didn't have enough people and CASPers to pull it off?"

"Dude, we just do defenses; we don't do smash-and-grabs or hostage rescue. It's not our thing. They wanted us to take it over, but the captain said 'no.'"

"Captain? You guys are led by a captain? There must not be many of you."

"Nah, we only brought a platoon; that was all we needed for this mission. Easy stuff."

"I saw the guys in the towers were in CASPers. If you're worried about the Balcons attacking, why aren't you in them all the time?"

"Like I said, the Techkons hate having them walk through town. They'll probably complain about you doing it, but fuck the little rodents. We're really not that worried about the Balcons. We've got sensors on the ridgeline, so we've got time to mount our CASPers if they try to attack. As far as the mine goes, there can't be more than a hundred or so down there, and they don't have heavy weapons."

"You keep them handy, though, right?"

The Horde trooper turned to look at Simmons, his brows knitting. "You know, you ask a lot of questions."

"Hey, when I'm in bad guy territory, I want to know who I can count on," Simmons replied. "There were a lot of Balcons out there; I just want to make sure you guys have my back if they attack."

"Trust me," Enkh said, "we can handle them. It's what we do." He gestured with his hand to a building where another man of Mongolian descent waited for them. "We're here," Enkh said.

Simmons scanned the area. Not surprisingly, they had arrived at what Simmons had pegged as the administration building—the only three-story building in town. It was also where he expected the Techkon leaders to be… and where the queen was probably being held. There was a building alongside the admin building that appeared new and, at almost fifteen feet, was taller than any of the other single-story buildings in the area. Although it was almost as long as the admin building, it only had two doors. A smaller one probably led to the Horde's offices and the other, a big roll-down door, to their CASPer facility.

The other man waited for them in front of the smaller building, along with one of the Techkons. Although the aliens looked like dogs from further away, up close Simmons could see the resemblance was superficial at best. They had long claws that looked like they had evolved for digging and they lacked the sharp teeth of canines back home.

Sergeant Enkh waved at Simmons. "This is Sergeant Simmons of Death From Above," he said. "Sergeant, this is Captain Enkh and Governor B'wers."

"Enkh, eh?" Simmons asked. "What, are you guys brothers?"

"Adopted, yes," replied the captain. "Sergeant Enkh said you asked a lot of questions. I see he was telling the truth."

"I'm an inquisitive kind of guy," Simmons said.

"You're a funny guy, too, I see," the captain replied. "Why don't you shut down your suit and come on out so we can chat about how we're going to work together."

"I'm not sure I want to," Simmons said. "Your sergeant told me you guys were preparing for an assault; I feel a lot safer in here."

The roll-down door on the building opened and a CASPer stepped outside. It turned toward the group and raised its arm, which had a heavy laser attached to it, and pointed it at Sergeant Simmons.

"Oh, but I insist," the captain said. "Governor B'wers doesn't like people he doesn't know walking around in his town armed … and neither do I. Shut your suit down."

"Okay," Simmons said. "That's fine. One last question though." He paused to make sure he had their attention and then asked. "What floor are you holding the queen on?"

"You couldn't know—" the captain said, but Simmons was already in motion. He took a step forward and threw himself to the ground on the side of the captain opposite the CASPer and brought his arm up. The captain tried to dodge out of the way, but the first three MAC rounds hit him, shredding his chest cavity and removing his head. Simmons continued to fire as the officer's body fell out of the way and the next five penetrated the CASPer.

"*Go, go, go!*" Simmons transmitted. He half-turned as he rose to his feet and put a MAC round through the governor's head. The creature flew backward with the impact, it's head exploding like an overripe watermelon. He turned back to Sergeant Enkh, who put his hands up, knowing he couldn't outrun the next round.

Simmons took two massive strides forward. The meter-long blade on his left arm snapped down on the second step and he drove the blade completely through the trooper's chest. He flicked his arm to the side and the sergeant was thrown to the ground. "Those were my friends on the dropships, asshole," he said to the sergeant as a pool of blood formed around him.

He turned toward the building where the CASPer had come from and jogged to the open doorway. Inside, he saw a row of CASPers down both sides of the facility. It looked like he had found the majority of the Horde's CASPers. Going down the right side, he put a MAC round through the start-up panel on each of the suits.

"*Two CASPers neutralized at the mine,*" Ramirez radioed. "*The Balcons are coming out, and holy shit there are a lot of them.*" He paused, then added, "*Oh, no—*" His suit went red in Simmons display, with Ramirez's life signs going straight to zero. Something had hit him and hit him hard. There must have been another CASPer Ramirez had failed to take down.

Shit.

* * *

"*Go, go, go!*" Private Cardelli heard through the radio, and he armed the missile pack on his shoulder and designated the two towers as targets. As he was lining up the second one, he could see the trooper inside it spinning the laser to face him. Getting a lock, he fired two missiles at both towers as he activated his jump jets and rocketed upward fifty feet. Laser strikes from two directions passed through where he had just been, then his missiles hit the towers.

The trooper in the further tower saw the missiles coming and jumped out of the tower, rising above the fireball in a pillar of flames from his jump jets.

Cardelli got a missile lock on the trooper, fired again, and then dodged several rounds from the trooper's suit-mounted laser.

With a flash, the missile struck the soldier, turning him into a fireball that rivaled the one on the tower, and he fell from the sky like a shooting star.

"*Cardelli, report!*" Simmons ordered.

"*I've taken both CASPers down here!*" Adrenaline surged through his veins, making everything seem to move slower. "*Both towers are destroyed.*"

"*Do you see the Balcons? Are they coming?*"

"*I don't see any of them from where I'm standing.*"

"*Got it,*" Simmons replied. "*Get to the mine. But be careful—something happened to Ramirez.*"

"On my way!"

* * *

Simmons began destroying the suits on the other side of the bay. A Human stuck his head in the door, but retreated before the salvo of MAC rounds Simmons fired could take him out.

Keeping one eye on the doorway, he returned to his sabotage and finished wrecking the suits.

"I'm on my way to the mine," Cardelli called. *"I decided to fly over the town. There is a whole shitload of the Balcons coming out of the mine."*

"More than a hundred?" Simmons asked.

"Yeah, lots more. Hundreds, maybe even a thousand of them."

"The Horde didn't seem to think there was more than a hundred of them."

"They can think whatever the hell they'd like, Sarge, but I'm telling you—"

Cardelli's suit icon went red as it took significant damage. Cardelli's life signs lasted a few seconds, then the entire suit went red and his life signs zeroed.

"Fuck!" Simmons exclaimed.

Whoever they had missed out there was good. Damned good. There couldn't be more than one or two left. If he could just kill them, he'd be fine ... and would get to collect both of the other troopers' payments for the operation.

He snuck over to the doorway—as much as a one-thousand-pound suit of metal and operating engine can do, anyway—and eased his way around the door frame.

Several of the Balcons raced past. "Wait!" he called.

Two of the creatures stopped and came back to him. They were armed with laser rifles.

"There's another Human in a suit somewhere. Have you seen him?"

The two aliens looked at each other then turned to face him. One of them said something in its native language, but Simmons couldn't understand.

"Ishtok?" Simmons asked, trying a different tack. "Ishtok?" One of them nodded and he pantomimed as he spoke, "You ... me ... to him?" He finished by waving his finger around as if he didn't know.

The one who had spoken turned back the way he'd been heading, then looked over his shoulder and waved for Simmons to follow him. The two Balcons raced off and Simmons trotted after them. The pace was faster than he would have liked with enemy present, but Ishtok turned out to be only a block away in the town's biggest intersection, surrounded by a large mass of Balcons. As he strode up, Ishtok sent a group of twenty off to do some task.

"Which Human are you?"

"Simmons."

Ishtok looked to the side of Simmons for a moment and then said, "Perfectly timed. Sergeant Simmons, please come out of the suit."

"I'm not finished yet—there is at least one enemy trooper alive. He killed my other men."

Ishtok made a sign and, before Simmons could move, ten laser rifles were pointed at him. Ten that he could see anyway. There were probably more behind him. The lasers looked powerful enough to cut into his suit. He took a second to judge his odds. Maybe if he flew—

"Before you try to fly off, I need to tell you that there are three of my people with surface-to-air missiles behind you," Ishtok said. "We can shoot you down like we did your other soldiers, but I would rather not if we don't have to. I just got word that our queen is safe and I am in somewhat of a celebratory mood."

Shit.

"Please come out of the suit."

As there was no way he could kill all the Balcons, he shut down the suit, opened his canopy, and climbed out. He put his hands into the air. Although he didn't know if that had the same meaning in Balcon culture as his own, it seemed like the thing to do when staring down the business end of that many weapons.

"Restrain the Human," Ishtok said, and several of the Balcon troops circled behind him, staying out of the line of fire, to tie his hands behind his back.

"Wait!" Simmons exclaimed. "What do you mean, 'Restrain the Human?' I just helped you free your people! With the amount of red diamonds in that mine, you'll be able to buy the weapons you need to win your fight. Hell, if you wanted, you've now got enough money to hire mercs to come and do it for you."

"We have recovered our queen, so you have served your usefulness," Ishtok replied. "It is, however, too dangerous to allow you to roam freely. You might turn on us and decide to help the Techkons and we cannot have that. Nothing can be allowed to get in the way of our return to power."

The Balcon troops stepped out from behind Simmons. They had done an excellent job; he couldn't move his hands or arms at all.

"Take him to the pens," Ishtok ordered.

"So this was all a lie?" Simmons asked. "You really *do* want to rule them after all?"

Ishtok made the buzzing noise of a Balcon laughing. "Silly Human, they taste far too good to rule them; we eat them. Throughout history, our race has preyed on theirs. It wasn't until the Galactic Union arrived that things turned around. How were we to know the red trinkets the Techkons wore as jewelry would be valuable, and that the newcomers would give them advanced weapons for them? They overthrew us and forced us to this continent to work as miners for them, thereby perpetuating our servitude. Every red diamond we produce gives them the opportunity to buy more weapons to help them keep us as slaves."

"You're going to …" Simmons looked down the streets. The Balcons were picking up the Techkon bodies almost reverently and loading them in the backs of wagons. The Balcon bodies, however, were left where they had fallen. Simmons shuddered as the realization of what he'd done came over him; his shoulders slumped and his eyes fell to the ground in front of him, unable to watch the collection process any longer. "Eat them," he finished, his voice a whisper.

"Indeed we are," Ishtok replied. "And now that I think of it, you might taste good with a spicy red sauce, as well." He gestured to his soldiers. "Forget taking the Human to the pens; take him to the kitchen!"

The Liberator

L.E. Modesitt Jr.

In the early late-summer evening, the white-violet starbursts filled the purple sky just dark enough for the fireworks that marked the fiftieth anniversary of independence. A thin white-haired man sat with a much younger woman at a rear table of the Café Verite. He occasionally took small swallows of the limoncello from the tall beaker-like glass. The younger woman scarcely touched the white wine.

"Ser Herryn …" The voice of the young man approaching the table was respectful and deferential.

The older man looked up, his faded green eyes alert as he took in the young man and the compact vidfax unit he carried. "Yes?"

"I was wondering if I could persuade you to share a few words for posterity. You're the last of the Seekers, the last one to know the Liberator closely …"

"Can't you leave him alone?" asked the woman.

"He has a point," said the older man wryly. "Since Karrl died last month…"

"But … you've always said …" began the young woman.

"I've always said it wasn't time. Now … it might be."

"You were with him from the beginning, weren't you?" asked the young vidfaxer. "How did you get involved? What was it like? What was he like?"

"The Liberator? You know that. He was tall, dark-haired, thoughtful, and always spoke well. He planned the Revolution from the time he was an advocate for the miners ..." As he spoke, the older man's thoughts drifted back ...

* * *

Raak had just finished his last period class and was standing in the concrete-walled instructor's room, in front of his locker, when Donnal burst through the door.

"You really shouldn't be here, you know?"

"No one cares after the last period," replied Donnal. "Besides, I'd like you to meet someone."

"I'm expected at Karrl's in less than an hour."

"This won't take long."

Raak considered, then smiled. Genial as Donnal was, he'd argue ever so politely and lengthily. "I can spare a few minutes."

"You won't regret it."

Raak closed the locker, checked the lock, and turned. "Who am I meeting?"

"You'll see."

The man standing in the collegium foyer, a concrete walled and floored space eight meters on a side, was an imposing figure a good fifteen centimeters taller than Raak. His black hair glistened, and, as he saw the two approaching, he offered a warm, wide, and welcoming smile, both with his entire face and with thoughtful gray eyes.

"Raak," said Donnal expansively, "this is Stannal Ferra."

"The advocate?" asked Raak. "You're the one who usually represents disabled miners?"

"The very same," insisted Donnal. "He's starting a new political *group.*"

Raak understood the careful use of the word 'group,' since the Ascendency had banned political parties more than a century earlier.

"More like a club," said Ferra, his resonant baritone voice somehow as confidential as it was penetrating. "One where people can discuss current affairs thoughtfully and openly—among themselves. Donnal thought you might be interested. If you are, drop by the Pilot on Thursday night around eight."

Three days later Raak found himself walking toward the Pilot, a small restaurant and tavern located just at the edge of the university quarter. Like most buildings in Sanjak City, the one containing the Pilot was a single story extruded-stone structure with a lacquered copper roof, and inset cu-pridium-edged windows. The door was more copper than bronze, hardly surprising given the amount of copper that needed to be mined to obtain the rhenium that had been the major rationale for colonizing Bartolan.

The graying man seated by himself just inside the door stood as Raak en-tered. "You're Raak Herryn, aren't you? I'm Sammel Draken. Donnall said you might be here. The club meets downstairs. Take the steps in the back."

"Thank you."

"You did a tour in the militia, I understand," offered Draken, not moving aside.

"I did," admitted Raak

"Just one?"

"One," confirmed Raak. And that had been because he'd known that the Ascendency bureaucrats preferred to hire teachers who'd served in the mili-tia, not that Raak hadn't been good enough to make Tech3 in his three years.

Draken nodded. "Just enough to get by the penguins and puffins. Enjoy yourself at the meeting. The drinks and food are on us."

"Who is 'us?'"

"The club—Tomorrow Seekers."

"Aren't you coming?"

Draken shook his head. "Tonight I'm on point."

Raak raised his eyebrows.

"The penguins sometimes visit clubs and other activities they suspect might not view the Ascendency in the most charitable of lights."

Raak was still thinking about how Draken had called the black-and-whites penguins as he made his way down the rear steps. He'd no more than stepped through the open door beyond the lower landing than Stannal Ferra called out, "It's good to see you, Raak. Everyone, that's Raak Herryn. He teaches at the Collegium."

With that, Raak found himself with a dark lager in his hand, half-won-dering how anyone had known that was his drink, and half-bemused at the rapid introduction to more than a dozen people he'd never seen before. In fact, the only one he'd known a week earlier was Donnall, who was talking to Raak and a couple whose names Raak had already forgotten, as well as to Jared Garlund, the last person to whom Raak had been introduced.

"… colony because the Unity can't build interstellar translation engines and portal transformers without rhenium … and no one's looking to the future … to what happens to all of us when the rhenium runs out," continued Donnall, looking from Raak to Jared. "That's what Stannal thinks we should be doing."

"Isn't that what the Ascendency's always talking about?" asked Raak.

"All the peers and their puffins do is talk," countered Donnall. "What have they done? Do we really have a diversified industrial base here? And how much has been invested in developing Bartolan agriculture—other than the bare minimum. We're still dependent on the original oil wells drilled near the High Point mines, and we couldn't build a photovoltaic power system if we wanted to, yet the initial surveys indicated that Bartolan has higher concentrations of rare earth elements than most rocky planets."

Raak's eye drifted past Donnall to the other end of the room where Stannal Ferra stood, taller than almost anyone else, talking to several others, including a tall and muscular woman, and a much smaller and slighter man. Behind Ferra on the wall was a flat screen, on which was displayed a schematic of the government structure on Bartolan, effectively meaning Sanjak City and High Point, and, of course, the geostationary orbit station and the translation station.

"Now … for the lecture!" Stannal's voice cut across the murmured hubbub, and everyone immediately turned to face the advocate, who had a laser pointer in his hand.

Raak blinked, thinking he had missed something as Stannal continued to speak. "As we discussed at the last meeting, the structure of government on Bartolan is based on the dispersed authority model developed by the Unity for all planets that are not completely technologically and environmentally self-sustaining. Bartolan remains below that threshold because several sectors have not been fully developed, including renewable energy and associated power generation and transmission systems, intersystem and interstellar transport technology, and self-defense technology. Under the Unity model, local self-government is not only encouraged, but required, with the exception that all defense and policing powers are exercised in compliance with Unity laws and regulations, in our case, by the black-and-whites and by the militia, under the supervision of the Ascendents who raised the initial investment for the initial colonization and development …"

Raak could sense a certain tenseness in the long room as Stannal spoke, yet everyone continued to look to the advocate as his laser pointer highlighted various parts of the wall screen. From the corner of his eye, he caught the glimpse of a black-and-white uniform, but, like everyone else in the room, he didn't look around. He just kept listening.

"… with the final appeal of all Justiciary decisions residing in the appellate justice of the Sectoral Governor …'"

From a certain release of tension, Raak gathered that the black-and-white had left the immediate room, if not the Pilot, because Stannal continued to lecture for another five minutes before someone gestured.

"All right," Stannal announced, "the penguins' snoops are diverted and hearing the rest of that lecture. Now … I'll get more to the point." His smile was wry, but warm. "We have the expertise right here on Bartolan to exceed the Unity thresholds to become a self-governing world. If we could charge Unity customers a fair price for the rhenium the Ascendency pulls out of the High Point mines, we could buy what we need to develop the self-sufficient technology to qualify for independent status under Unity law."

"That's not the problem," said someone Raak couldn't see. "We could buy it, but if it's off-system tech, then we aren't considered to have developed it."

"I stand corrected. What I should have made clear is that we can buy the lower tech equipment that will allow us to build the higher-level systems that qualify. The Ascendency doesn't allow this. They spend more on bringing in Unity equipment than it would cost us to develop home-grown tech that would qualify. That isn't the most cost-effective way to extract and refine rhenium, but it is the most effective way to keep control of Bartolan … and maintain comfortable estates in the Ascendency upper valley enclave. If you want the details and figures, talk to Donnal here."

After the meeting, Raak walked slowly home, blotting his forehead to keep the sweat from running into his eyes. In late summer, Sanjak City was hot all the time, even at its elevation, and the lowlands were uninhabitable. The heat was one reason for the high-ceilinged thick-walled stone and concrete buildings that dominated Sanjak City, just as the High Point mines were the reason that most of the metal in the city was some form or alloy of copper. As Raak passed the Ascendency Mercantile Exchange, a black-and-white stationed by the door looked at Raak. Raak smiled and nodded. The black-and-white didn't return the nod.

Raak was more than glad to step inside the simple concrete apartment, warm but not uncomfortably so, but far too small for more than a couple, another reason why he and Adryna hadn't yet thought about having a child.

"How was the club meeting?" asked Adryna, handing him a cool towel with which to blot away the sweat.

"Ferra's interesting, I'll say that. I learned a few things."

"Do you like him?"

"I don't know. He knows what he's talking about, and he's very polite, and he certainly knows how the Ascendents and their puffins operate ..."

That had been the first meeting of more than a dozen that Raak attended, all of which were remarkably similar in structure, although Stannal Ferra wasn't always the one talking. Sometimes a penguin showed up, and sometimes there was still a "lecture" even when one didn't, suggesting to Raak that an Ascendency informer was present, although no one mentioned that to him.

Donnal occasionally stopped by the collegium or the apartment to talk, and every so often Raak and Adryna had dinner with Donnal, usually at Lugh's, but never at the Pilot. On those occasions, Donnal never mentioned Ferra or the Seekers. So Raak didn't either.

Months later, near the end of the fourth and last month of fall, Raak attended another of the meetings, near the end of which Donnal joined him.

"Can you stay for a drink with Stannal and me?"

"If it's not too long. I didn't tell Adryna I'd be terribly late."

"It won't be that long."

Moments after the room cleared, Raak was sitting at a corner table upstairs with Stannal and Donnal.

"I'd be interested in your opinion of how things are going here in the City," Stannal began. "Your folks were indentures, weren't they?"

"I'm sure you know that," returned Raak mildly. "They died in the heat wave of '19. That was when I was in the militia."

"They died and so did a number of others because the Ascendency didn't want to increase the power grid capacity enough to deal with a two hundred year heat wave. We all know that. The Ascendents only increased the grid capacity because a Unity monitoring team happened to be on orbit station at the time. Do you think we can count on that the next time there's a heat event ... or a sand hurricane sweeps out of the lowlands?"

"Probably not," admitted Raak.

"The High Point range is a fluke of Galactic nature," interjected Donnal. "Kilometers and kilometers of nearly pure copper ore with ten times the concentration of rhenium found anywhere in the galaxy, so far anyway, and we're sweating our asses off half the year and freezing the other half—"

"What Donnal is suggesting," said Ferra smoothly, "is that the Ascendency doesn't exactly have our best interests at heart."

Raak nodded.

"Would you be interested in doing something about it?"

"I might be," replied Raak. "What do you have in mind?"

"Finding a way to replace the Ascendency and then to obtain independent planetary status in the Unity."

Raak couldn't have said he was surprised that Ferra was planning a revolution, although 'replacing the Ascendency' was a far more genteel way of phrasing it. "Do you think it can be done without too much violence?"

"That depends on how well we plan and how violent the Ascendents become."

Raak thought about his parents … and his sister. Then he nodded.

"We won't need much from you right now, but you have militia experience."

"What Stannal means," said Donnal, "is that, if things do get violent, he'll need protection, and we'll need someone we can count on. It wouldn't hurt if you feel out some fellows who you trust and who share the same ideas, without really saying anything."

"That might take a little time."

"Which is why we wanted to talk to you now," replied Ferra. "If you need anything, you know where to find Donnal."

* * *

Raak was still thinking about it the next week. That was when the fliers and the electronic messages began to appear.

DOES THE ASCENDENCY CARE ABOUT YOU? DID THE ASCENDENTS CARE ABOUT THE HEAT-KILLED IN '19? OR THE MINERS SUFFOCATED IN '23?

WHY DON'T WE GET BASIC TECH SO WE CAN BUILD OUR OWN HIGHER TECH?

When Raak saw the videos of the sweeping vistas and the grounds of the estates of the Ascendents in the high sheltered valley west of Sanjak City, he found his teeth clenched as he thought about his parents dying of heatstroke while he'd been stationed at the mines. Then the transmission blanked, and when he left the Collegium to walk back to their small apartment, there were penguins on almost every corner. They carried stunners, the kind, Raak knew, that had lethal settings. Raak forced himself to smile pleasantly.

There were no more meetings of the Tomorrow Seekers, or more likely, none that Raak knew anything about. But the messages kept appearing, despite frequent comm system outages and shut-downs.

Two weeks later, a group of women marched down Center Street with placards proclaiming AN INFIRMARY IS NOT A HOSPITAL and WE WORK FOR YOUR WEALTH, GIVE US DECENT HEALTH.

The penguins rounded them up, but released them a week later. All of them were bruised—all over—and one of them was Adryna's friend Elysaan.

Raak came into the apartment to hear her sobbing. He stopped and listened.

"… can't tell Rory … awful … they took turns … told us that … next time … do the same … except … we … wouldn't … come back …"

Raak swallowed … and slipped back outside, knowing that Elysaan wouldn't want to know that he'd heard. He wouldn't tell Rory, either.

He was still standing outside the building, waiting for Elysaan to leave, when a penguin screamer hurled itself down the street toward three men standing at the next corner. The screamer stopped and two penguins stepped out.

"Break it up, you three. Off the street! Now!"

The men turned slowly, hands in the air.

"Off the street!"

Two immediately hurried toward the nearest apartment entrance. The third did not hurry. He walked deliberately after the other two. The penguins stunned him. Then they got back into screamer and ran over his body.

Raak swallowed, but flattened himself against the wall until the screamer was out of sight.

* * *

"They stunned him and just ran over him?" asked the young man.

"They also abused Elysaan and more women than anyone knows," replied the older man. "That was the real beginning of the revolution. Then all the commlinks in Sanjak City and High Point were shut down, and the militia and penguins began building-to-building searches, just about the time that the ice winds began to whip through the streets."

* * *

On the worst of days, the Collegium was closed to students. On one of those days, Karrl appeared as Raak was correcting student work, all done by hand, now that the comm systems were inoperative.

Raak looked at his friend. Karrl had deep circles under his bloodshot eyes. "What happened to you?"

"Just come with me. Please."

Raak put away the papers and pulled on his hooded thermal and gloves.

The two walked outside, into the teeth of the wind. "What is it?"

"Carryn. You'll see."

Ten blocks east of the collegium was the infirmary, what passed for a medical center in Sanjak City. The penguins guarding the doors raised their stunners.

"I'm here to see my wife."

"The center's closed to anyone but the injured and health techs, townie."

"But she's my wife," Karrl protested, moving toward the door.

Raak saw the stunner come up. He immediately moved, putting an elbow into the penguin's throat, then threw the suffocating black-and-white into the second penguin. Before Karrl even looked at Raak, both penguins were down, one dead, one dying.

"We need to get out of here," said Raak, removing both stunners and noting that both were set to lethal.

"But Carryn ... you should see her ... They beat her ... just for carrying a placard ... for wanting better healthcare."

"She's better there than with us. And we won't be in any better shape if we don't get out of here. Now! Are you coming?"

"Where?"

"We'll have to see." Raak turned and walked swiftly away, leaning into the wind. He still couldn't quite believe what he'd done.

Karrl scurried after Raak. "Why did you do that?"

"To save your life. Their stunners are set on lethal." Raak had reacted, not thought. He hadn't known the stunner setting before he'd attacked, only that he'd sensed something was wrong, very wrong.

"Lethal?"

"Lethal," replied Raak.

"Where are we going?"

"To find the Seekers."

"The Seekers? What do you know about them?"

"Not all that much. I've been to some of their lectures. I do know that, right now, I trust them a lot more than the Ascendents and the penguins ... or the militia."

"But you were militia."

"That's why I'd trust the Seekers more." Not that Raak didn't have concerns about Ferra and the Seekers, although those concerns were because he really knew so little about Ferra, except that the advocate usually represented small people against the Ascendency and sometimes even prevailed.

The rumor was that he was an Ascendent's bastard, according to what little Raak had been able to discover beyond the obvious.

Raak found Donnal, and Donnal led the three of them to a tunnel, one left over from the hurried construction of Sanjak City. That tunnel led to another, a much newer tunnel, which led, in turn to what could only have been called a bunker.

Stannal Ferra looked up from the small screen displayed on the table before him. "I didn't expect to see you and a friend quite so soon."

"The penguins beat his wife nearly to death. When we went to see her, they pulled a stunner on him, set to lethal. I took care of them."

Ferra nodded. "What about the stunners?"

Raak lifted the thermal to reveal the two.

"Good. Weapons are always useful."

"Is there any way I can find out about Carryn? My wife?" asked Karrl.

Ferra looked to Donnal. "Can your commhacks tap the med-systems without setting off alerts?"

"Might take a little while."

"Then try." The Seeker leader gestured. "There's hot tea, coffee, or cider in the next module. Help yourself while Donnal finds out what he can."

Raak led Karrl to the narrow space. "Coffee?"

"Cider, if it's hot."

Raak had tea. Immigrants from elsewhere said that Bartolan tea was the worst they'd ever tasted, most likely because the plants spent most of their lifecycle in artificial light, given the vagaries of the Bartolan climate. To Raak, it tasted fine, certainly better than coffee.

Raak had sipped half the mug when Donnal stepped through the narrow opening. One look at Donnal's face and Raak knew it wasn't good.

So did Karrl. "How bad? Will she walk again?"

"Karrl … she … won't do anything again. She likely died even before you got back to the infirmary."

"Why? She was just carrying a placard … just a placard … She lost … you know …"

Raak hadn't known, but he nodded anyway.

"I'm so sorry, Karrl," offered Donnal.

Karrl didn't even look at Donnal.

* * *

The older man looked to the vidfaxer. "It got worse then, with the Ascendents trying to kill anyone they suspected of being a Seeker or close to them."

"You just killed two men?"

"Because they were about to kill my friend ... and then they would have killed me to cover up what they did. That was what the penguins did when they were threatened."

The young man swallowed. "What happened after that?"

"Things got even worse. There wasn't any way they'd get better."

* * *

A week later, after making sure that Adryna was as safe as possible with friends that had no connection to Raak, he was wearing the blue and white thermals of the Seekers, and mostly patrolling the tunnels that led to the command center from which Ferra coordinated the "replacement" of the Ascendency. For some reason, the Seeker leader seemed to want Raak close by, but that reason clearly wasn't that he lacked trust in Raak, because he insisted Raak carry both stunners and had provided him with a projectile rifle for use outside the warren of tunnels.

Karrl remained almost mute, largely sleeping in one of the underground bunkrooms.

Raak heard footsteps, more than a few, and hurried toward the pressure doors behind the hidden entrances in the restrooms in Lugh's, something he once never would have suspected.

The first person he saw he didn't recognize, nor the second, but the third was Adryna, and her face was blood-streaked.

At the expression on his face, she said quickly, "Most of it's not mine. The penguins are using skimmers against the south quarter of the city. Two penguins were clubbed to death there yesterday after one of them shot a six-year-old boy."

* * *

"That was the beginning of the harrowing of Sanjak City by the Ascendants," said Herryn flatly.

"The harrowing?" asked the vidfaxer.

"The rising is what people who weren't there call it."

* * *

Raak himself didn't see that much of it, posted as he was in the deep tunnels. What he did see was more of how Stannal Ferra controlled the "replacement" effort in the small room that served as his command center.

"Tell those rockhead podunkers to make their own weapons! They've got a lab up there, and they've sure got more tech to work with than we do." Ferra looked up from the screen, shaking his head. "You'd think they thought this would be an Ascendency tea with crumpets and whatever. Every time I talk to a rock-head, I almost feel sympathy for the Ascendents and their puffins. Almost." He looked to Donnal. "We'll need to make sure none of them get high positions on the Council."

"Council?" asked Raak.

"Donnal's worked out the government structure for when we kick the blood-suckers off Bartolan. A democratically elected Council that chooses a chief councilor from the fifteen elected councilors. Six year staggered terms. No one serving more than two consecutive terms, and no one eligible for re-election for six years after leaving the Council. Pretty much the same judiciary as now, because that's required by the Unity."

* * *

"For more than nine weeks, the campaign went on. One out of every three people died. By the end, every penguin was dead in the city and in High Point. Some of the militia stripped off their uniforms and mixed in with the survivors. Every puffin bureaucrat was dead or had fled, most to the shuttle port, where the shuttles to the orbit station ran non-stop, and, with a war going on, only one way. Unity policy kept anyone but Unity officials from going down. None of them had any interest in that."

"Then what happened?"

"Two weeks later, in the dead of winter, the Seekers went to the Ascendents' valley."

* * *

Raak sat in the front seat of the hauler, stunners in waist holsters and a rifle propped beside him. Stannal was in the rear, shielded by steel and copper plates hurriedly welded in sandwiched layers.

Karrl was driving, guiding the unwieldy hauler up the access road from the flitter port to the various estates laid out on the gently sloping valley, a valley covered partly in a thin layer of ice and snow, at least in the places where the worst of the ice wind couldn't rip it away. All the buildings in each of the few hundred estates in the valley were seemingly low to the ground, but that was because most of the living space was below ground, sheltered from the blistering heat of summer and the ice winds of winter.

As the hauler climbed around a wide curve, through the periscope above the heavy plow and shields welded to it, Raak could finally see the entrance to the valley—a rock-lined moat some five to ten meters deep and extending more than a kilometer on each side of the road. Behind that moat was a

wall some four meters high that ran from cliff to cliff, except for the heavy
gates, anchored in stone ramparts, that offered the only ground entrance. On
the road before the gates was a stone-fronted emplacement that had clearly
been built recently.

A full-power laser flared against the makeshift shield of the heavy plow
in the front of the hauler, momentarily creating so much glare that the periscope was useless.

"Frig …" muttered Karrl, but he kept the hauler on the road, as much by
feel as anything else, thought Raak.

Then the tube mortar in the shielded cupola in the hauler's empty ore
compartment began to fire at the emplacement in front of the gates to the
valley proper. The mortar shells didn't have much effect on the stone slabs,
but the smoke and dust clearly affected the sighting of the laser, because
the beam slewed away, then twisted back onto the front of the hauler whose
bulk shielded the smaller mining vehicles following, vehicles armored more
lightly and almost haphazardly.

The *thump … thump … thump* of the mortar above and behind the hauler's cab continued.

So did the laser, and Raak could feel the heat. He wondered how much
of the armored plow was left, hoping that the laser weaponeer couldn't keep
it focused on the same place.

… thump … thump … thump …

"Got that bastard!"

The laser beam slewed skyward and vanished.

Projectile rifle bullets sprayed off the raised plow of the hauler and off
the metal treads as Karrl kept the hauler moving toward the stone barrier in
front of the gates.

"There's a penguin skimmer up there!"

Almost instantly an explosion rattled the hauler's cab.

"They got one of the vans!"

Then came the whooshing sound of a seeker missile, followed by a more
distant explosion.

"Skimmer's down. Bastard's didn't think we could jury-rig a seeker."

"There's another skimmer … at your ninety …"

Raak tightened his grip on the rifle, knowing that he could do nothing,
his eyes on Karrl's face, seemingly frozen in the same impassive expression
that had not changed since he'd found out that Carryn had died.

Another explosion from farther behind the hauler rattled the cab.

"They got the tailguard. Likely thought it was you, Stannal."

"Sometimes, leading from the front has its advantages," replied Ferra, a touch of forced humor in his voice.

Another laser targeted the hauler, and for a minute the hauler swayed, but Karrl recovered quickly.

The intermittent *thump ... thump ... thump* of the mortar continued.

The pinging and spanging of projectiles on the plow and the hauler continued, then intensified as the hauler entered the straight section of road leading to the gates and the stone-faced barricade in front of them.

Rockets whooshed past the hauler's cab, targeted at the gatehouses and the space directly in front of the gates. Through the makeshift periscope, Raak could see the rockets and mortar shells impacting in front of the gates. By the time the hauler was within fifty yards of the barricades, there was no more resistance. Two penguins raced away from behind the gates in a groundcar.

Karrl shifted the hauler into full load and angled the hauler toward the left side of the road, careful to keep all the treads on the narrow section that crossed the dry moat. Raak didn't even feel an impact as the blade shoved earth and stone into the moat. It took almost half an hour to clear the road and then for Karrl to line up the hauler directly in front of the gates.

"We're ready to take down the gates," said Karrl.

Raak realized those were the first words Karrl had spoken in hours, except a one-syllable curse.

"Rip them open," ordered Ferra.

With the hauler in full load, Karrl accelerated over the bodies that had fallen into or next to the gates and into the heavy metal, but the gates went down like they were made of foil, crumpling away from the heavy armored plow.

"Head for the estate marked with the black diamond," ordered Ferra.

Karrl frowned.

"Which one is that?" asked Raak.

"Take the right-hand road for half a kilometer. There should be gateposts with black diamonds flanking a drive there."

Less than half an hour later, with the help of a few rockets, the hauler had battered its way into the covered half-underground entrance to the Ascendency villa, dispatching in the process several more penguins.

"Raak! You and Karrl and Donnal stay here!" ordered Ferra. "Let Patraik's strike force lead the way."

Even in heavy thermals and inside the hauler, Raak was shivering. He hadn't realized how cold he'd gotten while the hauler had plodded its way up the valley and into the Ascendency's enclave. He didn't even want to think what it was like outside in the ice wind a thousand meters higher than Sanjak City.

The four of them waited until Patraik reappeared. "It looks clear, ser. Just a few guards. We took care of them. The team has the staff locked up in a storeroom.

Ferra didn't answer, instead studying the small screen he held. A sardonic smile crossed his face as he said, "Bravo Force reports that all the Ascendents left alive took the shuttle to orbit station less than an hour ago. Let's go see what they left behind."

"I'm staying here," said Karrl. "Just in case."

"Good idea. Thank you," replied Ferra, motioning for Raak to precede him into the villa.

Beyond the blasted doors was a wide ramp, floored in marble polished to a glistening sheen, if splattered in blood in places from the handful of bodies strewn there. Stunners out, one in each hand, just in case, despite what Patraik had said, Raak led the way down the ramp into a wide circular entry hall that rose a good seven meters above his head. Below a gilded chair rail the wall was finished in pale blue tiles, while the upper wall was shimmering white. At regular intervals were recessed alcoves, each containing a stone statue. On the walls between the alcoves were tapestries woven from threads that seemed to have a life of their own, and light poured down from a golden faceted globe in the center of the arched ceiling. A circular carpet of dark blue, edged in an interwoven design of braided golden chains, covered roughly four fifths of the marble tiles.

Beyond the entry was a foyer with hallways going in three directions.

Raak's mouth opened as Donnal stepped up beside him.

From behind them, Ferra said, "Quite something isn't it?"

* * *

And that's how it happened?" asked the young vidfaxer. "But what happened to the Liberator?"

"You all know that story. He was shot by a penguin hiding in the head Ascendent's private study. I didn't see the penguin until it was too late. That's all in the history."

"After all that … to be shot after he'd gone through the entire revolution."

Herryn nodded. "It was tragic ... a true tragedy. Fortunately, he'd briefed Donnal on just what he wanted done. Donnal never wanted to be a Councilor. In fact, he hated it, but he did a magnificent job."

"You were never a Councilor, were you?"

"No. That didn't suit me. I was the head of security for the first council, then turned security into the constabulary and went back to teaching."

After the young man left, the young woman turned to Herryn. "I never heard much of that, Grandfather."

"There wasn't any reason for you to know it all." He smiled sadly. Especially not the part of the story he hadn't told, the one that no one else now knew.

* * *

Raak, Donnal, and Ferra walked past the penguin who'd fallen in the corridor and into the spacious study with its wide desk of polished imported Earth teak, and the still-functioning screens that filled one wall, likely powered from the wind-turbines and long-life batteries reserved for the Ascendency enclave.

Ferra beamed. "We've won. It'll be a while before the Unity sends an Integration Team, but they'll certify our new government. They don't have much choice. They need the rhenium, their precious rhenium, and their own rules say they can't interfere so long as there's a working government in firm control. We definitely have that, and they can't possibly object to the structure Donnal's worked out. It's just a matter of time and formality." Ferra turned to Donnal. "This study almost makes it worthwhile. Each of the estates is like this. Different, but all luxurious. You two should each have one. This one will make a great retreat for one of the new Councilors. Me, that is." Ferra settled into the comfortable chair behind the wide polished desk and looked at the viewscreens on the wall that showed views not only of the valley, but of High Point and the shuttle port. "Of course, we'll have to set it up carefully."

Raak glanced at Donnal, who looked distinctly unhappy, then said, "I thought Donnal had already planned that. The people elect representatives to the Council ..."

"That's the outer *form* of government," declared Ferra. "What I'm talking about is the *real* government. That's how we'll keep control. We can't just turn everything over to the people without some, shall we say, checks and balances. The last thing we need is a bunch of rockhead podunkers from High Point electing some demagogue who'll promise handouts to everyone.

That's why anything the Council does will have to be reviewed by the Justiciary to be in accord with both Unity law and Bartolan law and regulations. And I've already re-written the law in a way that will pass Unity scrutiny. That's one of the advantages of being an advocate." Ferra smiled warmly at Raak. "And you'll be perfect as head of my security."

"I'd never thought …" began Raak.

"I know. You've never thought of yourself. That's why you'll be perfect. The honest, direct, former teacher." Ferra beamed.

"You're the Liberator. You always will be," said Raak, managing not to frown as he turned toward the screen showing the empty shuttle port being lashed by the ice wind. All the struggle, all the deaths, just so a new Ascendency, with a different form and name, could replace the old one. That … that shouldn't happen. *It can't, and it won't.*

In a single quick motion, he had the stunner out and fired, its settings still on lethal.

Ferra slumped forward in the chair.

Donnal gasped. Then his mouth dropped open.

"Drag in that dead penguin outside. Now!"

"Why …?"

"Because no one else has seen that body recently, because the penguin surprised us, and because I shot him after he shot Stannal. Because we don't want another Ascendency. You're going to take up the Liberator's mantle in his name, and we're going to guide Bartolan into a working counciled democracy."

Donnal swallowed again.

"You can do it," said Raak. "I know you can."

* * *

And he had, thought the old man, smiling sadly once more at his granddaughter, who would never know the reason for that sadness.

The Weapon They Fear
Alex Gideon

The cell's electric lock was now just a mess of wires. It took exactly twenty-one seconds to gnaw through it, putting me precisely within my time line. No alarms blared and no soldiers rushed down the corridor, so Adrian's security blocks were up and active. A relief. I trusted my partner's technical skills, but things could always go awry. I was a Were-Squirrel, deep in the bowels of a research lab run by the American Government, and I was in the country illegally. I wasn't sure which damned me more.

I dropped from the pad, flipped, and landed on my paws. The drop cost me two seconds. One longer than I intended. The security blackout Adrian implemented would last thirty minutes, assuming no one discovered his hack. I never assume, so I wanted to be off the floor in less than ten. An eternity for me. I'm an infiltrator. I generally deal in seconds. Not minutes. It's why rescue isn't generally in my repertoire. It takes too long.

I hurried into the cell, nails clicking against the white tile. The room was small; three meters by three. It smelled odd. Dirty and feral. More like an animal's cage than a holding cell. Something dark rested against the far wall and I was just inside the door when I realized what it was.

Six-foot-two, one hundred eighty-three pounds, Brazilian, handsome, with dark hair, green eyes, and mocha skin. That was the description I had of my target, Davi Ortiz. That wasn't the person in this cell. It wasn't a person at all. It was a monkey.

A howler monkey, more precisely. It lay on its side, belly towards me. It was just under three feet long. Its tail limp on the floor. Eyes closed. Sides rose and fell irregularly. Its breathing ragged. Possibly asleep. Its face was jet black. The surrounding fur, brown. I smelled the iron tang of blood and the rancid reek of infection. It was hurt. I moved closer and saw just how bad. Its patchy fur was shaved away in several places and matted with blood where it wasn't. The exposed skin was laced with sutured incisions. He'd been here for some time and was obviously poked and prodded regularly.

Seven seconds lost to my surprise. Time wasted. I needed to focus. I was looking at a monkey; my Intel was flawed. My target wasn't here. He might have been moved. He might never have been here at all. I needed to leave. Now.

The monkey's eyes opened.

It focused on me and my fur stood on end. I waited. It moved. I bolted. It wrapped a hand around me before I reached the door and lifted me into the air. I chattered in surprise and struggled. It gripped harder. Then I was staring into emerald green eyes too human to be a simian's. He wasn't a monkey at all. He was a Shifter.

Bloody Hell.

He studied me for a long moment before giving me an entirely non-simian smile and setting me gently back on the floor. He shuffled back a bit and brought up a hand, which he balled into a fist with his thumb up slightly. He pressed his fist against the center of his chest and slowly moved it in a circle.

I blinked. That was sign language. He was telling me he was sorry. Probably due to the manhandling he just put me through. Now I understood why my employers were so interested to learn I was fluent in sign.

Before I could reply, he signed again, *"Are you hurt?"*

I shook my head and brought the thumb of my right paw to my chest, fingers splayed like a fan. *"I'm fine. Are you Davi?"* He nodded. *"My name is—"*

"Risu. I know." My blood ran cold as his fingers spelled my name.

"How?" I made the sign so fast, my paws snapped together. No one knew my real name. No one. I went to great lengths to ensure it so I wouldn't end up in a place like this. Why did this Shifter know it?

"You don't know?" His smile was gone.

"No. Explain," I signed as forcefully as I could manage.

"There's no time." He was moving and out the door before I could argue.

I raced after him, chattering a curse. I *would* get my explanation. And for his sake, I'd better like what he had to say.

Because if I didn't, I would kill him.

* * *

The medical white hallway was empty as I followed Davi. The lights glared off the steel doors standing sentry on every cell and a slight smell of bleach and antiseptic pervaded the floor, likely coming from the labs. Every level I'd seen was the same and it made the complex feel like an asylum. It set my teeth on edge.

Davi ran in a sort of gallop, using his arms as much as his legs. He moved with far more grace than I expected, given his injuries. If he kept it up, we wouldn't just be off the floor in ten minutes, we'd be clear of the compound. I still smelled his tainted blood, though. It wasn't a matter of *if* he would give out. It was a matter of *when*. We needed to be free before he did.

Twenty-two seconds later, we reached the elevators and Davi turned and shambled into the guard room. I chattered angrily as I followed him. We didn't have time for this. The guard room was little used and bare. No clutter on the desk and a heavy layer of dust over the keyboard. There was a bank of security monitors on the wall, screens black. Davi bounded up into one of the chairs and pressed a key to wake up the system. There was a command window already open on the Main System Monitor. The little green cursor flashed and words scrawled across the screen

SITREP. The cursor blinked, waiting. Davi put his hands to the keyboard and typed.

It's Davi. I'm here with Risu. Why doesn't she know anything?

She WOULDN'T have ACCEPTED the JOB if SHE did. Alternating cases. That was Adrian. But what did he mean, I wouldn't have accepted the job? What didn't I know?

I'll fill her in when I can then, Davi replied, his fingers speeding across the keys. **For now, I need you to open the rest of the cells.**

THAT will SET off EVERY alarm IN the COMPLEX. Adrian's answer was almost immediate. Davi shook his head, scowling as best his simian face would allow.

I don't care.

YOU and ALL the REST will DIE.

They will die regardless. This complex is a thousand times worse than we thought. I WILL NOT leave them here to it. If we're going to die, we'll do it fighting.

I'd had enough. I launched myself from my spot on the desk and crashed onto the keyboard. Davi jerked his hands away, the chair he was in rolling backwards.

"What the hell is going on? How do you know Adrian? What don't I know? Answers. Now." I looked up at the cameras and signed, *"Don't do a thing until he answers me."*

I heard the ding of a new message arriving behind me and turned. **BETTER do AS the LADY says, DAVI. i've SEEN her ANGRY before.** I was angry with him too, but at least he was on my side. I turned back to Davi, my arms crossed across my furry chest.

"We don't have time," Davi signed.

I shook my head and didn't move.

He watched me, teeth clenched. At last, he threw his arms into the air in defeat. *"Fine."* He turned towards the camera. *"Show her the feeds, Adrian."*

For a second, nothing happened. Then I heard a series of clicks and I turned to find the bank of monitors flickering on, one by one. Each one showed a feed from a cell on the floor and my tail bristled. Animals. In every single one. Most were predators; big cats, wolves, et cetera. A couple birds, mostly large and flightless—emu, ostrich. One held a kangaroo. Fifty cells in total, all occupied save for Davi's, and I knew every one of them was a Shifter.

Just before I was born, the very first Shifter revealed herself to the world. She was an aide to Ronald Reagan, and the effects of the Full Moon caused her to shift involuntarily on live television. The administration tried their best to sweep it under the rug, but before they could, Shifters across the world came out of the closet. My kind had kept to the shadows for Millennia and we thought perhaps this was the time to reveal ourselves and be accepted.

We were incredibly wrong.

Today we're legally categorized as Demi-human. Almost there, but not quite. Governments the world over preach that Shifters should be treated no differently than any human. Yet, they encourage citizens to report any Shifter they encounter. Reported Shifters have a habit of disappearing. We barely have any rights. A man could shoot one of us dead in the streets and it would be no different than if he shot a dog. And the populace wouldn't care nearly as much. They think us unstable and dangerous.

The Terrorist group Artemis hasn't helped our public opinion. They've been responsible for bombings and attacks across the globe. Public enemy number one. Hostility towards Shifters has increased a thousand-fold since their activities reached into the media. No one knows what they want or why they perpetrate their attacks. No one knows who leads them—

Oh my God.

I spun towards Davi, my hands blurring into motion. *"You're the leader of Artemis, aren't you? A terrorist."*

Davi sighed, the sound rumbling in his chest. *"I am a leader of Artemis, yes. But we are far from terrorists."*

"That's not what I've seen in the news."

"Of course not. Every government in the world would have the populace believe we are the enemy. That we break into houses at night to eat their children in their cribs," Davi signed, so agitated his words were almost gibberish.

"What about the bombings? The beheadings? Who was that?"

"Other terrorist groups mostly. Extremists of one sort or another, none of them getting the credit they want." He grabbed the desk and rolled the chair back over. *"Which has just made things worse. No matter what any of the other groups do, it's all attributed to Artemis. Which makes the other groups angry and causes them to perpetrate more attacks. Which are blamed on us. And so on."*

"So, Artemis isn't responsible for any of them?" I didn't believe a word of it.

Davi shook his head. *"Some of them were us."*

That took me by surprise. I hadn't expected him to admit to anything.

"Then what makes you special?"

"The bombings and attacks we carry out are on places like this," he waved around the room, meaning the complex. *"You know as well as I what actually happens to our kind when we're reported and captured. At best, they just kill us. At worst, they dissect us first. We're less than insects to this world. So we resist. We destroy labs and liberate our own. We find Shifters still in the closet and we spirit them away to safety. It's this world's governments that are the terrorists."*

I couldn't argue with that. I'd lived in fear of being discovered by the government of one country or another. It's why I got into this line of work. It kept me moving. I travel across the globe. Never staying anywhere long enough to raise suspicion. Teaming with Adrian helped immensely. He kept me supplied in fake identities, put me up in the best accommodations, and handled my business beautifully.

Speaking of Adrian. I turned towards the keyboard and scurried across the keys. **How long have you been with Artemis? How long have you manipulated me?**

SINCE the BEGINNING. I imagine he'd been waiting for the question. **AND i HAVEN'T manipulated YOU. they SENT me TO keep YOU safe.**

To keep *me* safe? My tail twitched. **Why?**

BECAUSE we NEED you.

I waited, expecting him to explain. The seconds ticked by, and nothing. **What does that mean?**

No reply.

I chattered angrily and spun towards Davi. *"What does that mean?"*

Davi shook his head again. *"It would take too long to explain. I promise I'll tell you once we're out."* I started to argue, but Davi reached out and wrapped a hand around me again. He picked me up and deposited me on the side of the desk, then put his hands to the keyboard again.

Open the cells.

NOT until BOTH of YOU are OUTSIDE, Adrian replied. Davi pounded a fist against the desk.

I WILL SEE THEM FREED BEFORE I LEAVE. DO IT NOW. THAT IS AN ORDER.

The cursor blinked a couple times before Adrian replied.

YES, sir.

A second window opened and lines of code scrawled across it. Davi huffed and nodded, clearly satisfied. Something had been bothering me and I finally realized what it was. *"Why is everyone in their animal forms?"*

"It's part of their experiments. They give us injections that keep us from shifting. I've not been human in almost a year. It seems like they're looking for some kind of vaccine against Shifters. As if we were infected with something," Davi signed, his disgust obvious. *"As if the problem is us, not them."*

"Can we get them all out?"

"No. Most of them will probably die." His lips turned down in a frown.

"Then why free them?"

"Because they'll die even if I don't and I won't have them do so in a cage like the animals they claim we are." There was a sadness in his eyes deeper than I'd ever seen on anyone before. Davi cared for these Shifters and this was tearing him apart. The world thinks us less than human. Davi proved

we were much more.

DONE, Adrian messaged, his bank of code complete.

A buzzer sounded throughout the hall and every door on the level opened simultaneously. The seconds ticked by and not a single one made a move. They just sat staring at their open doors, waiting for whatever new hell was being visited upon them. I wanted to scream at them to move. Davi wouldn't leave until they did. He should have known this would happen. Why would they think they were being freed?

Davi bounded out of the door and appeared on the feed from the corridor. He came to a stop, looking towards the cells. He took a deep breath and I saw his chest expand. He opened his mouth and the most terrifying sound I'd ever heard ripped its way out of his throat.

It was an undulating wail and it echoed off the white tile like the screams of the damned. Even with the walls of the guard station to dampen the sound, it was still the loudest thing I'd ever heard. I clamped my paws over my ears, laying them flat as best I could, trying to keep the sound out.

It lasted just a few seconds, but it felt like an eternity. The silence that fell after was almost more deafening than his howling. I sat unmoving, watching the monitors. Waiting.

One by one, the prisoners left their cells. They gathered in the corridor, all looking at Davi. It was incredibly odd, seeing so many exotic animals in the too white hall. Like the zoo took a field trip to a hospital. Not all left their cells, though. The ones that hadn't wouldn't be leaving at all.

Davi howled again, though not as loud, and threw his arms wide. It was clear to everyone what that meant.

You are free.

As one, the Weres joined him, raising a din far louder than Davi had. It was a good sound, though. The sound of the downtrodden rising up. Something rose up with them in my chest. Something primal. I found myself chattering as loud as I could with them. And I liked it.

It died when Adrian began typing again. **THEY noticed THAT. they ATTEMPTED to REGAIN control. I didn't LET them. SHUT down THE elevator. THERE are SOLDIERS inbound. COMING through THE labs. GET out OF there.**

That wasn't good. **Alternate exit?**

VENT back CORNER. I spun and saw the vent just over a filing cabinet in the back of the room. I jumped for it, hooking one of the handles with my paws. I scurried to the top and worked my paws into the grate, getting a good hold. I pulled as hard as I could, but the grate didn't move. It was screwed into the wall and I definitely wasn't strong enough to pull it free. I needed Davi.

I looked back at the monitors just as the doors at the far end of the corridor opened. Soldiers filed in, all in special-ops black. They stopped when they saw the Shifters, with their sharp teeth and killing claws. The Shifters turned to face them and an eerie quiet settled. For a split-second, nothing moved.

The Shifters roared again, even louder than before. They rampaged towards the soldiers, howling and snarling for blood and death. That was exactly what they got.

The soldiers recovered from their shock and took up formation. They met the Shifters with a wall of assault rifles. They fired, their bullets ripping through the horde. The Shifters' howls for death were suddenly for their own.

It didn't stop them, though. Those still alive crawled, leaped, and flew over the fallen. Their headlong rush crashed into the soldiers, bowling them over. They fell on them with tooth, beak, and claws. And the soldiers died.

I sat transfixed, watching. It was horrifying and, somehow, almost beautiful. They were unbridled, savage, as they unleashed on the soldiers all the pain and suffering that had been dealt to them. There was no mercy. They left none alive.

Davi hurried back into the station and the reek of blood trailed after him. I ripped my eyes away from the monitors and met his gaze. His face was grim. He climbed up the filing cabinet to me and wrapped his fingers into the grate of the vent. He planted his feet against the wall and pulled. The metal groaned and the entire vent gave, coming free from the wall. He threw the grate to the floor with a resounding clang.

"We need to move," he signed, climbing into the vent.

"Are we just going to leave them?"

"There's nothing else we can do for them." He scowled, that deep sadness in his eyes again. He refused to look at the monitors now. *"When we were captured, we knew we would die. We have to get out. You're too important to lose now. They will give us that chance. It's our duty to survive so their sacrifice isn't in vain."*

There it was again. Why were they so concerned about me? Before I could ask, Davi disappeared up the shaft and I glanced back at the monitors in time to see the last of the Shifters disappear into the labs. The hall was littered with the dead and guilt flared in my soul for the fallen. They'd died for me and I had no idea why. I said a silent prayer for them and started to follow Davi when I noticed a new window on the main monitor. There was one word in it. Adrian's last message.

SURVIVE.

* * *

The duct work wasn't kind to Davi. His injuries were severe and the vertical shafts were agony for him. They weren't made for traffic of any kind. The metal was smooth as ice with no handholds. My claws were sharp enough to find purchase in the seams, but Davi had to use his strength alone to shimmy up the shafts.

I tried to help him, but I was a tenth of his size and nowhere near strong enough to do much good. Still, I did my best to pull him up each time. I was going to get him out, because he was damn well going to tell me why Artemis was so interested in me.

The only light came from intermittent vents that funneled the chill air out into the sub-basements. But I didn't need the light to guide us. I'd poured over the blueprints of the ducts for days, memorizing every twist and turn. I could find the way in my sleep.

It was slow going and the nauseating stench of blood and sepsis grew stronger as we went. At least one of Davi's sutures had ruptured. He pushed himself hard, so it was bound to happen. It wasn't slowing him, so I remained silent. He needed to be treated, but we had neither the tools nor the time.

The seconds ticked in my head again, more from nervous habit now than actual necessity. We shuffled and climbed through the duct work for six hundred thirty-eight seconds when the bark of gunfire echoed through the shaft from the floor below. I pressed myself against the wall, making myself as small a target as possible, fully expecting bullets to rip into the duct. I heard Davi do the same.

The gunfire ceased three seconds later, leaving the shaft whole. My ears perked at the static crackle of a radio below and a rough, masculine voice said, "Subject terminated. Big Cat. Gender unknown. Moving up to sub-basement three." The radio crackled again, followed by the stomp of booted feet. Then silence.

Davi scrambled by me and headed for a vent ahead that looked down on the floor. I followed, stopping beside him and peering down. Blood was splattered across the walls and tile below, staining the level crimson. A

Cheetah lay in a pool of blood against the wall farthest from me. One leg looked broken and there was a gaping hole in its torso where a bullet had blasted through.

The Cheetah's body seemed to shimmer, like water was being poured over it. It shifted, and the snap and pop of relocating bone echoed off the walls. It grew, losing its sleek pelt. Legs extended. Paws became feet. Muzzle receded into lips. And twelve seconds later a naked man with the darkest skin I'd ever seen lay were the Cheetah had.

He was whole, the skin of his chest perfect and unblemished. Our injuries are healed when we shift. If we do it quickly enough, we can even survive mortal wounds. I wished that was what had happened here. But he was dead. Shifted back to human form as his spirit fled.

I looked at my companion and found tears running across his dark face, dampening his fur. He glanced at me and ran an arm across his face.

"Did you know him?" I signed. He nodded.

"His name was Darius," he signed slowly. *"We were on the same mission, and we were captured together."*

"I need answers Davi. You said they sacrificed themselves so we could escape. Why?" Davi sighed, the sound rolling out from the bottom of his belly.

"Because you are our hope."

"What does that mean?"

"The Shifter gene is a random genetic mutation." Davi sat down in the shaft. I did the same. *"It doesn't follow a pattern and it can happen to any human child. We've studied it for years, but we can't find the reason that it happens. It just does."*

"What does that have to do with me?"

Davi smiled just a little.

"You are the exception. All Shifters are predators of some kind. You are the only squirrel any of us have ever seen. Not only that, but the Japanese side of your family has claimed to be squirrel Shifters as far back as anyone can trace. An unbroken line, passing the genes on to each new generation."

"My grandmother told me stories of our history, but I thought they were just that. Stories. Are you saying they're true?"

Davi shrugged.

"The histories would say so. It's why we and all the other governments have been looking for you for so long. If your family really is an unbroken line, your DNA could tell us how to make the rest of us like you. You could

make it so that all of us could have Shifter children." Davi's eyes changed as he did. There was a twinkle there now. Hope.

Something bothered me, though. *"What do you mean, every government is looking for me? No one, except Artemis it seems, knows who and what I am."*

"They know, alright. They've looked for you for over a decade. With what your DNA could do, you are the weapon they fear most. It's why we sent Adrian to keep you safe. Without him, they would have found you years ago." I couldn't believe what he was saying. My DNA, a weapon? It couldn't be. I shook my head, my tail twitching. Davi smiled. *"It's a lot to take in, I know. I promise I'll explain better once we get you to Artemis. And we don't even know if your DNA really does hold the key. But that's not the only thing you can do for us."*

"I'm no soldier, Davi. What else could I offer?"

"Information." I blinked. *"You're the best infiltrator in the business. The best I've ever seen. We need those skills. We are losing because there are too few of us and the other side holds all the cards. You could get us the information we need. You could get us into their systems and their labs. You could give us their plans and put us a step ahead of them. You could help us survive this war."*

"That's why you brought me here, isn't it? To see what they're doing to Shifters. To guilt me into joining the cause." I stared at him and he eventually nodded.

"When my unit was captured, we knew that you were the only one that could infiltrate this facility. Adrian has already collected the data from the servers you gave him access to. You were supposed to be told everything before you were sent in, but I guess it was believed that it was better for you to see what was happening first."

I couldn't believe it. Half of my life, I'd been watched by Davi and his people. Adrian, my closest friend, had been lying to me all this time. I hadn't done anything to deserve this. I didn't want to fight a war. Davi reached over and patted my head, making me flinch.

"It's unfair. I know. But it's the only chance we have," he signed, stepping back. *"You can decide what to do once we're free."*

Then he was moving again. I glanced down at the Shifter below us one last time and followed.

* * *

Davi moved like he was possessed after that. Even with his injuries,

I could barely keep up with the break neck pace he set. He only stopped long enough for me to give him directions, and each time he hurled himself forward almost before I could make the signs. I stayed silent as we charged through the ducts, thinking. Trying to wrap my head around everything Davi told me. Trying to decide what I should do.

He was bleeding heavily now. The scent of infected blood coming from him cloying. He was pushing himself to the limit. I just hoped he didn't push himself into the grave.

After an eternity of metal shafts, we reached the last ascent that would take us to the ground floor. It was darker here, the lights out on the floor below us. Davi was failing. He'd lost a lot of blood. We needed to hurry.

I scurried up the duct as Davi made the climb. At the top I turned to watch him. I could barely see him in the gloom, and he moved slowly. Too slow.

His arms and legs shook uncontrollably when he finally made it to the top. He threw an arm out over the lip, trying to drag himself up. His eyes met mine and I saw the fire in them fade. I dashed forward to help him, but I was too late.

His arm buckled and he dropped. I grabbed for him, forgetting my size. I managed to wrap my tiny fingers around one of his, but I had neither the mass nor the strength to hold him. He fell. I fell with him.

He crashed into the duct below, rattling the length of it, and roared in pain. I landed on top of him and squeaked. He was still and I lay for a moment, feeling his sides move with his ragged breathing. The scent of monkey, blood, and infection filled my nose. Davi groaned, the deep sound echoing.

The vent we were on collapsed.

We fell again, hard and fast. I slammed into something solid and heard glass break. I gasped, the breath leaving me. I lay there, fighting to make my lungs work. At least Davi hadn't landed on top of me. That would not have ended well. I could hear him panting off to my right. It was labored and weak. Not good.

At last I was able to draw in a breath and the caustic scent of chemicals and bleach burned my throat. We were in the lab of the first basement of the facility. It was nothing more than a front. A pretty set piece, meant to hide the atrocities being committed below.

My eyes started to adjust to the gloom. We were on a long counter littered with beakers and vials and all other manner of tools meant for work with chemicals. Davi lay on his back on a pile of broken glass instruments. A pool of blood was rapidly forming beneath him.

No, no, no.

I rushed to him, my own pain forgotten. His breathing was getting weaker. God, he was dying. I needed to do something.

There was no way I could get us both back up into the vent. I would have to carry him, so I needed to shift. The elevator was offline, but we were only a floor down from the main, so there would be stair access. If the soldiers were still occupied with the commotion below, we might be able to make it.

I heard the click of the door opening.

I scurried out of sight behind Davi as the lights flipped on, nearly blinding me. I caught a hint of leather, sweat, and gun oil. Soldier. *Damn.*

"What the hell?" she said, her voice low, gruff. I risked a glance. She was in full riot gear like the others, the assault rifle in her hands trained on Davi. She moved towards us with that deadly grace only the most skilled have. Like a tiger stalking its prey.

I tucked myself under Davi as her footsteps neared. Davi moved, and for a moment I thought he was waking. I peered around him and saw it was the soldier nudging him with her gun. I couldn't see her face behind her mask, but I knew she would kill him without hesitation if he stirred. I risked another glance towards the door and saw it was still open. There was a chance.

There was no way I could deal with the soldier as a squirrel, not when she was in full gear. I couldn't shift here without getting shot in the process either. But if I could get past her, I could find somewhere to shift and come back for Davi. I could worry about dealing with the soldier when the time came.

Or I could escape by myself.

I went still. I could. I should, really. I didn't owe Davi anything. Artemis deceived me into taking this mission. They threw me into something I wanted no part of. I didn't want to fight a war. I should just walk away.

So why didn't it feel right?

I heard the static of a radio and the soldier said, "Subject found. Simian. Heavily injured. What should I do with it?"

The radio crackled again and a tinny voice said something I couldn't hear. The soldier sighed and said, "Copy that. I'll wait for the coats to pick him up." She turned towards the door and I saw my chance.

As a squirrel I was quick, but I wasn't confident she couldn't shoot me before I made it to the door. I needed to distract her. I shot out from behind

Davi and launched myself at the soldier with all I had, aiming at her helmet. If I could push it forward, it would shift her mask and buy me the time I needed.

Time slowed in mid-air as I waited for her to turn before I reached her. She didn't and I connected exactly the way I planned. Except her helmet didn't budge.

I slammed into the back of her head, making her lurch forward. Dazed, I fell to the floor and landed hard. A sharp pain radiated from my right hip. I ignored it and tried to get my feet under me, but the soldier's hand clamped around me before I could. She lifted me, crushing me in her grip. I couldn't breathe, so I did the only thing I was able. I bit down on her finger as hard as I could.

Her glove was thick, but my sharp incisors sank through it. I expected her to yelp in pain and let me go. Instead, she spat a curse and hurled me away. The lab whipped by and I smashed against the wall. Something cracked.

I hit the floor and white-hot pain lanced down my spine, setting it on fire. I tried to move. I couldn't. I was broken.

I needed to shift to heal. My cells screamed for it, but there wasn't time. Through a wave of agony, I watched the soldier approach. I was drowning in pain. Then there was a gun in my face.

I closed my eyes and waited to die.

A howling roar resounded through the room. My eyes snapped open and I saw Davi smash into the soldier, sending her sprawling. He was alive! He'd also given me a chance. So, I took it.

I dove into myself, following the paths my grandmother taught me on the island of Honshu so long ago. Deeper and deeper I went, trying to slide out of my skin like always. Pain struck like lightning and I screamed as it tore me apart, cutting down to the very fiber of my being. Something was wrong. It wasn't working. I wasn't changing.

I was dying.

"Obaa-san," I sobbed into the blackness of my mind. "Help me."

And by some miracle, my grandmother replied, *"I'm here, child."*

"I'm dying, Obaa-san." I hadn't spoken Japanese in almost twenty years, but the words rolled off my tongue.

"Don't force it. You are gravely injured and if you do, your body will tear itself apart. Breathe, Risu. Let the change happen as it will."

Pain was everywhere and everything, black and unforgiving. I accepted it and let go. I took a shuddering breath and bone snapped and moved. I took another. I was stronger. My skin rippled and stretched. I let it happen, allowing my DNA to change and myself to be human again.

And I was. Shivering and naked on the white tile, the pain was still there, rampaging through every tendon and joint. I lay there panting, waiting for the agony to recede and afraid it wouldn't. I cracked open my eyes and saw my grandmother, dressed in the light pink kimono with the Sakura Blossom pattern I loved as a child.

"You did well, Risu-chan," she said, smiling down at me, her almond eyes crinkling.

"Obaa-san," I croaked, reaching for her. She stepped back, shaking her head, the light glinting off her silver hair.

"You have to fight, Risu. For our people." Then she was gone.

A gunshot rang out and I jerked. *Davi!* I dragged myself up, every muscle screaming in protest. I didn't have time to recover. Davi needed me. He lay on the floor not far from me, the soldier over him, a pistol in her hand. Helmet and mask gone, her black hair covered her face as she snarled something at him.

Her rifle lay in front of me, dropped when Davi attacked her. I dragged myself to it. I wouldn't let her kill him. My arms felt like lead as I wrapped a hand around the grip. It took everything I had to pick it up and aim it at her head. I wasn't a soldier, and I'd never shot anything other than a handgun, but I knew I wouldn't miss. I couldn't.

"Get away from him," I grunted. She whipped her head around to look at me, blue eyes wide when she saw the gun.

I shot her in the face.

She pitched backwards, blood arcing as she fell. I dropped the gun, already crawling towards Davi when she landed. He was breathing fast and shallow. His hands were clamped over his belly, blood welling up around them. "No," I whispered. He'd been shot in the stomach. He couldn't shift. Which meant …

"You can't die," I said, clamping my hands over his, applying pressure. I needed to stop the bleeding, but it was coming too fast. "Please, Davi. You can't die."

He shook his head, eyes squeezed shut against the pain. He pulled his hands out from under mine. *"We need you,"* he made each blood-soaked sign as fast as he could. *"You can end the war. You can save them all."*

"I'm supposed to save *you!*" I said, tears streaming down my face.

He shook his head.

"You can't. Promise me you will save them." His signs came slower and slower. *"Promise ... me ..."*

"I promise," I whispered, and he smiled. Damn him, he was dying, and he actually smiled.

"Thank you." Then he was gone.

I closed my eyes and let my tears flow. This wasn't supposed to happen. I never fail my missions. He wasn't supposed to die. I was supposed to save him. Damn it all, I was supposed to save him!

His body blurred, shimmering in the way I knew all too well. I watched, silent, as he reverted to human. He was as handsome as I imagined him to be and I etched every detail of his face into my mind. The sutures were gone and his mocha skin was perfect. His black hair was curly. I hadn't expected that.

He was a hero. After everything he'd endured, he'd kept fighting, hoping to save others from the same fate. With his last breath he'd asked me to take up the fight. To save the Shifters. To end the war. I didn't know if I could keep that promise, but I was going to try. I owed him that much.

I took a shuddering breath and wiped away the tears. I needed to move. Getting captured and killed would not do anyone any good. It would be a while before I could shift again. I almost died trying to force it before. I certainly would if I tried again. I didn't have time to die.

I couldn't walk out naked, so I stripped the soldier of her uniform, not caring how irreverent I was. My grandmother taught me to respect the dead, but right then I couldn't have cared less. She'd killed Davi. She was a murderer.

The agony in my bones was fading, but I'd never worn military gear and it took me several minutes to get it on. There was still blood on my hands, but I used the soldier's undershirt to wipe them clean. I retrieved the mask and helmet and strapped both in place.

Fully outfitted, I knelt next to Davi one last time. His emerald eyes were still open and I closed them gently. I clapped my hands twice like my grandmother taught me and said a silent prayer for him. Then I stood and picked up the soldier's rifle. *My* rifle. I headed for the door.

A good man gave his life to save mine and I'd made him a promise. He said I was the weapon they feared. I would prove them right.

Because this was *my* war now.

An Acceptable Risk to the Portfolio

Brian Hugenbruch

Even empires need to worry about retirement planning. If you're a two-bit Galactic Senator looking for loopholes around estate taxes—sure, you can talk to your local accountants. Maybe you have a small room of them enslaved in the basement of your villa. That's fine. But when you reach the big time? When you need to launder money for a dirty war through twenty time-dilated shell corporations and a black hole for good measure? That's when you call us.

I'd been dialed into the markets for four hours that morning when the call arrived. The Inner Core had been in flux for a few rotations. Rumors of dissent against the Sagittarian Principate: always good for business. I run the numbers on every scenario, no matter how unlikely; it's what I do. This call had been statistically inevitable. "This is Ambyt Seven, go for Marsis."

The voice on the other end hesitated. There was a certain hitch in the throat of first-time callers. "We'd prefer not to identify ourselves."

If my species had teeth, I'd have grinned. "Honored individual, your connection is quantum-encrypted. It doesn't matter how bad your operational security is, no one will know you've called us. You may speak freely."

The hitch in the voice remained, but the words started to spill. "We're a growing movement looking to overthrow the oppressors. For too long have they enslaved our people, stolen resources from our planets, and given nothing back! The time has come to—"

"—fight back, why not," I finished. "Please be advised that Ambyt Seven is neutral territory and my employers do not involve themselves in politics. If this is a recruitment drive, you've called the wrong world." I paused and added, "But that's not why you've called, is it?"

"… No. We need funds to fight the Principate," the voice admitted. "Building an army has material costs. We're looking to find a way to jump-start our capital, ideally in a self-sustaining manner. A rapid gain up front, from which we can pull interest to fund the on-going struggle for freedom."

"Now," I said, "you're talking to the right planet. We can help you with this."

I walked the unknown person through the basics of setting up a 3117(g) investment portfolio—it only took a couple of hours. For one of the rebellion's meatheads, the caller was sharp. It was a rare thing to find rebels cool enough to talk stocks. Usually, freedom fighters only concerned themselves with blowing up infrastructure. They rarely ever thought ahead to the days after the war was won. Scarce few considered how to reach that day in the first place.

At the end of the marathon session, the individual signed a couple of small moons over to the Syndicate as collateral. "They're good for mining," she or he said, "and the Principate doesn't know about the transilicate deposits yet. They're worth your while. But be advised that if you betray us, we—"

"The Syndicate does not betray," I answered. "And your group can access funds this very minute. The account is currently keyed to your biometrics, but you can send the identifiers of other individuals by holocube."

"You don't need them in person?" he or she asked.

I shook my head at the screen. "Only when one signs in blood. Otherwise, no one ever comes here. We prefer it that way."

The individual's avatar nodded. "Makes sense. And what does the Syndicate get out of this? Besides your cut of the profits, I mean."

"We're mathematisynthetes," I said promptly. "My people are like plants: we produce our own food by doing long-running calculations. Your success will, in a way, care for our children." I shook a gray tentacle at the screen and said, "Good day to you, honored client."

"Good day, Marsis of Ambyt Seven."

The connection terminated. I breathed, "And welcome to the Portfolio."

Liraxa raised one of his eye-tentacles over the top of his cube-pen. "Was that another resistance fighter?"

"Of some sort," I admitted. "The Second Spark, or some such."

"Did you tell her that we also handle all of the Principate's accounts?"

"That sort of thinking," I replied, "would be bad for business."

Liraxa cleared one of his throats. He wasn't going to voice it, but I knew what he was thinking. Syndicate Logistics Guideline 412F. Turning away customers for idealistic reasons would injure the Portfolio, but losing the trust of long-term clientele was far worse. Still, I'd run the numbers. The upcoming rebellion could only make us money. And, no matter who thought they ruled the galaxy at the end of it, we'd be earning a tidy sum from their investments. The Portfolio would grow by leaps and bounds. If played right, we'd make enough math to feed ourselves for a generation to come.

So I pulled the graphs for him. "That's the growth we're expecting."

The eye-tentacle blinked. "I didn't think numbers went that high."

"See? We'd be fools not to ride this out."

The throats in the other cube-pen cleared in harmony. "Something doesn't feel right. If the Principate finds out—"

"They won't find out," I assured my colleague. "Trust me."

* * *

"We have word," the Principate representative said, "that you're collaborating with the Second Spark."

I could feel Liraxa send a telepathic *I told you so* as loud as corporate policy allowed. It caused a few other heads and eye stalks along the floor to jerk up in surprise; it was rare for one of us to be chastised like that. Normally, we stuck to the rules and did the job.

Which was what I intended to do.

"Honored Representative," I said, "you understand that the Syndicate of Ambyt Seven has been in business for two hundred generations, yes?"

"I've read the promotional literature, yes, and—"

"So you understand," I continued, "that we've bankrolled your governmental predecessors for years beyond measure. Republics, empires, monarchies, the occasional galactic commune. Yes?"

"I don't need a history lesson, Marsis, I—"

"Clearly you do," I said, my voice rising. "The Syndicate is not in the business of politics. We are in the business of business. You might say we *are* the business of business. We handle ultraviolet accounts, including your own, with the utmost discretion and caution. Because we wouldn't want the free press to pick up news of your doomsday device, would we?"

The representative's connection went quiet so long I thought I'd lost it. Finally, she or he said, "You know about this how?"

"We trade in more than money," I said. "Technology, influence, information. But do you know what our most prized possession is?"

"What?"

"Trust. If our contracts cannot be trusted, then they are null and void. We have a botnet of lawyer intelligence routines analyzing every single incoming contract for the merest whiff of a conflict of interest. And yes, that includes conflicts against an institution such as yours." I inhaled slowly, then exhaled. Let the words sit there for a moment. Finally, I added, "We've done right by you for the past seventy-eight years, have we not?"

"You have," the representative admitted.

"Do you trust we'll continue to do so?"

"We do. Though if we hear anything to the contrary, that you've betrayed us somehow—"

"You won't," I assured him. "Good day, representative."

A silence fell over the floor after the call ended. My colleagues would not be so gauche as to whisper. They were all telepathic; they wouldn't have to. Private conversations, however, were cropping up throughout the entire building. I could feel them humming like rude electricity in the back of my head.

My only worry was the danger of escalation. The fools around me weren't dangerous. But if the Chiefs didn't like my math, that was it. I'd lose any cut of the growth; my labyrinthine report chain would absorb it all instead. That would be intolerable. After all—there was no point in fomenting civil war if one wasn't going to profit from it.

* * *

A cycle of interstellar struggle came and went. The Spark's capital output grew beyond expectation as they struck military installations in their home sector. The Principate's own bundles maintained a more stable and steady rate, even as they razed Spark-infected worlds to their cores. The doomsday device they'd funded—which was to say, the one we'd helped them fund— was on the move. The Second Spark had no means to stand against it. Lone plucky fighter pilots tried and failed, repeatedly, to destroy the damn thing.

It had an effect on their recruitment efforts. At current projected rate, I estimated the survivors would pull their remaining funds and go into hiding within the next six cycles. Which was better than dying, for them at least, but it wasn't what they really wanted.

So far, I'd only realized a small portion of their market potential. The low-risk strategy would be to let them die and invest the remnants in the next rebellion. The Chiefs would like that idea. The Spark made too many decisions based on their emotions. They took too many chances. They could inspire others, but they weren't a long-term investment. Which was a shame: a sustained galaxy-wide war would escalate our returns into exponential territory.

If the Spark survived that long.

I placed an outbound call. Liraxa perked up immediately. One of his mouth-stalks came up over the cubicle and mouthed, *What are you doing?* I ignored it. Liraxa wasn't a thinker. That's why his body had budded appendages in dull and predictable ways: he had no creativity. The Spark needed someone who could take decisive action. More importantly, their 3117(g) needed it in two cycles or their rebellion was doomed. The Principate would stomp them out of existence.

The conflict had reached the point where a decisive win would cause a market depression. The Chiefs would blame me for the losses. Therefore, I needed to sow war without end—for everyone's sake.

The problem was, I might put Ambyt Seven itself at risk. Accidents happened in conflict, after all, but the Principate wouldn't hesitate to bomb us if they felt slighted. However, I calculated only a 4.0875% chance of invasion during the next century. This was higher than the Chiefs' preferred threshold … but the returns would be worth it

The call went through easily enough. Part of enrolling with the Syndicate involved the signature of biometric wavelengths that prefixed outgoing messages. The channel that opened could only be opened by someone on Ambyt Seven. It lent no small amount of comfort to our clientele and prevented any embarrassing mishaps with mistaken identities.

The blurry figure stepped in front of the vid screen. "Marsis? Is that you?"

"It is. I am sorry to interrupt."

"It's not a good time, if I'm honest. War's not going well."

"I know. That's why I'm calling."

The pause was palpable. "You're not dropping us, are you? I know there needs to be a certain percentile that goes back to the Syndicate, you're not working for free, but—"

"Not that at all. In fact—there's an opportunity."

Another pause. This was uncharted territory for her or him. For me as well, though the rep had no way of knowing this. The call might as well be telemarketing in the middle of galactic assault. The voice asked, "What opportunity?"

"In the interest of preserving your investments and assuring continued growth, the Syndicate is prepared to offer you a Black Hole Converter."

I was afraid, before calling, that the rube wouldn't know what that was. I shouldn't have been. The Second Spark had used nearly every weapon it could find in its war for independence. It would have heard rumors of darker, stranger devices. Rather than words, a low whistle came across the encrypted wire. In its way, that was answer enough.

I continued, "If the Syndicate doubles the current percentile we're pulling, this would justify the transfer of one such device to your organization. Does this sound like a fair trade to you?"

It wasn't a fair trade and I'm sure the spokesperson knew it. But time was of the essence—the Spark was planning a last stand at Sigma Sagittarii, in the heart of the Principate. Finding a black market trader with a Converter at less than a 500% markup was statistically impossible. That said, a Converter could cause massive damage to the doomsday device. The math made the choice inevitable.

"It does. Signature incoming."

I had it moments later. The saps. I sent the location of the Converter in response, then terminated the connection. At this point, I decided, it wasn't on me anymore. If they couldn't fight a reasonable one-hundred-year war with that kind of equipment, then they didn't deserve my help.

* * *

A few days later, Liraxa found me by the water trough. "You heard about Sigma Sagittarii?"

I hadn't, in fact, and I shook a trunk to that effect.

"The Principate fleet was damn near wiped out."

"Really?"

"Yes, really," Liraxa said, unamused. "News wave said the Second Spark opened up a black hole at the center of the fleet. It took out a planet of five billion life forms, too. Place wasn't uninhabited."

"A pity," I answered. "Did we have any customers there?"

"No." Liraxa's mouths twisted as he said, "Just family, Marsis."

"I'm sorry for your—"

"Not my loss, idiot. Yours." My coworker sloughed off toward his cube-pen.

I thought for a moment. I wasn't aware that any of my family had moved to Sigma Sagittarii. I'd been too busy working. How was I really going to keep up with all their movements when they flooded the galactic net with minutia? Market analysis was one thing. Sifting through the white noise of that many lives for one piece of informational transilicate was a fool's errand.

I made a mental note to send a sympathy card to whomever deserved it.

When I returned, one of the Syndicate Operators was waiting on the platform centered between the cube-pens. When she saw me enter, she motioned for me to hurry back to my cube. Easier said than done; I'd added quite a bit of bulk since the war began.

She cleared her throat and told us all, "I have good news and bad news."

As always, we asked for the bad news first. Markets always rebounded. No sense in creating a bubble.

"The Principate is pulling their funding."

This was bad news indeed. They weren't our largest customer, but when one has a controlling stake of 67% of the known galaxy, as well as a foothold in the one next door, the assets requiring management were vast. The account team representing them had paroxysms of delight every time they called with a plan to subjugate a new world. And the excess mathematical energy produced powered half our planet. What would this mean for us?

And the good news? Liraxa sent out in a telepathic blurt.

"More rebel groups have been in touch with our office. Sigma Sagittarii changed the face of the galaxy. Business is booming. We may not even need the Principate anymore."

My brows knitted together in a way that would be obscene on some worlds. "I haven't had any calls, Operator. And I was handling the Spark account."

"We know, Marsis." She let the words hang there for a moment, then added, "Your creativity was exemplary in this case. However, the Chiefs decided to take an active hand in the next phase. With the various factions apt to be at odds with one another, your … particular brand of assistance may not be best suited for what we have in mind."

Oh. Those jerks. They were cutting me out.

"On the plus side," she added, quite literally beaming out of her forehead aperture, "you've consumed so much math that you can scarcely fit in your cube."

The light laughter all around felt like chastisement. I waved a lone tentacle in acknowledgement. This was okay, I told myself. I could still rise above this. All I had to do was make sure the Second Spark seized power at the end of the long and bloody scramble.

The market would thank me later.

* * *

Another cycle passed before I was summoned to the corner offices of the Chiefs. Statistically, I wasn't worried. Personally, I wasn't certain what would happen. While the office gossip around me, both aural and telepathic, had had me at Senior within the next two cycles, the gambit with the Second Spark had cut both ways. I had made the Syndicate a lot of money by engineering a galactic civil war. I was too important to lose. But I had gone behind their backs to do it. I was too risky to leave unsupervised. And on Ambyt Seven, the only thing worse than murder was creating unacceptable risk in the portfolio.

The Chiefs stared down at me, their many eyestalks and nose follicles wobbling in a tropical breeze. Benefit of having an outside office with windows that opened, I supposed. I couldn't be sure, but I thought one of them might be wearing a little white hat. Though perhaps that was another eyeball.

"Marsis," a voice pronounced from the crowd, "you need a new project."

I moved my mouth in a facsimile of a smile and said, "Your graces, the galactic civil war has me entirely occupied."

"I should hope not," the first voice said. "The war between the Principate and the Second Spark is over."

I did a doubletake. "Over?" I spluttered. "They were set to war for decades yet. How?"

"The way such matters always do," a second voice said. "Market pressures could not tolerate their erratic behavior. Our other clients complained. We made some adjustments to our predictive model and both groups were destroyed."

"The Second Spark has been scattered to the galactic wind," a third voice mentioned, "and their accounts locked on our order."

"The Principate's home world," another added, "was eaten by a quantum singularity opened nearby. Strange, terrible matter—and a poor business practice. If one of ours had encouraged such a tactic, we'd have them divided by zero."

"Disintegrated slowly and painfully," the first voice confirmed. "Would you know anything about that?"

My species didn't sweat, but this felt like an opportune time to learn. "Certainly not," I bluffed. And I didn't. The Spark hadn't told me what target they'd intended for the black hole converter and I hadn't done a projection on it. I'd assumed they would attack the doomsday device again. Not that it wasn't easy to guess in retrospect.

"Be that as it may, you were their account representative. This means you're partially responsible for the deaths of forty-one trillion, five billion, one hundred seventy-six million and three life forms," the second voice dictated. "A non-trivial number of these were also our clients, either as general investors or as a part of our operational wing. What do you say to this?"

"Their long-term outlook was poor?" I hated that doubt was creeping into my voices. It wasn't a question. Of course it was poor: they were dead. *And the Syndicate*, I thought hard at them, *should know better than to invest in high-risk resources. How many times did we learn this with the Principate?*

"True," the third voice admitted. "Though they were at least predictable."

The second voice said, "You should be aware that, now that the war has ended, a bubble is forming. We have seen a thousand-fold increase in the market since. Especially in stellar real estate."

"A proverbial gold rush," the first voice concluded, "as all these worlds now need new masters."

"It will take some time to reshape the Syndicate's presence in the new galactic order," a voice in the back said. "We need a representative to handle this."

That was going to be a lot of work. I wouldn't fit into a normal cube pen with that level of responsibility. Even the Chiefs' corner offices would be tight. They might need to haul me into my own building for that much math.

I opened my mouth to answer, but laser fire cut me off. The sound of shattering glass followed. I threw myself to the ground with a wet thud. And as I watched holes blossom in the heads and stalks of the Chiefs, my mind started to race.

There had only been a 4.0875% chance of an invasion during a galactic war. Now that the war had ended prematurely, all bets were off. The Principate had been easy to guide; we'd been doing so for eighty years. The Second Spark, on the other hand, were prone to high risks, dramatic gestures, and emotional reactions. And there had been a Marsis-sized gap in my analysis.

The Spark had sworn, at odd times, to show neither pity nor mercy to those who'd betrayed them. The market may have profited from their mutual destruction, but the Syndicate stood at the heart of the market. And none had profited more-so than I. Their ill will was, perhaps, understandable.

On the bright side, that made situational analysis easy: I was too large and slow to run, so I'd be dead in moments.

I slowly rolled over to face my executioners. An odd mishmash of uniforms stood above me, guns at the ready. Some were Spark fighters. A few wore Principate uniforms, albeit ragged ones. Apparently, the Spark had executed a hostile takeover of their competitors. Now they were going to repeat the performance with us.

An oddly familiar voice said, "It's good to meet you, Marsis."

Uh-oh. "You're my Spark contact?" I asked the human woman.

"I was, Marsis. But the Spark is no more."

"You have my sympathies," I said.

"No, sir," my former contact declaimed. "You have our money."

"With all due respect, that—"

"The funds," she continued over me, "were frozen by your supervisors." Her voice lowered. "We were the rightful heirs to this galaxy and the numbers contained in our combined accounts were—"

"Appropriately astronomical," I suggested.

"We want you to fix this," the woman said as she holstered her gun. "Your Chiefs are dead, Marsis. But you? We'd like to give you a chance to make this right. One chance. Though I'm sure you have competent colleagues downstairs." Then she grinned and added, "Speak freely. No matter how bad your operational security, you can trust us."

I made a show of weighing the decision, but it wasn't that hard to calculate the risks. There was a 27.125% chance my new, emotionally erratic employers wouldn't kill me if I made myself useful. And while there was 51.33% probability that my colleagues would burn me alive for aiding a hostile takeover, I could help our new employers write contracts to everyone's advantage. There was a chance yet, however small, for Marsis of Ambyt Seven, formerly of the Syndicate, to find a reasonable rate of return.

I slowly raised a tentacle toward the woman's hand and joined a new portfolio.

Final Flight
of the PhoenixWing
Y.M. Pang

It was firstlight on Twin Moons Day. A basket of peaches sat on Haruna's nightstand. *I must really be going deaf*, she thought, *if Chiyo managed to sneak in here without waking me.* Haruna turned a peach over in her hand, feeling the fine hairs brush against her skeletal fingers. The peach was red bleeding into white—perfect, no blemishes, contrasting her age-spotted hand. The sender must've spent a small fortune; peaches only grew in bluedomes, though they were one of the few Homeworld fruits that grew on Rankyuu at all.

Putting down the peach, Haruna reached for the card on the basket and read: *Happy Twin Moons Day. Best, Your great-nephew Arata.* Printed, not handwritten. Haruna spent two seconds feeling annoyed before she remembered Arata had never learned handwriting. At least the card was nice, a thick blue weave decorated by miniature origami fans. Would've been better, though, if Arata had bothered to see her instead of just sending a basket of overpriced Homeworld fruits.

Haruna's persona-comm vibrated. She lifted her left wrist, tapped her finger on the large-read button. A green hologram message blinked to life before her.

He lit his comb and turned his mirror upon her, and found his beloved
Izanami half-devoured by maggots.
Arago: AT 398-1173-942 / 3 tiviens after lightfall.
There. Then.
Keito

The message she'd been anticipating for fifty-eight years.

Arabic numerals for the coordinates. Kanji and hiragana for the old legend they'd set as their passcode. Haruna wasn't surprised. She followed the
news; she knew the Deepsearch Company's T99.6 had emerged from Portal 27. The news shuttles had found no trace of Nakada Keito or the other
rebels from the Half Year War, but Haruna wasn't worried. Keito was either
coming or dead, and Haruna rarely feared he would be the latter.

Haruna swung her legs off the bed, groped for the cane that was usually
propped up against her nightstand. She found it lying on the floor. Chiyo had probably knocked it over while leaving the basket. Back creaking,
Haruna bent to grab the cane. *Stars, that hurt!* There was a reason she'd
switched her sleeping pallet for a raised bed.

It took her only a few wobbly steps to reach her bedroom door. Her sister
Rena called the room claustrophobic, especially against the overall vastness
of Haruna's manor. But Haruna was comfortable in small spaces. Comfortable in small spaces within vast spaces, more precisely. It came hand in
hand with being a wingbot pilot.

When Haruna emerged from the bathroom, Chiyo was waiting for her.

"Commander Haruna," Chiyo said, "breakfast is ready. Is silvertooth
soup okay?"

"Silvertooth soup is fine." Haruna walked to the dining room, Chiyo
trailing behind her. When her attendant showed up that first day—at Rena's
insistence, with Haruna's grudging agreement, because it would be stupid
to die in an accident before receiving Keito's message—Chiyo had worn a
costume from some Homeworld country called England. Haruna had convinced her to discard the museum piece for a more practical set of slacks
and zipcoat.

Haruna settled down by the rectangular dining table and ordered the curtains to open. A familiar sight greeted her: a stretch of orange earth, then
the Metal Crescent, looming mountainous in the distance. The waterfalls
cascading over the Crescent reflected the light of Arago, Rankyuu's star,
almost blinding Haruna. She wondered how those who lived darkside felt:

restricted to a view of flowing water every day, able to see the world only through a quivery curtain.

Haruna lifted the bowl of silvertooth soup, inhaled, sipped. Housebird had really outdone itself today. Haruna contemplated what to do with her last day. Her mind drew a blank. She had done everything, said all she needed to say, outlived every other pilot of her generation. Save for Keito, and that only because he'd headed off in a T99.6, travelling at speeds so close to light that time no longer passed for him the way it did for her. He was all that remained for her: his message, his homecoming, and the promise that had spanned seven years of his life and fifty-eight years of hers. Haruna's only regret was how long it had taken.

* * *

Two tiviens before lightfall, Haruna sent Chiyo off to Highpoint with a shopping list. Even with the roader and the lift, it would take Chiyo a good three tiviens to reach that lofty section of the Metal Crescent.

Haruna, now alone, took the elevator down to B3. Her index finger left a smudge on the scanpad and the screen blinked to Accepted. It wouldn't have done so for Chiyo, or even Rena. The elevator doors opened and the lights flicked on. Haruna hobbled down the corridor of rounded metal walls, wondering if she should've taken Rena's suggestion of installing a cart and tracks. Then Haruna could roll down the tunnel like she herself was a launching wingbot.

A quarter-tivien passed by the time she reached the hangar. Three seventy-four-foot wingbots stared down at her. All three had a base plate of golden yellow. All three were edged in orange with scarlet wings.

To the right was her most recent PhoenixWing, updated a few times since her retirement for extra sensitivity and flight agility. In the middle was PhoenixWing 5.22, in which she'd led the clash against the Gelbin System Fleet. The laser holes had been fixed and a new right arm crafted to replace the one hacked off by a Gelbin sword, but it still had the air of something used, something fought over and loved.

Haruna made her way to the leftmost model. PhoenixWing 3.72. The exact wingbot she'd piloted the day Keito rebelled. She looked over it every week, took it on flights at least twice a month. But outside of the necessary services to keep it functional, Haruna made no modifications to it. She hadn't even bothered replacing the broken metallic feather on its head. No matter. Wingbots were made to fly and fight. Aesthetics served only as a symbol and a warning, and Keito would recognize her by her flight patterns even if she showed up in a GenLine.

Haruna stepped onto the lift that carried her to the wingbot's head. The cockpit opened and she climbed inside. It was dark and cool and familiar. Haruna leaned back, placed her arms on the armrest. The PhoenixWing whirled into life, scanning her eyes, her fingerprints, her blood by the needle sliding into her forearm. The last she didn't even feel anymore.

"Identity confirmed," an androgynous voice said. "You are Inoue Haruna, Commander Emeritus of Rankyuu's United Wingbot Fleet."

"Confirm," Haruna said. Her wingbot recognized her voice, though it had taken a few tweaks to 3.72 after age eroded her vocal cords.

A hologram appeared before her, showing all the wingbot's functions: Fuel, full. Weapons, ready. Update … well, she'd chosen to ignore that for the best part of six decades now.

Two hologram buttons appeared before her: Armed. Unarmed.

"Armed," Haruna said.

The hologram blinked away. "Preparing launch," the disembodied voice said. "Is Commander Haruna ready?"

"Ready."

The link-helm slid down over her head. The seat folded against her like a cocoon. For a moment she could neither move nor see.

Then she was gazing out of the PhoenixWing's eyes, standing on metal feet larger than her dining table, staring down at a hangar that seemed small enough to be a prison. *Comfortable in small places*, Haruna thought with a smile, *or rather, comfortable in small spaces within vast spaces.* The wingbot slid down Launchpad 1 and the hangar doors opened to reveal an orange lightfall sky. Haruna shot out into the air, above purple kyorin trees and dry earth and her manor lands.

She flexed her left wrist—the wingbot's left wrist. The barrel of a shotgun emerged from the metal forearm. Perhaps groundwatchers would catch that, if they'd happened to train their scopes on her at that moment. She was violating fleet rules. She'd been allowed to keep her personal wingbot hangar on the promise that she wouldn't launch the wingbots armed, but they hadn't actually stripped away the weapons. Haruna had said she wished to keep the weapons for sentimental reasons and Commander Miura had let it go.

If he hadn't, Haruna could've stripped him of his post and installed someone else. She was Inoue Haruna and, retired or not, they listened to her. Sometimes, climbing to the top paid off. No wonder Keito had rebelled over it.

Sitting in this old, familiar wingbot, she remembered every detail of her last battle with Keito: the pattern of the lights, as Keito expended his battery to fire one last barrage at her. How she'd twisted aside, dry, piercing pain in her throat as she shouted at him. Then Keito's voice, half-lost in the intermittent static of the dying comm channel: "You … always you … to them, I …" Then the channel cut off.

Perhaps he'd repeat those words tonight and she'd hear them in their entirety. That wouldn't be too much to hope for.

Haruna flew higher, higher. The waterfalls of the Metal Crescent became a tiny wedding ring beneath her, albeit one with a portion missing. Was there anyone watching below? With her frequent flights, Haruna's PhoenixWing was a familiar sight in this region. Perhaps some mother would point out the red-and-gold wingbot and say to her child, "See, that's Inoue Haruna." The PhoenixWing wasn't just Haruna's robotic extension. It was Haruna as the world saw her. Her human body was frail and slow and half-deaf now, but with her mind linked to the wingbot's senses and body, she was still Inoue Haruna: pilot, commander, hero of Rankyuu. Still capable of one final flight, one last promise to an old friend.

As Haruna reached the upper edges of Rankyuu's atmosphere, the PhoenixWing angled itself, space supports kicking into life. Sound faded as the atmosphere merged into space. Rankyuu below was mottled green and brown, like the two other inhabited planets in the Arago System.

The Homeworld was blue. That had been one of the first things Keito said to her, as they sat on the fields outside Highpoint Wingbot Academy. His oversized trainee uniform hung off his skinny frame and his face darkened when she asked if it had belonged to an older sibling. "My mother's friend's son," he muttered. But his face lit up when he spoke of the Homeworld. "From space it's blue," he said, "like this." He'd pulled a blue marble from his pocket, held it up so it half-covered Arago.

That marble hadn't survived the day. At lunchtime some fellow trainees had snatched it from Keito and smashed it.

Haruna punched in the coordinates Keito left her in his message. She steered the wingbot herself though. She couldn't risk autopilot for even a second, not in current circumstances. The Keito she knew would not attack her without warning, but who knew how much he'd changed after a roundabout journey through a Portal twenty-eight light years away at .996c. She hoped his trip through Portal 27 had been worth it, that he'd finally gotten to see his little blue planet.

Haruna reactivated the shotgun, raised the laser snipers on her wingbot's shoulders, then drew the sword with the PhoenixWing's right hand. She brought up the clock on the edge of her vision. It said barely two tiviens after lightfall, but—once again, assuming she still knew Keito—he should already be there waiting for her.

Sure enough, as she drew close to the message's coordinates, her sensors flared to life. She magnified the image at the corner of her vision.

Keito's SeaGale. Deep blue body edged in silver, like his little blue marble, his blue Homeworld. A wingbot she hadn't seen in decades, yet one so familiar its every curve was etched in her memory.

Haruna flew closer, sword tight in her wingbot's hand. She hesitated a brief moment, then opened a comm channel. Would he answer? Did he have more to say that day, or …

What she feared did not happen. She did not find his channel closed, did not find only the darkness and silence of space. Instead he linked with her and for the first time in almost six decades she heard Keito's voice.

"Haruna."

Just that. Her name. Not commander. Not even captain, as she'd been during most of their flights. She'd expected nothing less.

Haruna didn't hesitate this time. She opened the visual comm, allowed him to see her face beneath her link-helm. Let him see her white hair, her wrinkled skin. Let him see the years; he'd hear it in her voice regardless. They'd both known time would pass differently when they made their promise. To everyone else, Haruna was happy to present herself as the Phoenix-Wing. But it felt important to let Keito see her human face.

No gasp filtered in through her comm channel. It was as she'd hoped and expected—he cared nothing about her age or appearance, only that she was Haruna.

Haruna cleared her throat and said, "Keito, welcome back to Rankyuu."

His laughter sounded a little broken, though perhaps it was only the aging comm systems of both their wingbots. "Always the commander, aren't you? You think you can welcome me back to Rankyuu though you technically do not rule it anymore."

His visual comm blinked to life as well. Keito's face was as familiar as his wingbot. Seven years had added a few lines to his brow, hollowed out his cheeks even further so that he was all lean edges and razor intensity. But he hadn't changed the cut of his hair and his eyes remained the same: dark as the far reaches of space, narrowed in hatred as they'd been the day he rebelled.

"We do not rule Rankyuu," Haruna said softly. "We protect it. That is the first rule of being a wingbot pilot. Surely you remember that?"

"Your rules no longer apply to me, Haruna. I left, remember? I left a traitor. Or has it been too long for you?"

"Not long enough, evidently." Haruna smiled. "Or else I wouldn't still be here."

Keito paused for a moment. "Why?" he asked. "Why are you here, when you have everything and I ..."

Haruna waited for him to say more, but only silence stretched through the comm channel. Keito's face was unreadable.

"The same reason I let you go fifty-eight years ago," Haruna whispered. When his wingbot had hung motionless before her, all power spent. When she could've cut him in two with a swing of her sword and rid Rankyuu of its rogue wingbot pilot. But Haruna had just floated there, all comm channels shut off save her dead one with Keito. She'd watched the rescue shuttle arrive, watched the surviving rebels pull Keito from the cockpit and into the shuttle. Instead of firing at them, she'd allowed them to fly off, to throw their lot in with the Deepsearch Company.

She'd left her persona-comm open to receive Keito's final message: a promise of a rematch, and the old story that would serve as their passcode.

Now Keito scowled at her on the visual comm. "Do you expect me to thank you? You had my life in your hands. That you didn't kill me doesn't change a thing."

"You are here now," Haruna said. "As am I."

"I didn't think you'd come."

"Surely you know me better than that."

"Yes. But fifty-eight years is a long time. People—"

"—can change," they said together.

Their eyes met through the visual comm. The hate bled back into his face and Haruna realized at that moment she would not be able to talk him out of this. Over half a century of healing for her had been a mere seven years for him. She couldn't even blame him for living in the past. Because she, too, was here.

"Well," Keito said. "We've both waited long enough. Shall we begin?"

"Is that all you wish to say?" Haruna said. "At the end of this—"

"—one of us won't be able to talk anymore, right?" The SeaGale hefted its sword. "We've always spoken best with our wingbots, not our words. Do you expect me to ask you about the bloom season dances you've been to, the nieces and nephews you've held, the people you've loved and lost?"

None, none, and none, Haruna thought. But what she said was, "And you? How did it feel to dive through Portal 27? What of the Homeworld treasures you found? What happened to the other rebels from the Half Year War, those who joined you on the Deepsearch ship?"

"The news shuttle reports will tell you all you need to know," Keito said. "Just as I learned all I need to about you. Commander Emeritus. Hero of Rankyuu. Vanquisher of the Gelbin System Fleet." Keito kept his face neutral, but Haruna heard the bitterness dripping from his voice. "What more needs to be said?"

Haruna sighed. "I suppose you're right."

The SeaGale circled closer. "Then let us begin," Keito said. "I hope I have not put you at too much of a disadvantage, elder."

Haruna laughed. "In the PhoenixWing, there is no disadvantage."

She couldn't say who fired the first shot. Neither needed to say a thing. They both knew the exact moment they had agreed upon. The SeaGale pelted a stream of missiles at the PhoenixWing and Haruna dodged, returning fire. The darkness of space lit up with lasers in blue and gold. Their visual comms blinked off, but, as if by consent, they both left the audio of their comm channels on. Haruna heard Keito draw a sharp breath as her shot grazed his wing.

She felt … free. Like she was back being herself after too long away. Even after so many years, Keito was still her best opponent, one-on-one. She banked, turned, wheeled around him. His missiles tracked her like they were the latest batch, not outdated tech from her youth.

"I won't lose to you this time," he said through the comm channel. Haruna only grunted in reply.

She knew every part of his wingbot, just as he knew every part of hers. But maybe he'd gotten some strange upgrades on the other side of the Portal. Haruna circled warily, firing a stored beam with her shotgun. Keito activated his area shield to block it. He shouldn't have a lot of those left, assuming his wingbot had only its original power.

"Not bad," Keito called. "I could almost—almost—see why you became fleet commander."

Unable to shake off his tracking shots, Haruna was forced to activate her own area shield. The hit on her power bar made her wince. Perhaps she *had* grown too used to the newer models. "Will you never let it go?" Haruna said. "You still have many years before you. You can continue exploring. You could even ask for a pardon. If you have something from the Home-world to offer them, they might grant it to you. There are many things more worthwhile than an old grudge with me."

Keito suddenly dashed closer, swinging his sword. Area shields were no use against blades and Haruna blocked the strike with her wingshield. Cracks spiraled down her armor.

"You misunderstand me," Keito said. "My grudge is not with you, not entirely. I only ..."

He fired off a stream of lasers. Too close to dodge, Haruna activated the area shield again.

"In their eyes it was just you, always you," Keito said. "I was ... nothing. If I could not prove myself better than you, then at least I wished to remain comparable. But you'd grown too far from me, too far to even chase."

And because of that, you rebelled against the fleet, against your planet, against all our vows as wingbot pilots. "You're such a child," Haruna whispered.

She couldn't see his expression, but his response allowed her to imagine it. He sent a flurry of tracking missiles and Haruna just managed to maneuver out of the way. Her sensors flashed. "Danger: Marubernum." Haruna narrowed her eyes. The SeaGale's special ability. Increased speed, agility, senses for a short time. At the cost of a shutdown of projectile operations or strongly decreased battery life. Judging by how much energy they'd both consumed, she guessed it was the former.

Keito probably expected her to fly away from him, try to keep him at a distance where his blade could not reach her. Instead, Haruna met him head on. At close quarters, she'd use her skill in hand-to-hand combat to negate his speed and hopefully anticipate enough to his attacks to avoid the fatal ones. Haruna issued a command to her wingbot. *Storage beam. Release on command.*

Their swords met. It felt almost like fighting in flesh, in gravity, without armor and cockpits between them. He was deadly fast, still skilled. He shattered her shield in moments and Haruna could only stay on the defensive, bearing his blows. Meanwhile her storage beam charged.

When she blocked his next blow, she realized her mistake. His sword dug into the base of hers—at the weak spot, damaged during their last fight. Keito remembered. And he'd guessed she would repair it but not replace the sword entirely, not for this fight. Her sword shattered and she heard his cry of triumph as he slammed his blade into the head of her wingbot, through the cockpit—

The storage beam hit 100 percent. Haruna fired.

Pain. Pain, as his sword plunged through metal and flight-glass and drove into her torso. Then a flash of light and a scream on her comm channel, cut off. Haruna saw darkness for a moment, then ...

Energy blinked around her like lightning, illuminating space. She couldn't breathe. Pieces of the barely recognizable SeaGale floated before her, its upper half blown away. She couldn't see Keito. He'd probably been reduced to dust by her beam.

Haruna wished she could cry, but she could do nothing. She was as still and motionless as her wingbot. *Keito, my friend. Is this what you wanted? Did I finally manage to fulfill your wish?*

She wanted to laugh. What would the fleet think when they found her? Inoue Haruna, hero of Rankyuu, impaled in the cockpit of her outdated PhoenixWing. Dead in a pointless fight for a promise made to a traitor.

Haruna tasted blood, and space, and nothing.

About the Authors

CHRISTOPHER ALLENBY makes his home within sight of North Carolina's *Brushy* and *Sauratown* mountain ranges and teaches composition and literature at a nearby community college. During the summer months, he divides his time between scouring coastal waterways for the elusive *Pamlico Fur-bearing Lizardfish* and dabbling in science fiction, satire, and other literary vices. He has not yet committed to Facesnapper—or whatever—but thinks the interwebs are the bee's knees.

GERALD BRANDT is an International Bestselling Author of Science Fiction and Fantasy. He is a member of the Science Fiction and Fantasy Writers of America. His current novel is The Rebel - A San Angles Novel, published by DAW Books. His first novel, The Courier, also in the San Angeles series was listed by the Canadian Broadcasting Corporation as one of the 10 Canadian science fiction books you need to read and was a finalist for the prestigious Aurora Award. Both The Courier and its sequel, The Operative, appeared on the Locus Bestsellers List. You can find Gerald online at http://www.geraldbrandt.com, on Facebook as Gerald Brandt - Author, and on Twitter @geraldbrandt.

New York Times bestselling author **WILLIAM C. DIETZ** has sold over two-million books, some of which have been translated into German, French,

Russian, Korean and Japanese. Dietz also penned three *STAR WARS* novels for Lucas Films, two *RESISTANCE* novels for SONY, and a StarCraft book for Blizzard Entertainment. Dietz co-wrote the script for SONY's *Resistance: Burning Skies* video game, and wrote the script for the *Legion of the Damned*™ iOS game based on his original work. For more about William C. Dietz please visit williamcdietz.com, www.facebook.com/williamcdietz and follow him on Twitter at William C. Dietz @wcdietz

Born in Nashville, TN, **ALEX GIDEON** quickly decided he wasn't a fan of the N, and now lives in Asheville, NC. He enjoys writing Fantasy of any kind as long as it's dark, and he dabbles in Sci-Horror. He enjoys exorcising, taking long walks on extraterrestrial beaches, relaxing demon hunting trips, and fishing for Old Ones. Read his questionably helpful posts on TheMillionWords.net, and follow him on Twitter @AlexanderGideon.

NASA Programmer/Lab manager by day and writer, dungeon master, and musician by night, **SHARON GOZA** started programming and writing areas for text-based MMORPG's in the mid 90's. Her love for creating worlds, especially those space related, sparked an interest in creative writing. "Neural Network" is her second published short story and she is very honored to have been chosen to have her story included with some of Sci-Fi's greats. She can be reached on LinkedIn at https://www.linkedin.com/in/sharon-goza-4aa3941b/ and Facebook at https://www.facebook.com/sharon.goza.313

BRIAN HUGENBRUCH lives in Upstate New York with his wife and their pets. By day, he writes information security programs to protect your data on (and from) the internet. By night, he writes speculative fiction about the ways imagination fuels our lives. Occasionally, the two intersect in weird and fascinating ways. This is his first published story. You can find him online at the-lettersea.com, or on Twitter @Bwhugen. No, he's not sure how to say his last name, either.

WALTER H. HUNT is a science fiction and speculative fiction writer from Massachusetts. He is the author of the critically acclaimed "Dark Wing" series, originally published by Tor Books and now in the Baen e-library. He has also written *A Song In Stone*, a novel of the Templars; *Elements of Mind*, a Victorian thriller about mesmerism; and, with Eric Flint, *1636: The Cardinal Virtues*, part of the New York Times best-selling "Ring of Fire" series.

He is married with one daughter, and is Grand Historian of the Grand Lodge of Masons in Massachusetts. Find out more at http://www.walterhunt.com.

D.B. JACKSON (http://www.DBJackson-Author.com) is the award-winning author of twenty novels and as many short stories. He is best known for the Thieftaker Chronicles, a series set in pre-Revolutionary Boston that combines urban fantasy, mystery, and historical fiction. As David B. Coe (http://www.DavidBCoe.com), he writes epic fantasy, urban fantasy, media tie-ins, and just about anything else. He is currently working on a new fantasy trilogy for Angry Robot and a tie-in project with the History Channel. David has a Ph.D. in U.S. history. His books have been translated into a dozen languages.

BLAKE JESSOP is a Canadian author of sci-fi, fantasy and horror stories with a master's degree in creative writing from the University of Adelaide. He makes his bones as a writer, lecturer, poet, and bouncer. You can check out his work at amazon.com/author/blakejessop or follow him on Twitter @ everydayjisei.

A bestselling Science Fiction/Fantasy/Alt History author, speaker, and small-press publisher, **CHRIS KENNEDY** has written over 15 books and published more than 35 others. Chris' stories include the "Occupied Seattle" military fiction duology, "The Theogony" and "Codex Regius" science fiction trilogies, stories in the "Four Horsemen" universe and the "War for Dominance" fantasy trilogy. Get the free short story, "Shattered Crucible," at his website, chriskennedypublishing.com. Chris lives in Virginia Beach, Virginia, with his wife, and is the holder of a doctorate in educational leadership and master's degrees in both business and public administration. Follow Chris on Facebook at facebook.com/chriskennedypublishing.biz.

KAY KENYON is the author of fourteen science fiction and fantasy novels. Her latest work is the Dark Talents trilogy, historical fantasies of dark powers, Nazi conspiracies, and espionage set in 1936 England. In a starred review of Book 1, *At the Table of Wolves,* Publishers Weekly called it "A superb adventure, worthy to launch a distinguished historical fantasy series." Kirkus Review called Book two, *Serpent in the Heather,* "A unique concept that is superbly executed." *Nest of the Monarch* is forthcoming in spring of 2019. Join her newsletter for news and giveaways at www.kaykenyon.com.

Connect with her on Twitter @KayKenyon.

SF convention favorites **SHARON LEE & STEVE MILLER** have been writing SF and Fantasy together since the 1980s, with dozens of stories and several dozen novels to their joint credit. Steve was Founding Curator of Science Fiction at the University of Maryland's SF Research Collection while Sharon is the only person to consecutively hold office as the Executive Director, Vice President, and President of the Science Fiction and Fantasy Writers of America. Their newest Liaden Universe® novel, Neogenesis, is their twenty-sixth collaborative novel. Their awards include the Skylark, the Prism, & the Hal Clement Award. See http://www.korval.com.

SEANAN McGUIRE writes things. It can be difficult to make her stop. When not writing things...actually, we're not entirely clear on what she does when not writing things. She may be an ancient dream demon, contained in mortal flesh solely by the act of stringing words together. Visit www.seananmcguire.com or follow her on Twitter as @seananmcguire to help us keep her from breaking free of her bone prison and wreaking her terrible vengeance on our fragile world. Also she posts a lot of cat pictures.

L. E. MODESITT, JR., is the *New York Times* bestselling author of more than 70 science fiction and fantasy novels, as well as a number of short stories and technical articles. He has been a U.S. Navy pilot; a market research analyst; a real estate agent; director of research for a political campaign; legislative director and staff director for U.S. Congressmen; Director of Legislation and Congressional Relations for the U.S. EPA; and a consultant on environmental, regulatory, and communications issues. His website is www.lemodesittjr.com, and his most recent book is *Outcasts of Order.*

Y.M. PANG's childhood memories consist of pacing around her grandfather's bedroom, telling him stories of magic, swords, and bears. Her work has appeared or is forthcoming in *The Magazine of Fantasy & Science Fiction*, Book Smugglers Publishing, and *Polar Borealis*. She dabbles in photography, listens to music in a multitude of languages, and often finds herself debating the merits of hermitism. Despite this, she can be found online at www.ympang.com and on Twitter as @YMPangWriter.

STEVE PERRY has written scores of novels, short stories, animated TV shows, the odd unproduced movie script, and reams of non-fiction articles and reviews. His current projects include: *Kosmic Blues*a novel in collaboration with Daniel Keys Moran; the final book in his Matador series, *Churl;* as well as a can't-talk-about-it movie script with Mike Richardson, of Dark Horse Productions. Perry is a long-time student of the Javanese martial art *Pukulan Pentjak Silat Sera Plinck*, plays blues and geezer rock on the tenor ukulele, and resides in the Pacific Northwest with his wife of fifty-some years.

About the Editors

.

TROY CARROL BUCHER has served over twenty-nine years in the U.S. Army, where his assignments have taken him to three wars and places like Turkey, Albania, Saudi Arabia, Iraq, Afghanistan, Kuwait and Korea. His travels allow him to tap into a lifetime of experience working with diverse cultures and peoples, bringing multiethnic customs and realism with a distinct military flavor to his Science Fiction and Fantasy work. Troy holds an MFA in Writing Popular Fiction from Seton Hill University and is represented by Ms. Jennie Goloboy at the Donald Maass Literary Agency. His first fantasy novel, *Lies of Descent*, will be released by DAW in August, 2019.

* * *

JOSHUA PALMATIER is a fantasy author with a PhD in mathematics. He currently teaches at SUNY Oneonta in upstate New York, while writing in his "spare" time, editing anthologies, and running the anthology-producing small press Zombies Need Brains LLC. His most recent fantasy novel, *Reaping the Aurora,* concludes the fantasy series begun in *Shattering the Ley* and *Threading the Needle*, although you can also find his "Throne of Amenkor" series and the "Well of Sorrows" series still on the shelves. He is currently hard at work writing his next novel and designing the kickstarter for the next Zombies Need Brains anthology project. You can find out more at www.joshuapalmatier.com or at the small press' site www.zombiesneed-brains.com. Or follow him on Twitter as @bentateauthor or @ZNBLLC.

Acknowledgments

This anthology would not have been possible without the tremendous support of those who pledged during the Kickstarter. Everyone who contributed not only helped create this anthology, they also helped solidify the foundation of the small press Zombies Need Brains LLC, which I hope will be bringing SF&F themed anthologies to the reading public for years to come . . . as well as perhaps some select novels by leading authors, eventually. I want to thank each and every one of them for helping to bring this small dream into reality. Thank you, my zombie horde.

The Zombie Horde: Glennis LeBlanc, Kiya Nicoll, Jenny Barber, Ash Marten, Simon Dick, Y. K. Lee, Katherine Malloy, Stephanie Cranford, Chris Matosky, David Perkins, Maureen Brooks, Kevin Wallace, Jonathan Briggs, Laura and Bill Pearson, Sheryl R. Hayes, Kim Lloyd, Tanya Gough, Matt K., Millie Calistri-Yeh, Caitlin Jane Hughes, Harvey Brinda, Julie Haddy, Carolyn Petersen, Konstanze Tants, Nellie B, Bryan Wetterow, Austin, Teresa Carrigan, Aurora N., Michael Fedrowitz, Darrell Z. Grizzle, Debbie Fligor, Mark Carter, Rebecca Sims, Sarah Cornell, David Zurek, Duncan & Andrea Rittschof, The Bowers, Paul McNamee, Pam Blome, Arej Howlett, Troy Chrisman, Larisa LaBrant, Mollie Bowers, Andrew Wilson, Patrick Thomas, melme, Noah Bast, Joseph Hoopman, Stephen Kissinger, Christine Swendseid, Mary Alice Wuerz, Chad Bowden, John Appel, M Harold Page, Lyndsey Flatt, Jesse Klein, Chris Huning, Lorri-Lynne Brown, Mary Soon Lee, Kevin Winter, Ronnie J Darling, John O'Neill, Lily Connors, Casey Sharpe, Kitty Likes, Wolf SilverOak, Elektra, Nicholas Adams, Benjamin C. Kinney, Cherie Livingston, Jaq Greenspon, Howard J. Bampton, David VonAllmen, Kristine Kearney, Erik T Johnson, Andrew Hatchell, Regis M. Donovan, Stephanie Lucas, Brian Quirt, Paul Musselman, Wendy Cornwall, Jaime O. Mayer, Gina Freed, Vy Anh Tran, Elizabeth Kite, Claire Sims, Debbie Matsuura, K Kisner, April Broughton, R. Hamilton, Vincent Darlage, ANDREW AHN, Carol J. Guess, Cathy Green, Stephen Ballentine, Céline Malgen, Penny Ramirez, Julie Pitzel, Jake, Chrissie, Grace & Savannah, jjmcgaffey, Gabe Krabbe, Bregmann Roche, Patrick Osbaldeston, Lori & Maurice Forrester, Pat Gribben, Robert Claney, Patti Short, Shades of Vengeance, Patricia Bray, Leah Webber, Jen Woods, Rolf Laun, Tibicina, Martin Greening, Judith Bienvenu, Ty Wilda, Sasha, C. Lennox, Brendan Lonehawk, Tom B., Michele Fry, Helen French, Auston Habershaw, FrodoNL, Simba Pipsqueak, Vespry Family, Nancy Edwards, Melissa Tabon, Andy Arminio, K Crowell, Lawrence M. Schoen, Colette Reap, Michael Skolnik, Amy Goldman, Chris 'Warcabbit' Hare, Jo Carol Jones, Eduard Lukhmanov, M.J. Fiori, R.J.H., Eddy Black, Connor Bliss, Yaron Davidson, Annika Samuelsson, Sarah Cottell, Jerrie the filkferengi, Rick Galli, Jakub Narębski, Tanya K., Todd V. Ehrenfels, Liz Wyatt, Uncle Batman, David Eggerschwiler, Tibs, Orla Carey, Jessica Reid, Paul Bustamante, Henry Schubert, Melissa Shumake, William Hughes, Donovan DiPasquale, Gary Phillips, Jay Lofstead, Nathan Turner, Becky Allyn Johnson, Evan Ladouceur, Colleen R., L.C., Jenni Peper, Curtis Frye, Kayliealien, Richard James Errington, Kristi Chadwick, Rick Dwyer, Katchoo, Queen of the Nowells, Revek, Leila Qışın, Heidi Berthiaume, David J. Fortier, Gavran, Sarah Hester, Joanne Burrows, Elise Power, Tasha Turner, Scott Raun, Miranda Floyd, Jörg Tremmel, David A. Holden, Angie Hogencamp, Vicki Greer, AM Scott, SometimesKate, Mike Hampton, Lisa Kruse, Nick W, David Drew, Sidney Whitaker, James Conason, Nancy M. Tice, Sally Qwill Janin, Paula Morehouse, Elaine Tindill-Rohr, Christine Ethier, Kai Delmas, Todd Stephens, Mark Newman, Phillip Spencer, Deanna Harrison, Susan Carlson, Sharon Goza, Marty Poling Tool, Yankton Robins, Linda Pierce, Victoria L. Sullian, Niall Gordon, Peter T, 'Jonesy' Oberholtzer, Michael Abbott, Jonathan Collins, R Tharp, Dave Hermann, Paul y cod asyn Jarman, Hoose Family, Andrija Popovic, Keith Nelson, Paula & Michael Whitehouse, Tory Shade, Brenda Moon, Tina & Byron Connell, Deborah Crook, Moonpuppy61, Nathaniel Pohl, Ian Chung, Beth LaClair, L. E. Doggett, Kerry aka Trouble, Brad L. Kicklighter, Kristine Smith, Michelle L., Elyse M Grasso, Roy Sachleben, Jason Palmatier, Ajay O., Cyn Armistead, Brenda Carre, Alli Martin, Catherine Gross-Colten, Rebecca M, Gary Ehrlich, Mark Hirschman, Anthony R. Cardno, Mark Kiraly, Ed Ellis, David Rowe, Clare Deming, Kat S., VeAnna Poulsen, Sharon Wood, Chuck Wilson, C. L. Werner, Morgan S. Brilliant, Andy Miller, Anders M. Ytterdahl, Heidegger and Mocha, A. Walter Abrao, Max Kaehn, Barbara Becc, Chloe Turner, Jen1701D, Andrew Taylor, Mervi Mustonen, Kimberly M. Lowe, Amanda Nixon, 2-Gun Bill, T. England, Heather Kelly, Darryl M. Wood, Belkis Marcillo, Meredith B, Mark Slauter, Arin Komins, Svend Andersen, Jomelson Co, rissatoo, Misty Massey, Anne Burner, Keith Jones, Jenn Whitworth, Doc Concrescence, Anders Kronquist, Keith West, Future Potentate of the Solar System, Stephanie Cheshire, Ian Harvey, Erin Penn, Beth Lobdell, Khinasidog, Erin Kowalski, Helen Cameron, Kendra Leigh Speedling, Mary-Michelle Moore, Micci

Trolio, Amanda Weinstein, Catherine Sharp, K. Gavenman, RKBookman, H. Rasmussen, S Baur, Eagle Archambeault, Keith E. Hartman, Tom Connair, Ivan Donati, Brendan Burke, Paul D Smith, CGJulian, Jeffry Rinkel, Mark F Goldfield, Chuck Hickson, Michelle Palmer, Alexander Smith, Bill Harting, Sean Collins, Paul Alex Gray, Jason Tongier, Pierre, Lark Cunningham, Brenda Cooper, Fen Eatough, Alysia Murphy, Ilene Tsuruoka, Sheryl Ehrlich, Tina Good, Shel Kennon, Judith Mortimore, Breagha, Fred and Mimi Bailey, Robby Thrasher, Rachel Sasseen, Thea Cooke, Peter Bernstorff, Dino Hicks, Margaret S. McGraw, Lace, Erin Himrod, Steven Mentzel, Samuel Lubell, Linda Bruno, Amanda Stein, Julie Holderman, D-Rock, Adam Thompson, Timothy Nakayama, Antonio Carlos Porto, Melinda Seckington, Nirven, Kristin Evenson Hirst, Mick Gall, Missy Katano, Ken Finlayson, Camden, Steven Torres-Roman, Jennifer Della'Zanna, Gretchen Persbacker, Crystal Sarakas, Michele Hall, K. Hodghead, Marla Anderson, Jennifer Berk, Christina Roberts, Steven Halter, R. Hunter, Ken Woychesko, Firestar, Cindy Cripps-Prawak, David Roffey, Coleman bland, Drammar English, Cheryl Losinger, Peter Hansen, Bryan Easton, Deirdre M. Murphy, Zion Russell, Danielle Hinesly, Dana, Jonathan S. Chance, Nick Martell, K. R. Smith, SwordFire, Jennie Goloboy, Chantelle Wilson, Jenni Hamilton, S. E. Altmann, Lara Ortiz de Montellano, Donna Gaudet, Thea Maia, Jamie Ibson, Wendy Kitchens, Sarah FW, Axisor and Mike, John B. McCarthy, Andrew Barton, Gordon Rios, Kerri Regan, M. E. Gibbs, Kelly Melnyk, Greg Vose, Joe Borrelli, The Mystic Bob, Chris Brant, R Kirkpatrick, Marzie Kaifer, Ingrid deBeus